THE ARGENTINIAN'S BABY OF SCANDAL

SHARON KENDRICK

A PASSIONATE NIGHT WITH THE GREEK

KIM LAWRENCE

MILLS & BOON

® and TM are trademarks owned and used by the trademark owner
and/or its licensee. Trademarks marked with ® are registered with the
United Kingdom Patent Office and/or the Office for Harmonisation
in the Internal Market and in other countries.

First Published in Great Britain 2019
by Mills & Boon, an imprint of HarperCollins*Publishers*
1 London Bridge Street, London, SE1 9GF

The Argentinian's Baby of Scandal © 2019 by Sharon Kendrick

A Passionate Night with the Greek © 2019 by Kim Lawrence

ISBN: 978-0-263-27351-9

MIX
Paper from
responsible sources
FSC
www.fsc.org   FSC™ C007454

This book is produced from independently certified FSC™ paper
to ensure responsible forest management.
For more information visit www.harpercollins.co.uk/green.

Printed and bound in Spain
by CPI, Barcelona

THE ARGENTINIAN'S BABY OF SCANDAL

SHARON KENDRICK

This story is for Megan Crane,
with whom I shared an unforgettable trip
to the west of Ireland…
and for Abby Green—the diva of Dublin!

CHAPTER ONE

LUCAS CONWAY SURVEYED the blonde who was standing in front of him and felt nothing, even though her eyes were red-rimmed and her cheeks wet with tears.

He felt a pulse beat at his temple.

Nothing at all.

'Who let you in?' he questioned coldly.

'Y-your housekeeper,' she said, her mouth working frantically as she tried to contain yet another sob. 'The one with the messy hair.'

'She had no right to let anyone in,' Lucas returned, briefly wondering how the actress could be so spiteful about someone who'd supposedly done her a good turn. But that was women for you—they never lived up to the promise of how they appeared on the outside. They were all teeth and smiles and then, when you looked beneath the surface, they were as shallow as a spill of water. 'I told her I didn't want to be disturbed.' His voice was cool. 'Not by anyone. I'm sorry, Charlotte, but you'll have to leave. You should never have come here.'

He rose to his feet, because now he felt something, and it felt like the fury which had been simmering inside him for days. Although maybe fury was the wrong word to use. It didn't accurately describe the hot clench to his heart when he'd received the letter last week, did it? Nor the unaccustomed feeling of dread which had washed over him as he'd stared down at it. Memories of the past had swum into his mind. He remembered violence and discord. Things he didn't want to remember. Things he'd schooled himself to forget. But sometimes you were powerless when the past came looking for you...

His mouth was tight as he moved out from behind his desk, easily dwarfing the fair-haired beauty who was staring up at him with beseeching eyes. 'Come with me. I'll see you out.'

'Lucas—'

'Please, Charlotte,' he said, trying to inject his voice with the requisite amount of compassion he suspected was called for but failing—for he had no idea how to replicate this kind of emotion. Hadn't he often been accused of being unable to show *any* kind of feeling for another person—unless you counted desire, which was only ever temporary? He held back his sigh. 'Don't make this any more difficult than it already is.'

Briefly, she closed her swollen eyelids and nodded and he could smell her expensive perfume as he ushered her out of his huge office, which overlooked the choppy waters of Dublin Bay. And when she'd followed him—sniffling—to the front door, she tried one last time.

'Lucas.' Her voice trembled. 'I have to tell you this because it's important and you need to know it. I know there isn't anyone else on the scene and I've missed you. Missed being with you. What we had was good and I... I love you—'

'No,' he answered fiercely, cutting her short before she could humiliate herself any further. 'You don't. You can't. You don't really know me and if you did, you certainly wouldn't love me. I'm sorry. I'm not the man for you. So do yourself a favour, Charlotte, and go and find someone who is. Someone who has the capacity to care for you in the way you deserve to be cared for.'

She opened her mouth as if to make one last appeal but maybe she read the futility of such a gesture in his eyes, because she nodded and began to stumble towards her sports car in her spindly and impractical heels. He stood at the door and watched her leave, a gesture which might have been interpreted as one of courtesy but in reality it was to ensure that she really did exit the premises in her zippy little silver car, which shattered the peace as it sped off in a cloud of gravel.

He glanced up at the heavy sky. The weather had been oppressive for days now and the dark and straining clouds were hinting at the storm to come. He wished it would. Maybe it would lighten the oppressive atmosphere, which was making his forehead slick with sweat and his clothes feel as if they were clinging to his body. He closed the door. And then he turned his attention to his growing vexation as he thought about his interfering housekeeper.

His temper mounting, Lucas went downstairs into the basement, to the kitchen—which several high-profile magazines were itching to feature in their lifestyle section—to find Tara Fitzpatrick whipping something furiously in a copper bowl. She looked up as he walked in and a lock of thick red hair fell into her eye, which she instantly blew away with a big upward gust of breath, without pausing in her whipping motion. Why the hell didn't she get it cut so that it didn't resemble a birds' nest? he wondered testily. And why did she insist on wearing that horrible housecoat while she worked? A baggy garment made from some cheap, man-made fibre, which he'd once told her looked like a relic from the nineteen fifties and completely swamped her slender frame.

'She's gone, then?' she questioned, her gaze fixed on his as he walked in.

'Yes, she's gone.' He could feel the flicker of irritation growing inside him again and, suddenly, Tara seemed the ideal candidate to take it out on. 'Why the hell did you let her in?'

She hesitated, the movement of her whisk stilling. 'Because she was crying.'

'Of course she was crying. She's a spoiled woman who is used to getting her own way and that's what women like her do when it doesn't happen.'

She opened her mouth as if she was about to say something and then appeared to change her mind, so that her next comment came out as a mild observation. 'You were the one who dated her, Lucas.'

'And it was over,' he said dangerously. 'Months ago.'

Again, that hesitation—as if she was trying her hardest to be diplomatic—and Lucas thought, not for the first time, what a fey creature she was with her amber eyes and pale skin and that mass of fiery hair. And her slender body, which always looked as if it could do with a decent meal.

'Perhaps you didn't make it plain enough that it was over,' she suggested cautiously, resting her whisk on the side of the bowl and shaking her wrist, as if it was aching.

'I couldn't have been more plain,' he said. 'I told her in person, in as kind a way as possible, and said that perhaps one day we could be friends.'

Tara made a clicking noise with her lips and shook her head. 'That was your big mistake.'

'My big mistake?' he echoed dangerously.

'Sure. Give a woman hope and she'll cling to it like a chimp swinging from tree to tree. Maybe if you weren't so devastatingly attractive,' she added cheerfully, resuming her beating with a ferocity which sent the egg whites slapping against the sides of the bowl, 'then your exes wouldn't keep popping up around the place like lost puppy dogs.'

He heard the implicit criticism in his housekeeper's voice and the tension which had been mounting inside him all week now snapped. 'And maybe if you knew your place, instead of acting like the mistress of my damned house, then you wouldn't have let her in in the first place,' he flared as he stormed across the kitchen to make himself a cup of coffee.

Know her place?

Tara stopped beating as her boss's icy note of censure was replaced by the sound of grinding coffee beans and a lump rose in her throat, because he'd never spoken to her that way before—not in all the time she'd worked for him. Not with that air of impatient condemnation as if she were some troublesome minion who was more trouble than she was worth. As she returned his gaze she swallowed with confusion and, yes, with hurt—and how stupid was that? Had she thought she was safe from his legendary coldness and a tongue which could slice out sharp words like a knife cutting through a courgette? Well, yes. She had. She'd naively imagined that, because she served him meals and ironed his shirts and made sure that his garden was carefully weeded and bright with flowers, he would never treat her with the disdain he seemed to direct at most women. That she had a special kind of place in his heart—when it was clear that Lucas Conway had no heart at all. And wasn't the fact of the matter that he'd been in a foul mood for this past week and growing snappier by the day? Ever since that official-looking letter had arrived from the United States and he'd disappeared into his office for a long time, before emerging with a haunted look darkening the spectacular verdant gleam of his eyes?

She ran a wooden spoon around the side of the bowl and then gave the mixture another half-hearted beat. She told herself she shouldn't let his arrogance or bad mood bother her. Maybe that was how you should expect a man to behave when he was as rich as Lucas Conway—as well as being the hottest lover in all of Ireland, if you were to believe the things people whispered about him.

Yet nobody really knew very much about the Dublin-based billionaire, no matter how hard they tried to find out. Even the Internet provided little joy—and Tara knew this for a fact because she'd looked him up herself on her ancient laptop, soon after she'd started working for him. His accent was difficult to figure out, that was for sure. He definitely wasn't Irish, and there was a faint hint of transatlantic drawl underpinning his sexy voice. He spoke many languages—French, Italian and Spanish as well as English—though, unlike Tara, he knew no Gaelic. He was rumoured to have been a bellhop, working in some fancy Swiss hotel, in the days before he'd arrived in Ireland to make his fortune but Tara had never quite been able to believe this particular rumour. As if someone like Lucas Conway would ever work as a bellhop! He was also reputed to have South American parentage—and with his tousled dark hair and the unusual green eyes which contrasted so vividly with his glowing olive skin, that was one rumour which would seem to be founded in truth.

She studied him as the machine dispensed a cup of his favoured industrial-strength brew of coffee. He'd had more girlfriends than most men had socks lined up in a top drawer of their bedroom, and was known for his exceptionally low boredom threshold. Which might explain why he'd dumped the seemingly perfect Charlotte when she—like so many others before her— had refused to get the message that he had no desire to be married. Yet that hadn't stopped her sending him a Valentine's card, had it—or arranging for a case of vintage champagne to be delivered on his birthday? 'I don't even particularly *like* champagne,' had been his moody aside to Tara as he'd peered into the wooden case, and she remembered thinking how ungrateful he could be.

Yet it wasn't just women of the sexy and supermodel variety who couldn't seem to get enough of him. Men liked him, too—and old ladies practically swooned whenever he came into their vicinity. Yet through all the attention he received, Lucas Conway always remained slightly aloof to the adulation which swirled around him. As if he was observing the world with the objectivity of a scientist, and, although nobody would ever have described him as untouchable, he was certainly what you might call unknowable.

But up until now he'd always treated her with respect. As if she mattered. Not as if she were just some skivvy working in his kitchen, with no more than two brain cells to rub together. The lump in her throat got bigger. Someone who didn't *know her place.*

Was that how he really saw her?

How others saw her?

She licked lips which had suddenly grown dry. Was that how she saw herself? The misfit from the country. The child who had grown up with the dark cloud of shame hanging over her. Who'd been terrified people were going to find her out, which was why she had fled to the city just as soon as she was able.

She told herself to leave it. To just nod politely and Lucas would vacate the kitchen and it would all be forgotten by the time she produced the feather-light cheese soufflé she was planning to serve for his dinner, because he wasn't going out tonight. But for some reason she couldn't leave it. Something was nagging away at her and she didn't know what it was. Was it the strange atmosphere which had descended on the house ever since that letter had arrived for him, and she'd heard the sound of muffled swearing coming from his office? Or was it something to do with this weird weather they'd been having, which was making the air seem as heavy as lead? Her heart missed a beat, because maybe it was a lot more basic than that. Maybe it all stemmed from having seen someone from home walking down Grafton Street yesterday, when she'd been window-shopping on her afternoon off.

Tara had nearly jumped out of her skin when she'd spotted her—and she was easy to spot. At school, Mona O'Sullivan had always been destined for great things and her high-heeled shoes and leather trench coat had borne out her teacher's gushing prophesy as she'd sashayed down Dublin's main street looking as if she didn't have a care in the world. A diamond ring had glittered like a giant trophy on her engagement finger and her hair had been perfectly coiffed.

Tara had ducked into a shop doorway, terrified Mona would see her and stop, before asking those probing questions which always used to make her blush to the roots of her hair and wish the ground would open up and swallow her. Questions which reminded Tara why she was so ashamed of the past she'd tried so desperately to forget. But you could never forget the past, not really. It haunted you like a spectre—always ready to jump out at you when you were least expecting it. It waited for you in the sometimes sleepless hours of the night and it lurked behind the supposedly innocent questions people put to you, which were anything but innocent. Was that why she had settled for this safe, well-paid job tucked away on the affluent edge of the city, where nobody knew her?

She wondered if her gratitude for having found such a cushy job had blinded her to the fact that she was now working for a man who seemed to think he had the right to talk to her as if she were nothing, just because he was in a filthy mood.

She stilled her spoon and crashed the copper bowl

down on the table, aware that already the air would be leaving those carefully beaten egg whites—but suddenly she didn't care. Perhaps she'd been in danger of caring a bit too much what Lucas Conway had for his supper, instead of looking after herself. 'Then maybe you should find yourself someone who does know their place,' she declared.

Lucas turned round from the coffee machine with a slightly bemused look on his face. 'I'm sorry?'

She shook her head. 'It's too late for an apology, Lucas.'

'I wasn't apologising,' he ground out. 'I was trying to work out what the hell you're talking about.'

Now he was making her sound as if she were incapable of stringing a coherent sentence together! 'I'm talking about *knowing my place*,' Tara repeated, with an indignation which felt new and peculiar but oddly... *liberating.* 'I was trying to be kind to Charlotte because she was crying, and because I've actually spent several months of my life trying to wash her lipstick out of your pillowcases—so it wasn't like she was a complete stranger to me. And I once found one of her diamond studs when it was wedged into the floorboards of the dining room and she bought me a nice big bunch of flowers as a thank-you present. So what was I expected to do when she turned up today with mascara running all down her cheeks?' She glared at him. 'Turn her away?'

'Tara—'

'Do you think she was in any fit state to drive in that condition—with her eyes full of tears and her shoulders heaving?'

'Tara. I seem to have missed something along the way.' Lucas put his untouched coffee cup down on the table with as close an expression to incomprehension as she'd ever seen on those ruggedly handsome features. 'What's got into you all of a sudden?'

Tara still didn't know. Was it something to do with the dismissive way her boss's gaze had flicked over her admittedly disobedient hair when he'd walked into the kitchen? As if she were not a woman at all, but some odd-looking robot designed to cook and clean for him. She wondered if he would have looked like that if Mona O'Sullivan had been standing there whipping him up a cheese soufflé, with her high heels and her luscious curves accentuated by a tight belt.

But you dress like a frump deliberately, a small voice in her head reminded her. *You always have done. You were taught that the safest way to be around men was to make yourself look invisible and you heeded that lesson well. So what do you expect?*

And suddenly she saw exactly what she might expect. More of the same for the countless days which lay ahead of her. More of working her fingers to the bone for a man who didn't really appreciate her—and that maybe it was time to break out and reach for something new. To find herself a job in a big, noisy house with lots of children running around—wouldn't that be something which might fulfil her?

'I've decided I need a change of direction,' she said firmly.

'What are you talking about?'

Tara hesitated. Lucas Conway might be the biggest pain in the world at times, but surely he would give her a glowing reference as she'd worked for him since she'd been eighteen years old—when she'd arrived in the big city, slightly daunted by all the traffic, and the noise. 'A new job,' she elaborated.

He narrowed his stunning eyes—eyes as green as the valleys of Connemara. 'A new job?'

'That's right,' she agreed, thinking how satisfying it was to see the normally unflappable billionaire looking so perplexed. 'I've worked for you for almost six years, Lucas,' she informed him coolly. 'Surely you don't expect me to still be cooking and cleaning for you when you reach retirement age?'

From the deepening of his frown, he was clearly having difficulty getting his head around the idea of retirement and, indeed, Tara herself couldn't really imagine this very vital man ever stopping work for long enough to wind down.

'I shouldn't have spoken to you so rudely,' he said slowly. 'And that *is* an apology.'

'No, you shouldn't,' she agreed. 'But maybe you've done me a favour. It's about time I started looking for a new job.'

He shook his head and gave a bland but determined smile. 'You can't do that.'

Tara stilled. It was a long time since anyone had said those words to her, but it was the refrain which had defined her childhood.

You can't do that, Tara.

You mustn't do that, Tara.

She had been the scapegoat—carrying the can for the sins of her mother and of her grandmother before her. She had been expected to nod and keep her head down, never to make waves. To be obedient and hard-working and do as she was told. To stay away from boys because they only brought trouble with them.

And she'd learned her lessons well. She'd never been in a relationship. There hadn't been anyone to speak of since she'd arrived in Dublin and had gone on a few disastrous dates, encouraged by her friend Stella. She tried her best to forget the couple of encounters she'd shared with one of the farm hands back home, just before she'd left for the big city and landed the first job she'd been interviewed for. The agency had warned her that Lucas Conway was notoriously difficult to work for and she probably wouldn't last longer than the month but somehow she had proved them wrong. She earned more money than she'd ever imagined just by keeping his house clean, his shirts ironed and by putting a hot meal in front of him, when he wasn't gallivanting around the globe. It wasn't exactly brain surgery, was it?

On that first morning she had slipped on her polyester housecoat and, apart from a foreign holiday every year, that was where she'd been ever since, in his beautiful home in Dalkey. She frowned. Why did Lucas even *own* a place this big when he lived in it all on his own, save for her, carefully hidden away at the top of the vast house like someone in a Gothic novel? It wasn't as if he were showing any signs of settling down, was it? Why, she'd even seen him recoil in horror when his friend Finn Delaney had turned up one day with his wife Catherine and their brand-new baby.

'You can't stop me from leaving, Lucas,' she said, with a touch of defiance. 'I'll work my month's notice and you can find someone else. That won't be a problem—people will be queuing up around the block for a job like this. You know they will.'

Lucas looked at her and told himself to just let her go, because she was right. There had been dozens of applicants for the job last time he'd advertised and nothing much had changed in the years since Tara had been working for him, except that his bank balance had become even more inflated and he could easily afford to hire a whole battalion of staff, should the need arise.

But the young redhead from the country did more than just act as his housekeeper—sometimes it felt as if she kept his whole life ticking over. She didn't mind hard work and once he had asked her why she sometimes got down on her hands and knees to scrub the kitchen floor, when there was a perfectly serviceable mop to be had.

'Because a mop won't reach in the nooks and crannies,' she'd answered, looking at him as if he should have known something as basic as that.

He frowned. She wasn't just good at her job, she was also reliable, and no laundry could ever press a shirt as well as Tara Fitzpatrick did. It was true that sometimes she chattered too much—but on the plus side, she didn't go out as often as other young women her age so she was always available when he needed her. If he asked her to cook when he had people over for dinner she happily obliged—and her culinary repertoire had greatly improved since he'd arranged for her to go on an upmarket cookery course, after pointing out there were other things you could eat, rather than meat pie. As far as he knew, she never gossiped about him and that was like gold to him.

He didn't want her to leave.

Especially not now.

He felt the pound of his heart.

Not when he needed to go to the States to deal with the past, having been contacted by a lawyer hinting at something unusual, which had inexplicably filled him with dread. A trip he knew couldn't be avoided, no matter how much he would have preferred to. But the attorney's letter had been insistent. He swallowed. He hadn't been back to New York for years and that had been a deliberate choice. It was too full of memories. Bitter memories. And why confront stuff which made you feel uncomfortable, when avoidance was relatively simple?

Lucas allowed his gaze to skim down over the old-fashioned denim jeans Tara wore beneath her housecoat. Baggy and slightly too short, they looked as if they'd be more appropriate for working on a farm. No wonder she'd never brought a man back in all the time she worked for him when injecting a little glamour into her appearance seemed to be an unknown concept to her. And wasn't that another reason why he regarded her as the personification of rock-like reliability? She wasn't surreptitiously texting when she should have been working, was she? Nor gazing into space vacantly, mooning over some heartbreaker who'd recently let her down. Despite her slender build, she was strong and fit and he couldn't contemplate the thought of trying to find a replacement for her, not when he was focussed on that damned letter.

He wondered how much money it would take to get her to change her mind, and then frowned. Because in that way Tara seemed different from every other woman he'd ever had dealings with. She didn't openly lust after expensive clothes or belongings—not if her appearance was anything to go by. She wore no jewellery at all and, as far as he knew, she must be saving most of the salary he paid her, since he'd seen no signs of conspicuous spending—unless you counted the second-hand bicycle she'd purchased within a fortnight of coming to live here. The one with the very loud and irritating bell.

Lucas wasn't particularly interested in human nature but that didn't mean he couldn't recognise certain aspects of it, and it seemed to him that a woman who wasn't particularly interested in money would be unlikely to allow a salary increase to change her mind.

And then he had an idea. An idea so audacious and yet so brilliant that he couldn't believe it hadn't occurred to him before. Sensing triumph, he felt the flicker of a smile curving the edges of his mouth.

'Before you decide definitely to leave, Tara,' he said, 'why don't we discuss a couple of alternative plans for your future?'

'What are you talking about?' she questioned suspiciously. 'What sort of plans?'

His smile was slow and, deliberately, he made it reach his eyes. It was the smile he used when he was determined to get something and it was rare enough to stop people in their tracks. Women sometimes called it his killer smile. 'Not here and not now—not when you're working,' he said—a wave of his hand indicating the rows of copper pans which she kept so carefully gleaming. 'Why don't we have dinner together tonight so we can talk about it in comfort?'

'Dinner?' she echoed, with the same kind of horrified uncertainty she might have used if he'd suggested they both dance naked in Phoenix Park. 'You're saying you want to have dinner with me?'

It wasn't exactly the way he would have expressed it—but want and need were pretty interchangeable, weren't they? Especially to a man like him. 'Why not?' he questioned softly. 'You have to eat and so do I.'

Her gaze fell to the collapsing mixture in her bowl. 'But I'm supposed to be making a cheese soufflé.'

'Forget the soufflé,' he gritted out. 'We'll go to a restaurant. Your choice,' he added magnanimously, for he doubted she would ever have set foot inside one of Dublin's finer establishments. 'Why don't you book somewhere for, say, seven-thirty?'

She was still blinking at him with disbelief, her pale lashes shuttering those strange amber eyes, until at last she nodded with a reluctance which somehow managed to be mildly insulting. Since when did someone take so long to deliberate about having dinner with him?

'Okay,' she said cautiously, with the air of someone feeling her way around in the dark. 'I don't see why not.'

CHAPTER TWO

THE AIR DOWN by the River Liffey offered no cooling respite against the muggy oppression of the evening and Lucas scowled as they walked along the quayside, unable to quite believe where he was. When he'd told Tara to choose a restaurant, he'd imagined she would immediately plump for one of Dublin's many fine eating establishments. He'd envisaged drawing up outside a discreetly lit building in one of the city's fancier streets with doormen springing to attention, instead of heading towards a distinctly edgy building which stood beside the dark gleam of the water.

'What is this place?' he demanded as at last they stopped beneath a red and white sign and she lifted her hand to open the door.

'It's a restaurant. A Polish restaurant,' she supplied, adding defensively, 'You told me to choose somewhere and so I did.'

He wanted to ask why but by then she had pushed the door open and a tinny bell was announcing their arrival. The place was surprisingly full of mainly young diners and an apple-cheeked woman in a white apron squealed her excitement before approaching and flinging her arms around Tara as if she were her long-lost daughter. A couple of interminable minutes followed, during which Lucas heard Tara hiss, *'My boss...'* which was when the man behind the bar stopped pouring some frothy golden beer to pierce him with a suspicious look which was almost challenging.

Lucas felt like going straight back out the way he had come in but he was hungry and they were being shown to a table which was like a throwback to the last century—with its red and white checked tablecloth and a dripping candle jammed into the neck of an empty wine bottle. He waited until they were seated before he leaned across the table, his voice low.

'Would you mind telling me why you chose to come and eat here out of all places in Dublin?' he bit out.

'Because Maria and her husband were very kind to me when I first came to the city and didn't know many people. And I happen to like it here—there's life and bustle and colour on the banks of the river. Plus it's cheap.'

'But I'm paying, Tara,' he objected softly. 'And budget isn't an option. You know that.'

Tara pursed her lips and didn't pass comment even though she wanted to suggest that maybe budget *should* be an option. That it might do the crazily rich Lucas Conway good to have to eat in restaurants which didn't involve remortgaging your house in order to pay the bill—that was if you were lucky enough to actually *have* a mortgage, which, naturally, she didn't. She felt like telling him she'd been terrified of choosing the kind of place she knew he usually frequented because she simply didn't have the kind of wardrobe—or the confidence—

which would have fitted into such an upmarket venue. But instead she just pursed her lips together and smiled as she hung her handbag over the back of her chair, still pinching herself to think she was here.

With him.

Her boss.

Her boss who had turned the head of everyone in the restaurant the moment he'd walked in, with his striking good looks and a powerful aura which spoke of wealth and privilege.

She shook her hair, which she'd left loose, and realised that for once he was staring at her as if she were a real person, rather than just part of the fixtures and fittings. And how ironic it should be that this state of affairs had only come about because she'd told him she was leaving, which had led to him bizarrely inviting her to dinner. Did he find it as strange as she did for them to be together in a restaurant like this? she wondered. Just as she wondered if he would be as shocked as she was to discover that, for once. she was far from immune to his physical appeal.

So why was that? Why—after nearly six years of working for him when her most common reaction towards him had been one of exasperation—should she suddenly start displaying all the signs of being attracted to him? Because she prided herself on not being like all those other women who stared at him lustfully whenever he swam into view. It might have had something to do with the fact that he had very few secrets from her. She did his laundry. She even ironed his underpants and she'd always done it with an unfeigned impartiality. At home it had been easy to stick him in the categories marked 'boss' and 'off-limits', because arrogant billionaires were way above her pay grade, but tonight he seemed like neither of these things. He seemed deliciously and dangerously accessible. Was it because they were sitting facing each other across a small table, which meant she was noticing things about him which didn't normally register on her radar?

Like his body, for example. Had she ever properly registered just how broad his shoulders were? She didn't think so. Just as the sight of two buttons undone on his denim shirt didn't normally have the power to bring her out in a rash of goosebumps. She swallowed. In the candlelight, his olive skin was glowing like dark gold and casting entrancing shadows over his high cheekbones and ruggedly handsome face. She could feel her throat growing dry and her breasts tightening and wondered what had possessed her to agree to have dinner with him tonight, almost as if the two of them were on a date.

Because he had been determined to have a meal with her and he was a difficult man to shift once he'd set his mind on something.

She guessed his agenda would be to offer her a big salary increase in an attempt to get her to stay. He probably thought she'd spoken rashly when she'd told him she was leaving, which to some extent was true. But while she'd been getting ready—in a recently purchased and discounted dress, which was a lovely pale blue colour, even if it was a bit big on the bust—she'd decided she wasn't going to let him change her mind. And that his patronising attitude towards her had been the jolt she needed to shake her out of her comfort zone. She needed to leave Lucas Conway's employment and do something different with her life. To get out of the rut in which she found herself, even though it was a very comfortable rut. She couldn't keep letting the past define her—making her too scared to do anything else. Because otherwise wouldn't she run the risk of getting to the end of her days, only to realise she hadn't lived at all? That she'd just followed a predictable path of service and duty?

'What would you like to drink?' she questioned. 'They do a very good vodka here.'

'Vodka?' he echoed.

'Why not? It's a tradition. I only ever have one glass before dinner and then I switch to water. And it's not as if you're driving, is it?' Not with his driver sitting in a nearby parking lot in that vast and shiny limousine, waiting for the signal that the billionaire was ready to leave.

'Okay, Tara, you've sold it to me,' he answered tonelessly. 'Vodka it is.'

Two doll-sized glasses filled with clear liquor were placed on the tablecloth in front of them and Tara raised hers to his—watching the tiny vessel gleam in the candlelight before lifting it to her lips. *'Na zdrowie!'* she declared before tossing it back in one and Lucas gave a faint smile before drinking his own.

'What do you think?' she questioned, her eyes bright.

'I think one is quite enough,' he said. 'And since you seem to know so much about Polish customs, why don't you choose some food for us both?'

'Really?' she questioned.

'Really,' he agreed drily.

Lucas watched as she scrolled through the menu. She

seemed to be enjoying showing off her knowledge and
he recognised it was in his best interests to keep her
mood elevated. He wanted her as compliant as possible
and so he ate a livid-coloured beetroot soup, which was
surprisingly good, and it wasn't until they were half-
way through the main course that he put his fork down.

'Do you like it?' she questioned anxiously.

He gave a shrug. 'It's interesting. I've never eaten
stuffed cabbage leaves before.'

'No, I suppose you wouldn't have done.' In the flickering light from the candle, her freckle-brushed face
grew thoughtful. 'It's peasant food, really. And I suppose you've only ever had the best.'

The best? Lucas only just managed to bite back a bitter laugh as he stared into her amber eyes. It was funny
the assumptions people made. He'd certainly tried most
of the fanciest foods the world had to offer—white pearl
caviar from the Caspian Sea and matsutake mushrooms
from Japan. He'd eaten highly prized duck in one of
Paris's most famous restaurants and been offered rare
and costly moose cheese on one of his business trips
to Sweden. Even at his expensive boarding school, the
food had been good—he guessed when people were
paying those kinds of fees, it didn't dare be anything
but good. But the best meals he'd ever eaten had been
home-made and cooked by Tara, he realised suddenly.

Which was why he was here, he reminded himself.
The only reason he was here.

So why were his thoughts full of other stuff? Dangerous stuff, which made him glad he'd only had a
single vodka?

He stared at her. Unusually, she'd left her hair loose

so that it flowed down over her narrow shoulders and the candlelight had transformed the wild curls into bright spirals of orange flame. Tonight she seemed to have a particularly fragile air of femininity about her, which he'd never noticed before. Was that something to do with the fact that for once she was wearing a dress, instead of her habitual jeans or leggings? Not a particularly flattering dress, it was true—but a dress all the same. Pale blue and very simple, it suited her naturally slim figure, though it could have done with being a little more fitted. But the scooped neck showed a faint golden dusting of freckles on her skin and drew his attention to the neatness of her small breasts and, inexplicably, he found himself wondering what kind of nipples she had. Tiny beads of sweat prickled on his brow and, not for the first time, he wished that the impending storm would break. Or that this damned restaurant would run to a little air conditioning. With an effort he dragged his attention back to the matter in hand, gulping down some water to ease the sudden dryness in his throat.

'The thing is,' he said slowly, putting his glass down and leaning back in his seat, 'that I don't want you to leave.'

'I appreciate that and it's very nice of you to say so, but—'

'No, wait.' He cut through her words with customary impatience. 'Before you start objecting, why don't you at least listen to what I'm offering you first?'

She trailed her fork through a small mound of rice on her plate so it created a narrow valley, before looking up at him, a frown creasing her brow. 'You can't just throw more money at the problem and hope that it'll go away.'

'So we have a problem, do we, Tara?'

'I shouldn't have said that. It's nothing to do with you, not really. It's me.' She hesitated. 'I need a change, that's all.'

'And a change is exactly what I'm offering you.'

Her amber eyes became shuttered with suspicion. 'What do you mean?'

He took another sip of water. 'What if I told you that I'm going to be leaving Dublin for a while, because I have to go to the States?'

'You mean on business?'

'Partly,' he answered obliquely. 'I'm thinking of investing in some property there. I need to spread my money around—at least, that's what my financial advisors are telling me.'

'This wouldn't have anything to do with that letter, would it?' she questioned curiously.

He grew still. 'What letter?'

'The one...' The words came out in a rush, as if she'd been waiting for a chance to say them. 'The one which arrived from America last week.'

Lucas wondered if she'd noticed his reaction at the time. If she'd seen the shock which had blindsided him. It suddenly occurred to him how much of his life she must have witnessed over the years—a silent observer of all the things which had happened to him. And wasn't that another reason for keeping her onside? Bringing another stranger into his home would involve getting to know a new person and having to learn to trust them and that was something to be avoided, because he didn't give his trust easily. His mouth hardened and his jaw firmed. And it wasn't going to happen. No way. Not when there was a much simpler solution.

'I'm planning a minimum six-month stay and I'm thinking of renting an apartment because the idea of spending that long living in a hotel isn't what you'd call appealing.' He slanted her his rare, slow smile. 'And that's where you come in, Tara.'

'Where?' she questioned blankly.

'I want you to come to New York with me.' He paused. 'Be my housekeeper there and I'll increase your salary—'

'You pay me very generously at the moment.'

He shook his head with a trace of impatience. Who in their right mind ever pointed out that kind of thing to their employer? 'The cost of living is higher there,' he said. 'And this will give you the opportunity to try living in a brand-new city. This could be a win-win situation for both of us, Tara.'

He thought she might show excitement and more than a little gratitude, not a look of sudden suspicion, which hooded her eyes. Inexplicably, he found his gaze drawn to the delicate bowed outline of her lips, which he'd never really noticed before. Well, of course he hadn't. He'd never been this close to her before, had he? Close enough to detect her faint scent, which was like no other perfume he'd ever encountered. Nor realised that her clear skin was porcelain-pale apart from those few freckles which dusted the upturn of her nose. He shook his head, perplexed by the observation and by the inexplicable rise of heat in his blood.

'New York,' she said slowly.

'You said you wanted a change. Well, what greater change from Dublin town than living in the buzzing metropolis of Manhattan? Didn't you go on a trip there last Christmas?'

She nodded.

'And didn't you have a good time?'

Once again, Tara nodded. She'd saved up and gone with her friend Stella, who was a nanny in nearby Dun Laoghaire, and they'd done the whole New York holiday thing together. A fun-packed snow and shopping trip, marred only by the fact that Tara had fallen over on the ice rink outside the Rockefeller building and grazed both her knees. 'We had a very good time.'

'So what's stopping you from saying yes?' he probed.

Tara nibbled on the inside of her lip, reminding herself that her plan had been to get *away* from Lucas—not to sign up for more of the same. She needed to remove herself from the influence of a powerful man who was selfishly pursuing his own interests. He certainly wasn't thinking about what was best for *her* at the moment, was he? Only what was best for him.

And yet.

She ran her fingertip over the frosted surface of her water glass. If she looked at it objectively couldn't this be the best of all possible outcomes? A trip to a glamorous city she was already familiar with, without all the uncertainty of having to fix herself up with a job? Wouldn't a spell in America provide the inspiration she needed to turn her life around and decide what she wanted to do next?

But still she held back from saying yes because something seemed to have changed between her and

Lucas tonight. Something she couldn't quite put her finger on because she had no experience of this sort of thing. Was she imagining the tension which was stoking up between the two of them, like when you threw a handful of kindling on the fire? She certainly wasn't imagining the heart-racing feeling she was getting whenever she stared into his gorgeous green eyes— not to mention the fact that her body was behaving in a way which wasn't normal. At least, not normal for her. Her nipples were aching and there was a delicious syrupy feeling deep in the very core of her. She could feel a weird kind of restlessness she'd never experienced before, which was making her want to squirm uncomfortably on the wooden seat, and she was having to concentrate very hard not to keep wondering what it would be like to be kissed by him.

Was it because they were in the falsely intimate setting of a candlelit restaurant, making her wish she'd chosen somewhere brighter? Or because she'd stupidly decided to wear a dress and wash her hair—as if this were a real date or something? And now she was left feeling almost *vulnerable*—as if she'd lost the protective barrier which surrounded her when she was working at his house and cleaning up after him.

He was still studying her with an impatient question in his eyes, as if he wasn't used to being kept waiting. Come to think of it—he wasn't.

'Well?' he demanded.

'Can I have some time to think about it?' she said.

He looked surprised and Tara guessed that most women wouldn't have thought twice about accompanying their billionaire boss to a glamorous foreign city with the offer of a pay-rise.

'How long do you want?' he demanded.

Tara chewed on her lip. Should she ask her friend Stella's advice? She certainly didn't have anyone else to ask. She'd been so young when her mother died that she hardly remembered her and her grandmother had passed away just before she'd come to work for Lucas. 'A few days?' she suggested and gave a little shrug. 'Maybe you'll change *your* mind in the meantime?'

'If you continue to prevaricate like this, then maybe I will,' he retorted, not bothering to hide his displeasure. 'Let's just get the bill and go, shall we?'

'Okay.' She rose to her feet. 'But I need to use the washroom first.'

Still unable to believe she wasn't grabbing at his job offer with eager hands, Lucas watched as she walked through the restaurant, his gaze mesmerised by the curve of her calves, which led down to the slenderest ankles he'd ever seen. Suddenly he could understand why men living in the Victorian age had found them highly arousing.

He told himself to look away but somehow he couldn't. Somehow Tara Fitzpatrick's back view seemed to be the most beautiful thing he'd looked at in a long time, with those red curls spilling wildly over her shoulders. Her dress was slightly creased from where she'd been sitting but it was brushing against a bottom firmed by hard work and regular cycling—a realisation which was rewarded by an unwanted hardening at his groin. What the hell was happening to him? he wondered irritably. Was it simple physical frustration? Had

Charlotte's unexpected appearance at his house this afternoon reminded him just how long it had been since he'd had sex? He remembered their split, when he'd grown bored with her and bored with bedding her. Because despite the actress's undeniable beauty and sexual experience, hadn't making love to her sometimes felt as if he were making love to a mannequin? *And there hadn't been anyone since, had there?* Not even a flicker of interest had stirred in his blood, despite the many come-ons which regularly came his way.

With an impatient shake of his head, he glanced at his cell-phone to see what the markets were doing, but for once his attention was stubbornly refusing to focus and when he looked up, Tara was back. She must have attempted to brush the fiery curls into some kind of submission, because they looked half-tamed. Her eyes were bright and her air of youthful vitality made his heart clench with something he didn't recognise. Was it cynicism? He shook his head, confused now and slightly resentful because he'd come out tonight thinking this was going to be a straightforward exercise and it was turning into anything but.

'The bill, Tara,' he said impatiently. 'Have you asked for it?'

'I've done more than that.' She gave a wide smile. 'I've paid it.'

'You've paid it?' he repeated slowly.

'It's very reasonably priced in here,' she said. 'And it's the least I can do, since we came here in your car.'

As he followed her out of the restaurant—after a farewell even more ecstatic than their greeting—Lucas found himself trying to remember the last time a woman had offered to pay for a meal. Not recently, that was for sure. Not since those days when he'd had nothing and heiresses had sniffed around him like dogs surrounding a piece of fresh meat. When he'd been forced to leave his fancy school because there had been no money— or so he'd been told. But pride had made him refuse to accept the charity of women who had been hungry for his virile body. He'd fed himself. Sometimes he'd eaten the food left lying around after a meal in the directors' dining room. And sometimes he just used to go without. Tara had been wrong when she'd suggested he'd never eaten peasant food, he thought, the harsh reminder of those days making his jaw clench as his car purred smoothly down the quayside towards them.

But when he joined her on the back seat the bitter memories were dissolved by a rush of something far more potent. Lucas felt a beat of promise and of heady desire. Flaring his nostrils, he inhaled her subtle scent, which was more like soap than perfume. Half turning his head, he saw the brightness of her hair and suddenly he wanted to tangle his fingers in it. One slender thigh was placed tantalisingly close to his—a gesture he suspected was completely lacking in provocation— yet right now it seemed the sexiest thing he'd ever encountered. He swallowed as desire beat through him like an insistent flame and if it had been anyone else he might have reached out and caressed her. Touched her leg until she was squirming with pleasure and widening her thighs and whispering for him to touch her some more.

But this was Tara and he couldn't do that because she worked for him. *She worked for him.* She made his bed and cooked his meals. Ironed his shirts and kept his garden bright. She was an employee he wanted to accompany him to America. She wasn't a prospective lover—not by any stretch of the imagination. He stared straight ahead, attempting to compose himself as the traffic lights turned red.

Her heart pounding and her shoulders tense, Tara told herself to stop feeling so nervous as the powerful car purred through the city streets because *none of this was a big deal*. She'd just had dinner with her boss—that was all—and he'd just offered her a job in America, which was a massive compliment, wasn't it? She'd never been in his chauffeur-driven car before either, and travelling home in such luxury should have been a real treat. Yet she was finding it difficult to appreciate the soft leather or incredibly smooth suspension as they travelled through Dublin. All she could think about was how *different* Lucas seemed tonight and how her reaction towards him seemed to have undergone a dangerous and fundamental shift. From being a demanding employer, he seemed to have morphed into a man she was having difficulty tearing her eyes away from. For the first time ever, she could understand why he inspired such a devoted following among women. Suddenly, she *got* why someone as beautiful as Charlotte would be prepared to humiliate herself in order to wheedle herself a way back into his life.

And I don't want to feel this way, she thought. *I want to go back to the way it was before, when I tolerated him more than idolised him and was often infuriated by him.*

The car pulled into the driveway of his Dalkey house but instead of being relieved that the journey was over,

all Tara could feel was a peculiar sense of disappointment. Blindly, she reached for the door handle, her usually dextrous fingers flailing miserably as she failed to
locate it in the semi-darkness.

'Here,' said Lucas, sounding suddenly amused as he
leaned across her to click a button. 'Let me.'

Of course. The door slid noiselessly open because
it was an electronic door and didn't actually have a
handle! What a stupid country girl she must seem. But
Tara's embarrassment at her lack of savvy was exac-
erbated by a heart-stopping awareness as Lucas's arm
brushed against hers. She swallowed. He'd touched her.
He'd actually touched her. He might not have meant to
but his fingers had made contact and where they had it
felt like fire flickering against her skin.

Scrambling out of the car into an atmosphere even
stickier than earlier, she cast a longing look towards
the heavy sky, wishing it would rain and shatter this
strange tension which seemed to be building inside her,
as well as in the atmosphere. She scrabbled around in
her handbag to fish out her key but her fingers were
trembling as she heard a footfall behind her and Lucas's shadow loomed over her as she inserted it trem-
blingly into the lock.

'You're shaking, Tara,' he observed as she opened
the door and stepped into the house.

'It's a cold night,' she said automatically, even though
that wasn't true. But he didn't correct her with a caustic
comment as he might normally have done.

And the strange thing was that neither of them moved
to put on the main light once the heavy front door had
swung shut behind them, and the gloom of the vast hall-

way seemed to increase the sense of unreality which had been building between them all evening.

There was something in the air. Something indefinable. Tara felt acutely aware of just how close Lucas was. His eyes were dark and gleaming as he stared down at her and she held her breath as, for one heart-stopping moment, she thought he was going to kiss her. She felt as if he was going to pull her into his arms and crush his lips down on hers.

But he didn't.

Of course he didn't.

Had she taken complete leave of her senses? He simply clicked the switch so that they were flooded with a golden light, which felt like a torch being shone straight into her eyes, and the atmosphere shattered as dramatically as a bubble being burst. A hard smile was playing at the edges of his lips and he nodded, as if her reaction was very familiar to him.

'Goodnight, Tara,' he said in an odd kind of voice. And as he turned away from her, she could hear the distant rumble of thunder.

CHAPTER THREE

THE NEXT FEW days were an agony of indecision as Tara tried to make up her mind whether or not to accept Lucas's job offer. She tried drawing up a list of pros and cons—which came up firmly weighted in favour of an unexpected trip to America with her boss. Next she canvassed her friend Stella, who told her she'd be mad not to jump at the chance of joining Lucas in New York.

'Why wouldn't you go?' Stella demanded as she folded up one of the tiny smocked dresses belonging to the twin baby girls she nannied for. 'You *loved* New York when we went last Christmas. Apart from the ice-rink incident, of course,' she added hastily. 'And that man really should have been looking where he was going. It's a no-brainer as far as I can see, so why the hesitation?'

Tara didn't answer. She thought how lame it would sound if she confessed that something felt different between her and Lucas and that something unspoken and sexual seemed to have flowered between them that night. Or would it simply seem deluded and possibly arrogant to imply that Dublin's sexiest billionaire might be interested in someone like her?

But something *had* changed. She wasn't imagining it. The new awkwardness between them. The shadowed look around his eyes when she'd brought in his breakfast the morning after that crazy dinner, which had made her wonder if his night had been as sleepless as hers. The flickering glance he'd given her when she'd put the coffee pot down with trembling fingers before he'd announced that he was flying to Berlin later that morning and would be back in a couple of days—and could she possibly give him her answer about accompanying him to America by then?

'Yes, of course,' she'd answered stiffly, wondering why she was dragging her feet so much when she knew what she *ought* to say. She practised saying it over and over in her head.

It's a very kind offer, Lucas—but I'm going to have to say no.

Why?

Because... Because I've fallen in lust with you.

How ridiculous would that sound, even if it weren't coming from someone who could measure her sexual experience on the little finger of one hand?

But it was easier to shelve the decision and even easier when he wasn't around So Tara just carried on working and when she wasn't working, she did the kind of things she always did when Lucas was away. She swam in his basement pool and began to tidy up the garden for winter. She made cupcakes for a local charity coffee morning and went to Phoenix Park with Stella and her young charges. She listened to Lucas's voicemail telling her he'd be late back on Thursday night and not to bother making dinner for him.

And still the wretched weather wouldn't break. It was so heavy and sticky that you felt you couldn't breathe properly. As if it was pressing against your throat like an invisible pair of hands. Sweat kept trickling down the back of her neck and despite piling her rampant curls on top of her head, nothing she did seemed to make her cool.

On Thursday evening she washed her hair and went to bed, listening out for the sound of Lucas's chauffeur, who had gone to collect him from the airport. It wasn't even that late, but several days of accumulated sleeplessness demanded respite and Tara immediately fell into a deep sleep, from which she was woken by a sudden loud crack, followed by a booming bang. Sitting bolt upright in bed, she tried to orientate herself, before the monochrome firework display taking place outside her bedroom window began to make sense. Of course. It was the storm. The long-awaited storm which had been building for days. Thank heavens. At least now the atmosphere might get a bit lighter.

Another flash of lightning illuminated her bedroom so that it looked like an old-fashioned horror film and almost immediately a clap of thunder echoed through the big house. The storm must be right overhead, she thought, just as heavy rain began to teem down outside the window. It sounded loud and rhythmical and oddly soothing and Tara sank back down onto the pillows and lay there with her eyes wide open, when she heard another crash. But this time it didn't sound like thunder. Her body tensed. This time it sounded distinctly like the sound of breaking glass.

Quickly, she got out of bed, her heart pounding and

her bare toes gripping the floorboards. What if it was a burglar? This was a big house in a wealthy area and didn't they say thieves always chose opportunistic moments to break in? What better time than amid the dramatic chaos of a wild thunderstorm?

Pulling on her dressing gown, she knotted the belt tightly around her waist and wondered if she should go and wake Lucas. Of course she should—if he was back. Yet she was dreading knocking on his bedroom door in a way she would never have done before she'd agreed to have dinner with him. Back then—in that unenlightened and innocent time before she'd started to fantasise about him—she wouldn't have been in an angsty state of excitement, wondering what she'd find. She knew he didn't wear pyjamas because she did his laundry for him. And that was the trouble. She knew so much about him and yet not nearly enough.

Quietly, she pushed open her bedroom door and crept along the corridor, her head buzzing. At least she'd made up her mind about how to deal with his job offer—because no way could she join Lucas in America now, not if she was harbouring stupid ideas about what it would be like to…to…

She cocked her head and listened. Was that the creak of a footstep on the stairwell she could hear, or just the normal sounds of the big house settling down for the night? It was difficult to tell above the sound of the drumming rain. Peering over the bannister, she could see light streaming from Lucas's room on the floor below and she crept downstairs towards it.

She had just reached his door when a figure appeared at the top of the stairs and Tara nearly jumped out of her skin when she realised that Lucas was standing there wearing nothing but a pair of faded denims, which he had clearly just slung on, because the top button was undone. And his chest was bare. Gloriously and deliciously bare—his washboard abs as beautifully defined as the powerful curves of his forearms. Tara felt the sudden flip of her heart and was furious with herself—because wasn't it shocking to be noticing something like that at a time like this? She was supposed to be investigating a night-time disturbance, not eying up her half-naked boss like some kind of man-hungry desperado.

'Lucas!' she breathed. 'It's you.'

'Of course it's me—who else did you think it would be? Father Christmas?' he snapped. 'And what the hell are you doing, creeping around the place like a damned wraith?'

She was still flustered by the sight of him wearing so few clothes, and her reply came blurting out, the words tumbling over themselves in their eagerness to be said. 'I… I heard a crash from downstairs and I thought it might be…' she shrugged '…a burglar!'

'And you thought the best way to deal with some potentially violent nutter was to confront him with nothing more effective than an indignant look in your eyes?' His gaze bored into her. 'Are you out of your mind, Tara?'

Tara licked her bone-dry lips. Yes, that was a pretty accurate description of the way she was feeling right now. But she could hardly tell him the reason why, could she? She could hardly explain that her fixation about him had been so great that it hadn't left room in her head for anything else, and certainly not common sense. 'So what was the crash?' she questioned. 'Did you find out?'

Lucas scowled, aware that his body was hardening in a way which was *not* what he wanted to happen. And the reason for his suddenly urgent desire was the most perplexing thing of all. Tara was standing there in some passion-killer of a dressing gown, which looked as if it had been made from an old bedspread, and yet a powerful sexual hunger was pumping through his veins. It defied all logic, he thought—just as his behaviour had done in the few days since they'd been apart. He'd been busy in Berlin, buying fleets of electric cars and planning to lease them out to businesses at a highly profitable rate. He'd had several high-powered meetings with the German transport minister and had been taken to an entrancing *Schloss*, situated outside the capital, where busty blondes had served them foaming tankards of beer. Yet all the time there had been a constant soundtrack playing in his mind as if it was on some infernal loop and giving him no peace. It had begun with Tara and ended with Tara and had involved plenty of X-rated images of how her pale and freckled body might look if it were naked in his bed.

Why the hell was he thinking so graphically about a woman he'd never even given a second glance to before?

Somehow he managed to drag his thoughts back to the present, realising that she was regarding him with a question in her eyes, and somehow he managed to dredge up a memory of what she'd asked him. 'It was something breaking in the kitchen,' he informed her tightly. 'You'd left a window in the pantry open and the wind made some figurine fall.'

'Oh, dear.' She bit her lip. 'I'd better go and tidy it up.'

'No. Leave it until morning,' he said firmly. 'You shouldn't be clearing up broken china at this time of night—though the ornament is beyond repair, I'm afraid.'

Tara nodded, her mouth working with an unexpected flare of emotion, despite all her mixed feelings about where that little statue had come from. She'd only put it there because she'd been planning to clean it tomorrow. 'Can't be helped.'

'Was it something special?'

It wasn't the kind of thing he usually asked and for a moment she almost told him about the figurine of St Christopher—the patron saint of travellers—which her mother had taken with her when she'd left for England, setting out on a life which was supposed to be so different from what she'd left behind. But why would you start explaining a woman's broken dreams to a man who probably wasn't really interested—and a man who was only half dressed? Wouldn't that lead to questions and then yet more questions, which might end up with her revealing telltale details about her background? And nobody wanted to hear those, least of all herself. She might as well write on a placard: *This is why I am such a freak.* She shook her head and turned away but not before the salty prickle of tears had stung her eyes.

Had Lucas seen it? Was that why his voice suddenly gentled in a way she'd never heard before?

'Tara?' he said.

Impatiently fisting away the tears, Tara didn't know what she'd been expecting but it wasn't for Lucas to turn her around to look at him. It was just a hand placed on her upper arm, through the thick barrier of her dressing gown. The type of reassuring gesture anyone might make to someone who was on the verge of crying, but it didn't feel remotely like that. It felt...*electric*. Tara had grown up in a house where physical contact was frowned upon, where nobody actually *touched* each other—and nobody had touched her in years. Was it that which made her response to Lucas so instant? Her blood was heating, like syrup on an open flame, and her body felt as if it were dissolving from the inside out. She sucked in a shuddered breath and somehow it seemed inevitable he should pull her into his arms. It was comfort, she told herself. That was all.

But it didn't feel like comfort. It felt like heaven. Like a taste of something she'd never quite believed in. He was so big and powerful—so warm and strong—that it seemed only natural to let her head fall to his shoulder and for her breath to fan the silken skin of his neck. Tara had no idea how long that wordless embrace lasted. It might have been a few seconds but, there again, it could have been longer. Suddenly he pushed her head away so he could look at her, his eyes searching her face long and hard, and she'd never seen him look so disorientated. As if he were in some weird kind of dream and was expecting to wake up at any minute.

But he didn't wake up—and neither did she. They remained standing in the same spot, staring into each other's eyes as if it were the first time they'd ever seen each other.

'You'd better go back to your own room,' he said unsteadily.

Afterwards, Tara would ask herself what had possessed her to behave in such an uncharacteristic way.

Was it the certainty of knowing she wasn't going to be
working for him much longer which made her throw
caution to the wind? Or just the fact that she'd never
felt like this before—as if her body were on fire with
a burning need too powerful to be ignored? For once
she wanted to cast aside the roles she'd been given in
life. To forget the person she'd been taught to become.
Obedient Tara. Wary Tara. The woman who had never
stepped out of line because that way lay danger and
she had been fearful of what might happen if she refused to comply.

But now there was no fear, only an audacity which
felt newly minted and exhilarating.

'Why?' she questioned.

Her question hung in the air.

'You know why,' he ground out.

And somehow she did. Even though she had no experience of such matters, Tara could tell that Lucas Conway wanted her in exactly the same way as she wanted
him. It was explicit in the tension which radiated from
his powerful body and the hectic gleam which was glittering from his eyes. Her mouth was dry as she gazed
at his lips and the temptation to kiss them was just too
strong to resist. Because those lips held the tantalising
promise of something else—something she was keen
to explore. Suddenly she reached up to wind her arms
around his neck, her thumbs stroking the dark waves of
hair which covered the base of his neck, and she heard
him suck in a breath.

'Go to bed, Tara,' he growled.

Again, that boldness. That strange, uncharacteristic boldness as she repeated her own guileless question. 'Why?'

'I don't want to take advantage of you.'

'We're not playing a game of tennis, Lucas.'

'You know what I mean,' he growled. 'I'm your employer.'

'Not right now you're not,' she declared fiercely. 'Unless you're planning on demanding I go and fix you a midnight snack or iron a shirt for you.'

An unexpected smile curved at his lips as Lucas realised how his humble housekeeper seemed determined to confound all his expectations tonight—in fact, to blow them clean away. She'd fearlessly come downstairs to tackle a potential thief like some kind of modern-day warrior queen. With her pale skin and red curls streaming down her back like a pre-Raphaelite painting, she looked fragile and ethereal and yet she was turning him on. Very, very much. And suddenly he couldn't stem his desire any longer, not with her slim body so near and her mouth so tantalisingly close. He angled his head to kiss her, wondering if he was breaking some kind of fundamental rule. Some unspoken moral code. And then he cursed himself for even posing such a stupid question. Of course he was. Big time. He knew that. But knowing didn't change anything—how could it when she was kissing him back with a hunger which felt as fierce as anything he'd ever encountered?

Her lips were as soft as petals and he could sense all the sweet promise in her slim young body. Already he felt as if he wanted to explode. As if he could tear that ugly dressing gown from her body and do it to her right there, up against the wall outside his bedroom. Yet something held him back and not just because this was the first time and instinct told him to savour it, in case there wasn't a repeat. There was also part of him—a growingly distant part of him, admittedly—which wondered if one of them was going to suddenly come to their senses. As if something would suddenly shatter this strange spell and leave them facing each other with an air of disbelief and embarrassment.

But that wasn't happening. The only thing on the agenda right now was that the kiss was growing deeper—and the first tentative thrust of her tongue was making his groin grow deliciously hard. Hell. What kind of sorcery was she wielding when she was doing so little? And why was her body still hidden from his hungry gaze, beneath the folds of that unspeakable dressing gown?

Pulling his mouth away from hers, he saw nothing but dazed compliance in her eyes and was unprepared for the ecstatic thundering of his heart in response. When was the last time he'd felt this...*excited* about having sex with a woman? Was it because this was the last thing he'd ever imagined happening, or because she was so different from anyone he'd ever been intimate with?

He thought about leading her to his bedroom in a way he'd done with other women countless times over the years, when instead he did something which had never happened before. Picking her up, he planted his foot in the centre of the door and kicked it wide open.

'Lucas!' breathed Tara, her voice sounding almost shocked as he carried her towards his bed, which was softly illuminated by the glow of a nearby lamp.

'What's the matter, Tara?' he growled. 'Don't you like the masterful approach?'

She shook her head so that her curls shimmered down her back like a halo of fire and he could see her licking her lips before her next words came out with a rush of bravado. 'I don't like you kicking the paintwork when I'm the one who has to clean it!'

He laughed—which was extraordinary because he didn't usually associate humour with sex—but his mirth was quickly forgotten as he lowered her to her feet. Pulling open the sash of her dressing gown, he narrowed his eyes on discovering she wasn't naked underneath. Far from it. A baggy T-shirt of indeterminate colour hung to the middle of her lithe thighs. 'You certainly aren't dressed for seduction,' he observed wryly as he peeled it over her head.

'I'm right…right out of silk negligees,' she breathed as he smoothed his hands down over her ruffled curls.

Once again, he could hear a trace of vulnerability behind her flippant response and so he kissed her some more while he dealt with his zip, which was straining almost painfully over his hardness. He waited for her to offer to help him, but she didn't—and maybe that was a good thing. He wasn't sure he trusted anyone to touch him when he was this close to coming.

Kicking off his jeans, he urgently peeled back the duvet, sinking her down onto the mattress and wrapping his arms tightly around her so that they were skin-on-skin. He could hear her gasp as his erection sprang against her belly and for one last time he heard a whisper of warning in the recesses of his mind. *Are you sure you're doing the right thing?* But her long legs were tangling with his with unashamed excitement and when he slid his hand between her thighs, she was so wet and warm and slippery. He wasn't sure at all, he realised, but the only power on earth which could stop him now was Tara herself and, judging by the way she was writhing beneath him, that wasn't going to happen any time soon.

'Oh,' he said, his voice dipping with approval as he whispered his fingertip over the engorged little bud which was slick with desire.

'Oh,' echoed Tara as a shimmer of incredible sensation swept over her. Was this what had been spoken about with such venom when she'd been growing up? The most wicked thing in the world which could bring with it terrible consequences?

He lowered his lips to hers again and the sweetness of his kiss made her heart want to burst from her chest. How was it possible to *feel* this good? She closed her eyes in ecstasy as he began to kiss her breasts, his tongue flicking against one nipple so that it peaked into his mouth as if it had been made for just that purpose. She quivered as his fingertips skated over her skin, leaving a trail of goosebumps in their wake as he explored her breasts and belly and the jutting bones of her hips. Suddenly she wanted to touch him back in the same intimate way but she was shy and scared—wondering if her inexperience would put him off and bring this all to an abrupt end.

She thought: *Am I going to be passive about this, or am I going to be a participant?* For the first time in her life, couldn't she just go with what she wanted to do rather than thinking about what was the *right* thing to do? Fired by a fierce tide of hunger, she whispered her hand down his spine and then drifted her fingertips to the flat planes of his stomach. Did he sense she was going to move her hand further down to explore his hardness for the first time? Was that why he gave a low laugh of expectation?

In the soft light she could see the pale pole of his hardness contrasted vividly against the burnished hue of his olive skin and Tara wondered why she wasn't feeling the fear she had expected on seeing an aroused man for the first time in her life. Because this felt perfectly natural, that was why. This was what was *supposed* to happen between a man and a woman.

Tentatively, and with the lightness of touch which made her such a good pastry-maker, she started to stroke him—but he endured the exploratory skate of her fingers for no more than a minute before shaking his head.

'If you carry on doing that, this will not end well,' he growled softly, reaching out for a foil packet on the locker and tearing it open with impatient fingers. Then he lifted her up to position her over him, so she was intimately straddling him, his tip nudging against her new-found wetness.

Tara gasped as he splayed his hands over her breasts, his thumbs playing with her thrusting nipples, which instantly made her want to squirm with pleasure—although she wasn't exactly in the ideal position to do any squirming.

'Ride me, Tara,' he urged huskily. 'Ride me.'

She didn't get a chance to tell him she didn't really know what he was talking about because, suddenly, he was pulling her down onto him so that his erection was pushing deep inside her, as if he was done with talking and couldn't wait a second longer. Pushing up right into her so that he filled her completely, and the warm rush of unexpected pleasure was slightly off-set by the unexpected shock of what was happening to her body. She could feel her muscles tense and the briefest split of pain. She closed her eyes and when she opened them again, she found Lucas staring up at her with an expression of disbelief on his rugged features and something else.

Was it regret?

Or was it anger?

'You're a virgin?' he bit out.

Breathlessly, she nodded.

He said something she didn't understand—she thought it might be in Italian, though what did she know?—and it sounded incredulous. He put his hands on either side of her hips and for a moment she thought he was going to remove her from his body and tell her to get out. But he didn't. With a look of intense concentration on his face, he flipped her over onto her back while he was still inside her, displaying a skill which spoke volumes about his experience. And once she was on her back he smoothed away the wild disarray of curls from her face and stared down at her.

'I think I'd better be the one in charge from now on, don't you?' he said thickly.

She nodded, terrified of saying the wrong thing. Ter-rified he was going to stop. Because she couldn't bear that—not when those amazing feelings were building up inside her again and he was bending his head to kiss her more deeply than before. And she was floating now. Floating off into a sweet and strange new world where nothing existed except the sensation of Lucas Conway thrusting deep inside her, his mouth capturing hers in kiss after kiss. He moved slowly at first and then faster—as if her body was sending out an unspoken command which he correctly interpreted and acted upon.

She didn't think it would happen. Not the first time. She might have been innocent but she'd read all the magazine articles, like everyone else. And when it did, her orgasm was nothing like she'd expected. Because how could she ever have anticipated that something could feel this good? As if the sweet spasms which were racking her body had transformed her, so that for a moment she felt as if she'd redefined what it meant to be human.

Her fingers dug into the damp skin at his back and she kissed his neck over and over again as his own movements changed. His thrusts became more urgent and she heard his shuddered groan just before he collapsed on top of her. She wrapped her arms around him and in that moment she felt as if she'd tumbled into paradise and never wanted to leave. But nearly six years of a boss-employee relationship couldn't be dissolved in a couple of minutes and the unmistakable balance of power between them hadn't changed. So she lay there perfectly still and waited to hear what Lucas had to say.

CHAPTER FOUR

TARA STARED OUT at the sodden morning to where the previous night's storm had left the garden completely battered—as if some giant malevolent fist had pummelled the shrubs and flowers and left them leafless and sad. Gloomily surveying the damage to her previously well-tended shrubs, she found herself wondering if Lucas was in the air by now. If he was already beginning the process of forgetting her. Probably. No doubt it would be a speedy process in his case—less so in her own, she suspected—as she remembered the awkward words which had followed their passionate bout of sex.

It had been the worst conversation of her life—though of course she'd been too young to remember her grandmother telling her that her mammy was dead, which she supposed she must have done. Worse even than the time she'd discovered the truth about her tarnished legacy— not from the person who *should* have told her, but from a sniggering trio of bullies on a freezing cold school playground in the rural wilds of Ballykenna.

Nope. She sighed as she turned away from the window. It had been an all-time low to hear Lucas's chilly statement as he'd coolly detached himself from her satiated and naked body and rolled to the other side of the bed, his voice as distant as the great space which had suddenly appeared between them. And, just as she must have done twenty times over—she found herself reliving that post-sex scenario, word by excruciating word.

It had started with Lucas. A flat, hard assessment which had allowed no room for manoeuvre.

'That should never have happened.'

The trouble was that on one level she had agreed with him. It shouldn't. While on another level...

The flip side of the coin was that she'd been lying there, basking in emotion and reaction and a million other things besides. She'd felt fulfilled and relieved—yes, relieved—grateful that she was capable of feeling all the stuff other women felt and that her body was functioning just fine. For a few crazy, misplaced minutes before her boss had spoken, she'd actually been thinking that maybe she *could* go to New York with him, after all. That perhaps they could carry on doing... well, doing *this*. All right, it hadn't been the most conventional beginning in the world—but the world wasn't a conventional place these days and who was to say they couldn't have some kind of relationship, even if it didn't last? But Lucas hadn't wanted to hear that. He hadn't wanted to hear anything which smacked of eagerness. Presumably what he'd wanted was an unflappable response which echoed his own sentiments—one which reassured him that she wasn't about to start reading something into a foolish act of passion which meant nothing in the grand scheme of things.

'No,' she'd said slowly. 'I suppose it shouldn't.'

'I can't believe what we just did. I just can't believe

it.' He had shaken his tousled dark head. 'I should have—'

'Honestly, Lucas, you don't have to explain,' she had butted in quickly, her voice sounding much sharper than usual and he'd turned his head to look at her in surprise, as if thinking she didn't usually talk that way to him, which of course she didn't. But then, they weren't usually lying buck-naked in bed, were they? And because she couldn't bear the thought of him voicing any more regrets and leaving her with nothing but uncomfortable memories of her first ever sexual experience—which happened to have completely blown her away—she had somehow forced a smile to her lips. She'd even managed a half-shrug, glad that her expression was mostly hidden by the thick fall of her curls. 'Things got out of hand, that's all. It's not a big deal. Really.'

'But you were a *virgin*, Tara.'

'So what? Everybody is a virgin at some point in their life. I had to lose it some day.'

'But not with...'

His words had tailed off but she'd wondered what he had been about to say. Not with someone like me, probably. Someone who was completely out of her league. A commitment-phobe billionaire who normally dated the kind of women most men lusted after, not a skinny redheaded employee who'd hardly even been kissed before.

'I can't offer you anything, Tara,' he had continued fiercely. 'If that's what you're thinking.'

How *dared* he presume to know what she was thinking? Hiding her hurt behind righteous indignation, Tara had decided to fight against the negative opinion he seemed to be forming of her.

'You thought I was holding out for the man I'd one day marry?' His look of surprise had told her she'd judged it correctly. 'That I wanted to trade my innocence for a big white dress and a triumphant march down the aisle? You think the only reason we country girls come to the city is because we're looking for a husband? Well, don't worry, Lucas. I'm not—and if I was, I wouldn't choose someone who clearly has no intention of ever settling down. Just like I'm not expecting anything to come of this. You're right—it shouldn't have happened and it certainly won't happen again. For one thing, you're off to New York, aren't you? And I'm staying here in Dublin to find myself another job, which was always the plan.'

Unlike that night over dinner, this time he hadn't attempted to persuade her to stay and Tara felt angry at herself for having supposed he might. And hurt, too. That was the stupid thing. Her heart gave a funny little twist. He obviously couldn't wait to put as many air miles between them as possible. She'd thought she couldn't possibly feel any worse than she did, and then he had proceeded to rub salt into the wound by being unusually considerate.

'Look, I don't want you to feel you have to rush into anything.' His words had been careful but he had seemed oblivious to the irony in them as he'd reached out to glance at his watch. 'You must use the house here in Dalkey for as long as it takes you to find a job you really like. I'll be away for at least six months and I don't want you feeling as if you've got to grab the first thing which comes to hand just to get away from here.'

He'd made her feel like a charity case but somehow

Tara had hidden her humiliation behind a tight smile as she'd scrambled off the bed. 'Thanks, I appreciate it.'

'Tara?'

'What?' Her voice had been toneless as she'd turned around to answer his deep command. And wasn't it crazy how the human spirit continued to hope no matter how much the odds were stacked against it? Hadn't she secretly been praying he was going to tell her to get right back into bed when one look at the shuttered indifference on his face had told her that any such hope was pointless? 'What is it?' she'd said.

He had shrugged, even though she'd been able to see his body shift uncomfortably on the bed and the rigid outline of his erection beneath the sheet had been abundantly clear. She had felt herself blush and had been grateful that the dim light of the room had hidden her embarrassment.

'Nothing,' he'd growled. 'It doesn't matter.'

So she had picked up her abandoned dressing gown and T-shirt and returned to her room without another glance at the naked man on the rumpled bed, and if she'd thought he might come running after her—well, he hadn't done that either.

In the morning she'd overslept—which she *never* did—and when she'd gone downstairs, she'd found a note lying on the table. A simple note. A note which was damning despite its air of considered politeness. Or maybe because of it.

Tara,
In view of what happened last night, I've brought my trip to New York forward by a few days. I'm sure you'll understand the reasons why.

> *Good luck with all that you do—you've been*
> *the best housekeeper I've ever had and any refer-*
> *ences I provide will reflect that opinion.*
>
> *I've paid you in advance for six months, so take*
> *your time choosing your next position.*
> *Lucas*

What position was he talking about? she'd wondered with a mild tinge of hysteria as she'd crumpled the note in her palm before hurling it into the fire where it had combusted into a bouquet of bright flames. The one which involved her straddling him before taking him deep inside her body?

But recriminations and casting blame were going to get her nowhere. She needed to think clearly and objectively and, most of all, she needed a new job. She went to a couple of employment agencies and scrolled through the newspapers for domestic vacancies, but nothing compared to working for Lucas. She even went on a couple of interviews but her heart wasn't in it and despite her glowing references she was turned down for both jobs, which didn't exactly do wonders for her self-esteem.

She was longing to confide in Stella but something held her back. Was it because she thought her friend might be shocked by what she'd done—essentially enjoyed a night of casual sex with her employer? Stella couldn't be more shocked than she was herself, Tara thought grimly as she polished the fine furniture in Lucas's sitting room, trying to keep herself busy. And she discovered very quickly that it was easy to procrastinate. To act as if nothing had really changed, except that it had.

Something had *really* changed.

Her periods had always been as regular as clock-work and so she was concerned from the very first day of being late. But there again, it was weird how your mind did its best to protect you by concealing the truth and cloaking it in all kinds of possibilities. She told her-self that there'd been so much upheaval lately it was no wonder she was a little out of sorts. She blamed the sud-den dip in the temperature as autumn suddenly swept through the city. She managed to keep these various myths alive for a whole fortnight. It was only when she'd been unable to keep her breakfast down, or her lunch for that matter—and Stella had popped round unexpect-edly to find her sitting white-faced in the kitchen—that the whole horrible truth came tumbling out, though it still needed a little prompting.

'So. Are you going to tell me what's going on, Tara?' her friend demanded. 'About why you're looking so awful and acting so distracted?'

Licking her tongue over bone-dry lips, Tara prepared to say something she was glad her grandmother wasn't alive to hear. Or her mother for that matter. 'I'm...preg-nant.'

There were a few astounded seconds while Stella ap-peared to be having some difficulty digesting what she'd just been told. 'I wasn't aware you were seeing anyone,' she said at last, carefully. 'Have I missed something?'

And here it was. The horrible reality. Did she try to dress it up into acceptable bite-sized chunks so that her friend might understand? Tara wondered desperately. No, there wasn't a single chunk of this which could in any way be described as acceptable. In the end she managed to condense it down into a couple of bald sentences which she still found difficult to believe.

'I had sex with Lucas,' she said. 'And I'm expecting his baby.'

'You had sex with Lucas Conway?'

'I did.'

'You're kidding me?'

'I'm afraid I'm not.'

Stella shook her head from side to side, her thick black hair gleaming in the autumn afternoon sunshine. 'I wasn't even aware you fancied him!' she exclaimed, blinking at her in astonishment. 'Or that you were his type!'

'I didn't. And I'm not.'

'So what happened?'

Tara shrugged and the bitter taste in the back of her throat only intensified. 'I still can't quite work it out.'

'Well, *try*, Tara.'

Tara worried her teeth into her bottom lip before meeting her friend's incredulous gaze. 'He said something pretty mean to me, which focussed me into thinking I should get a new job.'

'Which I've been saying to you for ages,' said Stella darkly.

'He told me he didn't want me to leave—'

'Please don't tell me he *seduced* you so you'd change your mind?'

Tara shook her head. 'Of course he didn't. It wasn't like that.'

'Then just how was it, Tara?'

How could you put into words something which had flared between the two of them over dinner that evening? Something which had changed the way they were with each other, so they'd suddenly gone from being boss and employee to a man and a woman who were achingly aware of the other? Even if you could, it wasn't something you'd dare admit to a friend, for fear of coming over as slightly deranged—or even stupid. Both of which were probably true in her case. 'It just happened,' she said simply. 'I can't explain it.'

There was a pause and Stella's eyes bored into her. 'So now what happens?'

This was the question which really needed answering and Tara knew that there was no alternative than to face the thing she was dreading more than anything else.

'I'm going to have to go to New York and tell him.'

CHAPTER FIVE

THE WORLD AS he knew it had just come to an end but Lucas kept his expression blank as he finished reading the letter the attorney had given him. It had shocked and sickened him—the final sentence dancing before his eyes—but somehow he kept it together. He could feel the punch of his heart and the faint clamminess at his brow, but his hands were steady as he folded the piece of paper carefully and slipped it back inside the envelope.

'Do you have any queries, Mr Conway?' the lawyer was asking him. 'Anything you'd like to discuss with us, regarding the contents?'

A million things, thought Lucas grimly—and then some. But they were the kind of questions which couldn't be answered by some anonymous attorney he could see was burning up with curiosity. Not when he could manage to work out the most important bits for himself.

And suddenly it was as if a heavy mist had lifted and everything which made up the sometimes confusing landscape of his past suddenly become clear. It explained so many important things. Why his 'father' had always been so cruel to him and why his mother...

His mother.

He felt a twist of something which felt more like anger than pain as finally he understood why he'd never felt as if he belonged anywhere. *Because he didn't. His parents were not his parents and he was not the man he'd thought himself to be. Everything had changed in the time it took to read that letter.*

And yet nothing had changed, he reminded himself grimly. Not really. He was still Lucas Conway, not Lucas Gonzalez. A pulse flickered at his temple. And no way was he ever going to call himself Lucas Sabato, his birth name. He shook his head. He was the man he had set out to be. A truly self-made man.

'We had some difficulty tracking you down after your father's death,' the lawyer was saying smoothly. 'Given that you'd changed your name and settled in Europe. And given, of course, that you were estranged from your family.'

Behind his desk the man was looking at him with a hopeful expression, as if waiting for Lucas to put him out of his misery and reveal why he had been so keen to conceal his true identity for all these years. Lucas felt his mouth flatten.

Because he had no intention of enlightening the lawyer.

No intention of enlightening anyone.

Why should he? His inner life had always been his and his alone—his thoughts too dark to share. And they had just got a whole shade darker, he realised bitterly, before pushing them away with an ease born of habit. Much simpler to adopt the slick and sophisticated image he presented to the world—the one which discouraged people to dig beneath the surface. Because who in their right mind wanted to explore certain and unremitting pain?

Hadn't that been one of the unexpected advantages to becoming a billionaire at such an early age—that people were so dazzled by his wealth, they didn't stop to explore his past too deeply? Or rather, people became so obsequious when you were loaded, that *you* were able to control how you wanted conversations to play out. He was good at evasion and obfuscation. He didn't even tell people where he'd been born—sidestepping curious questions with the same deft touch which had enabled him to become one of the youngest billionaires in all Ireland. His accent had helped to obscure his background, too. It had been difficult to place—his cultured New York drawl practically ironed out by years of multilingual schooling in Switzerland. And Ireland had provided the final confusing note—with the soft, lilting notes he had inevitably picked up along the way.

'Thanks for all your help,' he said smoothly as he rose to his feet, tucking the envelope into the inside pocket of his jacket.

He was barely aware of the lawyer shaking his hand or the secretary outside who stood up and smoothed her pencil skirt over her shapely bottom as he passed by, her hopeful smile fading as he failed to stop by her desk. Outside he was aware of the faint chill in the air. The reminder that fall was upon them. After a busy couple of weeks of business meetings, things had looked very different this morning when he'd lined up another apartment viewing, intending to stay in the city for a minimum of six months. Yet there was no reason to change that plan, he reminded himself. No reason at all. He hadn't been back here in years because he hadn't wanted to run into his father, but the man who had erroneously claimed that title was now dead and he wasn't going to let that bastard reach out from beyond the grave and influence him any more. Why *not* reclaim the city of his youth and enjoy it as he had never been able to do before?

With a quick glance at his watch, he set off by foot to meet the real-estate agent. He walked along Fifth Avenue, his body tensing as he stared up at the Flatiron building he hadn't seen since he'd been, what...fourteen? Fifteen? That had been the last time he'd spent his school vacation here. That particular homecoming had ended in the usual violence when his father had raised his fist to him but Lucas had turned his back and simply walked away, trying to block out the sound of the other's man's taunts which had been ringing in his ears.

'Not man enough to fight?'

It had been a flawed assessment because for the first time ever, Lucas had felt too *much* of a man to fight back. He'd filled out that summer and his muscles had been hard and strong. The almost constant sport he'd done at his fancy Swiss boarding school had made him into a fine athlete and deep down he knew he could have taken out his adoptive father, Diego Gonzalez, with a single swipe.

And the reason he hadn't was that because he was afraid once he started, he wouldn't know when to stop. That he would keep punching and punching the cruel bully who had made his life such a misery.

So he had carried on walking and not looked back.

The only other time he had returned had been for his mother's funeral, when the two men had sat on opposite sides of the church without speaking. With the cloying scent of white lilies making him want to retch, Lucas remembered staring at the ornate scrolling on the lavish coffin, realising he'd never really known the woman he'd thought at the time had given birth to him. And he had been right, hadn't he? He hadn't known her at all.

But he wasn't going to dwell on that. He had spent his life rejecting the past and he wasn't going to change that now.

Deliberately focussing his attention on the here and now, he saw a woman standing up at the lights in front of him and the tawny colour of her hair made him think about Tara, even though that was something else he had decided was off-limits. He'd told himself that it had been a mistake. That maybe it had happened because he'd been thrown off-balance by what had lain ahead of him in New York. But at least he had let her down gently and no real harm had been done. And as she'd said herself—she'd had to lose her virginity some time.

Yet his eagerness to put her out of his mind hadn't been the plain sailing he'd expected. His night-time dreams had been haunted by memories of her slim, pale body and the delicious tightness he'd encountered as he had entered her. He would wake up frustrated and angry—with a huge erection throbbing uncomfortably between his thighs.

He still couldn't quite believe he'd had sex with her—his innocent housekeeper. Someone who, despite her fiery curls, had always seemed to blend into the background of his life, so that he hadn't regarded her as a woman at all—just someone to cook and clean and scrub for him. But she'd been a woman that night in his bed, hadn't she? All milky limbs and hair which had glowed like fire as the storm had flashed through the sky with an elemental force which had seemed to mimic what had been taking place in his bed. He found himself recalling the passion with which she'd kissed him and the eagerness with which she'd fallen into his arms. And then the unbelievable realisation—of discovering he was her first and only lover.

How could he have been so reckless?

His uncomfortable preoccupation was interrupted by the vibration of the cell-phone in his pocket and when he pulled it out his fingers froze around the plastic rectangle as he saw the name which had flashed up onto the screen. He shook his head in slight disbelief, as if his thoughts had somehow managed to conjure up her presence.

Tara.

Quickly, he calculated the time in Dublin and frowned. Getting on for ten in the evening, when normally she would have been laying the table for his breakfast, before retiring to her room at the top of the house. Of course, he wasn't there to make breakfast for, so she was free to do whatever she wanted, but that wasn't the point. The point was that she was ringing him.

Why was she ringing him?

He couldn't think of a conversation they could possibly have which wouldn't be excruciatingly uncomfortable, but, despite wanting to let the call go to voicemail, he knew he couldn't ignore her. He might wish he could take back that night and give it a different outcome but that wasn't possible. And she'd been a faithful employee for many years, hadn't she? Didn't he owe her a couple of minutes of conversation, even if it was going to be something of an ordeal? What if there'd been a burglary—a bone fide one this time, not just some holy statue crashing to the floor in the middle of a storm?

He felt an unmistakable wave of guilt as his thumb hit the answer button. 'Tara!' he said, his voice unnaturally bright, and he thought how usually he would have greeted such a call with a faint growl—the underlying message that he hoped she had a good reason for ringing. 'This is a surprise!'

'Is it a bad time to ring?'

She sounded nervous. Maybe she was remembering that other time when she'd called him and he'd been abroad, with a model called Catkin. Despite the warning look he'd given her, Catkin had picked up his phone and answered it, her voice laughing and smoky with sex. He remembered Tara's stuttering embarrassment when she'd finally come on the line and the way the model had sniggered beside him, loud enough to be heard. And with that loathsome demonstration of feminine cruelty, she had unwittingly put an end to their relationship.

'I'm dodging pedestrians on Fifth Avenue, Tara,' he said lightly. 'So you may have trouble hearing me above all the traffic noise.'

'Oh.'

She sounded flat now and he thought how their easy familiarity seemed to have been replaced by an odd new formality as he asked a question which sounded more dutiful than caring. 'Nothing's wrong, I hope?'

Her response was cautious. As if she was picking out her words—like someone sorting through the loose change in their pocket while searching for a two-euro coin. 'Not exactly.'

Not exactly? What the hell was that supposed to mean? *Please don't start telling me that you miss me or that—God forbid—you've decided you're in love with me.* 'No burst pipes in the basement?' he enquired, his forced joviality not quite hitting the mark.

'No, nothing like that. Lucas, I have… I have to talk to you.'

He could feel his heart sink because this sounded exactly as he'd feared. He'd had too many of these conversations in the past with women unable to recognise that their needs were very different. That the sex they'd shared meant nothing—it was just sex. She probably wanted to see him again, and soon—while he most definitely wanted to close the page on it. 'I thought that's exactly what we *were* doing,' he said smoothly.

'No. I don't mean a phone call. I mean face to face!' she burst out, her voice tinged with a desperation he'd never heard there before.

'But I'm in New York, Tara,' he told her, almost gently, because if he was going to have to let her down—which he suspected he was—then he needed to be kind about it. Because wasn't it his own damned fault that his housekeeper was now clearly pining for him? 'And you're in Dublin.'

'No, I'm not,' she corrected, sounding a little more confident now. 'I've just flown into LaGuardia.'

'LaGuardia?' he echoed incredulously. 'You mean you're in New York?'

'Obviously.' Her voice became terse.

Afterwards Lucas would wonder how he could have been so stupid, but that was only afterwards, when the hard, cold facts had finally percolated into his disbelieving brain. Maybe it was the double whammy of finding out the truth about his parentage which had sucked all the sense and perception out of him. Which meant he was able to shelve the glaringly obvious reason why Tara Fitzpatrick had taken it into her head to follow him to America, and to give a nod of acknowledgement to the curvy real-estate agent who had appeared outside the main entrance of the apartment block.

'Look, I haven't got time for this now, Tara. I'm meeting someone. Hi, Brandy,' he said, forcing a smile before putting his mouth close to the phone and hissing into it. 'Can you take a cab from the airport?'

'Of course I can!' She sounded angry now. 'I'm not a complete fool.'

'Meet me in the bar of the Meadow Hotel at seven. We can talk then.'

He cut the call and walked up the stairs towards the elegant town house, where the agent was slanting him a great big smile.

CHAPTER SIX

DESPITE ALL HER BRAVADO, Tara wondered if Lucas had deliberately chosen to meet her in the most inaccessible bar in New York. It was situated deep in the bowels of the fanciest hotel she could ever have imagined—a place which instantly made her feel overheated, overdressed and scruffy. She'd worn a thick sweater with her jeans because it was autumn and the city was supposed to be colder than Dublin—but the temperature inside the hotel made it feel more like summer and consequently there were little beads of sweat already appearing on her brow and stubborn curls were sticking to the back of her neck, like glue. And she couldn't take the sweater off because she had only a very old vest top on underneath.

After convincing the granite-faced doorman that her appointment was genuine, she was instructed to put her anorak and old suitcase in the cloakroom, where she was given a look of frank disbelief by the attendant. Her long scarf she kept draped round her neck out of habit, like an overaged child still clutching a security blanket. Tucking her ticket into her purse, she walked through the huge foyer—past impossibly thin women on impossibly high heels who were smiling adoringly into the faces of much older men—and never had she felt quite so awkward. Several times she had to ask for directions and was made to feel even more self-conscious for not knowing where she was going. As if showing any kind of ignorance meant you'd failed a test you hadn't even realised you were taking.

Eventually she found the bar, which was situated down a dimly lit passageway—dimly lit and daunting with its understated display of quiet opulence and a lavish oriental feel. Standing in front of a display of coloured glasses and bottles, a barman was vigorously shaking a cocktail mixture as if it were a pair of maracas, playing to the group of businessmen sitting on tall stools at the bar in front of him. It was definitely a man's room but Tara was met with nothing but disparaging glances, indicating that without the clothes, the sophistication or the glamour, she was the wrong kind of woman to drink in a place like this. And didn't that simple fact acknowledge more clearly than words ever could just how awful the predicament in which she now found herself?

Where *was* Lucas? she thought, with a tinge of desperation as she sat down at a vacant table in the corner of the room and snuck a glance at her watch. And who was this woman called Brandy he'd been meeting when she'd telephoned him from the airport? She felt her self-esteem take another dramatic nose-dive as a familiar voice broke into her reverie.

'Tara?'

Thank heavens. Her heart pounded with relief. It was Lucas and he must have entered the room without her noticing because he was standing right beside her. She could detect his subtle scent as his shadow enveloped her, making her acutely aware of his powerful body. As befitted the sophisticated environment, he was wearing a suit, a crisp shirt and a tie—but, despite the elegant exterior, Tara knew all too well what lay beneath the sophisticated city clothes.

And suddenly he was no longer her soon-to-be ex-boss who had migrated to the opposite side of the globe, but the man with whom she'd shared all kinds of intimacies. The man with whom she had lain naked—skin next to warm and quivering skin. Who had stroked her eager body with infinite precision and licked his tongue over her puckering nipples. Had she really lost her virginity to the man she'd worked for and never looked twice at for all those years? Had he really thrust deep inside her as he'd taken her innocence and introduced her to that terrible and exquisite joy? How did something like that even *happen*?

Her heart began to race even faster. It was one thing being in Dublin and deciding that telling him to his face was the only way to impart her unwanted news—but now she wondered if she had been too hasty. Should she have sent him an email, or a text, even though it would have been an extremely impersonal method of communicating that she was carrying his baby? Suddenly what she was about to tell him seemed unbelievable—especially here, in this setting. Because this was his world, not hers. It was quietly moneyed and privileged—and it was pretty obvious that she stuck out like some country hick with her home-knitted scarf and cheap jeans.

'H-hello, Lucas,' she said.

'Tara.'

His voice was non-committal as he gave a brief nod of recognition, but as he turned to look at her properly Tara almost reeled back in shock because his face looked *ravaged*—there was no other word for it. The faint lines which edged his mouth seemed deeper—as if someone had coloured them in with a charcoal pencil. And despite the dim golden glow cast out by the tall light nearby, she could detect a bleak emptiness in his green eyes. As if the Lucas she knew had been replaced by someone else—a cool and indifferent stranger, but one who was radiating a quiet and impenetrable fury. Lucas was no even-tempered, angelic boss, but she'd never seen him looking like this before. What was responsible for such a radical change? Was he angry that she'd turned up without warning and was this to be her punishment—being given the ultimate cold shoulder for daring to confront him like this?

Well, his reaction was just too bad and she wasn't going to let it get to her. She couldn't afford to. She wasn't some desperate ex-lover chasing him to the far ends of the earth because she couldn't accept their relationship was over, but the woman who was carrying his baby. She needed to do this and she would do it with dignity.

'I know this is unexpected.'

'You can say that again.' He sat down opposite her, loosening his tie as he did so, but his powerful body remained tense as he looked at her. 'Have you ordered yourself a drink?'

Now was not the time to explain that she'd been too intimidated by the ambidextrous barman to dare to open her mouth, aligned with the very real fear that buying something here would eat dangerously into her limited budget. 'Not yet.'

'Would you like to try one of their signature cocktails?' He fixed her with an inquiring look and she knew him well enough to recognise that his smile was forced. 'They come with their own edible umbrella and are something of an institution.'

She tried not to look ungrateful, even though she found his tone distinctly patronising. But he was summoning a waitress who was travelling at the speed of light in her eagerness to serve him and Tara told herself not to be unreasonable. She had to look at it from his point of view. They'd had some bizarre unplanned sex and now it must look as if she were trying to gatecrash his new life. Because he still didn't know why she was here and what she was about to tell him—and it was going to come as a huge shock when he did.

So the sooner she did it, the better.

Nervously, she cleared her throat. 'Just a glass of water would be fine for me.'

The darkness on his face intensified, as if he had suddenly picked up on some of the tension which was making her push nervously at the cuticles of her fingernails, like someone giving themselves a makeshift manicure. He glanced up at the eager server who was hovering around his chair. 'Bring us a bottle of sparkling water, will you?'

'Coming right up, sir.'

And once they were on their own, all pretence was gone. The courteous civility he'd employed when asking her what she wanted to drink had all but disappeared.

All that was left in its place was a flintiness which was intimidating and somehow *scary*, because it suddenly felt as if the man sitting opposite was a complete stranger, and Tara shifted uncomfortably on the velvet seat, dreading what she had to tell him.

'So. I'm all ears. Are you going to tell me why you're here, Tara?' Those curiously empty green eyes fixed her with a quizzical look. 'Why you've made such a dramatic unannounced trip?'

Tara sucked in a deep breath, wishing that the water had arrived so that she could have refreshed her parched mouth before she spoke. Wishing there were some other way to say it. She sucked a hot breath into her lungs and expelled it on a shudder. 'I'm… I'm having a baby,' she croaked.

There was a silence. A long silence which even eclipsed Stella's reaction when she'd told her the news. Tara watched Lucas's face go through a series of changes. First anger and then a shake of the head, which was undoubtedly denial. She wondered if he would try bargaining with her before passing through stages of depression and acceptance—all of which she knew were the five stages of grief.

'You can't be,' he said harshly.

Tara nodded. This was grief, all right. 'I'm afraid I am.'

'You can't be,' he repeated, leaning forward so that his lowered voice was nothing more than a deep hiss of accusation. 'I used protection.'

Tara licked her lips, pleased when the server arrived with their bottle to interrupt their combat, although the silence grew interminably long as she poured the water and it fizzed and foamed over two ice-filled crystal glasses. It was only when the woman had gone and Tara had forced herself to gather her composure long enough to take a deep and refreshing mouthful that she nodded. 'I realise that. And I also understand that the barrier method isn't a hundred per cent reliable.'

Incredulously, he looked at her. 'The *barrier* method?' he echoed. 'Who the hell calls it that any more?'

'I read it in a book about pregnancy.'

'When was it published? Some time early in the eighteenth century?'

Tara urged herself to ignore his habitual sarcasm, which right now seemed more wounding than it had ever done before. This was way too important to allow hurt feelings and emotions to get in the way of what really mattered, which was the tiny life growing inside her. But neither was she prepared to just sit there and allow Lucas to hurl insults at her, not when he was as much to blame as she was. *And I don't want to feel blame,* she thought brokenly. *I don't want my baby to have all the judgmental stuff hurled at it which I once had to suffer.*

She put her glass down on the table with a shaky hand and the ice cubes rattled like wind chimes. 'Being flippant isn't going to help matters.'

'Really? So do you have a magic formula for something which *is* going to help matters, because if so I'm longing to hear it?'

'There's no need to be so...*rude*!'

He leaned forward so that the tiny pulse working frantically at his temple was easily visible. 'I'm not being rude, I'm being honest. I never wanted children, Tara,' he gritted out. 'Never. Do you understand? Not from when I was a teenage boy—and that certainty hasn't diminished one iota over the years.'

She told herself to stay calm. 'It wasn't exactly on my agenda either,' she said. 'But we're not talking hypothetical. This is real and I'm pregnant and I thought you had a right to know. That's all.'

Lucas stared at her, half wondering if she was going to suddenly burst out laughing and giggle, *'April Fool,'* and he would be angry at first, but ultimately relieved. He might even consider taking her up to his hotel room and exacting a very satisfying form of retribution—something which would give him a brief respite from the dark reality which had been visited upon him in that damned lawyer's office. But this was October, not April, and Tara wouldn't be insane enough to fly out here without warning unless what she said was true. And she wasn't smiling.

He thought about the ways in which he could react to her unwanted statement.

He could demand she take a DNA test and quiz her extensively about subsequent lovers she might have dallied with after he'd taken her innocence. But even as he thought it he knew only a fool would react in that way, because deep down he knew there had been no lover in Tara Fitzpatrick's life but him.

He could have a strong drink.

Maybe he would—because the time it took to slowly sip at a glass of spirit would give him time to consider his response to her. But not here. Not with half of New York City's movers and shakers in attendance and a couple of people he recognised staring at him curiously from the other side of the room. He wasn't surprised at their expressions, because never had anyone looked more as if they shouldn't be there than Tara Fitzpatrick, with her thick green sweater the colour of Irish hills and her striking hair piled on top of her head, with strands tumbling untidily down the sides of her pale face.

He saw that her ridiculously over-long scarf was wound around her neck—the multicoloured one she'd started knitting when she first came to work for him and which had once made him sarcastically enquire whether she ever planned to finish it. 'I don't know how to cast off,' had been her plaintive reply, and he had smiled before suggesting she ask someone. But he wasn't smiling now.

Was he ashamed of her? No. He'd broken enough rules in his own life to ever be described as a conformist and he didn't care that his skinny housekeeper was sporting a pair of unflattering jeans rather than a sleek cocktail dress like the few other women in the bar. And besides, hadn't he just discovered something about himself which would shock those onlookers in the bar and fill them with horror and maybe even a little pleasure at hearing about someone else's misfortune, if they knew the truth about him? The Germans even had a phrase for that, didn't they? Schadenfreude. That was it.

He needed to get away from these blood-red walls, which felt as if they were closing in on him, so he could try to make sense of what she'd told him. As if giving himself some time and space would lessen the anger and growing dread which were making his heart feel as heavy as lead.

'We can't talk here,' he ground out, rising to his feet. 'Come with me.'

She nodded obediently. Well, *of course* she would be obedient. Hadn't that been her role ever since she'd entered his life? To carry out his wishes and be financially recompensed for doing that—not to end up in his bed while he gave into an unstoppable passion which had seemed to come out of nowhere.

'Where are we going?' she questioned, once they'd exited the bar and were heading back down a dimly lit corridor towards the foyer.

'I have a room here in the hotel.'

'Lucas—'

'You can wipe that outraged look from your face,' he said roughly as he slowed down in front of the elevator. 'My mind is on far more practical things than sex, if that's what you're thinking.'

'Would you mind keeping your voice down?' she hissed.

'Isn't it a little late in the day for prudery, Tara?'

'I'm not being a prude,' she said, in a low voice. 'I just don't want every guest in this hotel knowing my business.'

He didn't trust himself to answer as he ushered her into the private elevator and hit the button for his suite. In tense and claustrophobic silence they rode to the top, his thoughts still spinning as he tried to come to grips with what she'd told him. But how could he possibly do that, when he'd meant what he said? He'd never wanted to be a father. Never. His experience of that particular relationship had veered from non-existent to violent— and he'd never had a loving mother to bail him out. At least now he knew the reason why, but that didn't make things any better, did it? In many ways it actually made them worse.

'In here,' he said tersely as the doors slid noiselessly open and they stepped into the penthouse suite of the Meadow Hotel, which was reputed to command one of the finest views of the Manhattan skyline. It was growing dark outside and already lights were twinkling like diamonds in the pale indigo sky. Most people would have automatically breathed their admiration on seeing such an unparalleled view of the city. But not Tara. She barely seemed to notice anything as she stood in the centre of the room and fixed those strange amber eyes on him.

'I came because I felt you had a right to know,' she began, as if she had prepared the words earlier.

'So you said in the bar.'

'And because I felt it better to tell you face to face,' she rushed on.

'But you didn't think to give me any warning?'

'How could I have done that without telling you what it was about?' She was quiet for a moment. 'I wanted to see your face when I told you.'

'And did my reaction disappoint you?'

'I'm a realist, Lucas. It was pretty much what I thought it would be.' She sucked in a deep breath. 'But I want you to know that this has nothing to do with any expectations on my part. I'm just giving you the facts, that's all. It's up to you what you do with them.'

Lucas flinched, suddenly aware of his heart's powerful reaction as he acknowledged he was to be a father. But it clenched in pain, not in joy. 'Brandy,' he said harshly. 'I'll order strong tea for you, but I think I need brandy.'

Her reaction was not what he'd been expecting. He'd thought she might be slightly pacified by him remembering the way she liked her tea—but instead she turned on him with unfamiliar fury distorting her face. 'Can't you leave your girlfriend out of it for a minute?' she flared. 'Can't we at least have this discussion in private without you talking to her?'

'Excuse me?' He narrowed his eyes. 'I'm afraid you've lost me, Tara. I haven't a clue what you're talking about.'

'You were meeting someone called Brandy when I called you from the airport!' she accused.

It might have been funny if it hadn't been so serious but Lucas was in no mood for laughing. 'That's the name of the house agent, not my girlfriend,' he gritted out, but her chance remark put him even more on his guard. Was she already showing signs of sexual jealousy? Already planning some kind of mutual future which would be a disaster for them both, despite her fiery words to the contrary? Well, the sooner he disabused her of that idea, the better. 'The drinks can wait. Why don't you take a seat over there, Tara?'

Tara didn't want to take a seat. She wanted to be back at home in her iron-framed bed in Dublin, where she could see the sweep of the Irish sea in its ever-changing guises. Except that it *wasn't* her home, she reminded herself painfully—it was Lucas's. She bit her lip. But it was the closest she'd ever come to finding a place where she felt safe and settled—far away from all the demons of the past. 'I'd prefer to stand, if it's all right by you,' she said stiffly. 'I've been sitting on a long flight for hours and I need to stretch my legs.'

He nodded but she couldn't miss the faint trace of frustration which briefly hardened his eyes. Was he finding it difficult to cope with the fact that, since she was no longer technically his employee, he could no longer order her around as he wanted?

'As you wish,' he said. His drink seemingly forgotten, he stared at her. 'So where do we go from here?'

She wished he would show more of the emotion she'd seen in the bar a little while ago. It might have been mostly anger and negativity but at least it was *some* kind of feeling—not this icy and remote person who seemed nothing like the Lucas Conway she knew.

But she didn't know him, did she? Not really. And not just because he kept so much of himself hidden that people called him a closed book. You couldn't really know someone you worked for—not properly—because their interactions had only ever been superficial. Yes, she'd witnessed different sides of his character over the years—but ultimately she'd just been a person on his payroll and that meant he'd treated her like an employee, not an equal.

Had he ever treated his girlfriends as equals? she wondered. Judging by the things she'd witnessed over the years she would say that, no, he had not. If you were heavily into equality, you didn't pacify dumped exes by giving them expensive diamond necklaces rather than an explanation of what had gone wrong. *And you are not his girlfriend,* Tara reminded herself bitterly. *You are just a woman he had sex with and now you're carrying his baby.*

His baby.

Her fingers crept to touch her still-concave belly and she saw him follow the movement with the watchful attention of a cheetah she'd once seen on a TV wildlife programme, just before it pounced on some poor and unsuspecting prey.

'How...pregnant are you?' he questioned, lifting that empty gaze to her face.

He said the word *pregnant* like someone trying out a new piece of vocabulary, which was rather ironic given that he was such a remarkable linguist. And Tara found herself wanting to tell him that it felt just as strange for her. That she was as mixed up and scared and uncertain about the future as he must be. But she couldn't admit to that because she needed to be strong. Strong for her baby as well as for herself. She wasn't going to show weakness because she didn't want him to think she was throwing herself in front of him and asking for anything he wasn't prepared to give.

'It's still very early. Seven weeks.'

'And you're certain?'

'I did a test.'

'A reliable test?'

Silently, she counted to ten. 'I didn't buy some dodgy kit at the cut-price store, if that's what you're hinting at, Lucas. I'm definitely pregnant.'

'Have you seen a doctor?'

She hesitated. 'No. Not yet.' Would it sound ridiculous to tell him that she'd baulked at going to see the friendly family doctor in Dalkey—himself a grandfather—terrified of how she was going to answer when he asked her about the father of her baby? Terrified he would judge her, as people seemed to have been doing all her life.

She watched as Lucas walked over to the cocktail cabinet—a gleaming affair of beaten gold and shiny chrome—but he seemed to think better of it and turned back to face her, that remote expression still making his face look stony and inaccessible.

'So what do we do next?' He raised his dark brows. 'Any ideas? You must have had something in mind when you flew all this way to tell me. You want to have this baby, I take it?'

Tara screwed her face up as a blade of anger spiked into her and for a moment she actually thought she might burst into tears. 'Of course I want this baby!' she retaliated. 'What kind of a woman wouldn't want her baby?'

She wondered what had caused that look of real pain to cross his face and thought it ironic that if they had some of the closeness of real lovers, she might have asked him. But they weren't *real* lovers. They were just two people who had let passion get the better of them and were having to deal with the consequences.

'So is it a wedding ring you're after?' he enquired caustically. 'Is that it?'

'I've no desire to marry someone who finds it impossible to conceal his disgust at such a prospect!'

'I can't help the way I feel, Tara. I'm not going to lie. I told you I never wanted children,' he gritted out. 'And the logical follow-on from that is that I never wanted marriage either.'

'I didn't come here for either of those things,' she defended. 'But at least now I know exactly where I stand.'

Her fingers tightened around the strap of her bag, which was still tied diagonally across her chest like a school satchel—in case anyone had tried to mug her. 'And since I've done what I set out to do, I'll be on my way.'

'Oh, really?' Dark eyebrows shot up and were hidden by his tousled dark hair. 'And where do you think you're going?'

She drew her shoulders back proudly. 'Back to Dublin, of course.'

He shook his head. 'You can't go back to Dublin.'

'Oh, I think you'll find I can do anything I please, Lucas Conway,' she answered, and for the first time in many hours she actually found comfort in a sense of her own empowerment. 'And you can't stop me.'

But it was funny how sometimes your own body could rebel and that you had no idea what was going on inside you. Maybe it was the economy flight which had been extremely cramped, or perhaps it had something to do with the dreadful food she'd been served during that journey, which she personally wouldn't have given to a dog. Add to that her see-sawing hormones and troubled emotions and no wonder that a sudden powerful wave of nausea washed over her.

Did her face blanch? Was that why Lucas stepped forward, an unfamiliar look of concern creasing his face as he reached out towards her? 'Tara? Are you okay?'

There was no delicate way to say it, even though it was an intimacy she had no desire to share with a man who'd shown her not one iota of compassion or respect since she'd got here.

She swayed like a blade of grass in the wind. 'I think I'm going to be sick!' she gasped.

He muttered something in French—or was it Italian?—and Tara moaned in dismay as he caught hold of her before she fell, lifting her up into his arms. Last time he'd carried her it had been a shortcut to his bed—and hadn't that been the beginning of all this trouble?—but this time he merely carried her to the nearest bathroom so she could give into the intense nausea which was gripping her. And as she bent over the bowl and started to retch he was still there, brushing away the curls which were dangling around her face, even though she tried to push him away with her elbow.

'G-go away,' she gasped, mortified.

'I'm not going anywhere.'

'I don't want you seeing me like this.'

'Don't worry about it, Tara,' he drawled. 'I've been on enough school football trips to have witnessed plenty of boys being sick.'

'It's not the same,' she moaned.

'Stop talking.'

She did but it took a while before she felt better—which was presumably why she allowed Lucas to dab at her face with a deliciously cool cloth. Then, after a moment of cold, hard scrutiny, he handed her some paste and a spare toothbrush.

'Wash up and take as long as you like. Call me if you need me. I'll be right outside.'

Tara waited until he had closed the bathroom door behind him, and as she staggered to her feet to the mirror she looked in horror at the white-faced reflection staring back at her. Her eyes were huge and haunted and her hair couldn't have been more of a mess, which was saying something. She tugged at the elastic band so that her curls tumbled free and shook her head impatiently.

What had she *done*?

Thrown up in front of a man who didn't want her here. Given him news he didn't want, a fact which he'd made no attempt to hide. Even worse, she was thousands of miles from home.

Past caring about her old vest top, she peeled off her too-hot sweater, splashed her face with water and then vigorously washed her hands until the suds stopped being grey. Then she brushed her teeth until they were minty-fresh and removed a hotel comb from its little packet of cellophane. It was slightly too small to properly attack her awry curls but she managed to marginally tame them before going over to the door. Whatever happened, she would cope, she thought grimly. Look what her mother and her granny had done during times when having a baby out of wedlock was the worst thing which could happen to a woman. She dug her teeth into her lip. It was true that their lives had been pretty much wrecked by circumstances but they had *managed*. And she would manage too.

Pushing open the door, she found Lucas waiting outside, his body tense and his features still dark with something which may have been concern but was underpinned with something much darker.

His question was dutiful rather than concerned. 'How are you feeling?'

'Better now,' she informed him stiffly.

'I'll ring for the doctor.'

'Please don't bother. I don't need a doctor, Lucas. Women often get sick when they're pregnant. I'd just like you to call me a cab and I'll stay in the hostel I've booked for tonight—and tomorrow I'll see about getting the first flight back to Ireland.'

He shook his head and now there was a look of grim resolution in his eyes. 'I'm afraid that's not going to happen, Tara.'

She tilted her chin in disbelieving challenge. 'You mean you're going to physically stop me?'

'If I need to, I will—because I would be failing in my duty if I allowed you to travel around New York on your own tonight, especially in your condition,' he agreed grimly 'There's only one place you're going right now and that's to bed.'

'I'm not—'

'Oh, yes,' he said, in as firm a voice as she'd ever heard him use. 'You most certainly are. There's a guest suite right along the corridor. I've put your things in there. And it's pointless arguing, Tara. We both know that.'

Tara opened her mouth to object but he was right because she recognised that resolute light in Lucas's eyes of old. She'd seen it time and time again when he'd been in the middle of some big negotiation or trying to pull off a deal which nobody had believed could ever happen. Except that he made things happen. He had the wherewithal and the clout to mould people and events to his wishes. And didn't part of her *want* to lie down on a soft bed and close her eyes and shut out reality? To have sleep claim her so that maybe when she opened her eyes again she would feel better.

But how was that going to work and what could possibly make this situation better? She had let history repeat itself and she knew all too well the rocky road which lay ahead. But none of that bitter knowledge was a match against the fatigue which was seeping through her body and so she nodded her head in reluctant agreement. 'Oh, very well,' she mumbled ungratefully. 'You'd better show me the way.'

Lucas nodded, indicating the corridor which led to the guest accommodation, though he noticed she kept as far away from him as possible. Yet somehow her reluctance ignited a flicker of interest he wasn't prepared for and certainly didn't want. He frowned. Maybe it was because women didn't usually protest about staying in his hotel suite or try to keep him at arm's length like this. He was used to sustained adoration from ex-lovers, even though he was aware he didn't deserve such adoration. But women would do pretty much anything for a man with a big bank account who gave them plenty of orgasms, he thought cynically.

He'd tried to convince himself during the preceding weeks that the uncharacteristic lust he'd felt for Tara Fitzpatrick had gone. It *should* have gone by now. But to his surprise he realised it hadn't and he was discovering there was something about her which was still crying out to some atavistic need, deep inside him. Even when she was in those ill-fitting jeans and a vest top, he couldn't help thinking about her agile body. The pale breasts and narrow hips. The golden brush of freckles which dusted her skin. He remembered the way he had lowered her down onto his rocky hardness and that split-second when he had met the subtle resistance of her hymen. And yes, he had felt indignation that she hadn't told him—but hadn't that been quickly followed by a primitive wash of pleasure at the thought that he was her first and only lover?

His throat grew dry as he continued to watch her. The red curtain of curls was swaying down her back, reminding him of the way he'd run his fingers through their wild abundance, and the hot punch of desire which had hardened his groin now became almost unendurable.

Yet she was pregnant. His skin grew cold with a nameless kind of dread—a different kind of dread from the one he had experienced in the lawyer's office. She was carrying his child.

And in view of what he had learned today—wouldn't any child which had sprung from his loins have an unknown legacy?

He opened the bedroom door and saw the unmistakable opening of her lips as her roving gaze drank in the unashamed luxury of her surroundings and it was a timely reminder that, despite her innocence, she was still a woman. And who was to say she wouldn't be as conniving as all other women, once she got into her stride? 'I hope it meets with your satisfaction,' he drawled. 'I think you'll find everything in here you need, Tara.'

Did she recognise the cynical note in his voice? Was that why she turned a defiant face up to his?

'I'm only staying the one night, mind.'

He wanted to tell her that she was mistaken, but for once Lucas kept his counsel. Let her sleep, he thought grimly—and by morning he would have decided what their fate was to be.

CHAPTER SEVEN

TARA OPENED HER eyes and for a moment she thought she'd died and gone to heaven. She was lying in a bed—the most comfortable bed she'd ever slept in—in a room which seemed composed mostly of huge windows. Windows to the front of her and windows to the side, all looking out onto the fairy-tale skyline of New York. She blinked as she levered herself up onto her elbows. Like giant pieces of Lego, the tall buildings soared up into the cloudless October sky and looked almost close enough to touch. Sitting up properly, she leaned back against the feathery bank of pillows and looked around some more—because last night she'd been too dazed and tired to take in anything much.

It was…amazing, she conceded. The ceiling was made of lacquered gold, the floors of polished parquet, so that everything around her seemed to gleam with a soft and precious life. On an exquisite writing desk stood a vase of pure white orchids so perfect that they almost didn't look real. And there, in one corner of the room, was her battered old suitcase, looking like a scruffy intruder in the midst of all this opulence.

She flinched.

Just like her, really.

Lucas must have put a glass of water on the bedside table and she reached out and gulped most of it down thirstily. On slightly wobbly legs she got out of bed and found the en-suite bathroom—a monument to marble and shiny chrome—and, after freshening up and brushing her hair, thought about going to find Lucas. She needed to talk about returning to Ireland and he needed to realise that she meant it and he couldn't keep her here by force. But her legs were still wobbly and the bed was just too tempting and so she climbed back in beneath the crisp sheets and before she knew it was dozing off.

She was woken by the sensation of someone else being in the room and her eyelids fluttered open to find Lucas standing beside the bed, staring down at her. His jaw was unshaven and the faint shadows shading the skin beneath his vivid green eyes made it look as if he hadn't had a lot of sleep. Black jeans hugged his narrow hips and long legs and his soft grey shirt was unbuttoned at the neck, offering a tantalising glimpse of the butterscotch-coloured skin beneath. Tara swallowed. It should have felt weird to have her one-time boss standing beside her bed while she lay beneath the duvet wearing nothing more than a baggy T-shirt, but somehow it didn't feel weird at all.

This is my new normal, she thought weakly. The same normal which was making her breasts sting with awareness as her gaze roved unwillingly over his powerful body. *Because this man has known you intimately,* she realised. *Known you in a way nobody else has ever done.* She felt a clench of exquisitely remembered desire, low in her belly, and before she could stop them vivid images began to flood her mind as she remembered how it felt to encase him—big and hard and erect. Despite everything she'd been brought up to believe, it hadn't felt shameful at all. It had felt *right*. As if she hadn't known what it really meant to be alive and to be a woman—until Lucas Conway had entered her and she'd given that little gasp as brief pain had morphed into earth-shattering pleasure.

Her heart was thumping so hard she was afraid he might notice its fluttering movement beneath her T-shirt and so she sat up, her fingers digging into the duvet, which she dragged up to a deliberately demure level, just below her chin. Only then was she ready to give him a cautious nod. 'Good morning.'

He returned the nod but didn't return the sentiment. 'Did you sleep well?'

'Very well, thank you.'

'Good.'

They stared at each other cautiously, like two strangers forced into close proximity. Tara cleared her throat, wishing she could get rid of the sense of there being an unexploded time bomb ticking away unseen in one corner of the room. But maybe that was what babies really were. She forced her attention to the pale sunlight which splashed over the wooden floor. 'Is it late?'

'Just after eleven.'

'Right.' Her fingers didn't relax their hold on the duvet. 'I need to start thinking about leaving—and it's no good shaking your head like that, because I don't work for you any more, Lucas. You can't just tell me no and expect me to fall in with your wishes, just because that's what I've always done before.'

His eyes narrowed and she saw the hard light of the practised negotiator enter them, turning them into flinty jade colour. 'I wouldn't dream of laying down the law—'

'You've had a sudden personality change, have you?'

He completely ignored her interjection, and didn't respond to the humour which was intended. 'We need to talk about where we go from here,' he continued. 'Just hear me out, will you, Tara?'

Once again she shifted awkwardly but the movement didn't manage to shift the syrupy ache between her thighs, which was making her wish that he would tumble down on top of her.

And where did that come from?

Since when had she become so preoccupied with sex?

She swallowed.

Since the night Lucas Conway had introduced her to it.

With an effort she dragged her thoughts back to the present, wondering why he was talking so politely. He must want something very badly, she thought, instantly on her guard. 'Okay,' she said.

He traced his thumb over the dark shadow at his jaw, drawing her unwilling attention to its chiselled contours. 'Would you like coffee first?'

'I'm not drinking coffee at the moment, thank you. I've already had some water and I think you're playing for time. So why don't you just cut to the chase and tell me what's on your mind, Lucas?'

Lucas's jaw tightened with frustration. It was easy to forget that she'd been working for him and sharing his house for years. Longer than he'd lived with anyone at a single stretch—and that included his parents. But despite the relative longevity of their relationship, Tara didn't really *know* him—not deep down. Nobody did. He made sure of that because he'd been unwilling to reveal the dark emptiness inside him, or the lack of human connection which had always made him feel disconnected from the world. Now he understood what had made him the man he was. He'd been given a kind of justification for his coldness and his lack of empathy—but that was irrelevant. He wasn't here to focus on his perceived failings. He was here to try to find a solution to an unwanted problem.

'You don't have any family, do you, Tara?'

She flinched. 'No. I told you at my interview that my grandmother brought me up after my mother died, and my grandmother has also since passed.'

Lucas nodded. Had she? He hadn't bothered probing much beyond that first interview, because if you asked someone personal questions, there was always the danger they might just ask them back. And Tara had impressed him with her work ethic and the fact that, physically, he hadn't found her in the least bit distracting. *What a short-sighted fool he had been.*

Because the truth was that she was looking pretty distracting right now—with those wild waves of hair bright against the whiteness of the pillow and her amber eyes strangely mesmeric as they surveyed him from beneath hooded eyelids.

'Why don't you put some clothes on?' he said, shooting the words out like bullets. 'And we'll have this discussion over breakfast.'

'Okay.' Tara nodded, not wanting to say that she didn't feel like breakfast—just relieved he had turned his back and was marching out of the room, wanting to be free of the terrible *awareness* which had crept over her skin as his green gaze had skated over her in that brooding and sultry way.

After showering and shrugging on an enormous bathrobe, she found him drinking coffee in the wood-panelled dining room—another room which was dominated by the Manhattan skyline and she was glad of the distraction.

'I can't believe the size of this place,' she said, walking over to the window and looking down at a green corner of what must have been Central Park. 'Why, even the bathroom is bigger than the hostel Stella and I stayed in last Christmas!'

'I'm not really interested in hearing how you saw New York on a budget,' he drawled. 'Just sit down and eat some breakfast, will you?'

As she turned around Tara was about to suggest it might do him good to stay in the kind of cramped accommodation which *most* people had to contend with, but then she saw a big trolley covered with silver domes which she hadn't noticed before. On it was a crystal jug of juice, a basket covered by a thick linen napkin, and on a gilded plate were little pats of butter—as yellow as the buttercups which used to grow in the fields around Ballykenna. She'd thought she wasn't hungry but her growling stomach told her otherwise and she realised how long it had been since she'd had a square meal. And she'd been sick last night, she reminded herself.

She walked towards the trolley to help herself but Lucas stayed her with an imperious wave of his hand.

'No. I don't want you collapsing on me again,' he instructed tersely. 'Sit down and I'll serve you.'

Tara opened her mouth to tell him she was perfectly capable of serving herself, but then a perverse sense of enjoyment crept over her as he offered cereal and eggs, fruit and yoghurt, and she sat there helping herself with solid silver spoons. Because if she allowed herself to forget her awful dilemma for a moment, this really *was* role reversal at its most satisfying! The food was delicious but she ate modestly, a fact which didn't escape Lucas's notice.

'No wonder you always look as if a puff of wind could blow you away,' he observed caustically. 'You don't eat enough.'

She buttered a slice of toast. 'My book on pregnancy says little and often if you want to try to avoid nausea.'

'Just how many books on pregnancy are you reading just now?'

'As many as I need. I know nothing about motherhood and I want to be as well prepared as possible.'

Wincing deeply, he sucked in a lungful of air. 'You say you want this baby—'

'I don't just *say* it. Lucas—I mean it,' she declared fiercely. 'And if for one moment you're daring to suggest—'

'I wasn't suggesting anything,' he cut across her, his expression darkening. 'And before you fly off the handle, let me make my views plain, just so there can be no misunderstanding. Which is that I'm glad you've chosen to carry this child and not...'

'Not what?' Tara questioned in bewilderment as his mouth twisted.

'It doesn't matter,' he snarled.

'Oh, I think it does.' She drew in a deep breath, putting her napkin down and realising almost impartially that her fingers were trembling. 'Look, we're not the same as we used to be, are we? We're no longer boss and employee.' She looked at him earnestly. 'I'm not sure how you'd define our relationship now—the only thing I'm sure about is that we're going to be parents and that means we need to be honest with each other. I'm not expecting you to say things you don't mean, Lucas, but I am expecting you to tell me the truth.'

The truth. The words sounded curiously threatening as they washed over him and Lucas stared at her. For a man who had spent his life denying and concealing his feelings, her heartfelt appeal seemed like a step too far and his instinct was to stonewall her. Yet he recognised that this was like no other situation he'd ever found himself in. He couldn't just buy himself out of this, not unless he was prepared to throw a whole lot of money her way and tell her that he wanted to cut all ties with her and his unborn child for ever.

He would have been a liar if he'd said he wasn't tempted...

But how could he do that, given the bitter reality of his own history which had been revealed to him by that damned lawyer? Wouldn't that mean, in effect, that he was as culpable as his own mother had been?

And look how that had turned out.

'Have you given any thought to how you see your future?' he demanded.

Tara shook her head. 'Not really. Have you?'

'Finish your breakfast first.'

But Tara's mouth felt dry with nerves and it was difficult to force anything else down, especially under that seeking green gaze—and she noticed he hadn't touched anything himself except two cups of inky coffee. 'I've finished,' she said, dabbing at her lips with a heavy-duty linen napkin.

He placed the palms of his hands on the table in front of him, looking like a man who meant business. 'So,' he said, his emotionless gaze still fixed on her. 'It seems there are several options available to us. We just have to work out which is the most acceptable, to both of us.'

Tara nodded. 'Go ahead,' she said cautiously. 'I'm all ears.'

He nodded. 'Obviously I will provide for you and the baby, financially.'

'Do you want me to do a dance of joy around the room just because you're accepting responsibility?'

His frown deepened. 'It's not like you to be quite so…irascible, Tara.'

Tara didn't know what irascible meant but she could guess. Should she tell him her crankiness stemmed from fear about the future, despite his offer of financial support? Surely even Lucas could work that out for himself. She studied the obdurate set of his jaw. Maybe that was hoping for too much. He was probably thinking about his own needs, not hers. And suddenly she realised that she couldn't afford to be vulnerable and neither could she keep second-guessing him. She was responsible for the life she carried and she needed to be strong.

'Why don't we just stick to the matter in hand?' she questioned coolly. 'Tell me what you have in mind.'

Was he surprised by her sudden air of composure? Was that why he subjected her to a look of rapid assessment? It was a look Tara recognised all too well. It was his negotiating look.

'You have no family and...neither do I,' he said slowly. 'And since I'd already made plans to stay in New York for the next few months, I see no reason to change those plans, despite the fact that you're pregnant.'

She thought how cleverly he had defined the situation, making it sound as if the baby had nothing to do with him. But perhaps that was exactly how he saw it, and Tara certainly wasn't going to push him for answers. She was never going to beg him, not for anything. Nor push him into a corner. 'Go on,' she said calmly.

'You could stay here and return to Ireland in time for the birth,' he continued. 'That would free you from unwanted scrutiny—or the questions which would undoubtedly spring up if you went back home.'

And now the surreal sense of calm she'd been experiencing suddenly deserted her. Tara could feel colour flooding into her cheeks as she pushed back her chair and sprang to her feet, her hair falling untidily around her face. 'I see!' she said, her voice shaking with emotion as she pushed a thick wave over her shoulder. 'You're trying to hide me away in a country where nobody knows me! You're ashamed of me—is that it?'

'If there's any shame to be doled out, then it's me who should bear it,' he retorted, though he seemed mesmerised by her impatient attentions as she brushed away her unruly hair with a fisted hand. 'I was the one who took your virginity!'

Was it her pregnancy which made Tara feel so volatile? Which made her determined to redefine his view of what had happened that fateful night, because didn't his jaundiced summary of events *downgrade* it? Or was it simply that she had carried the burden of shame around for a whole lifetime and suddenly the weight was just too much to bear? 'I wasn't some *innocent victim* who just fell into the arms of an experienced philanderer,' she declared.

'Thanks for the uplifting character reference,' he said drily.

'That wasn't how it happened,' she continued doggedly. 'That night we were just…'

'Just what, Tara?' he prompted silkily.

She stared down at her bare feet for a moment before lifting her heavy-lidded gaze to his. 'We were just a man and woman who wanted each other and status didn't come into it—not yours, nor mine,' she whispered. 'Surely you're not going to deny that, Lucas?'

Lucas was taken aback by her candour and surprised by his response to it, because an emotional statement like that would usually have made him run for the hills. Maybe it was the naïve way she expressed herself which touched something deep inside him—something which unfurled the edges of the cold emptiness which had always seemed such an integral part of him. For a moment he felt almost…*exposed*—as if she were threatening to peel back a layer of his skin to see what lay beneath. And no way did he wish her to see the blackness of his soul.

So that when his groin grew rocky it felt almost like

a reprieve, because wasn't it simpler to allow desire to flood him? To let lust quieten all those nebulous feelings he hadn't addressed since leaving the lawyer's office and which had been compounded by the bombshell Tara had dropped in his lap soon afterwards? He looked at the wild spill of her hair and her sleepy amber eyes. The towelling bathrobe she had pulled on was swamping her slender body in a way which should have been unflattering, but it only seemed to emphasise her fragility and suddenly he knew he wanted her again and he didn't care if it was wrong. Because the worst had already happened, hadn't it—what else could possibly eclipse the prospect of unwanted fatherhood?

Slowly yet purposefully, he walked across the dining room towards her and now her cat-like eyes weren't quite so sleepy. Their pupils had dilated so they looked night-dark against her pale skin.

'Lucas?' she questioned faintly. 'What do you think you're doing?'

'Oh, come on, Tara.' His voice dipped. 'You're a clever woman. Surely you've got *some* idea.'

He saw her touch her tongue to her mouth. Heard the sigh which escaped from her lips and a heavy beat of satisfaction squeezed his heart as he met her hungry gaze. He reached out and pulled her into his arms and instantly she melted against him, the quick tilt of her face silently urging him to kiss her.

So he did.

He kissed her for a long time—long enough for her to start wriggling distractedly, in a way which only stoked his growing desire. He covered her lips in kisses, then turned his mouth to her throat, loving the way her head fell back to give him access to her neck and revelling in the way her thick hair brushed so sensually against his hand. He undid the robe and bent his head to kiss her tiny breasts, flicking his tongue hungrily over her thrusting nipples. And when her hips circled in wordless plea against his aching groin, he inched his fingers up her thigh. Up over the silken surface of her skin he stroked her until at last he found her tight little nub and began to play with her and she was begging him not to stop. Until she was letting him back her up against the dining-room table and he was seriously thinking about sweeping all the crystal and silver and breakfast remains to the floor—and to hell with the mess—when he drew back and looked down into her dazed face.

'Let's go to bed,' he growled, his hands on her shoulders now.

Tara's throat constricted. Her breasts were aching and the syrupy heat between her thighs was making her wish he'd start touching her there again. She wished he hadn't stopped. That he'd just carried on with what he'd been doing and ravished her right there, in the dining room. She might have only had sex once before, but she badly wanted to do it again. She wanted to be carried along on an unstoppable tide of passion like the first time—she didn't want to have to make a *decision* about her actions.

But that was naïve—and short-sighted. She couldn't regard sex like candy—something she could just take when she felt like it. Not when there were so many issues they still hadn't addressed. Wouldn't that be totally irresponsible? There were a baby and a future to think of.

And without that baby she wouldn't be here in his arms like this, would she? She would be back home in Ireland while Lucas carried on with the rest of his life without her.

'No,' she said, shrugging his hands from her shoulders and taking a step backwards, even though her quivering skin still seemed to bear the delicious imprint of his fingers. With firm fingers she pulled the front of her robe together and knotted the belt tightly. 'This is not going to happen.'

His expression told her he didn't believe her. To be honest, she couldn't quite believe it herself.

'Are you serious?' he demanded.

'That's the whole point, Lucas,' she said, and suddenly her voice acquired a note of urgency as she stared into his beautiful face. 'I am. Very serious. I mean, what precisely are you offering me here?'

The flattening of his mouth told its own story. A cynical indication that he now found himself on familiar territory—that these were female demands being thrown at him, something which had been happening all his life. 'I should have thought it was perfectly obvious what I'm offering you, Tara,' he said. 'Sex, pure and simple. Because the bottom line is that we still want each other—surely you're not going to deny that?'

No. She couldn't deny what was obviously the truth—not when her nipples were pushing insistently against her robe, and his frustrated gaze indicated that their silent plea hadn't gone unnoticed.

'So why not capitalise on that?' he continued, with silky assurance. 'Stay with me here in New York and be my lover?'

The passing seconds seemed to drag into minutes as his words sank in. 'Your lover?' she verified slowly, thinking it was an inaccurate description when there was no actual *love* involved.

'Sure. It makes perfect sense. I can make sure you look after yourself and we can enjoy some pretty incredible downtime.' He gave a slow smile as his gaze travelled to the tiny pulse which was hammering at her neck. 'What's not to like?'

The fact he had to ask was telling, but Tara reminded herself that Lucas had never been known for his sensitivity to other people's feelings. She told herself he wasn't trying to insult her, or hurt her—he was just doing what he always did and taking what he wanted. And right now he wanted sex.

Perhaps if she'd been a different kind of woman she might have agreed. If she'd been worldly-wise she might have smiled contentedly and sealed the deal in the master bedroom of this luxury hotel suite. But not only was she inexperienced, she was also afraid. Afraid she would read more into physical intimacy than Lucas ever intended. Afraid of falling under his spell as she'd seen so many other women do and then being heartbroken when he tired of her, as inevitably he would. After all, this passion had happened so suddenly—it was likely to end just as abruptly, even if he hadn't already had a track record for short-lived affairs.

She still knew so little about him. He was the father of her child yet she didn't have a clue what his own childhood had been like, because he'd never told her. Just as he hadn't told her what—if any—role he wanted to play in their baby's life. Wasn't the sensible thing to do to stay here and address all these issues in a calm and collected way? Not let desire warp her judgement and threaten to turn her into an emotional wreck.

'Yes, I will stay here,' she said slowly and then, before he could touch her again and make her resolve waver, she started backing towards the door. 'But not as your lover, although I will continue to be your housekeeper.'

'My...housekeeper?' he repeated blankly.

'Why not? That was the role you originally offered me, before—'

'Before you spent the night in my bed?' he growled.

'It wasn't the whole night, Lucas. I left shortly after two a.m., if you remember.' She cleared her throat and forged on. 'If you're moving into an apartment you'll need someone in post here and nobody knows the job better than me. It'll allow us to get to know one another better and to think about what's best for the future.'

'Wow,' he said sarcastically. 'That sounds like fun.'

She told herself afterwards that he could have tried to persuade her otherwise, but he didn't. Of course he didn't. Maybe he was already having second thoughts. As he stood silhouetted against the Manhattan skyline, he seemed to symbolise cool, dark composure—while she felt churned-up, misplaced and frustrated.

'I'd just like us to be honest with each other. You know. Open and transparent. Surely that's not too much to ask?' But her voice was a dying croak and her cheeks burning hot, as she turned away from his mocking gaze and fled from the dining room.

CHAPTER EIGHT

'TARA.' LUCAS SUCKED in an impatient breath. 'What the *hell* do you think you're doing?'

A bright clump of hair was falling untidily into her eyes as the apartment door swung open and Tara stepped inside, dumping two bulging bags of groceries on the floor right by his feet.

'I'm bringing home the shopping,' she answered. 'What does it look like I'm doing?'

With a snort of something which felt like rage, Lucas picked up the bags and carried them into the kitchen, aware that she was following him and that his temper was building in a way which was becoming annoying familiar. He waited until he had planted the hessian sacks in the centre of the large table before turning round to confront her. She could be so stubborn! So infuriatingly hard-working! Maybe it had been a mistake to move out of the luxury hotel and into a place of his own, so that Tara could resume her housekeeper duties—especially if she was going to keep up this kind of pace. But she had insisted, hadn't she? Had set her lips in a firm and determined line, and Lucas had found himself going along with her wishes.

'You shouldn't be carrying heavy weights,' he objected.

'Two bags of shopping is hardly what I'd call heavy. Women in rural Ireland have been shifting far more than that for centuries.'

'But we aren't *in* rural Ireland!' he exploded. 'We're in the centre of Manhattan and there are plenty of services which will have stuff delivered right to your door. So why don't you use one of them?'

'What, and never go outside to see the day?' she retorted. 'Cooped up on the seventy-seventh floor of some high-rise apartment block so that I might as well be living on Mars?'

'This happens to be one of the best addresses in all of New York City!' he defended, through gritted teeth.

'I'm not disputing that, Lucas, and I'm not denying that it's very nice—but if I'm not careful I'll never get to see anyone and that's not how I like to live. I've discovered an old-fashioned Italian supermarket which isn't too many blocks away. And I like going there—I've become very friendly with the owner's wife and she's offered to teach me how to make real pasta.'

Remembering the Polish restaurant she'd taken him to in Dublin what now seemed like light years ago, Lucas silently counted to ten as Tara began putting away the groceries.

'At least you seem to be settling in okay,' he observed, watching her sweater ride up to show a narrow white strip of skin as she reached up to put some coffee beans in the cupboard.

'Indeed I am, though it's certainly very different from life in Ballykenna. Or Dublin, for that matter.

But it's not so bad.' She pushed tubs of olives and fresh juice into the refrigerator and bent to pick up a speck of something from the granite floor. 'And the people are the same as people everywhere.'

There was a pause as he watched her tuck an errant wave of hair behind her ear, which somehow seemed only to emphasise its habitual untidiness.

'You know, you're really going to have to do something about your appearance,' he said.

Her shoulders stiffened and, when she turned round, her amber eyes were hooded. 'Why?' she demanded suspiciously. 'What's wrong with it?'

He made a dismissive movement towards her outfit—a gesture provoked by frustration as well as disbelief that his life had been so comprehensively turned upside down by one annoyingly stubborn woman. He still couldn't get his head round the fact that she was pregnant, and not just because it was such an alien concept to a man who had never wanted a child of his own. It was compounded by the fact that she didn't look pregnant yet—and her body was as slim as it had ever been. Not that he'd seen any of it, he thought moodily. Not since that first morning, when they'd very nearly had sex on the dining-room table, before she'd had second thoughts and pushed him away.

What woman had ever refused him?

None, he thought grimly. Tara Fitzpatrick was the first.

The painful jerk at his groin punished him for the erotic nature of his thoughts, yet for once he seemed powerless to halt them. They'd been living in close proximity for almost three weeks yet not once had she wavered in her determination to keep their relationship platonic. He shook his head.

Not once.

At first, he'd thought her stand-off might be motivated by pride, or a resolve to get some kind of commitment from him before agreeing to have sex again, despite her defiant words about not wanting marriage. He'd thought the undoubted sizzle of chemistry which erupted whenever they were together would be powerful enough to wear down her defences. To make her think: what the hell? And then give into what they both wanted.

But she hadn't. And hadn't he felt a grudging kind of respect for her resilience, even if it was making him ache so badly every night?

Perhaps it was that frustration which had made him go out and find this apartment. Tara had been complaining that with fleets of chambermaids and receptionists and waiters, there was nothing much for her to do at the hotel—so he had ordered Brandy to come up with some more rental places for him to look at. Eventually she had found a penthouse condominium on West Fifty-Third Street, a place which had caused even his jaded palate to flicker with interest as Brandy had shown him and Tara through each large and echoing room. Eight hundred feet above the ground, the vast condo had oversized windows which commanded amazing views over park, river, city and skyline. There was a library, a wine room, a well-equipped gym in the basement and a huge pool surrounded by a vertical garden. Most women would have been blown away by the undeniable opulence and upmarket address.

But Tara wasn't like most women, he was rapidly coming to realise. She had been uncharacteristically quiet when he'd given her an initial tour of the building. He'd watched her suspiciously eying Brandy and she had then proceeded to exclaim that he couldn't possibly be planning to live in a place that size. He remembered the shock on Brandy's face—probably worried she was about to lose her commission. But that was exactly what he was planning to do, he had explained. In New York you needed to display the trappings of success in order to be taken seriously, and luxury was the best way in which to go about it.

'Wealth inspires confidence,' he'd told her sternly afterwards, but she had shrugged as if she didn't care and he thought she probably didn't.

'You still haven't told me what's wrong with my appearance!' Her soft Irish brogue voice broke into his thoughts as she closed the door of the refrigerator and, plucking her navy-blue overall from a hook on the back of the door, began to shrug it on.

He stared at her. Where did he begin? Aware of the volatility of her mood—something he guessed had to do with fluctuating hormones—Lucas strove to find the right words. 'In Ireland you used to cook dinner whenever I had people over, and I'd like to be able to entertain here, too. In fact, I've arranged to hold a small dinner next week.' He jerked his head towards the impressive vista of skyscrapers. 'Show off the view.'

'It sounds as if there's a "but" coming,' she observed as she did up the last button of her uniform.

Lucas sighed. Maybe there was no easy way to say this. 'That…that thing you insist on wearing,' he said, his gaze sweeping over the offending item and noticing for the first time that her breasts seemed a little bigger than before and that the material was straining very slightly across the bust. A pulse hammered at his temple. 'It's not really very suitable for serving guests.'

'But you never complained when I wore it in Dublin!'

'In Dublin, you came over as someone mildly eccentric—while here you're in danger of being classified as some kind of screwball.'

'Some kind of screwball,' she repeated, in a hollow voice. 'Is that what you think?'

He wasn't surprised to see her face whiten but he was surprised how uncomfortable it made him feel. 'No, it's not what *I* think and it wasn't meant to be an insult, Tara,' he amended hastily. 'Anyway, there's a simple solution.'

'Oh, really?' she said moodily.

'Sure. You can go shopping. Get yourself some new clothes. It's fixable. I'm happy to pay for whatever it takes.'

He thought that a man might reasonably expect to see a woman's eyes light up at the prospect of a lavish buying expedition when someone else was paying. But Tara failed to oblige. He could see her biting her lip and for one awful moment he thought she was going to cry and that made him feel oddly uncomfortable. Her face screwed itself up into a fierce expression but when she spoke, her voice was quite steady.

'Whatever it takes,' she repeated. 'You're saying you want me to buy new clothes to make sure that I look the part—whatever the part is?'

'That's one way of looking at it.' He flicked her unruly curls a glance. 'And maybe you could do something about your hair while you're at it.'

She drew herself up very straight. 'So what you're really saying is that you want to make me look nothing like myself?'

'That's a rather dramatic summary of what I just said, Tara. Think of it as making the best of yourself for once.'

'You certainly seem to have been giving it some thought.' Suddenly that fierce look was back. 'Yet you didn't even bother asking me what the doctor said when I went to see him yesterday, did you, Lucas?'

Lucas met the accusation in her eyes, his body growing tense. He knew he was still in denial about impending fatherhood. That he was doing what he always did when confronted with something he didn't want to deal with, or which caused him pain. He blocked it. Locked it away. Stored it in a dark place never to be examined again. But you couldn't keep doing that when there was a baby involved. No matter how much he tried to pretend it wasn't happening. He kept thinking that one morning he was going to open his eyes and discover that he was the same Lucas as before, one with no ties or commitments.

And that was never going to happen.

And lately he'd been experiencing the occasional flicker of curiosity—uneasy little splinters of thought which spiked away at him at the dead of night when he lay in bed, aching for Tara. He kept remembering the final line of the letter written by the woman who had subjected him to a life of misery. His mother. Except that she was *not* his real mother, despite the fact that she had spent her life pretending to be. Surely no real mother would have treated their child with such disregard and cruelty. And surely no real mother would have tried to justify their behaviour with the flimsiest of excuses. His mouth hardened with contempt. She had done it because she was desperate for the love of a man who didn't really want her. Because she had put her desire for Diego Gonzalez above everything else, hopelessly pursuing it with single-minded determination which had pushed her adopted son into the shadows. And that was what people did for *love*, he summarised bitterly as he processed the accusation Tara had just thrown at him. They manipulated and they lied.

'Okay. Tell me. What *did* the doctor say?' he said.

But his dutiful question seemed to irritate her more than please her and she answered it like someone recounting the words by rote. She and the baby had been pronounced perfectly healthy, she told him tartly, and she had been booked in for a scan the following week. Her eyes had narrowed like a watchful cat. 'Perhaps you'd like to accompany me, Lucas?'

'We'll see,' he said, non-committally, pulling back the cuff of his shirt to glance at his watch. 'I have a meeting scheduled, so I'd better run. And in the meantime, do you want to organise yourself a shopping trip?'

Tara met the faintly impatient question in his eyes and tried to tell herself he wasn't being unreasonable, though in her heart she wasn't sure she believed it. But then, she was mixed up and confused and out of her depth in so many ways. Frightened about the future and unsure about the present. Every morning she awoke to a slew of different emotions but she'd refused to let them show, knowing that bravado was the only way of surviving this bizarre situation.

Her feelings about Lucas didn't help and she thought how much easier it would be if she didn't want him so badly. If only she could blind herself to the certainty that he could break her heart. She sighed, because in many ways she couldn't fault him. He had accepted her demand for no intimacy with composure and then hadn't she driven herself half mad wishing he hadn't accepted it *quite* so calmly? Perhaps she'd imagined he would come banging on her door at night, demanding she let him in. Or just walk in without asking, slide in between her sheets and take her into his arms. And wasn't there a big part of her that wished he *would* adopt such a masterful role and take the decision right out of her hands?

But no. He'd found this apartment within walking distance of Central Park—with the assistance of the intimidating Brandy—and had booked her in to see a wonderful obstetrician in Lexington, who had immediately made her feel at ease. In some ways their familiar working pattern had simply been transferred to a brand-new setting, except that here she had no bicycle because even she had to concede that in New York it was too dangerous.

Yet despite their superficial compatibility, she recognised that he was still a stranger to her. Despite that one-off night of intimacy, she knew no more about Lucas Conway than when they'd been living in Dublin. Back then it hadn't been relevant—but now she was carrying his baby and it was. Didn't she have the *right* to know something about him?

'If I agree to smarten up my appearance to fit in with your billionaire image...' she hesitated, lifting her gaze to his '...will you agree to do something for me?'

His green gaze was shot with cynicism. 'Ah. This sounds like bargaining territory to me.'

'Maybe it is—but that's irrelevant. Because I know nothing about you. Do you realise that, Lucas? You're the father of my baby and yet you're practically a stranger to me...' As her words tailed off she heard a trace of vulnerability in her own voice. Did he hear it too? Was that why his face darkened? But he relented, didn't he? Even if he did clip out the words like bullets.

'What do you want to know?'

Everything. But Tara sensed that if she asked for too much, she would get nothing at all.

'What was in that letter?' she questioned suddenly.

'The letter?' he said, and she knew he was playing for time.

'You know very well which letter. The one you received just before you came out here.'

The one which made you act so strangely and look so haunted.

She hesitated and said it exactly as it was. 'Which made you look so angry. Who was it from, Lucas?'

It was then that Lucas realised just how much Tara Fitzpatrick *did* know about him. Probably more than any other living person. His mouth hardened. But that was the thing about having a housekeeper. You thought they just existed in the shadows of your life. You thought they were there simply to enable things to run smoothly—but in reality they were watching you and listening to you. Absorbing all the comings and goings like a detached observer. And although her pregnancy meant Tara could no longer be described as detached—didn't that make her entitled to know the truth?

A truth he had firmly locked away. A truth he had never talked about with anyone before.

His throat dried as he looked into the soft question in her eyes and suddenly he found himself wanting to confide in her—to share the ugly facts with someone. 'It was from my father's...' His mouth twisted as he said the word. 'His attorney.

'Your *father*?' She blinked at him in surprise.

He nodded. 'He died a few months back.'

'You never said—'

'Well, I'm saying now. There was no reason to tell you before,' he said. 'And before you look at me with that reproachful gaze—I didn't go to his funeral because I hated him and he hated me.' He paused for a moment, long enough to get his breathing under control but he could do nothing about the painful clench of his heart. 'They found a letter from my mother among his belongings. A letter addressed to me, which I never received, even though it was written a long time ago, just before she died. But it seemed she didn't have the sense or the wherewithal to give it to her own lawyer. She entrusted it to her husband, which was a dumb thing to do because he kept it all this time and I only got to hear about it after his death.'

Her face creased with concentration as if she was trying to piece together a puzzle of facts. 'So is New York where you were born?'

He shook his head, his laugh bitter as, unwittingly, she asked the most pertinent question of all. 'It's where I grew up. I don't know where I was born because last week I discovered that my mother and father weren't my real parents.'

'You mean...' she frowned again '...that they kept that fact hidden from you?'

'Yes, they did. Though there's a more accurate way of putting it. They lied to me, Tara. All through my life they lied.' He saw her wince. 'Because they couldn't bear to tell me the truth.'

'And was the truth so very awful?' she whispered.

'Judge for yourself.' There was silence for a moment before he shrugged, but his shoulders still felt as if they were carrying a heavy weight. 'The woman I called my mother was in her forties when she married a man who was decades younger. She was a hugely wealthy heiress and he was a poor, good-looking boy from Argentina—who happened to have a pretty big gambling habit. Her Alabama family cut her off when she married Diego and the two of them moved to Manhattan. In her letter she explained that he wanted a child but her age meant she was unable to give him one.' He gave a bitter laugh. 'So she did what she'd spent her whole life doing. She tried to solve a problem by buying her way out of it. That's when she bought me.' He gave a bitter laugh. 'My mother bought me, Tara. But when the deal was done she discovered that having me around wasn't the quick solution to her troubles she thought I would be. She'd bought me, but she didn't want me and neither did Diego. Suddenly I was in the way and a child isn't as easy to dispose of as one of the fancy sports cars my father loved to drive.'

And Tara stared at him dumbly, in horror and in shock.

CHAPTER NINE

'YOUR MOTHER *BOUGHT* YOU?' Tara demanded, eventually getting her voice back. 'She actually paid money for you?'

'She did.' His jaw tightened. 'I guess the illegal trade in selling babies has always gone on and back then it was pretty unregulated. She found someone who was willing to part with their infant child—for the right price, of course.'

'I can't believe it,' she breathed.

But Lucas seemed to barely hear her. It was as if having bottled it up—that he could do nothing to now stop the words spilling bitterly from his mouth.

'A child's memory only kicks in fragmentally,' he continued harshly. 'But I gradually became aware of the fact that he seemed to resent me from the get-go and then to hate me—only I could never understand why. It couldn't have helped that he obviously felt trapped in a marriage to a woman he clearly didn't love—only he loved her fortune too much to ever walk away.' But that hadn't lessened the tension, had it? His mother sobbing and kneeling on the floor in front of her younger husband, begging him not to leave her. And Diego gloating like a boastful schoolboy about the lipstick she'd found on his collar. Lucas snapped out of his painful reverie to find Tara staring at him, her eyes like two amber jewels in her pale face.

'What…happened?' she whispered.

He shrugged. 'They sent me away to boarding school in Europe to get me out of the way. And when I came home for the holidays…' he paused and maybe admitting this was the hardest part of all, harder even than the sharp blows to his kidneys '…he used to beat me up,' he finished, on a rush.

'But, surely he couldn't get away with something like that?'

'Oh, he was very careful. And clever, too. He only used to mark me where it wouldn't show.' He heard her sharp intake of breath and she opened her lips as if to say something, but he carried on—wanting to excise the dark poison which had lived inside him for so long. 'The summer I realised I could hurt him back was the last summer I ever came here and that's when I broke all ties with them.'

'But what about your mother?' she breathed. 'Do you think she was aware that Diego was cruel to you?'

He gave a cynical laugh as he gazed at her with weary eyes. 'Do you really think it's possible for a woman not to know when a child is being beaten within the home, even in a house as big and cold and dysfunctional as ours?'

'Oh, Lucas.' Her bottom lip had grown pinker from where she'd been worrying it with her teeth and he saw the genuine consternation on her face. 'That's terrible. I can't—'

'I didn't tell you because I wanted your sympathy, Tara.' Ruthlessly, he cut across her faltered words. 'I told you because you asked and because you of all people now have a right to know. Maybe now you can understand why I started a new life for myself and left the old one far behind. When my mother died my father was such a gambler it wasn't long before there was no money left to pay for my schooling in Switzerland, so at sixteen I got myself a job as a bellhop in a fancy Swiss hotel—'

'So that bit was true,' she interrupted wonderingly before offering an explanation to the frowning question in his eyes. 'There were rumours swirling around Dublin that you'd been a bellhop but I couldn't ever imagine you doing a job like that.'

For the first time, he smiled—and the rare flash of humour on his troubled face made Tara's heart turn over with an emotion she didn't dare analyse.

'You'd be surprised at what a comprehensive education it was,' he said. 'I watched and learned from all the customers who'd made money and a couple of them gave me advice on how to make it big. When I got to Ireland I changed my name and that changed everything. I worked hard and saved even harder and I had a little luck sprinkled over me on the way.' He gave a short laugh. 'Though maybe I deserved a little luck by then.'

But Tara didn't seem interested in the details about how he'd made his fortune. Instead she was frowning with intensity, as she did when she was trying to work something out, often a new recipe.

'I guess you did.' She hesitated. 'But going back to the letter.'

'I thought we'd moved on from the letter.'

Seemingly undaunted, she continued. 'Was there any information about your birth mother in it?'

'I know her name.'

'And have you…have you followed it up?'

'What do you think?' he snapped.

'Don't you think you might? I mean, you might have…' She shrugged. 'Well, you might have other relatives who—'

'I'm not interested in relatives,' he said coldly. 'I've had it with family. Surely you can understand why? And I don't want to talk about it any more.'

He stared at her almost resentfully, wanting to blame her for having unburdened himself like this, but the hard stir of his groin was making him think about something other than the past. The flood of desire was a welcome antidote to the pain which had resulted from his confession and had left him feeling as if someone had blasted him with an emotional blowtorch. And now he was empty and hurting inside. Did she sense that? Could she detect the hunger in his body which was demanding release? Was that why she walked over to where he was standing and wordlessly hooked her arms around his neck, pressing her face against his cheek and planting there a kiss so soft that it made his heart turn over with something nameless and unfamiliar? Something underpinned with danger, despite all its dark deliciousness.

He wanted to push her away and compose himself but his need for her was stronger than his need for equilibrium and he pulled her into his arms and held her close. His heart pounded. So close. The faint scent of her sex was already redolent in the air and something

inside him melted as instantly as ice hitting hot water.
Their gazes clashed for the nanosecond it took before
their lips fused and they shared the most passionate
kiss he could ever remember. And when there was no
breath left in his lungs, he reluctantly drew his head
away, his eyes silently asking her a question and she
answered it with a silent nod. This time she didn't call
a halt to what was happening as he laced his fingers in
hers. Instead, she let him lead her to the master bedroom, where he pulled the navy-blue ribbon from her
hair and all those unruly waves tumbled around her
shoulders with fiery profusion.

'Lucas?' she said, and he heard the uncertainty in her
voice—as if wanting him to define what was happening. But he couldn't. Or rather, he wouldn't. He would
never lie about his feelings for her. This didn't go deep.
It was one level only. Simple physical need. 'I want you,'
he said, very deliberately. 'That's all.'

Tara sucked in a ragged breath, wondering if it could
be enough. But it had to be enough, because nothing
else was on offer. And surely she could be grown up
enough to admit that she wanted him—unconditionally.
Surely she wasn't demanding words of love or commitment in order to enjoy sex with the father of her baby.
Her mouth dried. Some people might say they'd already
made progress in their relationship because he'd con-
fided in her—something which had never happened
before. He'd told her the awful truth about his upbringing—which made even her own seem less bad. Should
she have filled him in on some of her own, awful personal history? She thought not. Not then and certainly
not now when he seemed to need her very badly, and

all she wanted was to bring a little comfort and joy into his life. Hers, too. Was that so wrong?

'I want you, too,' she said shakily.

'But before we go any further, there's one thing we need to get straight, which is that I'm not offering undying love, or certain commitment. I can't put my hand on my heart and promise to be with you for the rest of my life, Tara,' he emphasised harshly. 'Because that's not what I do. You know that.'

She shook her head. 'I don't care.'

She could see his throat constrict as he undid the buttons of her uniform before quickly dispensing with the T-shirt and jeans beneath. And when he began to tug impatiently at his silk shirt, she found herself fantasising about what their baby might look like when it was born. Would it be a boy? she wondered yearningly as he lifted her up and laid her down on the bed. A boy who would grow up to be like his father—charismatic and powerful but with a dark side which was hiding so much pain? Or would it be a redheaded little girl, destined to be swamped by her own insecurities?

But her questions were forgotten as his naked body was revealed to her—all honed muscle and soft shadow and the subtle gleam of olive skin. His limbs were hair-roughened and his desire was achingly obvious and she should have been daunted but she wasn't. She stared at him with longing as the bed dipped beneath his weight and when he took her in his arms again, his skin felt deliciously warm against hers. Was it the conversation they'd just had which suddenly made Tara feel less of a conquest and more of an equal? Which gave her the courage to explore his body in a way she would never

have dared do before? Tentatively at first but with growing assurance, she stroked his skin, her fingertips running over washboard abs, down over the flat hardness
of his stomach, to whisper shyly at the dark brush of
hair beyond.

'Tara?' he said softly.

'What?'

'Don't keep doing that.'

'You don't like it?'

'I like it too much,' he growled.

'What…what shall I do instead?'

He gave a soft laugh. 'Part your thighs for me.'

She lifted her head as she did exactly that, their gazes
clashing as, very deliberately, he slipped his hand between her legs and began to finger the creamy-moist
folds with a light touch which sent a wild shudder
through her body.

'L-Lucas,' she breathed.

'Shh… Don't say a word. Just feel it. Feel what I'm
doing to you. It's good, isn't it?'

'Y-yes. It's very good.'

With delicate precision he strummed her where she
was wet and aching, until she was writhing helplessly
on the mattress and making unintelligible little gasps.
Sensation speared at her with each feather-light touch
as he propelled her towards some starry summit, so
that she felt like an unexploded firework which was
hurtling though the sky. And when the eruption came,
he entered her at the same moment—so she could feel
herself still clenching around his hardness as their bodies were intimately joined. It felt exquisitely erotic and
unexpectedly emotional and as she looked up into the

dark mask of his beautiful face, she touched her fingertips to his cheek.

'Lucas,' she said shakily, trying to bite back the soft words of affection which were hovering on her lips.

He stilled as he searched her face. 'It doesn't hurt?'

'No. It's…it's gorgeous.'

'I've never done it without protection before,' he husked. 'Never.'

She couldn't respond to his appreciative murmur because her eager body was short-circuiting her addled brain, making rational thought impossible as a second orgasm swept her up on a breathless wave. In fact there was no time to address his question until afterwards, when he had choked out his own pleasure and she could feel the sticky trickle of his seed running down her thigh in a way which felt deliciously intimate. Her heart was pounding and her skin was suffused with satisfied heat, but she forced herself to turn over to face the Manhattan skyline outside the window as she tried to get her muddled thoughts into some kind of order.

Because she could sense she was on the brink of something risky. Something which needed to be reined in and controlled. Yes, they'd just had the most amazing sex but in the middle of it hadn't Lucas gloated about never having had unprotected sex before while she'd been getting all emotional about him? And that was the fundamental difference between them. He required sex and nothing more and so she needed to be vigilant about her emotions. To make sure she didn't get sucked into a bubble of love and longing which would burst at the slightest provocation.

'Tara,' he said softly.

His finger was tracing a delicate path between her buttocks and she felt herself quiver in response. 'What?' she questioned, as casually as possible.

'I suspect what we've just done has made you change your mind about us being lovers.'

His assurance was as unshakable as his arrogance and she wanted to tell him that, no, she hadn't changed her mind at all. She wanted to declare that this had been another impetuous mistake which mustn't be repeated. But she couldn't keep running away from the consequences of her actions, could she? She couldn't keep letting sex 'happen' and then act like a scared little girl afterwards.

What she wanted was impossible. Like most people she wanted what she'd never had—in her case a secure home and a child raised within a loving family—despite all her proud protestations to the contrary. Lucas had offered none of these things and, having heard about his own childhood, she could understand why. It didn't matter that his parents hadn't been his birth parents—what mattered was that they had lied and been cruel to him. His whole upbringing had been built on a web of deceit and had destroyed his trust in other people. No wonder he was such a commitment-phobe who had never wanted marriage. No wonder he sometimes seemed to view women as the enemy, because to him they were. His birth mother had sold him and his adopted mother had lied to him and condoned her husband's violence towards him.

But he'd offered to support her and the baby, hadn't he? He hadn't said he wanted to be hands-on, but surely that was a start—a single block on which to build. She didn't know what the future held—nobody did—but there was no reason why they couldn't have a grown-up relationship within certain boundaries. Just so long as she didn't start weaving unattainable fantasises—and maybe for that reason alone, she needed to maintain an element of independence.

So she turned over and touched her fingertip to his face, tracing it slowly along the outline of his sensual lips. 'Yes, I'll be your lover,' she said. 'But I'm not going to give up my role as housekeeper.'

His eyes narrowed. 'Are you out of your mind?'

'Not at all. I need to work and that's my job. Otherwise, what am I going to do all day while you wheel and deal—go out to lunch and have my nails painted?' Her smile was serene as she met his disbelieving expression and she wouldn't have been human if she hadn't enjoyed that small moment of triumph. 'I've never had any desire to be a kept woman, Lucas, and I don't intend to start now.'

CHAPTER TEN

SUNLIGHT CAME STREAMING in through the huge windows, bathing Tara's body with a delicious glow, though the only thing she was really aware of was Lucas's hand, which was splayed proprietorially over one breast, while the other was tucked possessively around her waist. But possessive was a misnomer and any sense she *belonged* to him was simply an illusion, she reminded herself fiercely. The touchy-feely-couldn't-seem-to-keep-his-hands-off-her side of his character was just another feature of the fantastic sex they'd recently enjoyed. A physical reaction, that was all.

He was lazily stroking her nipple so that it was proud and aching, even though she had just gasped out one of the shuddering orgasms which had become so much a part of her daily life. Yet the crazy thing was that the man beside her felt as much of a stranger as he'd ever done—despite having told her about his childhood and despite having just been deep inside her body. Had she hoped that physical intimacy would automatically morph into mental intimacy? That the bond between them would grow stronger—maybe even unbreakable—the longer they spent together wrapped in each other's arms like this?

Yes, she had. Guilty on all counts. But what did she know about such matters when he was her first and only lover? Her mentor, too. In the most delicious way possible, he had tutored her in every aspect of sex. He'd taught her how to uninhibitedly enjoy her body and not to be shy about expressing her needs, but none of that seemed to have impacted on their relationship. Despite the physical closeness of sharing their bed each night and the often teasing banter they enjoyed much as before, nothing fundamental had changed within their relationship. Emotionally, at least, he was as detached as he had ever been.

Was that because, in spite of his obvious disapproval, she'd insisted in maintaining her role as his housekeeper—thus reinforcing the boss/employee dynamic which had always existed between them? She didn't think so. What else was she going to do all day if she wasn't cooking and cleaning—lie around in some cliché of a negligee waiting for Lucas to return from one of his business meetings? She would go out of her mind with boredom if she did that. Anyway, she didn't have a negligee—cliched or otherwise—because somehow she still hadn't got around to the shopping trip Lucas had suggested she take to avoid looking like 'a screwball'.

'Are you awake?' His murmured voice was soft against her hair.

Her thoughts still full of fundamental insecurities, Tara nodded. 'Mmm…'

The bedclothes rustled as he shifted, turning her round to face him so that their eyes were level and Tara prayed her face didn't give away her feelings. Feelings she was trying desperately hard to hide, because she knew Lucas was no stranger to the emotion she and countless women before her had experienced...

She was falling for him. Falling deep and falling hard.

She was scared to use the word *love* but it was the only one which seemed appropriate to describe the see-sawing of her feelings and the great rush of joy which powered her heart whenever he walked into the room. When he kissed her she sometimes felt she could faint with pleasure and when he made love to her, her happiness threatened to spill over. It didn't seem to matter how much she tried to deny what she was feeling, it made no difference. She wasn't sure how it had happened. If it was because he'd taken her innocence and made her pregnant.

Or because, beneath his glossy patina of success, he was wounded and hurting inside and that made her want to reach out to protect him?

He lifted a strand of hair and wound it slowly around his finger and Tara was reminded of one of those fishermen back home—the way they used to slowly reel in their catch, before leaving the floundering fish gasping for air on the quayside.

'You still haven't been shopping,' he observed.

'I know.' She shrugged her bare shoulders. 'But I haven't seemed to be able to find the time.'

'Then *make* the time, Tara. Better still. Why don't I schedule an appointment with a personal shopper and drop you off at Bloomingdale's? That way you won't be able to wriggle out of it the way you seem to have been doing.'

She blinked. 'What's Bloomingdale's?'

He frowned. 'You're kidding?'

'Lucas, this is a big city and I'm exploring it the best I can! I can't be expected to know every single name which trips off your tongue.'

'It just happens to be one of the best department stores in the city, possibly the world,' he commented drily. 'And I'll drop you off there tomorrow morning, on my way to work.'

'But we might not be able to get an appointment so soon,' she objected.

His brief smile managed to be both dismissive and entitled. 'Don't worry about that,' he drawled as he parted her thighs with insistent fingers. 'We'll get one. You haven't forgotten that you're cooking dinner for six on Friday, have you?'

'No, Lucas. I haven't forgotten. I've been racking my brains to come up with a menu for days.' She swallowed. 'And you doing that to me isn't exactly helping me work out what to give them for dessert.'

'Damn the dessert,' he growled.

But by the following morning Tara felt sick with nerves at the thought of presenting herself to a professional stylist, horribly aware of the plainness and age of her bra and pants and wishing she could skip the whole ordeal. Because it turned out that Lucas had been right and there were any number of slots available for a man like him at short notice.

Reluctantly, she joined him in the back of his car, which then proceeded to get snarled up in the early-morning traffic. It was stop-start all the way and Tara started to feel even more queasy. 'It's very stuffy in here.'

'I'll turn up the A/C.'

'I don't want any more air-conditioning. I want to get out and walk,' she croaked.

He shot her a quick glance. 'Are you okay?'

'I will be when I'm outside in the fresh air.'

'Fine. Come on, I'll walk you there.'

'Honestly, there's no need. I can find the store perfectly well on my own and I don't want you to be late for your meeting.'

'Tara,' he said patiently, his voice underpinned with a hint of impatience. 'It's pointless objecting. I'm taking you there. End of discussion.'

He tapped the glass and spoke to his driver, then helped Tara out of the car. She saw a glamorous woman blinking at her in bemusement as she stepped onto the sidewalk in her sweatpants and trainers, swamped by a big old anorak she'd brought with her from Dublin. But it was great to be outside, despite the stationary traffic and ever-hooting cars. As Lucas fell into a steady walk beside her, she thought how well he seemed to know the streets and when she remarked on this, he shrugged.

'I grew up near here.'

'Whereabouts?'

'It doesn't matter.'

'I think it does.' She came to a sudden halt and a speed-walking man who was holding a cup of coffee above his head had to swerve to avoid her. 'I'd like to see where you lived, please.'

Lucas bit back an exasperated retort, but he altered his steps accordingly, making no attempt to hide his displeasure. If it had been any other woman than Tara he would have refused point-blank. He would have delivered a rebuke which suggested that unless she started behaving as he wanted her to behave, their relationship would be over. But it wasn't any other woman. It was Tara and she was pregnant and therefore he could never completely finish a relationship with her because, one way or another, they would be tied through their child for the rest of their lives. He wondered if she had any idea how much that terrified him or if she'd begun to guess at the self-doubts which flooded through him. Was that why there had been a subtle shift in her mood lately? Why she'd become unpredictable and emotional. Had it just dawned on her that he could never be the man she probably wanted him to be? Why, only yesterday when he'd arrived home, her eyes had been red-rimmed from crying and she'd been unwilling to provide an explanation of what had upset her. It was only later that she'd blurted out about hearing a radio request show playing 'Danny Boy', after which she'd been overcome by a wave of temporary homesickness.

Deep down, he knew their situation was untenable in its current form. That in just over six months' time she would give birth to his child and everything would change. He realised that she wanted reassurance he would be there for her, and in the important ways he would. Providing for her financially was always going to be simple—but giving her the emotional support he suspected she needed was not. Why promise to be the man he could never be? Why bolster her hopes, only to smash them and let her down? Surely it would be kinder to let her know where she stood right from the start.

His footsteps slowed as he reached Upper East Side, his heart clenching as he came to a halt outside an opulent mansion which was edged by elegant railings and neatly trimmed greenery. Outwardly, it seemed that very little had changed. There were still those two old-fashioned-looking streetlights he'd used to stare down on from within the echoing loneliness of his childhood bedroom.

'This is it,' he said reluctantly, his gaze lifting upwards to the four-storeyed building.

'Gosh,' breathed Tara, loosening her long scarf as she craned her neck to look up at it. 'It's massive. You must have rattled around in it like peas inside a tin can.'

He gave a bitter smile. 'Oh, I don't know. Furniture and objects can occupy an astonishing amount of space and it's amazing what you can do with nineteen rooms and an unlimited budget. Especially when someone else is paying for it.'

'Nineteen rooms?' she verified incredulously. 'In New York?'

He nodded. 'The dining room was modelled on the one at the Palace of Versailles and there's a hand-painted ballroom with a pure gold ceiling—not to mention a corridor wide enough to ride a bicycle down.'

'Is that what you used to do?'

'Only once,' he said flatly. That had been the first time his 'father' had hit him. His nanny—one in a long line of indifferent women in whose care he'd spent most of his time—had spotted the bruise when he was getting ready for bed, readily accepting his explanation that he'd acquired it after falling over. Later he'd discovered that the nanny in question had been sleeping with Diego. He'd overheard an indiscreet maid exclaiming that the woman had been discovered naked with him on the floor of the library, a litter of used condoms beside them. All he could remember about that particular incident had been his mother screaming. And then sobbing as she had dramatically stabbed at her wrists with a blunt blade which had refused to cut.

Tara stared at him. 'You must have felt very isolated there. My own...' she ventured hesitantly, before plucking up the courage to say it. To reassure him that her own life hadn't been all roses around the cottage door. Well, it had—but there had been very sharp thorns on those roses. 'My own childhood was pretty isolated. In fact, my grandmother—'

'Look, I really don't have time for this,' he said, with an impatient narrowing of his eyes as he glanced at his watch. 'And I have an imminent meeting. The city tour is over and so is the glimpse into my past. Come on, let's get you to Bloomingdale's—it's only ten minutes' walk away.'

His dismissive attitude hurt. It hurt far more than it should have done, but that was a result of her own stubbornness—not something *he* had done. Because Lucas was just behaving in the way he'd always behaved. How many times did he need to say it for her to finally get the message that he wasn't interested in deepening their relationship? He didn't *want* to know about her past. What had made her the person she was. What had made her happy and what had given her pain. She was someone he was forced to spend time with because of the baby and someone he liked having sex with, but that was as far as it went.

So put up or shut up, she told herself fiercely as Bloomingdale's came into view—with all the differ-

ent flags fluttering in the autumn breeze and a quirk-
ily dressed brunette called Jessica waiting for them.
After initial introductions, she gave Tara a thorough
once-over before fixing her with a warm smile and
turning to Lucas.

'Don't worry, Mr Conway. She's in good hands.'

Lucas gave a brief nod. 'Thanks. Just do what it
takes. I'll be back tomorrow night in time for dinner,
Tara. Okay?'

Tara nodded and thought how crazy the whole situation was. Right up until they'd left the apartment that
morning they'd been hungrily exploring each other's
bodies—yet now, in the cold and clear light of day,
she was expected to give him a cool farewell, as if she
meant nothing to him.

Because she didn't.

'Right,' said Jessica, turning towards Tara as Lucas's car pulled away from the kerb. 'Let's get this fairy
dust working.'

It was an experience Tara had never thought could
happen to someone like her. Pushing all her troubled
thoughts resolutely from her mind, she felt positively
Cinderella-like as Jessica led her through all the plush
and beautifully lit departments, which were perfumed
with all manner of delicious scents. She'd been planning to purchase only a modest wardrobe but it seemed
Lucas had forewarned the personal shopper this might
be the case because she was overruled in pretty much
everything.

'I've never owned a shirt like this before,' she observed wonderingly, running her fingertips over the
delicate fabric. 'I'll save it for best.'

'Ah, but you'll need more than one,' responded Jessica, with a smile. 'Which means you won't have to.'

In the space of a couple of hours, Tara went from being someone who'd never owned a single silk shirt, to someone who now had several. For the snowy New York winter she snuggled into an oversized metallic anorak, its hood lined with shaggy faux fur, which Jessica told her was fresh off the runway, while for more formal occasions came a mid-length coat in midnight blue, the warmest coat Tara had ever worn. An accompanying cobalt scarf was plucked from a rainbow selection and Jessica's gaze travelled ruefully to the overly long home-knit, which lay abandoned on a nearby chair like a large and neglected woollen snake. 'You might want to find that another home,' she suggested gently.

Tara felt a momentary pang before being persuaded into the first of many dresses—slinky shirtwaisters and soft knits which Jessica said emphasised her slim frame. Next came boots—long boots and ankle boots— plus a pair of trendy shoes with lace inserts to go with a swingy chiffon shirt and boxy denim jacket. There were exquisite embroidered bras and matching thongs, as well as T-shirt bras with more practical pants. And Tara felt momentarily overwhelmed as she acknowledged that it had been Lucas's murmured appreciation which had made her revel in her own body instead of being ashamed of it. He'd never moaned about the state of her underwear, had he? Not really. He'd always been more concerned in taking it off than complaining about how faded it was.

She blinked away the sudden tears which had sprung to her eyes as she tried on the jeans which were an entirely different breed from the baggy ones which had always been her mainstay. Fashioned from soft and stretchy denim, they hugged her bottom but allowed for future expansion, though there was still no visible sign of a pregnancy bump. She wanted to tell the shopper that in a few months' time none of these gorgeous outfits would fit—but she could hardly start telling her personal business to a complete stranger, could she?

'It's been a pleasure doing business with you, Mrs Conway,' said Jessica as the session drew to a close.

Tara shook her head—despairing at her instinctive pang of yearning at the thought of being Lucas's wife. *It's because your own mother was never married,* she told herself. *Nor her mother before that. You're just secretly craving the respectability you never had, which made your own childhood such a misery. But things are different these days and nobody cares if a child is born out of wedlock.* 'I'm not Lucas's wife,' she said calmly. 'I'm actually his housekeeper—and I was wondering if you happen to sell aprons here?'

To Jessica's credit, she didn't look a bit fazed by what have been an unusual request. 'Of course,' she said. 'Come with me.'

The morning ended with a rock-star experience at the hair salon, where Tara sipped cinnamon-flavoured latte as large chunks were hacked from her curls. The result was…well, unbelievable, really—and several of the stylists had clustered around the mirror to say so. Her hair looked just as thick as before but it was more… manageable somehow. Little fronds framed her face and, where layers had been chopped into it, the colour seemed more intense and the texture more lustrous.

She was aware of heads turning as she left the salon in her brand-new jeans, pale jumper and the boxy denim jacket. And she'd never had that experience before. Of men's eyes following her as she slid into the back of the chauffeur-driven car which Lucas had ordered for her.

She remembered her grandmother's disapproval of fancy clothes—understandable given her own monastic upbringing, but a bit tough on a growing teenager who had been forced to wear second-hand outfits, which had only increased the amount of bullying she'd received.

The apartment was quiet and, since Lucas wouldn't be back until tomorrow, she had a whole day and a night without him. The only time she'd been on her own since she'd arrived here—which meant no distractions as she prepared for her very first dinner party in America. She looked down at the list of people he'd invited—an official from the Irish embassy and his wife, an Italian businessman named Salvatore di Luca and his girlfriend Alicia, and an 'unnamed guest' who seemed to have been added since last time she'd looked at it.

She wasn't going to deny that it was going to be weird serving Lucas and his guests and playing the role of servant, all the while knowing she would be sharing his bed once everyone had gone home. But surely it was better that way.

It had to be. Because if they stopped being lovers... She bit her lip and silently corrected herself. *When* they stopped being lovers, if the baby drove a wedge between them, or when he tired of her as history dictated he would—then surely it would be less traumatic not to have become used to being his partner in public, and then have that role wrenched away from her. Such a brutal change of circumstance would surely leave her feeling neglected, unloved and unwanted.

And hadn't she already experienced enough of those feelings to last a lifetime?

Smoothing down her pale cashmere sweater, she went into the kitchen, realising that she needed to get a move on with her planning. Without her stack of cookery books, she was forced to fire up her computer to look up some recipes online, but she scrolled through them uninterestedly.

Until suddenly she had a brilliant idea.

CHAPTER ELEVEN

THE FIRST THING Lucas heard when he walked through the door was the sound of music. His steps stilled and he paused to listen, even though he was running late. Irish music. Some softly lilting air which managed to be both mournful and uplifting at the same time—in the way of all Irish music. He frowned as he heard a peel of laughter which sounded familiar and then the chink of crystal, followed by more laughter.

With a quick glance at his watch he moved swiftly towards the library, quietly pushing open the door to see his guests standing with their backs to him, listening to something Tara was saying as she tilted a bottle of champagne into someone's glass.

He almost did a double-take as for a moment he felt as if the light were playing tricks on him, because the woman in question looked like Tara and sounded like Tara, and yet...

He screwed up his eyes.

And *yet...*

Surely that wasn't *Tara*?

Her hair was scooped on top of her head but for once there wasn't a riot of frizzy curls tumbling around her face. The sleek red waves were coiled like sleeping serpents—emphasising the slim, pale column of her neck. He swallowed, because her hair wasn't the only thing which was different. She was wearing a dress. And stockings. And... Again, he frowned. She had on some flirty little apron which made her look... She looked as if she was about to leave for a party where the specified dress code was Sexy French Maid. His groin grew rocky and he realised he didn't want to focus on her appearance, or the evening was going to become one long endurance test before he could take her to bed.

He realised his guests must have heard him for they were turning to greet him and as he apologised for his lateness he saw a wry look on Brett Henderson's face— because, as a world-acclaimed movie star and key member of British acting royalty, he wasn't used to being kept waiting.

But Lucas's somewhat garbled explanations about late planes and fog on the San Franciscan runway were cut short by a dismissive wave from the Irish Embassy official.

'Oh, don't you worry about that, Lucas—we've been fine here.' Seamus Hennessy beamed, and so did his wife, Erin. 'We're hardly missed you at all and Tara's been looking after us grandly, so she has!'

For the first time since he'd walked in, Tara turned to look at him and gave a shy smile, which contrasted with the sensual allure of her outfit, and Lucas was taken aback by the resultant shiver which rippled its way down his spine as he met her heavy-hooded amber gaze. He found himself wishing he could just dismiss

the guests, skip supper and take her straight to bed—
yet his need for her unsettled him.

'Do you all have drinks?' he questioned pleasantly.
'Good. Tara? I wonder if I could have a quick word in
the kitchen.'

He didn't say anything as they left the library and
neither did he comment as they passed the dining room,
even though he could see she must have gone to a lot
of trouble to lay the table for dinner. Unlit candles pro-
truded from centrepiece swathes of fragrant greenery
mixed with cherry-coloured roses, and all the crystal
and silver was gleaming beneath the diamond shards
of the overhead chandelier. He waited until they were
in the kitchen and completely out of earshot before he
turned on her and the feelings which had been growing inside him now erupted.

'What happened?' he demanded. 'You don't look
like you!'

Faint colour stained her cheeks as she glanced down
at her outfit before looking up again to meet his accus-
ing gaze. 'You mean you don't like it?'

'I told you to buy yourself some new clothes,' he
ground out. 'Not to look like the personification of
every man's fantasy maid.'

She screwed up her face. 'It's an apron, Lucas!' she
said crossly. 'And perhaps you ought to make your mind
up about where you really stand! You were always criti-
cising my old uniform for being too frumpy and now
you're complaining that this one is too sexy!'

Confused, he shook his head. 'It's the way you wear
it,' he said slowly.

'Or rather, the way you perceive it—which is your

problem, not mine. Make up your mind what it is you want because I haven't got the time or the appetite for this. And now, if you'll excuse me—' she lifted her chin in as haughty a gesture as he'd ever seen her use '—I really do need to get on with serving dinner.'

He wanted to reach out and stay her with a hungry kiss but something stopped him and it wasn't just pride. It was anger. And jealousy—and he didn't *do* jealousy or possession.

But the true and very bitter fact seemed to be that he *did*.

He forced himself to snap out of his foul mood and, since he often hosted dinners without a woman by his side, it shouldn't have been a problem. Seamus and Erin were easy company and Salvatore di Luca's latest squeeze worked for the United Nations and had some very illuminating things to say about the current political situation in Europe, which usually would have interested him. But for once he found his attention wandering and the biggest fly in the ointment was Brett Henderson flirting like crazy with Tara. And she wasn't exactly discouraging him, was she? Did she really have to simper like that as she told him how much she'd enjoyed the film in which he'd played a shape-shifting wizard?

Lucas was forced to watch as the mellifluous Englishman returned the love-fest by purring all kinds of compliments about his housekeeper's home-made lasagne.

'A really lovely woman in a nearby Italian store taught me how to make fresh pasta!' she was telling him proudly.

'What, here? In cynical old New York City?' joked Seamus.

'Tara has a particular naïve charm all of her own,' said Lucas coolly, and he couldn't miss the look of fury she directed at him as she brought out the tiramisu.

Eventually they all went home and Lucas tried to ignore the sound of Brett asking Tara for her email address. And it wasn't until Seamus and Erin had extracted a promise that the housekeeper would attend a ceilidh at the embassy that they finally took their leave.

The apartment seemed very big and very quiet as Lucas walked back into the library and found Tara clearing away glasses. 'Did you give Brett your email address?' he demanded.

'And if I did? Is that such a crime?' She straightened up to look at him and he had never seen such a look of quiet fury in her eyes. 'Unless you think...' She shook her head as if in disbelief. 'Unless you really think that I would encourage one man in a romantic fashion, when I'm in a physical relationship with another?'

Physical relationship. He didn't like the sound of that, but he supposed he couldn't doubt its accuracy. 'You were sending out all kinds of mixed messages tonight.'

'That's all in your head,' she retorted, bending towards the table once more. 'I was being friendly, that's all.'

'Leave that,' he said as she resumed putting crystal glasses onto a tray with such force he was surprised they didn't shatter.

'I'd rather do it now than in the morning.'

'I don't care—'

'No,' she interrupted suddenly and this time when she straightened up, the quiet fury in her eyes had been replaced with something stronger—something which blazed like fire. 'You couldn't have made that more plain if you'd tried! But maybe I'm fed up with the Lucas Conway approach to staff management! You taught me to cook something other than pie so I would be worthy of catering for your fancy guests and I ticked that off the list, didn't I? Then you decided to dress me up like one of those paper dolls you find in a child's magazine—and I went along with that, too. Heaven forbid that I should look like some screwball! But you're still not satisfied, are you, Lucas? And nothing ever *will* satisfy you, because basically you don't know yourself and you have no desire to learn about yourself, because you're a coward.'

The room went very silent. 'Excuse me?' he questioned, his words like ice. 'Did you just call me a coward?'

'You heard exactly what I said.'

Tara met his stony gaze and couldn't quite believe she'd done it but she couldn't back out now, no matter what the repercussions might be. Because she loved him and she wanted him to stop running away from his past—even if that meant the end of what the two of them shared. And even if it was, would that really be such a great loss? You couldn't really share anything with a man with no emotions, could you? A man who resolutely refused to allow himself to *feel* stuff.

'You can't live properly until you reconcile yourself with your past—and I don't think I can carry on like this until you do,' she breathed. 'Maybe you don't have any living blood relatives, but isn't that something which warrants a little investigation? Don't you want to know why your mother sold you? To find out who your real father is and whether either of them are alive? To discover whether she had any more children and if you have any brothers or sisters?' Her face suddenly crumpled. 'I know that when I—'

'No!' Furiously, he cut across her—the slicing wave of his hand a gesture of finality. 'I'm done with confessionals and I certainly don't want to waste any more of my evening listening to you, while you start unburdening your soul. To be honest, I'm tired, and I'm bored. I don't know how many times I've told you that I never wanted that kind of relationship and unless you can accept that, then I agree—we have no kind of future. So perhaps you might like to think about that. And now, if you'll excuse me—I'm going to bed. I'll see you in the morning.'

Tara's heart was pounding with shock as he turned and walked out of the library without another word. She could hear his footsteps going upstairs, along the corridor towards the master bedroom, and just for a moment she actually considered following him, until she drew herself up short.

Was she completely *insane*? He might as well have taken out a full-page ad in *The Washington Post*, saying, *Leave me alone*. He'd told her he'd see her in the morning, and he'd done it with that cold and condemning look in his eyes. That wasn't the action of a man who wanted to cuddle and make up—that was a man who had been pushed to his limits. He was angry with her—but not nearly as angry as she was with herself. How long was she planning to hang around and get treated like someone who didn't really matter? Because she *did* matter. Not just for her baby's sake, but for her own.

She crept along to the second bedroom, uncomfortably aware that this was only the second night they'd spent apart since they'd resumed their sexual relationship—and she thought how big and lonely the bed seemed without him. Predictably, sleep was a long time in coming and when it did, dawn was just beginning to edge into the sky because she hadn't bothered to close the drapes.

When she awoke, the apartment was completely silent and, quickly, she got out of bed, wandering from room to room looking for Lucas, knowing with a sinking sense of certainty that she wasn't going to see him. The lingering aroma of coffee and some juiced halves of orange were the only signs of his presence. He must have had breakfast and then left. She looked around to see if there was a note, but of course there wasn't. And a huge pang of stupid longing swept over her as she tried to imagine what it would be like if he *was* the kind of man who left little messages dotted around the place. Affectionate words or cartoons, scribbled onto Post-it notes and stuck to the front of the refrigerator or left lying on a pillow. But those things only happened in films. or between real-life couples who genuinely loved one another. He'd only ever left her a note once before—when he'd brought forward his New York trip after they'd slept together and he'd told her he'd give her a good reference!

Back then he couldn't wait to get away from her and she wouldn't be here now if that night hadn't produced a child. Lucas would have moved on. And so would she. She'd have found herself a job as housekeeper to someone else and would now be throwing herself enthusiastically into her new role. Perhaps the discovery that she could enjoy sex might have provided some hope for the future—making her wonder if one day she'd be able to enjoy dating men who were more suitable than Lucas Conway.

Her stomach turned over at the thought of being held in any other arms than his. It made her feel violently sick to think of any lover other than Lucas and the longer she allowed this situation to continue, the harder it was going to be to ever give him up. Because that time would come, most definitely—as surely as the sun rose over Manhattan each morning. They'd already had their first serious row and they'd both said some pretty wounding things. Maybe she should be grateful for his honesty. At least he wasn't encouraging her to build fanciful daydreams and maybe it was time she stopped trying to pretend that this relationship of theirs was going anywhere. Surely it would be better—for both of them—if they re-established the boundaries and negotiated a different kind of future. She swallowed, knowing that the only way to do that was to put distance between them.

For her to go home to Ireland. Back to where she belonged.

She cleared up the debris from the dinner party, then went into the en-suite wet room and stood beneath the cascading shower, trying to enjoy the moment, but the luxury products were wasted on her. She took extra time washing and drying her hair and even more time selecting what to wear. Which clothes to take and which to leave behind. She stared a little wistfully at the chiffon skirt and lace insert shoes; the silky dresses and impossibly fine cashmere sweaters. She loved those clothes—loved the way they made her feel—but they had no place in the life she was about to resume. So she took the shiny anorak, the jeans, the darker of the sweaters, the warmest dresses-as well as all of the underwear. Then she called a cab and checked she had money and her passport. It was only as she was leaving that she realised she couldn't just *go*—not without saying something. So she went slowly into the library where she picked up a pen and, with a heavy heart, began to write.

Lucas stared down at the note and a flare of something which felt close to pain clenched at his heart. But it wasn't pain, he told himself furiously. It was disappointment. Yes, that was it. Disappointment that Tara Fitzpatrick had just done a runner like some thief in the night. And after everything he'd done for her...

He tugged his cell-phone from his pocket and jabbed his finger against her number. It rang for so long that he thought it was going to voicemail, but then she picked it up and he heard that sweetly soft Irish brogue.

'Hello?'

'You're at the airport, I assume?' he clipped out.

'I am. I've managed to get the last seat on a flight which is leaving for Dublin in...' there was a rustle as, presumably, she lifted her arm to look at her watch '... twenty minutes' time.'

'So you're running out on me,' he said coldly. 'Without even bothering to tell me you were going. Now who's the coward, Tara?'

'No, Lucas,' she corrected. 'The cowardly thing to have done would be not to have picked up this call.'

He could feel control slipping away from him and he didn't like it, because hadn't his legendary control allowed him to make his world manageable? Hadn't taking command enabled him to rise, phoenix-like, from the ashes of his upbringing and forge himself a successful life? 'Why didn't you at least wait around until I was back from my meeting when we could have discussed this calmly, like grown-ups?' he demanded.

He heard a fractured sound, as if she was having difficulty slowing down her suddenly rapid breathing. But when she spoke she sounded calm and distant. Very distant. He frowned. And not like Tara at all.

'You once left me a note when you couldn't face having an important conversation with me. Do you remember that, Lucas? Well, it's my turn now—and I'm doing it for exactly the same reasons. I didn't want a protracted goodbye, nor to have to offer explanations, or listen to any more accusations. I don't want bitter words to rattle around in my brain and imprint themselves on my memory, when we need to keep this civilised. So I'll be in touch when I'm settled and you can see as much or as little of our baby as you want. That's all.' She drew in a deep breath before letting it out in a husky sigh. 'Don't you understand? I'm setting you free, Lucas.'

Something swelled up inside him like a growing wave—something dark and unwanted. How *dared* she offer him his freedom, when it was not hers to give? Did she consider him as some kind of puppet whose

strings she could tug whenever the mood took her—
just because she carried a part of him deep inside her?
The dark feeling grew but deliberately he quashed it,
because he needed to think clearly—his mind unob-
structed by neither anger nor regret. Because maybe
she was right. Maybe it *was* better this way. Better she
left when things were tolerably amicable between them.
Time and space would do the rest and once the dust had
settled on their impetuous affair, they would be able to
work out some kind of long-term plan. He would be
good to her. That was a given. He would provide her
with the finest home money could buy and all the child-
care she needed. And he would...

He swallowed, wondering why his throat felt as if it
had been lined with barbed wire which had been left
out in the rain. Even if fatherhood was an unknown
and an unwanted concept—that didn't mean he wasn't
going to step up to the plate and be dutiful, did it? To
be there for his child as his own father had never been
there for him.

And if he found that impossible?

Why *wouldn't* he find it impossible, when he had no
real template for family life? And wouldn't it then follow that he was probably going to let her and the baby
down, somewhere along the line?

He swallowed as Tara's accusations came back to
ring with silent reproach in his ears.

*'Don't you want to know why your mother sold you?
To find out who your real father is and whether either
of them are alive? To discover whether she had any
more children?'*

His mouth hardened. No, he didn't want to know

any of those things. Why should he? In an ideal world he would have gone back to the life he'd had before. The one with no surprises. No analysis. No whip-slim woman challenging him with those sleepy amber eyes. But it wasn't that simple. Nothing ever was.

He cleared his throat. 'Just let me know when you get back to Dalkey,' he said coolly. 'And please keep me up to speed with your plans. I will return to Ireland in time for the birth.'

CHAPTER TWELVE

RAIN LASHED LOUDLY against the window and a gale howled like some malevolent monster in the dark night. In the distance Tara could hear trees creaking and the yelp of a frightened dog. She rolled over and shivered beneath the duvet, trying to breathe deeply, and, when that didn't work, to count backwards from one hundred. Anything, really, which would bring the oblivion and ease she craved in the form of sleep, if only for a few hours.

Because it was hard. She wasn't going to lie. If this was what being in love was like, then she wanted it out of her system as quickly as possible. The pain was unbearable. Pain like she'd never known. As if someone were inserting a burning poker into each ventricle of her heart. And the torture wasn't just causing physical pain—it was mental too, because the memory of Lucas was never far from her mind. It hovered in the background of her thoughts throughout every second of the day. The knowledge that he was no longer part of her life was like a heavy weight pressing down on her shoulders, so that most of the time she felt weary, even when she shouldn't have done.

She missed his face, his body, his banter. She missed being in his arms at night, wrapped in all that warm and powerful strength as he made love to her, over and over again. Angrily, she clenched her hands into two white-knuckled fists. Because that was a ridiculously romantic interpretation of what had taken place. They'd had amazing and exquisite sex, that was all, and presumably that was what he did with all the other women who had shared his bed—which perhaps made their dogged pursuit of him more understandable. She was the one who had elevated it to a level which was never intended, with her fanciful words of *love*. And in doing that, hadn't she followed the path of so many foolish women before her—her mother and her grandmother included? For the first time in her life, she acknowledged that Granny might have had a point in her often expressed and jaundiced view about men, as she'd waved her stick angrily in the air.

'I tell you, they're not worth it, Tara! Not a single one of them!'

But, outwardly at least, Tara was determined to present a positive face to the world. She made sure she looked after herself—exercising sensibly, eating regularly and faithfully keeping all her appointments at the hospital, who pronounced themselves delighted with her progress. She even continued to dress in the new style which had been shown to her so comprehensively in New York. She liked the way the new clothes made her feel. She liked the soft whisper of silk and cashmere against her skin and she liked wearing trousers which actually fitted her, rather than flapping around her legs. If she'd learnt one thing it was that her body was nothing to be ashamed of and that there was nothing wrong with wanting to take care of her appearance.

It was only at night, under the forgiving cloak of darkness, that she cried big salty tears which rolled down her cheeks and fell silently into her sodden pillow. That she ached to feel Lucas beside her again, even though in her heart she knew that was never going to happen. And each morning she awoke to sombre grey Dublin skies, which seemed to echo the bleakness of her mood.

But she was strong and she was resilient, and, once she'd adjusted to her new life, things began to improve. Or rather, once she'd accepted that Lucas wasn't going to suddenly turn up and sweep her off her feet—that was the turning point. She knew then she had to embrace the future, not keep wishing for something which was never going to happen. There was to be no fairy-tale ending. Lucas wasn't going to suddenly appear on the doorstep, his face obscured by a bouquet of flowers with a diamond ring hidden in his pocket. He'd told her he would be back for the birth—which was still four whole months away—which gave her plenty of time to erase him from her aching heart.

Aware that his Dalkey house held too many poignant memories, she began to bombard local employment agencies with her CV and quickly found a job—though not, as originally planned, in a big, noisy family. With a baby of her own on the way, she decided it was better to keep focussed on that. Her new position was as housekeeper to a couple of academics, in their big house overlooking Caragh Lake, in beautiful County Kerry. Dana and Jim Doyle had both sat in on her interview, where Tara had been completely upfront about her situation.

'I'm pregnant and no longer with the father of my child. I don't know if that's going to be a problem for you,' she'd blurted out, 'but he is providing generous financial support for us both.'

'So do you really *need* to work?' Dana had asked gently.

'No, but I've always worked.' Tara's reply had been simple. She was unable to imagine the long days stretching ahead without some kind of structure to them, terrified of all those hours which could be devoted to pining for a man who didn't want her.

How long before she stopped feeling this way? Before her body stopped craving his touch and her lips his kiss?

She emailed Lucas her new address and he sent an instant response, asking if she had everything she needed. The answer to that was obviously no and yet, for some reason, the question infuriated her. Why did people keep asking her what she *needed* when she had a warm bed, a roof over her head, and a secure job, which was a lot more than many people had? Her needs weren't the problem but her wants were.

She stared into the mirror.

She still wanted Lucas—wasn't that the most agonising thing of all?

Her hand moving down to her growing bump, she told herself that these feelings would fade. They *had* to fade—because everything did eventually. The bullying at school—once unendurable—had leached from her consciousness once she'd left Ballykenna. Even the reason for that bullying—all the shame surrounding her ancestry—had receded, so that she hardly thought about it any more. And that had come about because she'd made a determined effort to erase it from her mind.

So do that now, with Lucas, or you'll spend the rest of your life as a ghost of a person, longing for something which can never be yours.

Tara bit her lip.

He was the father of her child. Nothing else.

Her mouth firmed.

Nothing.

As he was driven through the sweeping Argentinian landscape, Lucas felt the pounding of his heart. It was pounding like an out-of-control speed train. As he got out of the car he became aware that his mouth was dry and recognised that this was the closest he'd ever come to fear. Or maybe it was just apprehension. Glancing up at the big sign which read Sabato School of Polo, he took a moment to realise that someone must have heard the sound of his car and a man was walking towards him.

The man's build was much like his own—long-legged, strong and muscular—though the thick tumble of dark hair was distinctly longer. He wore casual riding clothes and leather boots which were dull with dust— an outfit which was in marked contrast to Lucas's own bespoke linen suit. But as he grew closer, Lucas found himself staring into a pair of dark-lashed and slanting green eyes, so unnervingly like his, as were the chiselled jaw and high slash of cheekbones.

And now the pounding of his heart became deafening as he acknowledged who it was who stood before him. His older brother. He swallowed. His only brother. For a moment neither man said anything, just stared long and hard, their faces set and serious. Two powerful tycoons confronted by the bitter reality of their past, which had somehow merged into the present.

'Alejandro,' said Lucas eventually.

The man nodded. 'I've spent a long time trying to find you, Lucas,' he breathed slowly.

And that was the main difference between them, Lucas acknowledged. That his brother's deep voice was accented, its lilting cadence emphasising the Spanish of his mother tongue. Lucas felt his heart clench, realising that his brother had known their real mother, while he had not, and he felt a bitter pang he hadn't expected before replying to his brother's statement. 'I changed my name,' he said, at last.

Alej nodded and then smiled, expelling a long sigh of something which sounded like relief. 'Want to tell me about it? Over a beer maybe, or even a ride? I don't even know if you ride—how crazy is that?'

For the first time Lucas smiled as he chose the latter option, even though he hadn't been on a horse in a while and even though his brother was an ex-world-champion polo player who could outride most people. But for once, he wasn't feeling competitive and he didn't care if Alej outshone him in the saddle. He wanted clarity in which to confront the past—not alcohol clouding or distorting the things which needed to be said. He wanted to hear the facts as they were, no matter how much they might hurt.

And they did hurt. No two ways about it. He had thought he was prepared for the pain which might be awaiting him when he heard the full story of how he came to be adopted, but afterwards wondered if perhaps he'd been naïve. Because was anyone ever really *prepared* for pain? Intellectually you might think you knew what to expect, but on a visceral level it always hit you with a force which could leave you breathless.

Hacking out over the lush green pastures, they rode for a long time, sometimes talking, sometimes lapsing into thoughtful silences, until the sinking sun had begun to splash the landscape with coral and Alej turned to him.

'You must be thirsty by now. Think it's time for that beer?'

Lucas nodded. 'Sure do.'

As if by unspoken consent, they urged their mounts into a fierce gallop as they headed back towards the stables and Lucas was glad for the sudden rush of adrenalin which surged through his veins. Glad too that the rush of air dried the tears he could feel on his cheeks.

His brother's car was waiting to take them to Alej's *estancia*, where his wife Emily was waiting with their baby Luis, and Lucas stepped into the warm family home and felt a rush of something he'd never experienced before. Was it envy or regret? he wondered. Because as Alej lifted the squealing Luis high in the air and the beautiful Emily stirred something in a pot which smelt delicious, Lucas realised that he too could have had this. A home and a family. With Tara. The woman who had encouraged him to come here. Who had made him dare raise the curtain on his past and look directly into the face of his brother and his troubled ancestry.

He swallowed as Emily handed him a frosted bottle of beer.

He could have had all this.

And he had blown it.

He didn't sleep well that night, even though the bed was supremely comfortable and the steak which Alej cooked for dinner the best he'd ever eaten, especially as it had been served with Emily's delicious spicy vegetables. But in the days which followed, he was given a tantalising taste of the country of his birth. He grew to understand it a little and to like it enormously so that by the time it came to leave, he experienced a distinct pang as he dropped a kiss on the baby's downy head and hugged Emily goodbye. He didn't say much as Alej drove him to the airport. He didn't need to. He knew that something powerful had been forged between the two of them during the past week, a bond which had been severed so many years ago but which had somehow, miraculously, endured.

At the airport the two men embraced. Then Lucas took one last look at the sweeping mountains he could see in the distance and, somewhere in his heart, knew he'd be back. 'You know, you and the family must visit me in Ireland.'

'*Por supuesto.*'

Once again their gazes clashed with the sense of something unspoken. And then he was in the aircraft and clipping his seat belt before the private jet barrelled along the runway and soared up into the cloudless sky. For a while Lucas stared down at the retreating rooftops of Buenos Aires, before settling back in his seat.

It was a long flight but for once he couldn't con-

centrate on work matters—even though he was able
to communicate with his assistant on the ground. And
somewhat predictably, when the plane touched down in
Dublin, it was to a grey and blustery day. He thought
how tiny Ireland seemed in comparison to the sweeping landscape of the country he'd just left. A pulse was
beating at his temple as he stared down at the email his
assistant had sent him earlier and, slowly, he gave his
driver the address. All during the car journey to Caragh
Lake, Lucas was aware of the racing of his heart and
sudden clamminess of his palms—as if his body were
trying to keep him focussed on what his mind was trying so hard to resist. But the dark thoughts kept flapping back, like insistent crows.

What if he couldn't do this?

What if she didn't want him? Could he blame her if
she didn't? His mouth hardened. And mightn't that be
best? Wouldn't that guarantee her some kind of peace,
even if peace was a concept he couldn't ever imagine
finding for himself? Not now, anyway.

Despite its size, the big house wasn't easy to find,
tucked away in a leafy lane and overlooking a beautiful lake. As Lucas lifted the heavy door knocker he
could hear it echoing through the large house and it
seemed to take for ever before he heard the approach
of oddly familiar footsteps, and when the door opened
he saw Tara standing there. His heart leapt. The new
Tara. The one with the feathery soft hair which made
her look so sleek.

She was blinking at him in disbelief. 'Lucas?'

He heard the strangled note in her voice but of far
more concern was the sudden blanching of her skin

and the way her eyes had widened. Because there was no welcome in their amber depths and no smile on her soft lips. And her next words compounded his thumping fears.

'What are you doing here?' she demanded.

'Isn't it obvious? I've come here to see you.'

'And now you have. See? And I'm fine.'

She went to push the door shut again but he held up the palm of his hand.

'Tara.' His voice softened. 'That's not what I meant and you know it.'

Her face had lost none of its suspicion. 'You didn't warn me you were coming.'

'I thought unannounced was better.'

'Better? Better for who? Yourself, of course—because that's the only person you ever think about, isn't it?' Her voice rose. 'Are you crazy, Lucas? Didn't you think it mightn't be suitable for you to just come *barging* in like this? I might have been cooking lunch for Mr and Mrs Doyle.'

He didn't feel it prudent to point out that he'd had one of his assistants find out when her bosses were attending a conference on marine science in Sweden, and had timed his flight to Ireland accordingly. 'And are you allowed no life of your own?' he questioned archly.

The corners of her unsmiling mouth lifted but not with a smile—more like a rueful acknowledgement of some grim fact. 'You're probably better qualified than anyone to answer that question, Lucas. But that's beside the point. Why are you here?' She sucked in a deep breath, her hand leaning on the door jamb. 'Why are

you here when you told me that you'd be back in time
for the birth and that's still sixteen weeks away, by Dr
Foley's reckoning.'

For the first time Lucas allowed his gaze to move
from her face to her body and he was unprepared for
the savage jolting of his heart. She looked...

His throat grew dry. He'd never really understood
the description 'blooming' when applied to a pregnant
woman, mainly because such a field was outside his
area of interest. But he understood it now. She was
wearing an apron covering a woollen dress of apple-
green, and he could see that her slender frame had
filled out. There was more flesh on her bones and her
cheeks were fuller and, if he ignored the faint hostility
in her gaze—which wasn't easy—he could see a radi-
ance about her which seemed to make her glow from
within. But it was the curve of her belly which made
his heart begin to race.

Hesitation was something unfamiliar to him but he
could sense he needed to be careful about what he said
next—more careful than he'd ever been in his life—because she was still prickling with hostility. 'I'm here
because I need to speak to you. To tell you things that
perhaps you need to hear.'

Tara flinched, trying to put a lid on the rush of emotion which was flowing through her body. Because this
wasn't fair. He'd told her he would see her for the birth,
which was months away—precious months when she
was supposed to be practising immunity when it came
to looking into his beautiful face, that shadowed jaw
and those emerald-bright eyes.

But she couldn't tell him that, could she? If she

hinted that she couldn't cope with an unexpected visit from him, then wouldn't that make her appear weak?

She had no idea what he was about to say since she hadn't heard very much from him since she'd left America. For all she knew he might be about to announce that he'd finally met the love of his life, despite having vowed that he didn't *do* love. But stranger things had happened and some gorgeous New Yorker might have possessed just the right combination of beauty and dynamism to capture the billionaire's elusive heart.

And if that were the case, then wasn't it better to get it over with?

'You'd better come in,' she said grudgingly.

She was achingly aware of his presence as he followed her into the hallway, wishing her thoughts didn't keep going back to that first night, when it had all started. If only you could rewrite the past. If, say, she hadn't let Charlotte in that day, then none of this might ever have happened. But you couldn't rewrite the past and, anyway, would she really want to go back to the Tara she'd been back then? The unfulfilled misfit of a woman who'd never known real pleasure? And yes, the flip side to pleasure was emotional pain—unbearable pain for quite a while now—but you learnt through such experiences, didn't you? You learnt to cope and you became stronger—strong enough to handle an unscheduled visit from the man whose child you carried.

'Would you like coffee?' she questioned, expecting him to say no.

But Lucas never did what you expected him to do.

'Actually, I would. I've missed your coffee, Tara.'

'I don't want any of your old flannel.'

His gaze was cool and unabashed. 'It isn't flannel. I'm merely stating a fact. Though they brew some pretty amazing stuff in Argentina.'

She blinked. 'Argentina?'

'Why don't you make the coffee first?' he said gently. 'And then we'll talk.'

Her instinctive fury at his reversion to the dominant role was supplanted by a natural curiosity but, grateful for the chance to get away from the distraction of that piercing green gaze, Tara hurried from the room. She returned minutes later, hating herself for having first checked her appearance in the kitchen mirror, because it wasn't as if she wanted to impress him, was it?

He was standing with his back to her, looking down over the sweeping emerald lawn and, beyond that, the darker green of the trees, through which you could see the silver glimmer of the lake and, fringing those, the gentle hills of Ireland. Something poignant shafted at Tara's heart but she forced herself to suppress it, because she needed to keep calm.

He turned to face her and she could feel an annoying shiver of awareness but she quashed it. With a hostess-like air, she indicated that he should sit down and watched as he lowered his powerful frame into one of the worn velvet seats which the non-materialistic Dana Doyle had told her they'd had for years. And when she'd given him his coffee, just the way he liked it, Tara perched on a more upright chair opposite, not quite trusting her trembling fingers to hold the water she'd poured for herself.

'So,' she said, with a tight smile. 'What is it that you want to speak to me about, Lucas?'

She was unprepared for the sudden darkness which crossed his rugged features, like a black cloud suddenly obscuring the face of the moon. And for a look of something she'd never seen in his eyes before, something which on anyone else she might have described as desolation. But Lucas didn't do desolation and she wasn't here to analyse his moods or to try to get inside his head. This was a matter-of-fact meeting and he probably wanted to discuss financial support for her and the baby.

He stared down at the inky brew in his cup and put it down untasted, before lifting his gaze to hers.

'I took your advice,' he said simply. 'And went to Argentina.'

CHAPTER THIRTEEN

'YOU WENT TO ARGENTINA,' Tara repeated slowly.

He nodded. 'I did.'

There was a momentary pause. 'And what did you find there, Lucas?'

She was staring deep into his eyes, her expression as distant as ever he'd seen it, and Lucas wondered if coming here unannounced had been a crazy idea. But he owed her this. He owed her the knowledge which had first shocked and then saddened him. And he owed it to himself to discover whether he had messed everything up.

'I found my brother there,' he said simply.

'You have a brother?'

'I do. His name is Alej—Alejandro Sabato— and he has a family of his own. His wife is English and she's called Emily and they have a young baby, Luis.'

'That's nice,' she said stiffly.

He wanted to tell her about the terrible pain in his heart because he'd missed her so much, but old habits died hard and for the time being he sought refuge in facts. 'He'd actually been trying to find me, but because I'd changed my name his investigators kept coming up with blanks. Anyway, he was able to fill me in on everything I needed to know.'

Her gaze was still steady. 'Which is?'

He shrugged his shoulders, for there was no easy way to say this, no acceptable way of defining the harsh facts surrounding his conception. 'My mother was a prostitute and my father was one of her clients,' he bit out. 'A drunken thief who used to spend long periods in prison, and when he was released he would come out, beat her up and make her pregnant.'

She licked her lips and he could see a swallowing movement in her throat. 'So how did you come—?'

'To be brought up in one of the most expensive parts of one of the most expensive cities in the world?' he supplied, and she nodded. 'My mother had given birth to Alej just a year earlier and she was having enough trouble feeding one child, let alone another. So she decided to sell me. I suppose it made perfect economic sense. She went to see someone in Buenos Aires—someone who put her in touch with a rich American heiress—'

'Your mother?' she interrupted breathlessly.

'No!' he negated viciously. 'Wanda Gonzalez never earned the right to call herself that during her lifetime, so I'm damned sure I'm not going to honour her with that title now she's dead.' He gave a bitter laugh. 'She had specified that she wanted a birth mother from Argentina, so that I would resemble my "father" as much as possible.'

'And did you?' she questioned curiously. 'Resemble him, I mean?'

He shook his head. 'Not really. We had the same hair colour, but that was about it—I was bigger, stronger, more powerful.' He gave a short laugh. 'And that's how I came to be brought up amid such great wealth in Manhattan, while Alejandro lived a very different life in Argentina—that is, until he escaped from abject poverty to become one of the world's greatest polo players.'

'Alejandro Sabato,' she ventured slowly, with a nod of her flame-bright hair. 'Yes, I've heard of him.'

'I'm sure you have. He was a bit of a poster-boy for the sport in his time. But I haven't come here to talk about my brother, Tara.'

She became instantly alert. 'No?' she challenged.

He wanted her to make this easy for him. To soften her lips into a smile. To send him a soft, unspoken message with her eyes so he could get up and walk right over there. Pull her hungrily into his arms and kiss her as he'd dreamt of doing ever since she'd walked out of his New York apartment. Because if he started kissing her and they began to make love, surely it would blot away some of the pain.

But something stopped him and it was the sense that this was the biggest deal he'd ever tried to pull off and he couldn't afford to get it wrong. Yet getting it wrong was a distinct possibility, even though he knew how to wheel and deal in a boardroom. When to talk and when to let silence work for you. He knew about joint venture capital, about leasing out cars or lorries which people couldn't afford to buy themselves, but he knew nothing about telling a woman that he loved her. And wasn't that the crux of what he really wanted to say to her? The most important thing.

No. First up he needed to acknowledge what she had done for him. To tell her some of the things he had felt.

Still felt. 'I wanted to be angry with my mother and to blame her for the life into which I was born,' he whispered. 'And for a while I was. But then I realised that she'd taken a bad situation and tried to make it better. It can't have been easy to give me away, but she did. And she did it for me, so I wouldn't starve—and so that Alej wouldn't starve either. She probably thought she was giving me the best chance she could—she wasn't to know that Wanda was weak and Diego was cruel.'

'Lucas,' she said, and for the first time he could hear a softening of her voice and saw concern pleating her brow, as if she had detected his pain and wanted to soothe it away.

But he shook his head to silence her because he needed to say it, to let it all out so it could no longer gnaw away at him.

'I would never have found this out if you hadn't encouraged me to find my brother,' he said. 'You are responsible for that, Tara. For the bond I now have with my brother. For the discovery that I have a nephew and a sister-in-law. But when I saw that family of theirs it was like a dagger to my heart.'

'Lucas!' she said, as if she could hardly believe he was saying stuff like this, and wasn't there a part of him who could hardly believe it himself?

'I realised then that I had been given the opportunity to have a loving family—with you,' he said huskily. 'And because of my pride and arrogance and my cold and unfeeling heart, I had probably blown it. But I'm hoping against hope that I haven't blown it and I'm asking you to give me another chance because… I love you, Tara.'

She was shaking her head as if she didn't believe it, but the brief clouding of her eyes told him she didn't *dare* believe it and he knew he wasn't in the clear yet.

'I love your spirit and the way you answer me back,' he continued softly, and his eyes crinkled. 'Even although sometimes that trait makes me as mad as hell. I like the way you're loyal and true and that beneath your often prickly exterior there beats a heart of pure gold.' He swallowed. 'The first time I made love to you, it was like nothing I'd ever experienced. The way you made me feel was completely alien to me —'

She pursed her lips together. 'That's why you couldn't wait to dash away the next morning and fly to New York early?'

'Because it scared the hell out of me,' he admitted. 'It made me feel vulnerable, in a way I hadn't allowed myself to feel for years. And then, when I told you stuff I'd kept bottled up for so long and you comforted me with your arms and with your body...' He swallowed. 'You just rocked my world. You're still rocking it. Even now when I told you about my real mother and father, you just accepted it calmly. I was watching your face and you didn't seem appalled, or shocked. You didn't start expressing fears about what bad blood I may have being passed onto our baby.' He saw her flinch. 'Listen to me, Tara, I know I handled it badly but I didn't know at the time *how* to handle it. But now I do. I'm asking you to forgive me and telling you that since you've been gone my life seems empty. To tell you that I want to marry you and spend the rest of my life with you. To give our child love and security, as well as to each other. To create a family. A real family. The kind of family which neither of us has ever had before. That is…that is if you feel you could ever love me too. So what do you say, Tara Fitzpatrick?'

Right then Tara was finding it impossible to say *anything*, she was feeling so choked up. Because Lucas might not be carrying a big bunch of flowers and a diamond ring, but he *was* telling her he loved her and he was asking her to marry him.

But he still didn't know, did he?

He didn't know everything about her because she'd kept her own guilty little secrets. And although she'd tried several times to tell him about her past—hadn't she been quietly glad when he'd cut her short? Hadn't that given her the justification she'd needed to bury it even deeper—to act as if she were Tara Goody-Two-Shoes—in which case, perhaps *she* was the coward, after all.

'I'm not the woman you think I am,' she said slowly.

'You're everything—'

'No. I'm not. Hear me out, Lucas. Please. Because this is important.' She stood up, because it was difficult sitting there in the piercing green spotlight of his gaze. So she walked around the Doyles' lovely old sitting room, with its faded furniture and leaf-framed view over the silvery lake, and gave a small sigh as she began her story. 'My mother was a nurse in England when she got pregnant by someone whose name I was never told.' Her voice grew reflective. 'She never saw him again, so she came back to Ireland with me and I was brought up by my grandmother, while Mammy went out to work. We lived pretty much hand to mouth, in a little cottage on the outskirts of Ballykenna, and when I was two, my mother got breast cancer—'

'Tara.'

'No, Lucas,' she said fiercely. 'Let me finish. She got breast cancer and it was very aggressive. It was obviously very sad but I can't remember much about it, or maybe I just blocked it out. She died very quickly and I was left in the sole care of my grandmother.' She swallowed as she made an admission she'd never dared make before, even to herself. To realise that just because someone went through the mechanics of caring for you, didn't mean that they liked you or loved you. Especially if you reminded them of their own failings.

'She was a cold and bitter woman,' she continued, with a wince. 'Though it took me a long time to find out why. To discover why she hated men so much and why she used to dress me like a frump.' She swallowed. 'And why the other children used to laugh at me behind my back.'

'Why?'

She drew in a deep breath. Here it was. The truth—in all its unvarnished clarity. 'My grandmother had been a nun and my grandfather a priest and their liaison was a huge scandal at the time, because my mother was the result of that liaison. Oh, they tried to hush it up but everyone knew. And I think that some of the burden of the guilt my grandmother carried around with her must have transferred itself onto me. It's why I was terrified of men and of intimacy until I met you, Lucas.'

She didn't know what she expected him to do, but she'd imagined *some* moment of reflection while he processed what she'd just told him. As if he'd need time to come to terms with her revelation and maybe to get his head around what a massive scandal it had been at the time. But instead he was getting up out of the faded velvet chair and crossing the room with a purposefulness which was achingly familiar to her. And when he put his arms around her and pulled her close, she started to cry and once she had started she couldn't seem to stop. The tears came hard and fast and Tara realised she was crying for all kinds of reasons. She was crying for the women of earlier generations who'd had to deal with judgement and being shunned. And she was crying for her poor dead mother who would never know her grandchild. Those tears were of sorrow, but hot on their heels came tears of gratitude, and joy—for being fit and healthy and carrying a child beneath her fast-beating heart. A child who...

She turned her wet face up to Lucas and saw compassion and love blazing from his green eyes and that gave her the courage to tell him. 'I love you, Lucas,' she whispered. 'So much. And yes, I want to spend the rest of my life with you.'

He nodded, but didn't speak, just drew his arms around her even tighter and for now that was enough.

It was more than enough.

EPILOGUE

'LUCAS...' TARA GAVE a luxurious stretch as she felt the warm lips of her husband tracking over her bare stomach, making her flesh shiver into little goosebumps. *Again.*

She swallowed down her growing desire, because they'd only just made love, hadn't they? Was it always going to be this good? she wondered dreamily.

'We'll...we'll be late for dinner.'

'Dinner isn't until nine-thirty,' he whispered. 'You know they eat late in Argentina.'

'Yes, but even so.' She fluttered her fingertips to his bare shoulders. 'We really ought to be getting dressed.'

'Say that with meaning, Tara.' There was a note of laughter in his voice as he moved to lie on top of her. 'And perhaps we will.'

Within minutes she was gasping out his name as he drove into her and he was kissing away the sounds of her helpless little cries as she came. But even though a deep lethargy crept over her afterwards, Tara forced herself to wriggle out from beneath Lucas's hard, honed flesh and head for the en-suite bathroom, because they had a whole delicious evening ahead of them. Quickly, she showered and, when Lucas took her place to stand beneath the powering jets, she returned to the bedroom to slither into a silky black jersey dress and matching pumps, before creeping along the corridor to where Declan was fast asleep, in a cot beside his bigger cousin, Luis.

For a moment she just stood there, gazing down at the dark heads of the two sleeping babes, and a great wave of love and contentment swelled up inside her. They were so lucky, she thought, with a sudden twist of her heart. So very lucky. All of them.

She and Lucas had been married in Dublin just before the birth of their beloved son, Declan. Her friend Stella had been bridesmaid and the celebrations had been memorable for many reasons, not least because Stella had rebuffed the advances of the Italian billionaire Salvatore di Luca, which was pretty much unheard of. And the guest of honour had been Brett Henderson—the actor who had caused Lucas to be so jealous in New York—who had offered to sing a song at their wedding, about love changing everything.

'He's clearly still smitten,' Lucas had grumbled, when she'd excitedly shown him the email.

'Rubbish,' Tara had disagreed. 'I think he just likes a woman with an Irish accent—in which case he'll have plenty to choose from at the reception! Our friends will never forgive us if we say no, Lucas. And besides, nobody could disagree with the sentiments of the song he's planning to sing, could they?'

And Lucas had no answer to that.

Their honeymoon had been postponed until Declan was six months old, when they went on an extended stay with Alej, Emily and Luis at their beautiful Argentinian *estancia*. The two women had hit it off immediately and it had warmed Tara's heart to see Lucas bonding with the brother he was quickly getting to know. Her husband was learning about the land of his birth, too, and had changed his name back to his birth name— not the one he'd seen written above a pub on the very first night he'd arrived in Dublin, completely alone. As Lucas Sabato he was building a mother-and-baby unit outside Buenos Aires, to support women and children who had fallen on hard times. Tara swallowed. To help prevent another helpless baby being given up because his mother couldn't afford to feed him...

And tonight they would eat outside beneath the stars with Emily and Alej and count every single one of their blessings.

She heard soft footsteps behind her and felt the whisper of Lucas's lips against her neck. His arm snaked around her waist and for a moment the two of them were silent as they stood looking down at their son.

'It's crazy,' said Lucas softly.

'What is?'

He shrugged. 'How I've gone from being a man with nothing to a man who has everything.'

She turned to look at him, an expression of bemusement on her face. 'Some people wouldn't describe a relatively young billionaire as a man with nothing.'

He shook his head. 'All the money in the world doesn't come close to the way I feel when I look at you, and Declan. Because you have given me all that is properly precious. You gave me courage to seek out my family and doing that has enriched my life. You have given me a beautiful son. But most of all, you've given me your love and that is priceless.' He tilted her chin, his voice a little unsteady. 'You are my everything, Tara Sabato, do you realise that?'

He had taken her breath away with his soft words and Tara had to dab furiously at her eyes to stop her mascara running. 'And you are my everything,' she answered fiercely. 'For the first time in my life I feel as if I have a real home and that you and Declan are the beating heart of that home. And I love you. I love you so much. You do know that, don't you, Lucas?'

Tenderly, Lucas stared down into the amber gleam of her eyes. The woman he admired more than any other. Who was strong and smart and brave and beautiful. His equal. His wife. His love. 'Do I know that?' He smiled as he wiped a mascara-coloured teardrop away from her freckled cheek. 'You betcha.'

* * * * *

A PASSIONATE NIGHT WITH THE GREEK

KIM LAWRENCE

CHAPTER ONE

ZACH HAD RECEIVED the message he had been waiting for while he was stuck in traffic. Sometimes a first-hand knowledge of the back streets of Athens, combined with a flexible attitude to rules, came in useful.

Zach possessed both.

For some of his formative years he had lived by his wits on those streets, finding it infinitely preferable to living with the grandmother who had resented having her daughter's bastard foisted on her, and the drunken uncle who had perfected bullying into an art form.

It took him just under half an hour and a few probable speeding fines to reach the hospital. He remained oblivious to the covetous stares that followed his long-legged progress from his car and through the building. It took him three more minutes to reach the intensive care unit where Alekis Azaria had spent three days in a medically induced coma after being successfully re-suscitated following his last cardiac arrest.

Zach, as the closest thing the older man had to either friend or family, had been there the previous day when they'd brought him out of the coma. Despite the warnings that he had chosen not to hear, he had fully anticipated that Alekis would simply open his eyes.

The consultant had explained this sometimes happened but admitted there was a possibility that Alekis might never wake up.

Given the fact that the Greek shipping tycoon's presence here was on a strict need-to-know basis, it was no surprise that the same consultant who had issued this gloomy prognosis was waiting for him now, at the entrance to the intensive care unit.

The medic, used to being a figure of respect and authority, found himself straightening up and taking a deep steadying breath when the younger, tall, athletically built figure approached.

Zach didn't respond to the older man's greeting; instead, head tilted at a questioning angle, he arched a thick dark brow and waited, jaw clenched, to hear what was coming.

'He has woken and is breathing independently.'

Impatient with the drip-feed delivery Zach could sense coming, he cut across the other man, impatience edging his deep voice.

'Look, just give it to me straight.'

Straight had never been a problem for Zach. His ability to compartmentalise meant personal issues did not affect his professional ability.

'There seems to be no problem with Mr Azaria's cognitive abilities.'

A flicker of relief flashed in Zach's dark eyes. Intellectual impairment would have been Alekis's worst nightmare; for that matter it would have been his own.

'Always supposing that he was fairly...*demanding* previously?' the doctor tacked on drily.

Zach gave a rare smile that softened the austere lines of his chiselled, handsome features, causing a passing pretty nurse to walk into a door.

'He is accustomed to being in charge. I can see him...?'

The cardiologist nodded. 'He is stable, but you do understand this is early days?' he cautioned.

'Understood.'

'This way.'

Alekis had been moved from a cubicle in the intensive care unit to a private suite of rooms. Zach found him propped up on a pile of pillows. The events of the last week had gouged deep lines in the leathered skin of his face and hollowed out his cheeks, but his voice still sounded pretty robust!

Zach stood in the doorway for a moment, listening, a smile playing gently across his firm lips.

'Have you never heard of human rights? I'll have your job. I want my damned phone!'

The nurse, recovering her professional poise that had slipped when she'd seen Zach appear, lifted a hand to her flushed cheek and twitched a pillow, but looked calm in the face of the peevish demand and stream of belligerent threats.

'Oh, it's way above my pay grade to make a decision like that, Mr Azaria.'

'Then get me someone who can make a decision—' Alekis broke off as he registered Zach's presence. 'Good, give me *your* phone, and a brandy wouldn't come amiss.'

'I must have mislaid it.' Zach's response earned him a look of approval from the flush-faced nurse.

Alekis snorted. 'It's a conspiracy!' he grumbled. 'So, what are you waiting for? Take a seat, then. Don't stand there towering over me.'

Zach did as he was bade, lowering his immaculately clad, long and lean, six-foot-five athletic frame into one of the room's easy chairs. Stretching his legs out in front of him, he crossed one ankle over the other.

'You look—'

'I look like a dying man,' came the impatient response. 'But not yet—I have things to do and so do you. I assume you do actually have your phone?'

Zach's relief at the business-as-usual attitude was cancelled out by his concern at the shaking of the blue-veined hand extended to him.

He hid his concern beneath a layer of irony as he scrolled down the screen to find the best of the requested snapshots he'd taken several days earlier for Alekis.

'So how long before the news that I'm in here surfaces and the sharks start circling?'

Zach selected the best of the head shots he had taken and glanced up. 'Who knows?'

'Damage limitation is the order of the day, then.'

Zach nodded and extended the phone. 'I suppose if you're going to have another heart attack, you're in the right place. I'm assuming that you will tell me at some point why you sent me to a graveyard in London to stalk some woman.'

'Not stalk, take a photo...'

Zach's half-smile held irony as he responded to the

correction. 'All the difference in the world. I'm curious—did it ever occur to you I'd say no?'

Zach had been due to address a prestigious international conference in London as guest speaker to an audience consisting of the cream of the financial world when Alekis had rung him with his bizarre demand, thinly disguised as a request.

Should he ever start believing his own press he could always rely on Alekis to keep his ego in check, Zach mused with wry affection as the short conversation of several days before flickered through his head.

'You want me to go *where* and do *what*?'

'You heard me. Just give the address of the church to your driver—the cemetery is opposite—then take a photo of the woman who arrives at four-thirty.'

'Try not to let it give you a heart attack this time,' Zach advised now, placing his phone into the older man's waiting hand.

'Waiting for you to deliver this picture didn't give me a heart attack. Seventy-five years of over-indulgence did, according to the doctors who tell me I should have been six feet under years ago. They also said that if I want to last even another week I should deprive myself of everything that gives life meaning.'

'I'm sure they were much more tactful.'

'I have no use for tact.'

Greedy floated into Zach's head as he watched the older man stare at the phone.

'She's beautiful, isn't she?'

Zach deemed a response unnecessary. There was no question mark over the haunting beauty of the woman captured by his phone. What he *had* questioned was not

Alekis's interest, but his own fascination, bordering on obsession, with the face he couldn't stop thinking about. Until, that was, he had realised it wasn't the face, it was the puzzle of her identity, the mystery of the affair, that had tweaked his imagination, not those golden eyes.

'I'm always willing to lend a hand to a friend in need. I assume that you have lost all your fortune and no longer have access to your own personal team of private investigators in order to have needed me? How did you know she'd be there at four-thirty?'

'I have had her followed for the past two weeks.' He looked bemused that Zach would ask such an obvious question. 'And hardly a team was required... Actually I had reasons for not wanting to use in-house expertise. I was employing someone who proved to be an idiot...'

'The same person you had following her?'

'And he can whistle for his money. He was utterly inept, took any number of photographs, mostly of her back or lamp posts. And as for *covert*? She noticed him and threatened to report him for stalking... Took *his* photo, then hit him with her shopping bag. Did she see you?'

'No, I'm thinking of taking up espionage as my second career. I had no idea I was signing up for such a dangerous task. So, who is this scary lady?'

'My granddaughter.'

A quiver of surprise widened Zach's dark eyes as his ebony lashes lifted off the angle of his cheekbones. He really hadn't seen that one coming!

'Her mother was beautiful too...' The older man seemed oblivious to Zach's reaction as he considered the photograph, his fingers shaking as he held it up. 'I think she has a look of Mia, around the mouth.' His hooded gaze lifted. 'You knew I had a daughter?'

Zach tipped his head in acknowledgement. He had of course heard the stories of the wild-child daughter. There was talk of drugs and men, but no one knew if Alekis had seen her since she'd married against his wishes, and so the story went that she'd been disinherited. This was the first time Zach had heard mention of a granddaughter, or, for that matter, heard Alekis speak of his family at all; though a portrait of his long-dead wife hung in the hallway of his palatial home on the island he owned.

'She married some loser, Parvati, threw herself away on him—to spite me, I think,' the older man brooded darkly. 'I was right. He was a useless waster, but would she listen? No, he left her when she got pregnant. All she had to do was ask and I'd have...' He shook his head, looking tired in the aftermath of emotional outburst. 'No matter, she always was as stubborn and...' His voice trailed away until he sat there, eyes half closed.

Zach began to wonder if he had fallen asleep. 'Sounds like the apple didn't fall far from the tree.'

To Zach's relief, the older man opened his eyes and directed a scowl up at Zach, which slowly faded. The smile that replaced it held a hint of pride. 'Mia was a fiery one. Like her mother to look at but...' His voice trailed away again.

If the likeness in the painting he had seen was accurate, Alekis's wife had been beautiful, though not in the same style as the granddaughter with the glowing amber eyes. Zach could see no similarity between the two. The portrait was of a beautiful woman with a beautiful face but not a face to haunt a man. Unlike the face of the woman with the golden eyes. She was Alekis's granddaughter—he was still struggling to get his head around that.

Alekis's lack of family had been something they'd had in common, part of their unlikely bond that had grown through the years. Now it turned out that there was family and he was assuming Alekis wanted to be reunited. If the older man had asked his advice, Zach would have told him it was a bad idea. But Alekis wouldn't ask or listen any more than Zach would have if someone had told him beforehand that reconnecting with his own past would leave him with memories that would offer no answers and no comfort.

'I suppose I could have made the first move. I was just waiting but she never...' He wiped a hand across his eyes and when it fell away Zach pretended not to see the moisture on the old man's cheeks.

The truth was, he was finding it uncomfortable to see the man he had always considered self-contained and unsentimental and way past being a victim of his emotions show such vulnerability. But then maybe that was what a reminder of his own mortality did to a man?

'I suppose everyone has regrets.'

'Do you?'

Zach raised his brows at the question and considered it. 'We all make mistakes,' he said, thinking of his grandmother staring out of the window with blank eyes on his last visit to the home. 'But never the same one twice.' Twice made you a fool or in love—in his eyes the latter made you the former.

He could not imagine ever allowing his heart, or at

least his hormones, to rule his head. Not that he was a monk; sex was healthy and necessary but he never mixed it with sentiment, which had given him a reputation for being heartless, but he could live with that. Living with the same woman for the rest of his life? Less so!

'I regret...but it's too late for that.' Alekis's voice firmed. 'I want to make amends. I intend to leave her everything. Sorry if you thought you were getting it.'

'I don't need your money.'

'You and your damned pride! If you'd let me help you'd have got to the top a lot quicker, or at least with a lot less effort.'

'Where would be the fun in that? And you did help. You gave me an education and your advice.' Zach spoke lightly but he knew how much he owed to Alekis, and so did the shipping magnate.

'A gift beyond price, wouldn't you say?'

Zach's lips quivered into an appreciative smile. 'You really are feeling more yourself, but the moral blackmail is unnecessary, Alekis.' He spoke without heat. 'What do you want me to do?'

'Bring her to me.'

The face with the golden eyes floated into his head and Zach felt some nameless emotion flare inside him at the idea of seeing that face again.

The older man was staring again at the image on the screen.

'Will you?'

Zach's thickly defined sable brows lifted. 'Bring, as in...?' He shook his head, adding in an attempt to lighten the rather intense atmosphere that couldn't be doing Alekis's heart any good, 'I'm assuming we are not talking kidnap here.'

'It shouldn't come to that.'

'That wasn't actually an offer.'

The older man didn't appear to hear him.

'Does she have a name?' Zach asked, pretending not to see the moisture the older man wiped from the corners of his eyes.

'Katina.' Alekis's lips tightened. 'Greek only in name, she was born in England. Her history is…'

Zach was amazed to see a look close to shame wash over the older man's face.

'She has been alone for a long time. She thinks she still is. I intend to make it up to her, but I'm concerned that the shock will…'

'I'm sure she'll cope,' Zach soothed, repressing the cynical retort on the tip of his tongue. Discovering you were set to become wealthy beyond anyone's wildest dreams was the sort of shock most people recovered from quite quickly.

'It will be a culture shock. She's about to become an heiress and the target of vicious tongues and gold-diggers. She'll need to be protected…'

'From what you say she seems pretty well able to protect herself,' Zach inserted drily.

'Oh, she's clearly got spirit, but it takes more than spirit. She needs to be taught how things operate,' her grandfather continued. 'And I'm stuck in here, which is why I'm—'

Zach, who had listened with growing unease at the direction of this, cut in quickly. 'I'd love to help but that sounds pretty much like a full-time job to me.'

His mentor gave a deep sigh that made Zach's teeth clench; the smile that accompanied it was a nice blend of understanding and sadness. 'And you have every right to refuse.' Another sigh. 'You owe me nothing. Please don't run away with the idea I'm calling in a debt. I will discharge myself and—'

Zach lowered his shoulders. He knew when he was beaten.

'You know, sometimes I forget it was *me* that saved *your* life.'

The first lesson you learnt on the streets was to look after number one, the second was walk, or preferably run, away from trouble. Zach's problem was bullies. He hated them, and seeing those knife-wielding thugs surrounding the foolish old guy who was refusing to hand over his wallet had produced a red-mist moment that had led him to run towards danger and not away from it.

Zach believed nothing positive could be achieved by reflecting on the past, but if he had, his objective view would have been that there hadn't been anything remotely brave about his actions. Though stupid had flashed through his head at the first cut that had slipped between his ribs.

He might have saved the older man's life, but Alekis had given him a life and until this point asked for very little in return.

He watched, an expression of wry resignation twisting his lips, as the man's air of weary defeat melted away in a beat of his damaged heart.

The elderly Greek's smile oozed smug satisfaction. 'If you're sure?'

'Don't push it,' Zach growled out, torn between exasperation that he had been so expertly manipulated and amusement.

'It is important to control the flow of information when the news does leak. I know I can rely on you for that. The media will be all over her like a rash. We must be ready; she *must* be ready. *Go away!*'

The loud addition was directed to an unwary nurse who, to give her her due, stood her ground.

'I'll leave him to you. Good luck,' Zach added as he rose to his feet. 'You can email me the necessary,' he added before the exhausted-looking patient could react to his intention. 'Just give me her details and I'll do the rest, and in the meantime you get some rest.'

Kat danced around her small office and punched the air in triumph, before controlling the fizz of excitement still bubbling in her veins enough to retrieve the letter that she had tossed in the air after she had read it.

She read it again now, anxious that she hadn't misinterpreted it. That really *would* be awful. The tension that had slipped into her shoulders fell away as she came to the end.

It really did say what she'd thought, but what puckered her smooth brow into a slight frown was what it *didn't* say. There was a time she was expected to be there, at the address of the law firm, but no clue as to *who* was looking forward to meeting her.

She shrugged. Presumably a representative of one of the individuals or businesses known for their philanthropy to whom she had pitched her appeal—or *wasted her time with*, as some of her less optimistic-minded colleagues and volunteers had put it. Fighting against the negativity, she'd pointed out that she wasn't expecting any one person or organisation to step into the breach, but if she could persuade a handful to make some sort of donation it could mean a stay of execution for the refuge once the local authority funding was pulled the coming month.

Who knew? This could be the first of many.

There was a short tap on the door before Sue, with her nose stud, stuck her orange-streaked head around the door. 'Oh, God!' She sighed when she saw Kat's face. 'I know that look.'

'What look?'

The older woman stepped inside the room and, after closing the door, said, 'Your "campaign for a good cause" face.'

Kat blinked. 'Do I have a…?'

'Oh, you sure do, and I love—we *all* love—that you're a fighter, but there comes a time…' She sighed again, her skinny shoulders lifting before they fell. 'You've got to be a realist, love,' she told Kat earnestly. 'This place…' Her expansive gesture took in the small office with its cardboard-box system of filing—there always seemed to be something better to spend the limited resources on than office furniture. 'It's a lost cause. I've got an interview Monday. Just giving you the heads-up that I'll need the morning off.'

Kat was unable to hide her shock; her face fell. 'You're looking for another job?' If Sue, who was as upbeat as she was hard-working, had already given in… *Am I the only one who hasn't?*

'Too right I am, and I suggest you do too. There's always bills to pay and in my case mouths to feed. I care about this place too, you know, Kat.'

Kat felt a stab of contrition that her reaction might be read as judgement. 'I know that.' But the point was she didn't know what it was to be like Sue, a single parent bringing up five children and holding down two jobs.

On the brink of sharing the good news, she pulled back and moderated her response. She didn't want to raise hopes if nothing came of this.

'I know you think I'm mad, but I *really* think there's a realistic prospect someone out there cares.'

The other woman grinned. 'I know you do, and I really hope life never knocks that starry-eyed optimism out of you.'

'It hasn't so far,' Kat retorted. 'And Monday's fine. I'll cover... Good luck.'

She waited until the other woman had left before she sat down at her desk—actually, it was a table with one wobbly leg—and thought about who she might be meeting. Whoever it was didn't hang around. The meeting was scheduled for the following morning and the letter had been sent recorded delivery.

Well, she could cross the two off her list who had already sent a sympathetic but negative response, so who did that leave?

But then, did the identity of the potential donor actually matter? What mattered was that someone out there was interested enough for a meeting. So there was no beacon of light at the end of a tunnel but there was a definite flicker. Her small chin lifted in an attitude of determination. Whoever it turned out to be, she would sell her cause to them. Because the alternative was not something she wanted to contemplate—failure.

So for the rest of the day she resisted the temptation to share her news with the rest of her gloomy-looking colleagues. Not until she knew what was on offer, or maybe she just didn't want to have anyone dampen her enthusiasm with a bucket of cold-water realism? Either way there was no one to turn to for advice when she searched her wardrobe for something appropriate that evening.

There wasn't a lot to search. Her wardrobe was what designers called capsule, though maybe capsule was being generous.

It wasn't that she didn't love clothes and fashion, it was just that her budget was tight and in the past used up by impulse *bargain* buys, which inevitably sat in her wardrobe untouched and were eventually donated to a charity chop.

After a mega charity shop clear-out at the beginning of the summer and an unseasonal resolution to avoid sale racks, she had adopted a pared-down wardrobe. There had been the *one* slip. She looked at it now, hanging beside the eminently practical items. She rubbed the deep midnight-blue soft cashmere silk fabric between her fingers and gave a tiny nod; it was perfect for tomorrow's 'dress to impress'.

Smiling because her moment of weakness had been vindicated, she extracted the dress that stood out among the white shirts, T-shirts, black trousers and jeans, and hung it on the hook at the back of the bedroom door. Smoothing down the fabric, she checked it for creases, but everything about the dress managed to combine fluid draping with classic tailoring and the look screamed designer. The only fault she'd been able to find that had caused it to be downgraded to a second was the belt loop that needed a few stitches.

It had fitted so perfectly when she'd tried it on and had been marked down so much that, even though her practical head had told her there would never be an occasion in her life where the beautifully cut dress would come into it, she had bought it.

If she'd believed in fate—well, actually she did; the problem, in her experience, was not always recognising the door left ajar by fate as a golden opportunity.

It took her a little longer to dig out the heels buried among the piles in the back of the wardrobe, and she was ready. All she needed now was to go through her plan of attack. If she wanted to sell her case, make it stand out amongst the many deserving cases, she needed facts at her fingertips and a winning smile and someone with a heart to direct it at. The smile that flashed out was genuine as she caught sight of her face in the mirror…her eyes narrowed and her forehead creased in a frown of fierce determination.

So her winning smile could do with some work!

CHAPTER TWO

Zach was expected. The moment he strode into the foyer his reception committee materialised. He was shown up to the empty boardroom by the senior partner—the only Asquith left in the law firm of Asquith, Lowe and Urquhart—and three underlings of the senior variety.

If Zach had thought about it—which he hadn't, because he'd had other things on his mind—he would have expected no less, considering that the amount of business Alekis sent this firm's way had to be worth enough to keep the Englishman's Caribbean tan topped up for the next millennium and then some, not to mention add a few more inches to his expanding girth.

'I will bring Miss Parvati up when she arrives. How is Mr Alekis? There have been rumours...'

Zach responded to this carefully casual addition with a fluid shrug of his broad shoulders. 'There are always rumours.'

The older man tilted his head and gave a *can't blame a man for trying* nod as he backed towards the door, an action mirrored by the three underlings, who had tagged along at a respectful distance.

Zach unfastened the button on his tailored grey

jacket and, smoothing his silk tie, called after the other man before he exited the room. 'Inform me when she arrives. I'll let you know when to show her up.'

'Of course. Shall I have coffee brought in?'

His gesture took in the long table, empty but for the water and glasses at the end where Zach had pulled out a chair. Watching him, the older man found himself, hand on his ample middle, breathing in. The sharp intake of stomach-fluttering breath came with an unaccustomed pang of wistful envy that he recognised as totally irrational—you couldn't be wistful about something you had never had, and he had never had the sort of lean, hard, toned physique this man possessed. His own physical presence had a lot more to do with expensive tailoring, which permitted him to indulge his love of good food and fine wine.

'The water will be fine.' Zach reached for one of the iced bottles of designer water to illustrate the point and tipped it into a glass before he took his seat.

The door closed, and Zach glanced around the room without much interest. The room had a gentlemen's club vibe with high ceilings and dark wooden panelled walls—not really his usual sort of environment. He had never been in a position to utilise the old-school-tie network, but he had never been intimidated by it and, more importantly, not *belonging* to this world had not ultimately hindered his progress. If he was viewed in some quarters as an outsider, it didn't keep him awake nights, and even if it had he could function pretty well on four hours' sleep.

He opened his tablet and scrolled onto the file that Alekis's office had forwarded. It was not lengthy, pre-

sumably an edited version of the full warts and all doc-
ument. Zach had no problem with that; he didn't need
the dirt to make a judgement. The details he did have
were sufficient to give him a pretty good idea of the
sort of childhood the young woman he was about to
meet had had.

The fact that, like him, she had not had an easy childhood did not make him feel any *connection*, any more
than he would have felt connected to someone who
shared a physical characteristic with him. But he did
feel it gave him an insight others might lack, the same
way he knew that the innocence that had seemed to
shine out from her eyes in the snapshot had been an illusion. Innocence was one of the first casualties of the
sort of childhood she had had.

She had been abandoned and passed through the
care system; he could see why Alekis thought he had
a lot to make up for—he did. Zach was not shocked by
what the mother had done—he was rarely shocked by
the depths to which humans could sink—but he was
mildly surprised that Alekis, who presumably had had
ways of keeping tabs on his estranged daughter, had
not chosen to intervene, a decision he was clearly trying to make up for now.

While many might say never too late, Zach would
not. He believed there was definitely too late to undo
the damage. He supposed in this instance it depended
on how *much* damage had been done. What was not in
question was the fact that the woman he was about to
meet would know how to look after herself.

She was a survivor, he could admire that, but he was
a realist. He knew you didn't survive the sort of child-

hood she'd had without learning how to put your own interests first, and he should know.

The indent between his dark brows deepened. It concerned him that Alekis, who would normally have been the first to realise this, seemed to be in denial. The grandfather in him was putting sentiment ahead of facts, and the fact was anyone who had experienced what this woman had was never going to fit into her grandfather's world without being a magnet for scandal.

As Zach knew, you didn't escape your past; you carried it with you and learnt to look after number one. When had *he* last put someone else's needs ahead of his own?

There was no occasion to remember.

The acknowledgement didn't cause him any qualms of conscience. You didn't get to be one of life's survivors by *not* prioritising your own interests.

And Zach was a survivor. In his book it was preferable to be considered selfish than a victim, and rather than feel bitter about his past he was in some ways grateful for it and the mental toughness it had gifted him, without which he would not have enjoyed the success he had today.

He responded to the message on his phone, his fingers flying as he texted back. He looked down at the screen of his tablet. The vividness of the woman's golden eyes, even more intense against the rest of the picture that seemed washed of colour, stared out at him before he closed it with a decisive click.

Maybe he was painting a bleaker picture. He might be pleasantly surprised—unless Alekis had deliberately hidden them, it seemed the granddaughter hadn't had any brushes with the law. Of course, that might simply mean she had stayed under the radar of the authorities, but she did seem to hold down a steady job. Perhaps the best thing the mother had ever done for her child was to abandon her.

There was the lightest of taps on the door before Asquith stepped inside the room, his hand hovering in a paternal way an inch away from the small of the back of the woman who walked in beside him.

This wasn't the fey creature from the misty graveyard, neither was it a woman prematurely hardened by life and experience.

Theos! This was possibly the most beautiful creature he had ever laid eyes on.

For a full ten seconds after she walked in, Zach's entire nervous system went into shutdown and when it flickered back into life, he had no control over the heat that scorched through his body. The sexual afterglow of the blast leaving his every nerve ending taut.

He studied her, his eyes shielded by his half-lowered eyelids and the veil of his sooty eyelashes. He felt himself resenting that it was a struggle to access even a fraction of the objectivity he took for granted as he studied her. He expected his self-control to be his for the asking, irrespective of a bloodstream with hormone levels that were off the scale.

He forced the tension from his spine, only to have it settle in his jaw, finding release in the ticcing muscle that clenched and unclenched spasmodically as he studied her. She was wearing heels, which made her almost as tall as the lawyer, who was just under six feet. She was dressed with the sort of simplicity that didn't come cheap, but to be fair the long, supple lines of her slim body would have looked just as good dressed in generic jeans and a T-shirt.

He categorised the immediate impression she projected as elegance, poise and sex…

Her attention was on the man speaking to her, so Zach had the opportunity to prolong his study of her. She stood sideways on, presenting him with her profile as she nodded gravely at something the other man was saying, eyelashes that made him think of butterfly wings fluttering against her soft, rounded, slightly flushed cheeks. It was a pretty whimsical analogy for him.

Stick to the facts, Zach, suggested the voice in his head.

He did, silently describing what he saw.

Her profile was clear cut, almost delicate. There was the suggestion of a tilt on the end of her nose, her brow high and wide. The fey creature in the snapshot had a face framed by a cloud of ebony hair; this elegant young woman's hair was drawn smoothly back into a ponytail at the nape of her neck to fall like a slither of silk between her shoulder blades almost to waist level. Dark and cloud-like in the photos, in real life it was a rich warm brown, interspersed with warm toffee streaks.

The slight tilt of her head emphasised the slender length of her swan-like dancer's neck; the same grace was echoed in her slim curves and long limbs, beautifully framed by the simplicity of the figure-skimming calf-length dress. The length of her shapely legs was further emphasised by a pair of high, spiky heels.

'I'll leave you.'

'Leave?' Kat echoed.

Zach registered the soft musicality of her voice as her feathery brows lifted in enquiry, then, the moment he had been anticipating, she turned her head. Yes, her eyes really *were* that impossible colour, a rich deep amber, the tilt at the corners creating an exotic slant and lending her beautiful face a memorable quality.

Kat had been aware of the man in the periphery of her vision, sitting at the head of the long table. Up to that point, good manners had prevented her from responding to her curiosity and looking while her escort was speaking.

She did so now, just as the figure was rising to his feet.

The first thing she had noticed about her escort was his expensive tailoring, his plummy accent and old-school tie. This man was equally perfectly tailored—minus the old-school tie. His was silk and narrow, dark against the pale of his shirt. But what he wore was irrelevant alongside the impression of raw male power that hit her with the force of a sledgehammer.

She actually swayed!

He made the massive room suddenly seem a lot smaller; in fact, she experienced a wave of claustrophobia along with a cowardly impulse to beg her escort to wait for her.

You're not a wimp, Kat, or a quitter. Appearances and first impressions, she reminded herself, were invariably misleading. She'd found the first man's air of sleek, well-tailored affluence and accent off-putting initially, and yet now, a few floors up, he appeared cosy and benevolent. In a few minutes this dark stranger might seem cosy too. Her dark-lashed gaze moved in an assessing covert sweep from his feet to the top of his sleek dark head. Or *maybe not*!

Unless you considered large sleek predators *cosy*, and there was something of the jungle cat about him, in the way he moved with the fluid grace, the restless vitality you sensed beneath the stillness that a feral creature might feel in an enclosed space.

Aware she was in danger of overreacting and allowing her imagination to run riot, she huffed out a steadying breath between her stiff lips.

'Good morning.' She gave her best businesslike smile, aiming for a blend of warm but impersonal.

Easier said than done, when there were so many conflicting emotions jostling for supremacy in her head. Not to mention the fluttery pit of her stomach. She had no idea what she had been expecting, but it hadn't been this, or him!

She never rushed to judgement. She prided herself on her ability not to judge by appearances, so the rush of antagonism she had felt the moment his dark eyes had locked on hers was bewildering—and it hadn't gone away.

Her heart was racing, and it wasn't the only thing that had sped up. Everything had, including her perceptions, which were heightened to an extraordinary, almost painful degree, though they were focused less on the room with its background scent of leather and wood and more on the man who dominated with such effortless ease.

She had taken in everything about him in that first stunned ten seconds. The man stood several inches over six feet, and inside the elegant suit his build was lean yet athletic, with broad shoulders that were balanced perfectly by long, long legs. The strong column of his neck was the same deep shade of gold as his face, the warm and vibrant colour of his skin emphasised by the contrasting paleness of his shirt.

He was sinfully good-looking, if your taste ran to perfect. Such uncompromising masculinity attached to perfect symmetry, hard angles and carved planes, a wide mouth that was disturbingly sensual and the dark-as-night eyes framed by incredible jet lashes set under dark, strongly delineated brows.

There was no reaction to the smile she somehow kept pasted in place. She told herself to keep it together as she struggled to make the mental adjustments required.

'Oh, God!' It wasn't the pain in her knee when she hit the chair leg that made her cry out, it was the sight of the carefully arranged contents of the folder she carried sliding to the floor. 'Sorry,' she muttered as she bent to pick up the scattered papers, jamming them haphazardly into the folder.

Walk, think and string two syllables together, Kat. It's not exactly multitasking! It's all on your phone so it's not a disaster!

Cheeks hot, she straightened up. Forget old-school tie, *this* was who she was dealing with. *Fine.* Except, of course, it *wasn't* fine; she *was* making an impression, but not the intended one. Having gathered the papers, she promptly dropped them again. She bit her tongue literally to stop herself blurting a very unladylike curse.

Zach watched her silky hair fall over one shoulder as she fumbled for the scattered papers. The action drew attention to the curve of her behind, and as the soft, silky dark material of her dress stretched tight so did his nerve endings.

He could not recall the last time he had needed to fight his way through a fog of blind lust. If Alekis had had a window into his mind at that moment he might have doubted casting him in the role of protector and mentor. Or maybe not. There was some sense in it. Who better to guard the fluffy chick than a fox? Always supposing the fox in question could keep his own baser instincts in check.

Not that this creature was fluffy, she was more silky-smooth. *Smooth all over?*

Calming down this illicit line of distracting speculation, he let the silence stretch. It was amazing how many people felt the need to fill a silence, saying things that revealed more than a myriad searching questions.

Unfortunately, and uncomfortably on this occasion, in a moment of role reversal his own mind felt the need to fill the silence.

Alekis trusted him. The question was, did he trust himself?

The moment of self-doubt passed; even taking the trust issue with Alekis out of the equation, the logic of keeping the personal and professional separate remained inescapable.

'Won't you take a seat?'

She responded to the offer with relief; her knees were literally shaking. 'Thank you.' At least the table between them meant she was not obliged to offer her hand. Instead, she tipped her head and smiled. 'I'm Kat.'

'Take a seat, Katina.' He watched the surprise flare

in her amazing eyes and slide into wariness before she
brought her lashes down enough to veil her expression
momentarily.

The use of her *full* name, which no one ever used,
threw her slightly. Well, actually, more than slightly.

He couldn't know it, but the last person to call her
that had been her mother.

For many years Kat had believed that while she could
hear her mother's voice in her head, her mother was not
gone...she was coming back. Nowadays the childhood
conviction was gone and so was her mother's voice. The
memory might be lost but she did know that her name
on her mother's lips had not sounded anything like it did
when this man rolled his tongue around the syllables.

'Th-thank you,' she stuttered. Recovering from the
shaky moment, she gathered her poise around herself,
protective-blanket style. 'Just Kat is fine,' she added
finally, taking the seat he had gestured towards and
reflecting that it wasn't at all fine.

Though she was normally all for informality, she
would have been much happier with a formal, distant
Miss...or *Ms* or maybe even, *hey, you*. It wasn't just
her physical distance she felt the need to keep from
this man. His dark gaze seemed able to penetrate her
very soul.

She forced herself to forget his disturbing mouth,
equally disturbing eyes, the almost explosive quality
he projected, and move past the weird inexplicable antagonism. She was here to make a pitch, and save the
precious resource that the community was in danger
of losing. This was not about her—she just had to stay
focused on the prize.

All great advice in theory, but in reality, with those eyes drilling into her like lasers... Were lasers cold? She pushed away the thought and tried to dampen the stream of random thoughts that kept popping into her head down to a slow trickle.

Reminding herself that a lot of people were relying on her helped; the fact she was distracted by the muscle that was clenching and unclenching in his lean cheek did not.

'Water?'

Repressing the impulse to ask him if he had anything stronger, she shook her head.

'I'm fine,' she said, thinking, *If only!*

Nervous was actually how she was feeling and this man was probably wondering why the hell she was here.

She cleared her throat. 'I'm sure you have a lot of questions?'

His dark brows lifted; there was nothing feigned about his surprised reaction. 'I would have thought *you'd* have a lot of questions.'

True, she did. She gave voice to the first one that popped into her head. 'What do I call you?'

It wasn't really a change of expression, but his heavy eyelids flickered and left her with the distinct impression this wasn't the sort of question he had anticipated. She took a deep breath and tried again.

'It really doesn't matter to us *who* you represent—when I say it doesn't matter I don't mean... We would never accept anything from a...an...illegitimate source—obviously.'

'Obviously,' Zach said, realising for the first time

that she wasn't wondering why she was there, because she thought she knew.

He was intrigued.

His eyes slid to her plump lips. Intrigued had a much better ring to it than fascinated.

'Not that you look like a criminal or anything,' she hastened to assure him.

His lips twitched. 'Would you like to see character references…?'

She chose to ignore the sarcasm while observing that even when his mouth smiled his eyes remained as expressionless and hard as black glass. There was no warmth there at all. She found herself wondering what warmed that chill, and then gathered her wandering thoughts back to the moment and her reason for being here, which wasn't thinking about his eyes, or, for that matter, any other part of his dauntingly perfect body.

'We are just grateful that you are willing to consider contributing.'

'We?'

She flushed and refused to be put off by his sardonic tone. 'This we…' Kat pulled the folder from her bag and pointed to the logo on the cover. 'The Hinsdale project and family refuge. *Dame* Laura…' she put a gentle emphasis on the title; it was hard to tell sometimes but some people were impressed by such things, not that she had to pretend pride or enthusiasm as she told him '…began it back in the sixties when there was just the one house, a mid-terrace, a two-up two-down. It was all a bit basic.'

'And now?'

'We have extended into the houses both sides, the

entire row, and can take thirty-five women at any one time, depending, obviously, on the number of children. In the eighties the chapel across the road came up for sale and we bought it. Now it houses the nursery and crèche, which is available for women when they have moved out. It also contains a drop-in centre, which provides legal help and so forth. Dame Laura was personally involved, right up to her death.'

Had her own mother found Hinsdale, or a similar place, both their lives might have been very different.

Zach watched the wave of sadness flicker across her expressive face. Letting this interview play out a little longer might be on shaky ground morally, but practically it would provide a swifter insight into this woman whom he was meant to be *babysitting*.

'And what is your role?' Zach was experiencing a strange reluctance to abandon his mental image of a person so damaged they never looked at anything other than their own self-interest—a person, in short, much like himself.

The frown that came with the unbidden flicker of self-awareness faded as he watched her beautiful face light up with a glow of conviction and resolution as she leaned forward in her seat, losing the nervousness as she answered proudly.

'I run the refuge, along with a great team, many of whom are volunteers, as was I initially. I began by volunteering at the crèche when I was at school, and after I left I was offered a salaried position. I like to think Dame Laura would have been proud of what we have achieved.' Kat had met the redoubtable lady once; she had been frail but as sharp as a tack and totally inspirational. 'Her legacy lives on.' Embarrassed, Kat swallowed the emotional lump in her throat and reminded herself that there was a fine line between enthusiasm and looking a little unhinged. 'We have a dedicated staff and, as I said, so many volunteers. We are part of the community and don't turn anyone away.'

'That must make forward planning difficult.'

'We build in flexibility—'

He felt a twinge of admiration that, despite the starry-eyed enthusiasm, she was not so naive that she didn't know how to sidestep a difficult answer.

'Is that possible fiscally?'

'Obviously in the present financial climate—'

'How much do you need?'

The hard note of cold cynicism in his interruption made her blink, then rush to reassure. 'Oh, please, don't think for one moment we are expecting you to cover the total shortfall.'

'As negotiating tactics go, that, *Kat*...' the way he drawled her name made the fine hairs on the nape of her neck stand on end '...was not good—it was bad. It was abysmal.'

Her expression stiffened and grew defensive. 'I came here under the impression that you *wanted* to contribute to the refuge.' She struggled to contain the antagonism that sparkled in her eyes as she planted her hands on the table and leaned in. 'Look, if this is about me... There are other people who could do my job. The important thing is the work.'

'Do you think everything is about you?'

Kat felt her face flush. 'Of course not, it just felt... feels as if you find me...'

'So you are saying you'd sacrifice yourself to save this place?'

She swallowed, wondering if that was what it was going to take. Obviously it was a price she would be willing to pay, but only as a last resort. *Crawl and grovel if that's what he wants, Kat.* She heaved a deep sigh and managed an *almost* smile.

'You don't like me, fine.' *Because I really don't like you.*

Zach watched the internal struggle reflected on her face. This was a woman who should never play poker. As a born risk-taker, he enjoyed that form of relaxation.

She left a space for him to deny the claim.

He didn't.

'But, please,' she begged, 'don't allow that to influence your decision. I am one person easy to replace, but there is a dedicated staff who work incredibly hard.' Breathing hard, she waited for a response, the slightest hint of softening, but there was none.

Her chin went up; she was in nothing-to-lose territory.

She flicked to the first page of the thin folder, except the first page was now somewhere in the middle so it took her a few moments to locate it. 'I have the facts and figures; the average stay of a client is...' With a sigh she turned the page of figures over. It wasn't the right one. 'The average doesn't matter. Everyone who comes is different and we try to cater to their individual needs. The woman who is my deputy first arrived as a client. She was in an abusive relationship...'

A nerve along his jaw quivered. 'Her partner hit her?'

The hairs on the nape of her neck lifted in response

to the danger in his deceptively soft question. Underneath the beautiful tailoring she sensed something dangerous, almost feral, about this man. A shiver traced a sticky path up her spine as she struggled to break contact with his dark eyes.

'No, he didn't.' He hadn't needed to. He had isolated Sue from her family and friends and had controlled every aspect of her life before she'd finally left. Even her thoughts had not been her own. 'It's not always about violence. Sometimes the abuse is emotional,' she said quietly. 'But she now works for us full-time, is a fantastic mum and was voted onto the local council. The refuge has helped so many and it will again in future, the cash-flow situation is—'

Her own earnest flow was stemmed by his upheld hand. 'I am sure your cause is very worthy, but that is not why you were invited here.'

'I don't understand...'

'I had never heard of your refuge, or your Dame Laura.'

As his words sank in, the throb of anger in her head got louder; her voice became correspondingly softer. 'Then why the hell am I here?'

It was an indulgence, but he took a moment to enjoy the flashing amber eyes that viewed him with utter contempt.

'I am here to represent Alekis Azaria.'

The name seemed vaguely familiar to Kat but she had no idea why. She leaned forward, arching a questioning brow. *'Greek...?'*

He nodded. He had seen several reactions to Alekis's name before, ranging from awe to fear, but hers was a first. She clearly didn't have a clue who he was.

'Like you.'

She frowned, then realised his mistake. 'Oh, not really. The name, you mean? Oh, I suppose I must have some Greek blood, but I've never been there. Are you…?' she asked, searching for some sort of explanation, some sort of connection to explain him and this interview.

'I am Greek, like Alekis.'

'So why did this man who I have never heard of invite me here?' The entire thing made no sense to her. 'Who is he?'

CHAPTER THREE

'HE'S YOUR GRANDFATHER.'

He watched as the bemused confusion drawn on her face froze and congealed. As her wide eyes flickered wide in shock.

It took a conscious effort for Zach to hold on to his objectivity as she gasped like a drowning person searching for air. She sucked in a succession of deep breaths.

'I have no family.' Her voice was flat, her expression empty of the animation that had previously lit it. 'I have no one, so I can't have a grandfather.'

He pushed away an intrusive sliver of compassion and the squeeze of his heart and hardened his voice as he fell back on facts, always more reliable than sentiment.

'We all have two grandfathers, even me.'

Another time she might have questioned the significance of the *even me* but Kat was in shock. The sheer unexpectedness of what he had said had felt like walking...no, *running* full pelt into a brick wall that had suddenly appeared in the middle of a flower-filled meadow.

'I don't even know who my *father* is, other than a

name on a birth certificate.' It had never crossed her mind to track down the man who had abandoned her pregnant mother. The decision to search for her mother had not been one she had taken lightly, though, as it turned out, she had already been five years too late. 'Why should I want any contact with his family?'

Zach narrowed his eyes, recalling the one line in the file on the man Alekis's daughter had married in defiance of her father's wishes. 'He might have a family, but I don't have that information.'

'I don't understand...'

'It is your mother's family, or rather her father, that I am representing.'

She listened to his cold, dispassionate explanation before sitting there in silence for several moments, allowing her disjointed thoughts to coalesce.

'She had a family...' She faltered, remembering bedtime stories, the tall tales of a sun-drenched childhood. Was even a *tiny* part of that fantasy based on reality? The thought made her ache for her mother, far away from home and rejected.

'Your grandfather is reaching out to you.'

Shaking her head, Kat rose to her feet, then subsided abruptly as her shaking legs felt too insubstantial to support her.

'Reaching...' She shook her head and the slither of silk down her back rippled, making Zach wonder what it would look like loose and spread against her pale gold skin. 'I don't want *anyone* reaching out to me.' Her angry amber eyes came to rest accusingly on his handsome face. She knew there was a reason she had never trusted too-good-looking men besides prejudice and the fact the man who had spiked her drink all those years ago had been the one all the girls in the nightclub had been drooling over. 'Is this some sort of joke?'

'It is real.' As real as the colour of those pain-filled, angry, magnificent eyes.

'He's rich?'

Her words did make it sound as though a yes would be a good thing. This was not avarice speaking, he realised, but anger. The former would have made his life a lot easier.

'He is not poor.'

Her trembling lips clamped tight, the pressure blanching the colour from her skin as she fought visibly for composure.

'My mum was… She was poor, you see…*very* poor.' She eyed him with contempt, not even bothering to attempt to describe the abject hand-to-mouth existence that had driven her mother to drugs and the men who supplied them. A man who looked like him, dressed like him and oozed the confidence that came from success and affluence could not even begin to understand that life and the events that trapped people in the living hell of degradation.

'Yes.'

One of the reasons she rarely mentioned her early years was the way people reacted. She mentally filed them into two camps: the ones that looked at her with pity and those that felt uneasy and embarrassed.

His monosyllabic response held none of the above, just a statement of fact. Ironic, really, that a response she would normally have welcomed only added another layer to the antagonism that swirled inside her head as she looked at him. By the second he was becoming the personification of everything she disliked most in a person. Someone born to privilege and power without any seeming moral compass.

Ignoring the voice in her head that told her she was guilty of making the exact sort of rush or, in this case, more a *stampede* to judgement that she'd be the first to condemn, she sucked in a deep sustaining breath through flared nostrils.

Despite her best efforts, her voice quivered with emotion that this man would *definitely* see as a weakness. '*He* didn't reach out to her...'

'No.'

Her even white teeth clenched. 'Where was *he* when his daughter needed him? If he makes the same sort of grandfather as he made father, why would I want to know him?'

'I don't know...' He arched a satiric brow and pretended to consider the answer. 'He's rich?'

Her chin lifted to the defiant angle he was getting very familiar with. It was a long time since Zach had been regarded with such open contempt.

Better than indifference!

The knee-jerk reaction of his inner voice brought a brief frown to his brow before he turned his critical attention to the play of expression across her flawless features. He had never encountered anyone who broadcast every thought in their heads quite so obviously before.

The concept of a professional guard would be alien to her. Though in her defence, this *wasn't* professional to her—it was very personal. He was getting the idea that everything with this woman might be.

For someone who compartmentalised every aspect of his life, the emotional blurring was something that appalled him.

'So you're of the "everyone has a price" school of thought,' she sneered.

'They do.'

His man-of-few-words act was really starting to get under her skin.

'I don't. I'm not interested in money and…and… *things!*'

He arched a satiric brow. 'That might be a more impressive statement if you hadn't come here with a begging bowl.'

She fought off the angry flush she could feel rising up her neck. 'That is *not* the same.'

He dragged his eyes up from the blue-veined pulse that was beating like a trapped wild bird at the base of her slender throat. This might be the moment he told himself to remember that the untouched, fragile look had never been a draw for him. He had no protective instincts to arouse.

'If you say so.'

His sceptical drawl was an insult in itself.

'I am *not* begging. This isn't for me.'

He cut her off with a bored, 'I know, it is for the greater good. So consider that for the moment—consider how much you could help the *greater good* if you had access to the sort of funds that your grandfather has.'

He allowed himself the indulgence of watching the expressions flicker across her face for several seconds before speaking.

'You see, everyone *does* have a price—even you.'

'There is no *even me*. And I'm not suggesting I'm a better person than anyone else!' she fired back.

Zach watched her bite her lip before lifting her chin and found himself regretting his taunt. As exasperating as her attitude was, she had just received news that was the verbal equivalent of a gut punch.

And she had come out fighting.

'If you say so.'

She blinked hard, not prepared to let it go. 'I *do* say so, and,' she choked out, 'I really don't want to know the sort of person who would abandon his daughter.'

'Maybe she abandoned him?'

The suggestion drew a ferocious glare. On one level he registered how magnificent she looked furious, on another he realised that he was now in uncharted territory—he was playing it by ear. Zach trusted his instincts; his confidence was justified but, in this instance, it had turned out to be massively misplaced.

The unorthodox role assigned to him had been unwelcome, but he had approached it as he would anything. He'd thought that he had factored in all the possibilities…had considered every reaction and how to counter them to bring about the desired outcome with the least effort on his part.

Pity she didn't read the same script, Zach!

In his own defence, it hadn't seemed unreasonable to assume that the idea of being wealthy beyond any person's wildest dreams would swiftly negate any anger the heiress might feel towards the absentee grandparent.

He had never found it particularly admirable when people were willing to disadvantage themselves for a point of principle. He found it even less so now, when those so-called principles were making his own life hard work.

Not that it crossed his mind that in the long run she would reject the fortune. She'd find a way to trick herself eventually into believing she wasn't betraying her principles. He just had to help her get to that point a little quicker.

'He was the parent,' she quivered out. 'Parents care for their children.'

'In a perfect world, yes.' But, as she of all people should well know, the world was not perfect. It took a very stubborn idealist to retain a belief system like hers in light of her personal experiences.

She gritted her teeth. 'It's got nothing to do with a perfect world. It's called unconditional love. Not that I'd expect someone like you to know anything about that.'

'You'd be right, I don't,' he lied, pushing away the image that had materialised without warning in his head. His mother's thin, tired face, her work-worn hands. The memory was irrevocably linked with pain, which was why he didn't think about it, *ever*. 'Do you?'

The sudden attack threw her on the defensive. 'I see women willing to lay down their lives for their children every day of my working life.'

'Does that make up for your own mother abandoning you?'

He ignored the kick to his conscience when she flinched as though he had struck her. The illusion of fragility vanished as her chin lifted and she looked at him with angry eyes.

'None of this is about my mother.'

'Are you trying to tell me you're not angry with her for dumping you? My mother left me because she died…and for a long time I hated her for it.' They were words he'd never even thought, let alone voiced before, and they came with a massive slug of guilt and anger that her attitude had dredged up memories he had consigned to history. 'And you expect me to believe that you were never angry that you got dumped on a doorstep somewhere?' Maybe she genuinely didn't remember and that was why she was able to continue to lie to herself.

'It was a car park of a doctor's surgery. She knew that someone would help me, that I'd be safe.'

Safe… He closed his eyes, trying to banish the poignant image in his head of a dark-haired child standing there waiting for a mother who never came back.

'Some people should not have children,' Zach condemned. He had decided long ago that he was one of them. It was too easy for a bad parent to scar their children, so why take the risk?

'She needed help, she had nowhere to go—'

'I find your determination to see this woman as some innocent victim slightly perverse. She was the one who walked away from your grandfather. And she was an adult, not a child.'

Unable to argue with the facts the way he presented them, she snapped back. 'If this so-called grandfather of mine is so anxious to make contact, why isn't he here? Why send you?'

'He's in intensive care.'

It was a slight exaggeration; according to his latest update, Alekis had been downgraded from high de-

pendency to whatever the medical equivalent was. He
was the next step up...the walking wounded, maybe?

Her reaction was everything he had expected from
someone who seemed to have *bleeding heart* stamped
into her DNA. Like a pricked balloon, her anger deflated with an almost audible hiss.

Her eyes slid from his. 'Well, I'm sorry about that,'
she mumbled stiffly. 'But I have no room in my life
for someone I despise—' She broke off as he suddenly
leaned back in his leather seat and laughed.

'That's it, of course!'

'What's *it*?'

'It's just I've been wondering who you remind me of.'

The suspicion in her eyes deepened. 'What are you
talking about?'

'Someone who doesn't understand the word *compromise*, who can't forgive anyone who lets them down—
in fact, anyone, even family, no, es*pecially* family, who
doesn't live up to their idea of what is right...' He arched
a dark brow. 'Sounding familiar?'

It took her a few seconds to divine his meaning. Her
horrified reaction was instantaneous. 'I am *nothing* like
my grandfather.'

'Well, that's an improvement. You admit you have
one now. I've never put much faith in the whole gene
thing. I might have to rethink it—you've never met the
man and yet in your own way you are as stubborn and
self-righteous as Alekis.'

'How dare you?'

'Easily.' He dismissed her outrage with a click of his
long fingers. 'Your grandfather couldn't forgive your

mother so he lost her. You can't forgive him and you're willing to reject him when he makes the first move.'

'A move that was twenty-four years coming!'

'Granted.'

Kat's head had sunk forward, her chin almost on her chest, so that her expression was hidden from him as she muttered, 'I'm nothing like him.'

'Prove it.'

She lifted her head in response to the soft challenge, making herself look at him, mainly because once their eyes were connected it was difficult to break that connection, she observed angrily.

'You are a very manipulative man.'

He gave what she considered a heartless laugh, which sadly didn't make it any the less attractive.

'I'm impressed. It takes most people much longer to figure that one out.'

'And by then it's too late,' she said bitterly as she realised it already was for her. Like it or not, she had been put in a position where she had to prove that the future of the refuge was more important than...what? She realised that it hadn't been spelt out yet what her side of any bargain would be.

'What does he expect from me?'

'Alekis?' His broad shoulders lifted in a negligent shrug. 'You should ask him that.'

She squeezed her eyes closed, then opened them wide. 'Do I have any other family?' The sudden possibility that she had an entire family out there, aunts, uncles, cousins, felt strange...and yet exciting.

'Not that I am aware of,' he said, feeling quite irrationally guilty when the spark faded from her eyes.

Another emotion broke through his defences that Zach couldn't put a name to, didn't even try. It took seconds for him to douse it, but the memory of that nameless feeling remained like a discordant echo as he responded to the question with evasion that came easily.

'But again, I suggest you should ask the man himself. I am not privy to all his secrets.'

She nodded. 'And if I do…see him…how does that work?'

Before he could congratulate himself on a job well done she gave a fractured little sigh and added, 'Does he have any *idea* what sort of life she led? The places, the men…?'

Without warning an image of the little girl she had once been flashed into his head again, along with a compulsion to ask, 'Do you remember?'

'She used to tell me stories.' Without warning her eyes filled with tears; the stories were true. 'Does he live on an island?' she asked, remembering the wistful quality in her mother's voice when she told those stories. 'He didn't want us and now I—I don't have a grandfather. I don't have anybody.'

He clenched his jaw as the plaintive cry from the heart threatened the professional distance he needed to retain. 'I know this has been a shock.'

She gave a bitter little laugh. *'You think?'*

Shock? Was that what you called making someone question everything she'd thought she knew about her life?

'Look, I have no vested interest in this. I am simply the messenger boy. You make your decision and I'll relay it.'

She took a deep sustaining breath and looked him straight in the eye. 'I'll do it.' *Oh, God, what am I doing?* 'So, what happens now? If I agree to see him, I'm assuming he can't come here...unless that was a lie?'

'He is ill.'

'So that is real?'

He actually took some comfort from the fact that she was not *quite* as naive as she appeared, though even if she turned out to be half as naive it would be cause for serious concern.

'I wasn't lying. Alekis is seriously ill.'

'Is he in pain?'

'Not that I know of. Do you want him to be?'

Her eyes flew wide in comic-book shock-horror fashion. 'What sort of person do you think I am?'

'I think you're—'

The driven quality in his unfinished words made her shake her head in puzzled confusion.

'You want to know what happens next?'

Diverted, she nodded.

'The plan is for me to take you to Tackyntha via Athens, where you will meet your grandfather before his next surgery.' The doctors had agreed with the utmost reluctance to Alekis's plan to meet them at the airport, and then only after he had agreed to have a full medical team with him.

She shook her head. 'Tackyntha?'

'It is your grandfather's home, an island.'

'Where my mother lived.'

'I presume so.'

'So, you want me to go to the hospital.'

The obvious solution, but Alekis was determined that when he met his granddaughter he would not be lying in a hospital bed. 'At the airport.'

'And what if I say no?'

'I'd say fair enough, though it's a shame because your cause sounded pretty deserving.'

'Do you work for him?'

His lips twitched. 'He did offer, but, no, I do not work for Alekis.'

'Does he think you can buy love? Buy me?' Her words had an angry, forlorn sound.

'That is not in my field of expertise.'

'What *is* your area of expertise?'

'Well, it's *not* babysitting reluctant heiresses.'

She responded to the barely concealed disdain in his observation with an equally snooty glare of her own. 'I do not require a babysitter, thank you.'

'Let me rephrase it. You need to learn the rules of the society you're about to enter.'

She pounced angrily on the refined definition. 'So that I don't embarrass my grandfather, you mean! Oh, to hell with this. My home is here. I'm needed here.'

'Really? You already told me that you are not irreplaceable. That you have a talented second-in-command whose task, I think, would be a lot easier if your refuge had financial security. Besides, being an heiress does not make you rich in the present, but you will be a target for shady gold-diggers and tabloid journalists, which is where I come in.'

'So, what are you—a bodyguard or a babysitter?'

'I am a man at the end of his patience,' he intoned grimly. 'Look, the options are you flounce off or give me the details so that I can arrange a bank transfer into your refuge's accounts.'

'And what do I have to do?'

'Come and say hello to a dying old man.' For starters, he added silently, before reminding himself that her future and her happiness were not his business.

Who said be careful what you wished for? Maybe, she reflected grimly, someone who had dreamt of finding a family only to have it feel… How *did* she feel?

Unravelling the confused tangle of emotions she was struggling with, Kat knew that a dream come true wasn't meant to feel this way. 'So, who would he have left his money to if he hadn't decided to make up for a quarter of a century and look for me?'

'Me, I would imagine. However, you can relax. I don't need it.'

Which explained the arrogant manner and the air of self-importance.

'If I do come with you to Greece, I will need some guarantees. Firstly, I need to know that the future of the refuge is guaranteed.'

'My word is not enough for you?'

Her eyes narrowed at the hauteur in his manner. 'In writing, for my lawyer to check over.' Her expression dared him to challenge the fact she had a lawyer. Well, Mike *was* a lawyer, though not hers, but lawyer sounded so much more impressive and businesslike than her friend from her baking class who'd like to be more.

'Agreed,' he said calmly. 'You can have the papers by the end of the day.'

'And I need to know that I can leave whenever I like.'

The idea that he or Alekis had any control over her

movements was something he allowed to pass. 'Two months.'

'What?'

'You will give your grandfather two months to get to know you. That only seems fair, wouldn't you say?'

Nothing about this seemed *fair* to Kat, who nodded. 'Two months.' She started to get to her feet and stopped. 'I don't know your name.'

'Enter the name Zach Gavros into your search engine and you'll find out all you need to know about me. Some of it might even be true.'

CHAPTER FOUR

SOMEONE FILLED KAT'S glass with the wine from the party-sized box that she was pretty sure Zach Gavros would have turned his autocratic nose up at. It was still in her hand as she slipped out of the room, where the mood was definitely party, and into the relative quiet of the office. Though no longer *her* office.

She had said goodbye to everyone earlier, fighting the emotional lump in her throat, reminding herself that she was the only one, barring Sue, who knew that this was a permanent parting. The goodbye was of the 'for ever' variety.

Maybe she would come back after two months, but it didn't seem fair for her to ask Sue to step down when or if she returned, so she was making a clean break. Which had left her with no real option but to tell Sue, considering she was relying on her deputy to step into her shoes, the task that wasn't as easy as she had hoped. While she had been convincing a sceptical Sue how perfect she was for the job and how smooth the transition would be, Kat realised just how true it was. She supposed everyone liked to think they were indispensable, that they would leave a hole, be missed, but it was depressing to realise that she was so easy to replace.

'You should go back to the party,' she said to Sue, who she had seen slip away a few minutes earlier. The older woman, who was bent over a carboard box of files, straightened up and nodded.

'I will, but I couldn't let you go without a last hug.'

Feeling the tears press against her eyelids, Kat blinked and turned her head, putting her half-full glass down next to a pile of books on a cabinet. 'Nice photos,' she said, her glance taking in the framed photos of her children that Sue had already arranged on what was now *her* desk.

Sue looked anxious. 'I hope you don't mind?'

'Of course not,' Kat responded, feeling guilty because she had minded– -just a bit.

'So, when do you want me to tell the others that you're not coming back from the *management course*?' Sue asked, framing the words with inverted commas. She had made no secret that she was mystified by Kat's determination to keep the truth under wraps, and Kat hadn't really known how to explain it herself. It was hard to tell other people about something that still seemed unreal to her. Besides, they might look at her the way Sue had initially, as though she'd changed or she were a different person.

Well, she wasn't, and she didn't intend to be. Kat was determined that, whatever happened, she would hang on to her own identity. If her grandfather or Zach Gavros thought they could mould her into something she wasn't, they would soon learn otherwise.

Of course, she had searched for his name. There was

plenty of information there to give her an insight into the man her grandfather had chosen to tutor her in how the super-rich behaved, and also a few significant gaps.

His past seemed something of a mystery, which had sparked a thousand conspiracy theories. A favourite being that he had underworld connections. Another that he was Alekis's bastard son, which would make him her... No, that *couldn't* be right, she decided, sure that there could be no blood connection between them.

There were almost as many stories of his financial genius and ruthless dedication to amassing wealth as there were to the sleek cars he drove, and the even sleeker women who lined up to have their hearts broken by him.

And to be fair, in a number of cases their public profiles and careers had been enhanced by their association with the man. Kat didn't feel it was fair, though, as an image floated into her head of her mother's grave as it had been when she'd finally found it. Overgrown, untended...lonely. Her mother's heart had not been as resilient as the women whose names had been associated with Zach Gavros, but she liked to think that her mother had finally found a man worthy of her love. The beautiful gravestone in the cemetery gave her hope.

Kat pushed away the intruding thoughts with a firm little shake of her head. She smiled at Sue.

'That's up to you. You're the boss.' A sudden whoop from the other room, where the party was still in full swing, made her turn her head. When she looked back, Sue was looking at her suitcase.

'That is one very small case for a new life.'

'Just what I was thinking.'

Both women turned to the owner of the pleasant voice—*pleasant* was a good description of the man who was standing in the doorway. A little above average height, he was fairish and good-looking. Mike's newly acquired and carefully tended beard made him look less boyish and gave him, according to him, the maturity his clients expected of a solicitor earmarked for partner in a successful practice.

'I did knock but nobody heard. Am I too early?'

'Perfect timing, and I always travel light,' Kat told them both truthfully, seeing no need to explain that it was a hangover from her childhood, when for years she had been utterly certain that the mother who had left her sitting on the car-park wall of a health centre would come back to her. Her faith had been absolute; she had kept her small suitcase stowed neatly under her bed, packed, ready for the day her mum would come to claim her. Which was probably why none of the early foster placements had ever stuck, and the couple who had been interested in adopting her had backed out. *Polite,* she'd heard them tell her case worker, but unable to respond to love. They hadn't understood that Kat didn't need a family, she already had one, though seeing as they had said she was a polite child she hadn't wanted to upset them by explaining this.

In the end she'd found her way into a long-term foster home. A mad, hectic household with a rare and marvellous couple who didn't expect love, they just gave it, and they never mentioned her case under the bed.

Kat still had a packed case under her bed that she didn't have to explain, because Kat didn't share her bed or her history with anyone.

'You know everyone is going to be gutted they didn't get to say goodbye properly.'

Kat smiled. For a day or two, a week maybe, they might miss her. Might even say some affectionate *remember when* things about her in the future, but people forgot and that, she reminded herself before she slipped into a self-pitying spiral, was the way it should be. She would be in a position now to help them more from a distance than she ever could have here.

'What shall I tell them when you don't come back?'

'That's up to you. Like I keep saying, you'll be the boss, you'll do things your way. Oh, sorry!' She straightened the photo her elbow had nudged. 'This one of Sara is so cute. She looks just like you.'

'So everyone keeps telling me.'

Kat placed it carefully back down. The photo was the reason why Sue would always be missed, never forgotten. She had family. Shrugging off the wave of sadness tinged with envy that threatened to envelop her, Kat picked up her case and reminded herself that she travelled light, something that Sue, with all her responsibilities, couldn't do. She was lucky.

'This is your office—you might even splurge on that new desk I never got around to getting. Nobody suspects, do they?' She nodded towards the door, behind which there was the gentle hum of laughter.

'Not a thing.'

'I must be a much better liar than I thought.'

No one had had any problem accepting that a philanthropist who wanted to remain nameless had appeared, and that he was willing to not only fund the shortfall, but very generously fund the expansion of an annex and playground they had always dreamt of, and send Kat on a management course. And why shouldn't they? Everyone loved a happy ending.

Sue's reaction to the full story had made her realise that in most people's eyes she had her own happy ending. She was an heiress; she was living the dream. The dream of so many children living in care.

Not hers. Maybe she just didn't dream big. She had never thought of castles…just somewhere small, enough money to pay the bills and a mum. Her little fantasies had never contained any male figures; her own father, she knew, had walked out before she was born, and the men in her mother's life afterwards, well, the moments of peace she remembered coincided with their absences.

The only male figure who had been a reassuring presence in her life had been her foster father, but when he had died completely unexpectedly she had seen first-hand how devastated his wife, Nell, had been.

So the options, it seemed to Kat, were between being involved with a man who turned out to a bastard who abused or deserted you, or a man who, to quote dear Nell, you 'loved so much you became half a person after you lost them'. Those heartbroken words had stayed with Kat, as had the haunted, empty look in her foster mum's eyes.

Neither of the above seemed an option anyone with half a brain would voluntarily choose, though maybe falling in love removed the choice?

She was open-minded about the power of love, but it was a power she had never felt and she didn't feel deprived. Actually, she'd started to wonder, if you *had* to have a relationship—and the world did seem to be constructed for pairs—a relationship without love might be the way to go?

A choice made for common-sense reasons with someone you knew was nice and dependable—like Mike?

It was ironic that lately she'd even been contemplating saying yes, the next time he asked her out. Though that wasn't going to happen now.

Mike picked up her case. 'You sure about this?' he asked, his expression concerned.

'Of course she is—it's like a fairy tale and she's the princess. Aren't you excited? Your life is going to change.'

Fighting the impulse to yell, *I liked my old life,* she lifted her shoulders in a delicate shrug, smiling to take the edge off her words.

'I quite liked the old one. I'm still a bit in shock,' she added, feeling she had to defend her lack of enthusiasm as she returned Sue's hug and gave a sniff. 'Stop that,' she begged the weeping Sue. 'I said I was not going to cry.'

She did, a little, and Mike, being tactful, didn't comment on her sniffles as they drove along. Instead, he kept up a desultory anecdotal conversation that required nothing from her but the occasional nod and smile until they reached the private airfield.

A barrier lifted as they approached, and they were waved through to a parking area that appeared empty apart from two limousines parked at the far end.

Mike lifted her case from the boot and turned to where she stood waiting, her slender shoulders hunched against a chill autumnal breeze. 'I've done some research, and your grandfather, Kat, he's mega wealthy.'

Kat nodded. She too had looked up her grandfather's name and seen the results that spilled out. Knowing that her mother had lived the life afforded by such unimaginable wealth and privilege and then been reduced to such a miserable, degrading existence somehow made her fate worse, and intensified the anger Kat felt towards the man who had refused, up to this point, to acknowledge he even had a granddaughter.

'So, I suppose we're never going to have that movie and take-away night.' Underneath the lightness of his words she glimpsed a genuine sadness that made Kat experience a pang of guilt, acknowledging her own selfishness.

She'd turned to Mike for help, knowing that he wanted to be more than a friend, and had not spared a thought for his feelings. Maybe Zach had been right: she *was* like her grandfather.

Horror at the thought made her respond with more warmth than she might have otherwise shown as she threw her arms around him in a spontaneous bear hug.

'We can keep in touch.'

Zach emerged from the limo to see the embrace. He tensed, his teeth grating together in a white unsmiling barrier as the pressure of outrage building in his chest increased. Waving away the driver and his bags, he kept his eyes trained on the couple, ignoring the whisper in the corner of his brain that suggested his reaction to Katina having a lover was a bit OTT.

The soft sound of her laughter reached his ears, low and *intimate*, he silently translated, feeling the rush of another nameless emotion that pushed him into action, and strode across the concrete. It was nothing to him if she had a lover or a string of them, but the information, he told himself, might have been useful. It wasn't like Alekis to leave out such a detail, so presumably he didn't know about this man either.

He did not doubt that Alekis would manage to separate them, but he found he could see a quicker and more efficient way to facilitate this.

'Good afternoon.'

Furious with herself for jumping guiltily away from Mike at the sound of Zach's voice, she laid a hand on Mike's arm.

'Hello.'

The warmth lacking in her eyes as she had acknowledged the tall Greek's presence was there as she turned back to her friend. 'Mike, this is Zach Gavros. I told you about him.'

She had actually told him very little of what she had learnt online, because, like Sue, Mike's recognition of the name had been instantaneous, though, unlike Sue, Mike's depth of knowledge was more focused on Zach's apparent financial genius than the number of hearts he'd broken. And he hadn't shown the same degree of interest in what the Greek would look like without his shirt as Sue.

Kat, whose Internet trawl had been extensive, and had thrown up pictures of Zach and his ribbed, golden torso on a private beach with a model wearing nothing but a pair of minuscule bikini bottoms, already knew the answer. As she looked at him standing there, in a dark suit topped by a long overcoat, open to reveal his snowy white shirt, she realised that the knowledge of what he looked like minus the tailoring made her cheeks heat.

'This is my friend, Mike Ross.' She tore her eyes from the sensual curve of Zach's mouth and focused on his cleanly shaven jaw while she caught her breath, as Mike stepped forward, hand extended, and for a horrible moment she thought Zach was not going to take it.

'Friend and lawyer. I hope everything was in order, Mr Koss.'

She wasn't surprised that Mike didn't respond. Zach Gavros sounded coldly aloof and slightly bored, and he was already looking over the other man's fair head to a uniformed figure who came across and took Kat's case.

Kat's temper fizzed. The man was rude! To compensate, she bent in and kissed Mike's bearded cheek, her voice huskily emotional as she spoke.

'I'll be in touch.' The warmth faded from her voice as she tilted her head up to the tall, hovering figure. 'Given his form, I needed to know that the money for the refuge is ring-fenced should my *grandfather* decide to chuck *me* out too.'

Zach's eyes narrowed on the beautiful face turned up to him. She was spoiling for a fight but he had no intention of obliging. 'Not the time or place for this conversation, I think—Mr Ross.' The nod was curt as he took her elbow.

She had little choice but to respond to the hand under her elbow. It was either that or be dragged along the concrete. She skipped a little to keep up with his long-legged stride before taking advantage of a slight drop in his pace to snatch her arm away.

Panting, she lifted both hands in an 'enough is

enough' gesture as she shook her head. 'Will you slow down? I can't breathe!'

Zach swore under his breath as she started to back away. In seconds she was going to provide the paparazzo he had so far shielded her from with a full-face shot if the two members of his security team zeroing in on the guy, who he knew from experience had the tenacity of a terrier without the charm, didn't reach him in time.

It was a risk Zach was not prepared to take.

He acted on instinct; the question was, *what* instincts?

He moved with speed that bewildered Kat, certainly gave her no opportunity to react as he dragged her with casual ease into his body.

There were no shallows in the kiss. It was hard, deep and possessive. Above the paralyzing shock, on one level she registered the taste of his mouth, the skill of his lips, the hardness of the body so close to her own, but those factors were drowned out by the level that was all shuddering pleasure and heat.

It ended as abruptly as it had begun.

Rocking back on her heels like a sapling in a storm, Kat opened her mouth and no words came. There was a disconnect between her brain and her vocal chords.

'Let's take the "how dare you?" outrage as read,' he drawled, sounding bored and smoothing back his dark hair with a hand that might have held the slightest of tremors as his head turned towards the shouts of protest being issued by the paparazzo as he was escorted away.

Kat followed the line of Zach's gaze, comprehension dawning. The colour rushed to her pale cheeks.

It wasn't as if you thought he'd been overcome by lust for your body, Kat.

'A shot of me kissing a woman is not worth much.'

'The market being saturated.'

'Whereas the face of a mystery woman fighting me off would be, and that guy may be scum, but he's not stupid,' Zach conceded. 'He has a nose for a story and there were some shots of me leaving the hospital after visiting Alekis. If he had made the link…'

Kat barely heard anything he said after his initial comment. 'I wasn't *fighting* you!'

'Never allow the truth to get in the way of a good headline,' he told her with a cynical smile. 'It's all about perception, trust me, and don't worry, the boyfriend didn't see.'

'He's not my boyfriend, and even if he was that would be none of your business.'

He clicked his long brown fingers. 'In that case, no problem.'

Actually there was, and it was a problem of his own making. His strategy had been effective but it came with a price tag.

His gaze sank to her lush lips.

The price was the frustration of starting something he couldn't finish, and finishing was obviously a non-starter. It would be a massive betrayal of the trust Alekis had put in him.

His expression concealed by hooded eyelids, he watched as she angrily tapped one foot clad in a spiky little ankle boot. There was an element of compulsion in the slow sweep of his eyes as they travelled up the long smooth curve of her calves covered in dark tights.

Not being able to see the outline of her thighs through the kicky little woollen skirt she wore somehow made it more sexy. Imagination was a powerful aphrodisiac.

'Plenty of problems,' she rebutted grimly.

Zach found himself agreeing.

'I do not appreciate being mauled by you whatever the reason.'

'You have a novel way of showing your lack of appreciation.' The memory of how soft and yielding she had felt, how well her curves had fitted into his angles, created a fresh crackle of heat that settled in his groin.

If she had needed a warning that he was dangerous, the slow, predatory half-smile that left his eyes cold would have provided it.

The gesture was casual, his hand did not even make contact with the skin of her cheek, but it was close enough for her to feel the warmth. She swayed away from it but, warning or not, she had no facility to prevent the image that surfaced in her head. It was a very specific image, sensory in its strength, long brown fingers moving over pale... She escaped the images in her head before she fell over, her breath leaving her parted lips in a raspy gush.

Well, that couldn't be good, could it?

Shame rushed through her as she lifted her chin. There was no way she was going to add herself to the long list of women who had made fools of themselves over Zach Gavros. For starters, she had too much self-respect, and secondly, a much too strongly developed sense of self-preservation.

History would *not* be repeating itself. That was not an option, she told herself, as an image of the sad, overgrown grave flashed into her head. It was an image that represented a life wasted. She was not her mother; *her* hormones were not in charge. If that meant staying a tight, buttoned-up, but safe virgin, it was a price she was happy to pay.

Kat might not know a lot about heart-racing excitement, but she did know she didn't need it and this man was the living embodiment of heart-racing.

His hand dropped; useless to deny this situation was eating into his reserves of self-control. It was going to get very tiring if he had to remind himself every five minutes that she was Alekis's granddaughter, and as such totally off-limits—a matter not just of respect but practicality.

He needed a distraction, not to mention a release for all the sexual frustration that was clawing low and painfully in his belly, threatening the legendary cool he had long taken for granted. And he knew just the distraction. Andrea Latkis, a very talented and ambitious lawyer on Alekis's Athens-based legal team. Not coy, she had made her desire to sleep with him clear. It was an invitation that he had always intended to accept, but they both had busy lives and their calendars had never been in sync.

It would never have occurred to Andrea to make adjustments to her calendar. He liked that about her, because neither would he, but then maybe drastic situations, or at least uncomfortable ones, required him to make some concessions.

Having come to this conclusion, he was able to experience the rush of heat he endured when Kat removed a glossy strand of hair from her plump lips with something that approached acceptance.

His problem was not Alekis's granddaughter, it was the fact that he had not scheduled a sexual outlet into his life for too long—hence this reaction to having a beautiful woman forcibly thrown into his orbit.

He could relax, though not too much, he cautioned, remembering how he had felt as she'd smiled at the boyfriend. At least there was one interpretation of that moment he could delete—he did not do jealousy.

'Your grandfather is looking forward to meeting you.'

Like ice cream in a heatwave, the antagonism and defiance in her face melted, leaving wide-eyed deer-in-the-headlights fear. He ignored the tightening in his chest that was perilously close to sympathy and looked around.

'Where's the rest of your luggage?'

'I just brought the essentials.'

'For an overnight trip? No matter, we can take your wardrobe in hand when we arrive, and I can arrange to have your belongings shipped over.'

She adopted a calm, no-compromise attitude as she explained, 'No. I intend to keep my London flat on.'

'Alekis has several properties in London. Your things can be moved into whichever you prefer.'

Clearly he had trouble recognising no compromise. 'I prefer my own place, and what do you mean by *take my wardrobe in hand*?' She stopped. She was talking to empty space. Zach had turned and was striding off, his elegant long-legged figure drawing glances to which he seemed utterly oblivious.

She had to trot to catch up with him. 'In hand?' she echoed in a dangerous voice before tacking on breathlessly, 'Will you slow down? We're not all giraffes,' she told him, thinking that a panther was probably a better animal kingdom analogy. His legs might be long but they were in perfect proportion to the rest of his lean, square-shouldered, narrow-hipped frame.

His mouth quirked as he angled a glance down at her lightly flushed face. 'Sorry, I'm not used to—'

She paused as a thoughtful expression flickered across his saturnine features

'Used to what?'

'Considering anyone else.'

There was nothing even faintly apologetic about his admission. *'Never...?'* Was anyone really that selfish? Kat struggled with the concept.

'You sound shocked.'

'That there are selfish people in the world?' She shook her head. 'I'm not that naive. It's just mostly people try to hide it.'

It wasn't as if he had never been criticised—he'd actually been called a lot worse than selfish—but this was the first time he had ever experienced an inexplicable impulse to defend himself. It wasn't as though her approval meant anything to him—it was an impulse that he firmly crushed as he pushed out coldly, 'There are also virtue-signalling martyrs in the world who, in my experience, rarely try and hide it.'

He heard her sharp intake of breath as she came to an abrupt halt. He took a couple of strides before he stopped and swung back. She was standing there, hands fixed on her hips, her head thrown back as she stared up at him through narrowed amber eyes.

'Are you calling me a martyr?' Her eyelids fluttered as her eyes widened with astonished indignation.

He arched a sardonic brow and heard the sound of her even white teeth grating.

'If you can't take a little constructive criticism, Katina—'

She recognised he was baiting her but not before a strangled *'Constructive!'* had escaped her clenched lips; then she managed a smile of jaw-clenching insincerity. 'Then I suppose I should say thank you, and I promise you that any further *constructive* comments from you on my behaviour will be treated with the same degree of appreciation that I'm feeling now!'

His low, quite impossibly sexy rumble of appreciation—was it possible for a laugh to make you tingle?—had her tumbling from sarcastic superiority back to tingling sexual awareness.

She looked away quickly, embarrassed and confused by her reaction to a laugh, and took a moment before she trusted herself to look up again. When she did the mockery she had come to expect had faded from his lean face, replaced not by sympathy but something that came close to it.

Zach had not got to where he was without possessing an ability to read feelings, so recognising the fear underlying her tough stance was nothing more than he would have expected. What he didn't expect was the surge of irrational guilt attached to the surfacing need to offer her some sort of reassurance.

'I know this must feel frightening, being plunged into an alien environment, but you know, it does us all good to step outside our comfort zone once in a while.' He stopped, his expression closing as he realised how far outside his own comfort zone he was straying. There was a very good reason he didn't wander around emoting. In the financial world, empathy had a way of revealing your own weaknesses.

In his private world it had never been an issue. His relationships, if you chose to call them that, were about sex, not establishing an emotional connection.

The unexpected softening of his tone hit Kat in a weak spot she hadn't even known she had. If he had opened his arms she'd have walked into them wanting...*what*?

When did I turn into the sort of girl who needed a big strong man to turn to?

She let her breath out in a slow, slow hiss, tilted her chin and gave a cool smile. She hadn't turned into that girl and she never would.

'Please don't insult my intelligence by pretending you care,' she snapped back, ignoring the voice in her head that said she was using him as a scapegoat.

The weakness might be hers, but he had exposed it.

'Or do you even know how to spell empathy?'

'Well, if I need to borrow some, I'll know where to come.'

'Meaning?'

'You really are the original bleeding heart. How many men have figured out the way into your bed is by being weak and needy and...*damaged*?' he sneered.

She sucked in an outraged breath through flared nostrils and stalked past him, tossing over her shoulder, 'You are worse than disgusting!'

The sardonic arrogance stamped on his features

faded as she walked across the tarmac, her angry posture as graceful as a ballroom dancer's, chin up, her long neck extended, narrow shoulder blades drawn back. He might arguably have won the brief war of words, but the triumph felt hollow. Something possibly to do with the fact his body, reacting independently of his brain, was sending painful slug after slug of raw hunger in response to the movement of her slim body.

Theos, but this woman was killing him, or rather the lusting after her was.

He might consider her out of bounds but there were plenty that wouldn't. His task was getting less enviable with each passing moment.

CHAPTER FIVE

Any of the pleasure Kat might have felt at the sheer novelty value of the travelling style of the rich and famous was ruined for her by the thought of what lay ahead when they landed.

Every time she thought of the man who had left his only daughter to suffer a life a step from the gutter, icy anger rose up in her like a tide. She was not used to such feelings and they made her feel physically sick.

What did he want from her? Forgiveness? A second chance? Kat did not feel she had either in her.

The emotions surging and churning inside her must have shown on her face because at one point during the flight an attendant came and discreetly pointed out the bathroom facilities.

Happy to play along with the assumption she was a poor flyer, Kat vanished in the restroom for a few minutes of solitude she didn't really want—it left too much time for her dark thoughts.

Trailing her hand under the water and looking at herself in the illuminated mirror, she found it easy to understand the attendant's assumption she was about to throw up. She looked terrible, the emotional tussle in her head reflected on her face. She felt bad enough to wish for a foolish split second that Zach, who had fallen into conversation with one of the pilots as they'd boarded and vanished with him, was actually there to distract her—and that was pretty bad!

Nothing as dramatic as the kiss, of course. That had definitely been a step too far, she decided, a dreamy expression drifting into her eyes that she had no control over as she trailed her fingers across the outline of her lips, before snatching them away a moment later with a self-conscious grimace as she realised what she was doing.

When she retook her seat, despite her assuring the attendant she was feeling much better, the woman suggested she should alert Mr Gavros to the situation.

Kat hastily assured her that the only situation was her need to catch up on some sleep.

The attendant reluctantly complied, leaving Kat alone with her own thoughts and her rising sense of panic and trepidation for the rest of the flight. Zach didn't reappear until after they had landed; actually she didn't see him first, she *felt* his presence.

Even though she hadn't looked around she knew the *exact* moment he had appeared. It made her fumble as she released her seat belt and got to her feet, smoothing down her hair and straightening the row of pearly buttons on the square-necked sweater she wore tucked into the belt that emphasised her narrow waist, then stopped because her hands were shaking. The amount of adrenaline circulating in her bloodstream was having a dizzying effect. A situation not improved when she lifted her chin and was no longer able to delay the moment she looked at him.

He had lost the coat and jacket and was standing there, looking elegant and as relaxed as someone as driven as him could. Also, overpoweringly sexy. She blamed the enclosed space and the slight tingle left on her lips from that kiss.

'Where... How...?' She stopped, hating the breathy delivery, and ran a tongue across her dry lips and lifted her chin and husked out, 'Is he...my...*grandfather* here?'

The toughness she had adopted was paper thin; something about the way she stood there looking as vulnerable as hell and too proud to show it awoke something in a tiny, previously dead corner of Zach's heart. He tensed as some nameless emotion clutched at him, making his voice abrupt when he finally responded.

'He's waiting in a hotel next door to the terminal, but don't worry, it'll be private.' Alekis had taken over the penthouse floor to ensure privacy for the meeting, and presumably space for the specialist team on hand with defibrillators.

Zach just hoped this meeting was not going to be memorable for all the wrong reasons.

Her lips tightened. 'I hope he doesn't expect me to pretend, because I won't. I'll tell him what I think of him.'

Her words jolted loose a memory. He remembered saying as much to himself before he'd walked back into the seedy apartment that for seven years had been what some would laughingly call his home. His nostrils flared now as he remembered the sour stale stench that had hit him as he had opened the door.

He was a realist; he hadn't anticipated any sort of

an apology or even regret, just an acknowledgement of what they had done. It had become obvious very quickly that he wasn't going to get even that. He'd found his grandmother in her bed, hair matted, unwashed; her eyes had had a vacant look as she'd stared at him without recognition.

Of his uncle there had been no sign. Clearly when free bed and board was not worth the effort of living with a woman with what the doctors had diagnosed as advanced dementia, he had vanished. Later, Zach had discovered he had not got far. It seemed he'd picked a fight with the wrong solitary, weak-looking person, who, it had turned out, had not been alone. His uncle had died of his head injuries three days later—a sordid end to a sordid life.

He pushed away the memory and simultaneously dampened an uncharacteristic need to say something comforting, and almost definitely untrue, to soothe the conflict he could see in those golden eyes.

He couldn't see this meeting being comfortable.

'You mean you can pretend?' He had rarely encountered honesty of the variety she possessed in a world where it was rare for people to speak the truth. She stood out. His eyes slid down her body. She stood out for a lot of reasons.

'He is a stranger and he hurt my mother. He doesn't mean anything to me.'

'Then tell him that. The funding for your refuge is guaranteed.'

Kat found his response bewildering. Was he trying to play devil's advocate? 'You know I can't. He's ill, he might...'

The hand on her shoulder was light but strangely comforting. Finding Zach Gavros comforting in any sense of the word must mean she was in a worse state than she'd thought.

'If I say something and he dies…how am I supposed to live with that?' she choked out.

'Alekis is tough and he has an army of medics on hand. Anything that happens is *not* your responsibility,' he added, suddenly angry as hell with Alekis for putting his granddaughter in this position. 'By this evening you can be swimming in the sea.'

She gave a sudden smile that lightened her expression as she responded to the tip of his head and walked towards the exit. 'That would be something. I can't swim.'

'I'll teach you.' She was looking as startled by the offer as he felt.

'Don't be nice to me or I'll cry.'

'Relax, I'm never nice. Ask anyone. Living on an island, swimming is a necessary survival skill.' As was keeping women like this one an emotional mile away, women who couldn't believe that sex could be just that, women who wanted something deeper and more meaningful, women who needed an emotional depth he simply didn't have.

It was an exaggeration to say the hotel was next door to the airport, but it was conveniently close.

'It's very nice,' she said, keeping up the same flow of polite conversation she had during the car transfer. It helped maintain the illusion of normality but was, she realised, starting to sound desperate.

Actually, the hotel, part of a luxury chain she had vaguely heard of, was *extremely* nice in a plush, up-market way.

'Thank you.'

She threw a questioning look up at Zach's austerely handsome profile. 'The chain is a relatively recent purchase. It was a bit tired, but it's amazing what a refurb can do.'

'You own it?' Well, that explained the manager who was rushing out to greet them before personally escorting them to the private entrance to the penthouse floor, where the elevator door was flanked by men wearing suits and dark glasses who spoke into the headsets they were wearing.

Kat hesitated before she stepped inside the lift, taking a moment to pull her shoulders back and lift her chin.

Stepping in after her, Zach felt a twinge of admiration. It was impossible not to. She looked as though she were walking into a lion's den, but, my God, she was doing it with style!

The swishing upward ride took seconds and then the doors were silently opening.

'He is as nervous as you.'

Kat lifted her eyes. 'I seriously doubt that. I feel like I used to when I hid.' She had always had a hiding place ready when the loud voices had started, a place to crawl into and try to be invisible.

No hiding place now, Kat! Just do it!

He sensed she had not even realised what she had said, words that might not have made sense to many but, as someone who had tried very hard to be invisible, he knew that she was talking of an experience similar to, but he *really* hoped not the same as, his own.

He found himself hoping grimly that the mother who had abandoned her had retained enough motherly feeling to protect her child from violence, the sort that had scarred his own youth.

The golden eyes lifted to his. 'I'm afraid I won't be able to stop myself, that I'll say something really bad—I'm so angry,' she whispered, pressing a hand to her breastbone as if to physically hold in the storm of emotions raging there.

'Don't be afraid. You've a right to be angry.' Maybe she would have the apologies and explanations he'd been robbed of.

'I thought you were team Alekis.' *He has a beautiful mouth*... The thought drifted through the tangled knot of thoughts in her head as she stared at the sensually carved lines... Had he *really* kissed her? The memory, like everything else, had an unreal quality.

'You won't say anything to hurt him. You're too... *kind*.' He allowed himself the comment because he spoke as an objective observer. He was not here to get involved in the relationship between grandfather and granddaughter. He carried the inescapable taint of his own family with him through life without getting involved in someone else's family conflict.

The way he said *kind*, he made it sound like a defect—not that Kat felt kind as her attention narrowed in on the figure seated in a large chair that made her think of a throne, placed centre stage in the room.

She'd seen photos online, but this man was older, much older, yet even with a craggy face, drawn, with fatigue deepening the shadowy bags beneath his eyes, you could sense the power coming off the man. Then, a second later, she saw the eyes beneath the thick white eyebrows were filled with tears.

The wave of emotion that hit her was so unexpected and so powerful that all the other emotions seething inside her were swallowed up. This was her grandfather—her family.

'Katina?'

She pressed a hand to her trembling lips as the figure in the chair held out his arms. 'I am so s-sorry, Katina.'

Zach watched her fight to hold on to her antagonism and fail.

Even the relatively short time he had spent in her company meant that it didn't cross Zach's mind that her capitulation had anything at all to do with personal gain. This was about her generous spirit, and her longing for a family, or at least her idea of what a family was.

She was homesick for an idea.

The world called Zach reckless, a risk taker with a golden touch, but it was a lie. He never risked anything he was not willing to lose. Money was not important to him in itself. Lose a fortune, make a fortune—these were not things that would ever keep him awake. They were challenges, a test of mental agility.

True recklessness was what she possessed. It was the open-hearted way she ran towards the possibility of family and love, risking having her illusions shattered.

Zach admired it, and it appalled him.

Was he team Alekis? No, but neither was he the objective observer he wanted to be. Somehow this woman had awoken a protective instinct in him. He didn't want

to feel this way as he watched her cover the space between her and the old man, before dropping with graceful spontaneity to her knees beside the chair.

He turned abruptly and left, reminding himself that
he was not part of this drama as he stepped into the elevator, pushing away feelings he didn't want to name,
let alone feel.

Part of Kat didn't want to let go of her anger: it felt like
a betrayal to her mother, but it had gone, burned away
in that explosion of feeling. She'd practised her cold
words but how could she be mean when he looked so
frail and sounded so tearfully penitent? Though she
got a glimpse of the iron man who people feared when
he imperiously waved away someone who appeared to
check his blood pressure.

A moment later the first man came back with rein-
forcements. Several nurses in uniform and the dapper
figure in the three-piece suit did not react to the scowl
directed at him.

'I really must insist. These readings...'

For the first time, Kat realised that there were leads
trailing under her grandfather's suit, which were presumably giving readings in the connecting room.

'All right—all right!'

Kat wondered if his capitulation had anything to do
with the beads of sweat along his upper lip when he
caught her hand.

'As I was saying, it is a small gathering. Nothing too
formal, drinks and mingling...'

Saying? she thought, playing catch up. She couldn't
recall him saying anything about a *gathering*, but then

the short, emotionally charged conversation was a bit of a blur.

'A small press presence…'

Her heart started to pound and she felt sick.

'Don't worry, they are friendly, all invited. One of the advantages of owning an island is that it is easier to keep out undesirable guests.' The claw-like hand tightened on her own, crushing her fingers. 'You're an Azaria, you'll be fine.'

The medics closed in, wielding scary-looking syringes, and she backed away, unable to tell him that she *wasn't* an Azaria and she didn't fit into this life.

As she walked into the lift, the feeling of sick unease in the pit of her stomach grew. What had she just agreed to? Had she agreed to anything? She didn't want to go to a *gathering*, whatever that meant, formal or otherwise.

As the lift doors opened, Zach peeled himself away from the wall he had been leaning against and stood there, hands in his pockets, looking at her.

'You look like you need a drink.' And maybe a hug? He banished the aberrant thought. He was not a *huggy* person, and with Kat hugs would not stay comforting for long. His long fingers flexed as he saw the image in his head of them sliding under that top and over her warm skin.

'I'd prefer a few explanations. Gathering? Press?'

'Ah.'

'So you know what this is about?' She wasn't sure if she was relieved or resentful.

'Basically we are talking cocktail party. Alekis invites a few tame journalists a few times a year, lets them mingle with what is actually quite an eclectic bunch—'

Her voice, shrill with panic, cut across him. 'I can't mingle.'

He didn't look impressed. 'Rubbish. Here's the car now.'

She shook her head. 'No. I'm not going anywhere until you tell me what is going on.'

'We need to control the flow of information. Denying rumours will only—'

Her eyes flew wide in alarm. 'What rumours?'

His eyes lifted. 'A story will appear tomorrow confirming that your grandfather had a heart attack. This is a story that would normally dominate headlines for weeks, excite a predictably hysterical reaction and hit market confidence.'

'You couldn't stop this story?' Kat felt a bit guilty that she was relieved this was about market confidence and not about her.

There was a ruthless quality to the thin-lipped smile he gave in response that made her shiver. 'I planted the story.'

The addition of *obviously* was silent, but quite definitely there. Confused by that as much as his admission, she shook her head. 'But you just said—' she began, feeling her way.

'I said *normally*. On this occasion Alekis's illness will be buried by the much more exciting information that he has been united with his long-lost granddaughter.'

'So, you're using me.'

She sounded shocked by the discovery. His dark brows flattened into a line of exasperation above his obsidian stare.

'This was not my idea.' He wasn't trying to deflect

her anger, but he decided it might be a good thing that she recognised that even at death's door her grandfather was not a warm and cuddly person.

It was bizarre he had to spell it out, but despite her upbringing, inexplicably it seemed to come as a shock to her that anyone had motives that were not pure and elevated.

He wasn't going to be the only one to notice her lack of guile and sophistication, but he might be the only one who wasn't trying to use it to his own advantage. You did not have to be psychic to predict that if she didn't toughen up, and quick, she was going to be a soft touch for every hard-luck sob story going. He hoped for her sake she was a quick learner, or else she was in for some painful lessons in human nature.

She glanced towards the building behind them. 'He?'

'Alekis delegated, but yes, the plan is his. It's nothing sinister. We're controlling the flow of information. Or would you prefer some tabloid breaks the story, sensationalising it? Perhaps digging up an old lover to publish a kiss-and-tell?' He saw no benefit from telling her that this might happen anyway. There were going to be disgruntled ex-lovers coming out of the woodwork once the news of the heiress hit. 'This way your exposure is controlled. Hiding you away would have photographers in helicopters flying over Tackyntha with telephoto lenses.'

Her startled eyes looked up at him as she slid into the car. 'People will want to take my photograph?' she said as he joined her.

'Are you trying to be facile?'

She shook her head.

He sighed and pushed his head into the leather headrest. 'Belt up, Katina.'

She did and sat there looking shell-shocked.

Zach waited until the car moved away and into the traffic before he spoke. 'You are going to be one of the wealthiest women in Europe, Katina. People will all want to know what you had for breakfast, what your favourite colour nail varnish is. They will discuss what you're wearing and speculate on your sexuality, whether you have an eating disorder or a drug problem.'

He watched as the horror of the reality hit home, feeling like a bastard, but better a bastard on her side than one who could exploit the vulnerability on display in her wide eyes and trembling lips.

She half rose in her seat before subsiding, no parachute, no escape—*no escape*. 'Oh, God!' she groaned, closing her eyes. 'I can't do this.'

'Yes, you can.'

His firm, unsympathetic rebuttal made her eyes fly wide as she directed a glare of simmering dislike at him. She had seen lumps of granite with more empathy than he possessed.

'The way you handle yourself these first few weeks is important, will set a pattern. Alekis's wealth means people don't have automatic access to you. I can put up some barriers to protect you.'

She pushed away the images of walls around a gold-lined cage that flashed through her head, telling herself not to be such a drama queen. There was plenty to be nervous about without inventing things.

'You hide away and people will assume you have

something to hide. We need to create the illusion you are open,' he explained, digging deep into his reserves of patience as he explained what was obvious. 'While telling them essentially nothing.'

Her dark feathered brows lifted. *'We?'*

'All right, you. One of the first things you need to remember is trust no one, *no one*,' he emphasised grimly. 'Not *everyone* you meet will be out for a piece of you,' he conceded.

'Just ninety per cent of them. What a relief!' She quivered. He was really selling this lifestyle. 'I'm not stupid, you know. I might even be able to work out which knife and fork to use. I am a fast learner.'

'That remains to be seen. I won't pretend it isn't going to be a steep learning curve.'

'Oh, I really wish you would pretend that it is.'

He responded to her attempt at humour with a hard look. 'But you will learn to judge. Learn your own style. Until you do, that's what I'm here for.'

She fixed him with a narrow-eyed glare. 'So you mean you'll put the words in my mouth and tell me what to wear.' She folded her arms across her chest and directed a belligerent stare up at his face. 'I'm not a puppet.'

'No. From where I'm sitting you are…' He completed the sentence in a flood of angry-sounding Greek before finally dragging a hand through his dark hair as he sat there, lips compressed, dark eyes burning.

'I don't understand Greek.'

'I said,' he gritted out, 'I am trying to protect you, but if you would prefer I throw you to the wolves…?'

As their eyes connected, glittering black on gold, a

strange little shiver traced a slow, sinuous path up her tension-stiffened spine.

'What is this? Set a thief to catch a thief, or in this case a wolf to catch a wolf?' It was true, there was definitely something of the lean, feral predator about him, which she could see might appeal to some women.

'For your information, I have not spent my life in a protective bubble and I've been coping without a guardian angel—which, for the record, is *definitely* major miscasting—all my life. I resent being treated like a child.'

Were you ever a child? he wondered as his glance moved in an unscheduled slow sweep over her slim, tense figure, oozing hostility, before coming to rest on the outline of her lips. The dull throb in his temples got louder as he saw faceless wolves drawn to the delicious invitation of their plump pinkness.

The barrier of his clenched teeth did nothing to shield him from a fresh onslaught of painful desire. Alekis had put him in a 'rock and hard place' position. He couldn't lay a finger on her without betraying the trust the older man had, for some reason, placed in him and he couldn't walk away, either.

'So, we are going to the island.'

'It doesn't take long by helicopter.'

Kat felt reluctant to admit she'd never flown in one. 'And do your family live there too? Is that how you know Alekis?'

A look she couldn't quite put a name to flickered in his eyes. It was gone so quickly that she might have imagined it.

'No, my family do not live there.'

'But you have family…?' she asked, remembering how he had spoken about his mother's death. 'They were there for you after your mother died?'

'You think because our mothers are dead that gives us something in common? It does not.'

She flushed. If he'd tried to embarrass her, he'd succeeded. Did he think she didn't know they came from two different worlds? That she needed him to point out they had nothing in common, that he had been raised in a world of wealth and privilege that she knew she would never fit into.

Being orphaned was always an awful thing for any child, but in Zach's world there were cushions…nannies, good schools. None could replace maternal love, but it helped if you had the support structure of a family, especially one that meant you didn't stand out because your clothes were not the latest fashion, or you had no holiday to talk about at the start of a new school term.

'You really do worry about family, don't you? Well, relax—yes, I *did* have family.' His lips curled in a cynical smile of remembrance. 'An uncle who is now happily dead and a grandmother who is a great deal pleasanter now that she doesn't remember my name, or, for that matter, her own.'

Shock reverberated through his body, none of it showing on his still shuttered face as he realised he had just revealed more to her than he had to another living person. Not even Alekis knew the details about his life before they had met, and here he was spilling his guts to this woman, with her ridiculous sentimentality, virtually inviting her to walk around in his head!

Was this a new symptom of sexual deprivation?

She looked at his bleakly beautiful face and felt her heart squeeze with sympathy. His comment had been sparing in detail, but you didn't need to have worked with children caught in the firing line of family conflict to recognise that Zach's childhood had not been what she'd imagined.

'I'm so sorry,' she said, wondering uneasily how many of her other assumptions about him were wrong.

'There is no need to be sorry,' he sliced back coldly. 'It is the past.'

Did he really believe it was that easy? she wondered, remembering all the times when she was growing up that she had wished that her past were a painless blank. That she didn't have the snatches of memories that made her sad, while filling her with a nameless longing.

Glancing at his shuttered face, she recognised that she had pushed him as far as she could on the subject. She changed tack. 'So, what is your connection to Alekis?'

'I wonder about that sometimes myself.'

Before she could voice her frustration at this deliberately unhelpful response, he added, 'Your grandfather helped me when no one else would.'

'So, a financial loan...?' she probed.

His eyes were hidden by his half-lowered lids but the smile that quivered on his sensually sculpted mouth intrigued her. 'Not as such, but I remain in your grandfather's debt. I doubt very much if I would be where I am today without his intervention.'

'Where would you be?'

'I sometimes ask myself that, but not often. I prefer

to deal with the here and now, and in the here and now I consider myself in Alekis's debt.'

'Do you like him?'

His dark brows drew together in a straight line above his aquiline nose. 'He has many qualities I admire and many faults I accept.' His dark eyes had a mesmeric quality as he captured her gaze and there was an intensity in his words as he spoke. 'The door to the world you are about to enter is rarely opened to outsiders. I was an outsider, so maybe Alekis thought I was well placed to help your transition.'

'So you're not an outsider now?'

'I have never been a joiner.'

Did he *ever* give a straight answer? she wondered. 'But you want me to join.'

He shook his head. 'That will be your choice. I want you to be aware of the pitfalls. To learn how to—'

'Blend in?'

He gave a sudden laugh, deep and uninhibited. It melted his expression into a smile that made him look years younger and made the bottom of her stomach dissolve. She realised that if this man ever made the effort to charm there wasn't a woman alive who could resist.

Including me!

Now there was a fact to keep her awake at nights.

'What is so funny?'

'The idea of you blending in anywhere.' The laughter died from his face, leaving something much darker, much more intense, more dangerous, she realised, than mere charm. 'You're an exceptionally beautiful woman.'

His deep voice was like rumpled velvet, warm, sensuous and will-sapping. She had no idea how long she

sat there staring at him before the blare of a car horn
jolted her back to reality.

The reality being that Zach possessed a voice that
really ought to carry a danger warning! Ah, well, the
next time, should there be a next time, she would be
prepared and not look like such an idiot.

She broke the seductive hold of his dark, mesmeris-
ing stare, though the effort filmed her skin with sweat
as she snapped out contemptuously, 'Don't be stupid!'

Obviously she knew she wasn't *bad* to look at, but
exceptionally beautiful was not a term used for a woman
who had a mouth that was way too big for her face, a
gap between her front teeth and the sort of body that
looked great in clothes but without them… She hated
her bony collarbones and she didn't see how anyone
could consider the visible angles on her hips feminine.

Her reaction to him stating the obvious seemed
strange. You could be excused for assuming, given her
reaction, that no one had ever told her how beautiful
she was before. Even if she had had lovers who left a
lot to be desired, he thought scornfully, the woman
had a mirror.

'Even if you could blend in you shouldn't. You should
carry on being yourself, as much as is possible.'

She looked bemused by the advice. 'Who else would
I be? I think you worry too much. I'm used to being the
odd one out. The kid in care with the wrong clothes.'

If the comment had been made in an attempt to gar-
ner sympathy, Zach would not have felt any. He did not
want to now, and yet as he looked at her he experienced
less sympathy but a sudden deep anger for the childhood she had been robbed of. And yet she seemed to

have her own set of values that nobody had been able to take from her.

Could he say the same? *Maybe she had come to terms with her past more than he had his?*

He pushed the thought away; the past was something he did have to come to terms with. It was gone and buried. Not only could he not imagine himself discussing it so openly as she did, but he could not imagine wanting to.

CHAPTER SIX

'YOU CAN OPEN your eyes now. We're in the air.'

She did so, taking a breath and realising that at some point during the take off she had grabbed his hand and dug her nails in hard.

With a self-conscious 'Sorry... ' she released it, her brows twitching into a front of dismay as she saw the half-moon crescents standing out white in his olive skin. Pretending to tuck a stray strand of hair behind her ears, she rubbed the skin of her cheek, which was tingling from the warm brush of his breath. It was scary that her body was so sensitive to him.

'I've never been in a helicopter before.'

She just hoped the transfer would be as short as he had promised. Kat leaned forward in her seat to loosen the hair that had got caught down the neck of her sweater. As she leaned back, her glance connected with Zach's.

The lurch in her stomach had nothing to do with their mode of transport as the moment that vibrated with unseen electricity stretched. He was sitting close enough for her to see the network of fine lines that fanned out from the corners of his eyes and the dusting of dark stubble shading his jaw, the shadow adding extra emphasis to the hollows of his cheeks.

She breathed a little deeper, unconsciously leaning forward as her nostrils flared, picking up on the clean male scent that rose from his warm skin. Sensations she had no name for shifted inside her and she paused, like someone standing on the edge of quicksand, fighting the urge to jump in with both feet.

Just before she reached tipping point, she jerked back again abruptly. The sudden adrenaline rush continued to make her head spin. She flexed her fingers before closing both hands tight, trying not to think of that unacknowledged moment when she had been within a heartbeat of reaching out and touching his cheek. It had been an instinctive thing. Kat would have been happier not knowing she possessed such instincts.

And *much* happier not having the image in her head of them lying naked together. Shame mingled with real fear as she dragged her eyes away from the firm sensual line of his mouth. Maybe there was a faulty gene responsible for being attracted to bad men…and she had inherited it? It had always been her secret fear.

Zach's eyes were hooded as he watched her, reminding himself that the task assigned him by Alekis was keeping men out of her bed, not occupying it himself. It did not assuage the ache in his groin as he watched her pupils tellingly dilate until only a thin ring of amber remained.

The muscles in Zach's brown throat rippled as he swallowed, his heavy lids lowered over his eyes as he turned his head to direct his hooded stare out of the window. He had not experienced this sort of elemental response to a woman in a long time and knowing she felt the same attraction, when they were sitting this close and she was looking at him with those hungry eyes, was not making his life any easier.

He closed his eyes to shut out the temptation, but the ache in his body did not diminish as he breathed his way through the hot elemental surge of raw desire that he had to endure because he sure as hell had no control over it.

Kat sat there, heart pounding, throat dry, wondering if he was going to acknowledge the crackle of sexual tension that shimmered in the air between them or even do something about it. Trying to decide if she wanted him to or not.

She was actually on the point of saying something, exactly what she didn't know, when he closed his eyes, and within seconds gave the impression of man deeply asleep.

She had worked herself up into a state of breathless anticipation and he was asleep!

Her cheeks stung pink with mortified heat when she realised how close she had come to utterly humiliating herself. It had felt so real, so tangible. Had it *really* been in her imagination? she wondered, studying the strong lines on his face. Sleep had ironed out some of the austerity and hardness from his face and made him seem younger somehow.

It really was odd to find yourself attracted to someone you did not even like; in fact, actively disliked, she mused, suddenly sleepy herself as the tensions of the last few hours began to catch up with her. Perhaps the *odd* thing was that she had never felt this way before.

Or maybe *she* was just the oddity, a virgin because she'd never allowed anyone to get close enough to change the situation. There had been moments of uncomfortable self-awareness when she'd recognised that this was in part at least due to her deep-seated fear of abandonment, but it was an insight she pushed away.

The same way she'd been pushing away the glaringly obvious fact that she was attracted to Zach Gavros. Of course, denial had been a lot easier when she had been able to think of him as an arrogant two-dimensional figure, but getting a glimpse of his vulnerabilities was making that a lot harder.

Would these newly aroused feelings go back into hibernation once Zach vanished from her life?

Did she want them to?

Kat hadn't worked out the answer by the time her eyelids flickered closed and did not lift.

She knew it was a dream—she'd had it before many times, but not for a long time now. The heart-thudding, stomach-clenching sense of icy dread. Except it wasn't *her*—it was someone else she was watching, crouched small in her hiding place, waiting for the monster's hand to reach in and drag her out. Kat wanted to shout a warning to the little girl, but her voice wouldn't work. Her entire body felt paralysed. She was watching, waiting, helpless to stop what was about to happen.

I'm asleep...asleep...it's not real. She kept repeating the words in her head, fighting her way through the grey layers of sleep to the surface. The process was all consuming, exhausting, then she heard a sound and focused on it, dragging herself clear of the shadows.

As she opened her eyes an indistinct face seemed to be floating there. She watched the outline grow more defined and more solid. Zach was leaning forward in his seat, talking to her.

'We have arrived.'

She blinked, had a moment utter blank, before the memories all came rushing back. She pulled herself upright in her seat with a jerk. 'Oh, God! I must have fallen asleep.' She dragged her hands over her slippery, silky hair, anchoring stray tips behind her ears as she smoothed it.

'You were dreaming.'

'Was I?' she said, thinking, *You were watching me...* and feeling quite extraordinarily exposed.

'You don't remember?'

He was looking at her with what felt like uncomfortable intensity. 'Who remembers dreams?' she said, turning her head to look out of the window, determined that whatever she saw, if her grandfather ate off gold plates and showered in champagne, she was not going to display unworldly awe. She'd show Zach she could pretend as well as anyone.

Her decision incinerated at her first glimpse of her new island home. Temporary home, reminded the voice of caution in her head.

It helped that their arrival coincided with the start of a breathtaking sunset, which, as they came in to land, had just tinged the water with feathers of red.

The landing strip seemed close to the candy-coloured village with terracotta roofs they had flown over, appearing to be cut into the rock of a peninsula that projected into the sea. She doubted her grandfather's villa could be set anywhere more spectacular.

She glanced towards the backdrop of green mountains, looking for signs of a road that might lead to the villa.

'Is it far?' she asked, releasing her white-knuckled grip on the armrest and willing her stomach to stop churning as the helicopter set down and she released the breath held in her chest in a long sibilant sigh of relief.

He angled a questioning look at her face. 'Far?'

'To the house, villa, whatever—is it far from the village?'

An amused smile deepened the lines fanning out from his deep-set eyes. 'There is no village.'

'Town, then,' she said, irritated by his pedantic response.

'Not one of those, either.'

'But...' Her brows twitched into a frown. 'I saw...' Comprehension dawned and her eyes flew wide. 'You're telling me that was a *house*?'

The incredulous uplift of her voice on the word made his lips twitch.

'But where are the people?'

'There is a live-in staff, obviously.'

Still in shock, she watched as he turned to someone who had entered the helicopter; presumably the younger man had been waiting for their arrival. He tipped his head towards Kat and spoke at length in Greek with Zach, who responded in the same language, saying something that had the other man smiling and heading for the exit.

Zach turned his eyes, stilling on her averted face. She

was struggling to loosen the clip on her safety restraint. A hank of hair had fallen across her face and he experienced the strangest impulse to push it back. Would the skin of her cheek be as smooth and soft as it appeared?

His hands clenched into fists as though they held the silky tendrils, before he brought the line of speculation to an abrupt halt. The fact that the questions had been there to begin with was a massive wake-up call. Just a warning; he was in control and in no danger of losing it now.

If the thought lacked conviction, he refused to acknowledge it. Admitting it would have meant acknowledging a chink in his armour.

Freeing herself after a tussle, Kat lifted her head and found he was looking at her with an intensity that made her stomach flip. For a moment the charge in the air, imaginary or real, was back, and it took her breath away before, heart thudding, she managed to lower her lashes in a self-protective shield. Had she imagined that moment? Had it been a creation of her over-heated imagination? *Wishful thinking?*

The sly whisper vanished like smoke but not before her spine had stiffened in utter rejection, that she would want to unleash anything in him let alone... A tiny little shudder showered through her body as she moistened her dry lips. It was ludicrous, more than ludicrous, she told herself firmly, laughable!

Only she wasn't laughing.

'Your grandfather bought the island in the sixties, I believe. At the time there was a church, a couple of houses, but the only occupants were the goats. A goatherd came over from the mainland once every couple of weeks to tend them. So no evictions. The goats are still here too, but don't try hugging them. They are feral creatures, not tame, so approach with caution.'

Kat stared at his face. In profile, there was a strength to the angles and planes that touched her now that she'd told herself it was a purely aesthetic level of appreciation.

Yes, he was beautiful to look at, but he was also *not tame.*

Luckily, she had never been drawn to the untamed, or unpredictable.

There you go with the denial again, Kat, taunted the voice in her head. *Afraid you've got more of your mother in you than you admit to?*

'All right.' She set her shoulders. 'So what now?'

'Now I escort you to the villa and introduce you to your new home.'

Standing up, her head ducked, she followed him towards the open doors.

CHAPTER SEVEN

THE TWO CARS, the first carrying the minimal baggage and the second themselves, drew up onto the illuminated forecourt. Night had fallen with a speed she found confusing, a clear starlit night scented with the smell of the sea and wild thyme.

Zach, who had gone around to open her door, left her to the assistance of the driver and moved forward to meet the woman who appeared in the massive set of double doors that were flung open to welcome them.

Dressed in a tailored black dress that suited her curvy figure, the woman was average height. It was hard to tell from this distance if the silver streaks in her dark hair were natural or a fashion statement. The chignon it was arranged in appeared as smooth and immaculate as the rest of her.

Kat felt travel-worn and untidy by comparison. She tucked the stray strands of hair behind her ears and told herself if she started worrying about what impression she made on everyone here she'd be a nervous wreck within the week.

Zach's voice drifted across the space to Kat; it sounded warm.

'Selene.'

As she watched from where she stood beside the car it seemed to Kat there was a genuine affection in his greeting as he put his hands on the shoulders of the woman, who Kat judged to be in her forties, and kissed her cheeks.

The rapid interchange was in Greek, and, as the woman glanced over in her direction several times, it didn't seem paranoid to assume they were discussing her.

Get used to it, Kat, she told herself as they began to walk back towards her.

'Katina, this is Selene Carras, your grandfather's housekeeper. This, Selene, is—'

'You have a look of Mia, my dear.'

Kat's cautiously polite expression melted in wondering disbelief. Eyes sparking eagerness, she sounded incredulous. 'You *knew* my mother?'

'Indeed I did.' The smartly dressed woman's kind brown eyes crinkled deeply at the corners as she smiled, her teeth as white as the double row of pearls around her neck. 'My own mother was the housekeeper on the island before me. When we were girls your mother and I would play together during her school holidays before we got older and…she was missed greatly by many.'

Emotion filled Kat's throat. There had never been anyone in her life she could speak to about her mother, never anyone she could ask all the questions she wanted, *needed* to ask.

'She used to tell me stories when I was little about an island where the sun always shone and the sand on the beaches was white. I thought they were stories. I never thought…' When her throat clogged with unshed tears of emotion, she turned her head, blinking hard, embarrassed less by the overspill of emotion than by the fact Zach was witnessing it.

Though, ironically, it was Zach who unwittingly came to her rescue.

'Did I hear dinner mentioned?'

'Of course, Mr Zach, but first things first. I will show Miss—'

'Kat, please,' Kat begged, not caring if this was etiquette or not.

The woman tipped her head. 'I will show Kat to her rooms, give her time to freshen up and then I'll have dinner served in half an hour?' She glanced from Kat to Zach, taking their silence as agreement, and continued cheerfully. 'Mr Zach will bring you down to dinner.' She glanced at him before explaining. 'The house is not exactly compact and it takes a little time to get your bearings.'

Not compact!

If the hallway they entered was any indication, the place was massive!

Underfoot the marble glowed while, high above, the massive antique chandeliers glistened. The central sweeping staircase ran up to the gallery above and then upwards to another floor.

It was Zach's voice, deep and inflected with dry irony, that interrupted her shocked silence.

'Alekis is not really a fan of less is more, and he really thinks that size matters. There isn't a room in the place that you couldn't have a game of cricket in. Well, not really my game, but…'

'It didn't stop you trying.' The older woman touched Kat's arm. 'The rooms *are* a little large.'

Kat only dimly registered the interchange.

'Ah.' Zach breathed and paused when he saw what had stopped her in her tracks.

'She is beautiful,' Kat said, staring.

'Your grandmother, I believe.'

Kat, her eyes wide, glanced at him and then back at the portrait in the heavy gold frame. It was positioned on the far wall lit by several spotlights. She took a step closer to study the woman, one she had never met or even knew existed.

This woman was her grandmother.

The roots she had been longing for all her life, Kat realised, were here. But did she belong? This was all so alien.

'My grandmother?'

The woman in the painting was wearing a classic shift dress that would have looked fashionable today, the knee-high boots elongated her legs and her dark hair was dressed in a slightly bouffant updo. With her dark eyes outlined by kohl, her rosebud lips pale and her lashes spiky and long, it was an iconic sixties look.

'She looks like Mum…' The face that she thought she remembered floated into her head. 'I *think*?'

Zach could not see her face, just hear the almost quiver in her voice, but it was the set of her narrow shoulders and the emotions he could feel literally radiating from her that made something twist hard in his chest. Something he refused to recognise as tenderness. An equally unfamiliar impulse to offer comfort made him move forward.

He had been so focused on the solitary figure staring up at the painting that he didn't realise he wasn't
the only one affected by the poignant image she made,
until the housekeeper wrapped her plump arm around
the younger woman's slender shoulders. The touch was
brief but enough to draw a smile of warm gratitude from
Kat as the older woman moved away.

Spontaneous expressions of support and comfort
were not really in Zach's comfort zone. Far better, he
decided, watching the moment, to leave it to those with
more experience with touchy-feely stuff. Despite his in-
eligibility he found the feeling that he'd been cheated
out of the feel of her warm skin lingering, digging deep
enough to make him ache. Everything between them
seemed to come back to one thing: this desire that never
quite went away and flared in an unpredictable way.
Problematic but not anything he couldn't deal with—he
had never allowed his appetites to rule him.

The housekeeper studied the portrait. 'She did, more
so as she grew up.'

Kat sent her another look of teary gratitude. 'I don't
have any photos, just what I remember, and I'm not sure
how much of that is real,' she admitted.

Listening, Zach found himself wanting to tell her she
was lucky; he wished his own memories of his childhood were open to misinterpretation, but his were all
unpleasantly real.

'This way.'

'I'll show her the way,' he heard himself say.

'Really?' Selene shook her head and recovered her
poise. 'Of course.'

'This is a lot for you to take in.'

Kat nodded. 'Pretty overwhelming. Until now I hadn't thought of my mother being here, not really.' She stopped as her throat closed over, not conscious that Zach had slowed to keep pace with her. 'Do you remember your mother?'

Midway up the sweeping staircase, he stopped. Puzzled by his rigid posture, so did Kat.

'Yes,' he said finally, and began to walk again.

'I wish I remembered more.'

He stopped again, this time at the top of the staircase, and looked down at her, his expression sombre.

'Be careful what you wish for.'

He *remembered*; he remembered a once beautiful woman worn down by single parenthood and the two or three jobs she'd needed to pay the rent on their apartment and keep him in clothes. She had always been tired, and Zach remembered promising her that one day she would not have to work. He would have a job that meant she could rest; rest had seemed like the ultimate luxury.

He never got the chance; he was ten when she died. For years he'd assumed it had been the exhaustion that had taken her life, a life that had been a constant, unrelenting grind. Only later he'd learnt by accident when he'd found her death certificate that she had succumbed to pneumonia. In her weakened condition she hadn't been able to fight the infection that had ravaged her body or afford the medicine that might have saved her.

Unable to explain even to herself this *need* in her to know more about him, more about the man who wore power so comfortably, she tentatively pushed. 'After your mother died you went to live with your grand-mother, and—?'

'Dimitri, my uncle.'

The bleakness in his voice was reflected in his face as he continued to speak. She had the impression that he had almost forgotten she was there as he continued.

'If she could love anyone, she loved him, in her way, though of course that love came a poor second to the bottom of a vodka bottle.'

'She didn't love you?' The question slipped out. She knew it was one she had no right to ask but anger pushed it through her caution.

'Me?' He laughed, the sound hard. 'She resented me almost as much as she had resented her own daughter. She forgot I was there for the most part and left me to Dimitri. Dimitri was a weak man who blamed the world for anything that went wrong in his life, and, like many weak men who could not take responsibility for their own actions, he was a bully. He used me as a punching bag.'

Kat felt the tears press against the back of her eyelids. He remembered every blow, every curse. She knew it without him telling her.

'I hate bullies!'

Her fierce declaration brought his eyes back to her face as she stood there, her hands clenched into fists, the empathy shining clear in her glorious eyes. He froze. What the *hell* had he just done?

What had begun as a lesson in caution had become some sort of soul-baring session. Feelings that he had put into cold storage had been resurrected. His jaw clenched. He had every intention of putting them safely back behind the mental ten-foot-high steel-reinforced walls that had taken him years of painstaking effort to construct.

'I remembered...' The housekeeper's voice drifted up the deep stairwell and they both turned as she mounted the first few steps.

Kat tore her eyes off Zach's curiously expressionless face.

The older woman, standing at the bottom step, was breathing hard as though she'd just run back.

'You mentioned photos—I have some. They are mostly from a few summers. I will look them out for you,' she promised. 'There used to be lots about the place.'

'Thank you,' Kat called down, genuinely touched by the gesture.

'This way,' Zach said, indicating the corridor to the left. He sounded distant and cold. She was assuming he was regretting opening up to her. It was pretty obvious he was not a man who was into sharing his feelings.

'So what happened to the photos of my mother?'

'Before my time,' he said abruptly, before adding, 'I'm not sure, but your grandfather will know.'

Unless he'd destroyed them, Kat thought, imagining the angry man trying to wipe his daughter from his life. The thought left her feeling deflated as she walked beside a silent Zach down what seemed like several miles of corridors until Zach stopped at a door.

'You're here.' As he spoke a maid emerged from the room. She seemed flustered when she saw them.

Zach said something in Greek that made her smile

and tip her head towards the room and say something in her native tongue before moving away.

'What did she say?' Kat asked.

'You're not going to learn if I keep translating for you.'

Kat, who had turned to follow the girl's progress down the wide corridor, turned back to Zach. He was a lot closer than she had anticipated. She took a hasty step backwards, nothing to do with retreat and a lot to do with self-preservation. His *closeness* had a disturbing effect on her nervous system.

'So how am I going to learn? Or is that the idea—to make me feel like an outsider?' She regretted the self-pitying addition the moment it left her lips, but in reality she felt as though she always would be an outsider here. It seemed impossible that she would ever fit in.

'You could take lessons.'

She noticed he didn't offer.

'Though they say immersion's the best way to learn a language.'

'Who's they?' she jeered, unimpressed.

'Experts.'

She snapped her fingers to express her opinion of experts. 'I call it stupid, a bit like saying throwing someone in the deep end is the best way to learn to swim.'

'But you can't swim,' he reminded her, picturing her in a very small bikini, emerging from waves. It was a very distracting image. 'Well, this is your suite.' He tipped his head and walked away. 'Half an hour, then.'

She wanted to ask where he was sleeping but stopped herself. It sounded too needy. She thought of saying she wasn't hungry but she realised she was actually starving. Nerves had meant she hadn't eaten a thing all day.

Kat walked in the room and leaned against the door. The room she had entered was furnished in the style of a French chateau, the walls peachy gold in colour, the stunning fireplace with its top-heavy carving dominating the room.

She found the opulent luxuriousness of it all fascinating. The antiques, the drapes, the handmade wallpaper. This was the embodiment of money being no object. It was clear there had been an effort made to inject some personal touches. Kat was appreciative of the flowers and candles. The antique furniture, probably worth a fortune, was all a bit too ornate to ever feel comfortable; her tastes were simpler.

The bathroom was a place where she didn't mind the extravagance. It was spectacular. Someone had already lit the candles around the massive copper tub. She was sorely tempted but was conscious of the time factor and Zach's parting words. Instead, she contented herself with washing her face—her make-up was long gone anyway. She applied a smudge of grey shadow to her eyelids, two flicks of mascara, and rubbed some clear gold on her lips. Her hair, after a severe brush, she left shiny and loose, before changing her top for a clean, though slightly creased, black silk blouse from her case, which somehow had arrived in the room before her.

With three minutes to spare she was outside the bedroom in the corridor, not pausing to analyse her determination not to have him step inside her room. It wasn't as if he was going to carry her through to the French-boudoir bedroom with its canopied bed that was probably a lot of women's dream. The same women probably dreamt of having a man like Zach throw them on it and make mad, passionate, head-banging love to them...or should that be *with* them?

She had never felt that her ignorance of head-banging sex was a disadvantage in life previously, but now she found herself wondering what she was missing.

'You don't want to know, Kat. It's not you.'

The echo of her announcement had barely died away before a voice very close by responded.

'What don't you want to know?'

Kat felt as if guilt was written all over her face, but she managed a very credible recovery. 'If they dress for dinner here.' It was, she decided, inspirational but, now that she thought about it, actually quite relevant.

'Well, there is no *they*, just us, and as you see...'

She accepted the invitation of his downward sweeping gesture and felt her tummy muscles quiver in help-less appreciation as she took in the pale shirt, open at the neck, and the black jeans that clung to his narrow hips and suggested the powerful musculature of his thighs.

The wash of colour lent a peachy glow to her skin as she put effort into controlling her breathing and dragged her eyes back to his face. His dark hair was damp, as though he'd just stepped out of the shower.

'That's good, then.' She turned and began to walk briskly away. He let her go a few feet before calling after her.

'Wrong direction.'

She compressed her lips. 'You might have said!'

He might have, but the truth was he had been enjoying her rear view too much. 'Sorry.'

'I'm not really a formal sort of person.'

'Alekis rarely entertains, but I'm sure he will want to show you off when he is discharged.'

She turned her head, falling into step beside him. 'He looked…frail. How ill is he, really?'

'He has a history of what I believe he euphemistically has in the past called "cardiac events". This time, however, he had more than one cardiac arrest. He is not a young man.'

'You mean he died?' His neutral delivery made it impossible for her to figure out if he would care one way or the other. She got it that some people didn't wear their heart on their sleeve, but this was ridiculous!

Did he think it was weakness to show emotion?

'So they tell me.'

'Should I…?' She shook her head. 'No, it doesn't matter—'

He hefted a sigh. 'Your first lesson is to stop thinking about what the right thing is, and think instead about what you want.'

She skipped a little to catch him up and angled a puzzled look at his profile. 'Do you mean you *never* do anything you don't really want to?'

'Why would I?' It was a question he had been trying to answer since Alekis had foisted the task of bringing his granddaughter home. A spreadsheet would have shown that any debt he felt towards Alekis was fully paid up by the knife he'd taken for him, but some things could not be defined by spreadsheets and analysis.

His instinct, honed by his visceral hatred of bullies, had saved Alekis's life, but Alekis had enabled him to rewrite his own life. He would always owe Alekis. It was not something that he could analyse, it was just something he accepted.

His eyes drifted to the cloud of dark hair, loosened now, that fell almost all the way down to her narrow waist. His acceptance meant he would never feel that silky hair slide through his fingers.

'Oh, I don't know, because it's the right thing?'

He dug his hands deep in his pockets. 'Who decides what the right thing is? But the answer is, no, I don't. You are looking at me as though you have just discovered a different species. I promise you, Katina, I am not the one that is different.'

'You make it sound like it's a bad thing to be different.'

'When different involves you believing in the Easter Bunny, Santa Claus and the basic goodness of your fellow man after the age of nine, then, yes, it is a bad thing, a very bad thing. I believe we are eating in here.' He paused outside an open doorway and gestured for her to precede him.

'You are the most cynical man I have ever met.' She paused on the threshold. 'Oh, this is pretty,' she exclaimed as she registered the table set before the open French doors. Light, gauzy window coverings were fluttering in the light sea breeze that caused the lit candles to flicker and dance. 'I thought all the rooms were massive here.'

'I thought, after the day you have had, you might like something slightly less...formal?' He had phoned ahead to ask for the staff presence to be kept to a minimum to give her some breathing space.

Her eyes flew to his face, then, aware that her pleasure at the small consideration was excessive, she turned and walked across to the open doors to breathe in the fragrance blowing in from the water.

'I can hear the sea!'

'Hard to escape it. We are on an island.'

She swivelled around to face him. 'Well, I have never lived on a private island so I can't be quite so bored about it as you.'

What amazed him was she appeared utterly oblivious to the fact that, standing there with the moonlit, star-studded sky as backdrop, the spider's-web-fine curtains blowing around her face like a bride's veil, she looked utterly beautiful.

In this era of air-brushed perfection, she stood out, not just for her natural beauty, but her total lack of artifice. The inner sexuality that she was totally oblivious of added another transfixing layer to her appeal.

The idea of enjoying that sensuality, of wrapping himself in it, and her hair, raised his core temperature several degrees, which made him a little more effusive than he might normally have been when Selene arrived before he could say something really stupid, like, *Let's skip the food and go to bed.*

'Wow, multitasking tonight, Selene? Isn't this a bit below your pay grade?'

Mouth prim, but smiling with her eyes, the housekeeper gestured to the two maids in uniform who appeared, pushing a trolley on wheels.

'I have followed your instructions. It will be informal, but I wanted to see personally that Kat is comfortable.' She nodded to the girls and said something in Greek that prompted them both to busy themselves with the items on the trolley.

Kat approached the chair that Zach held, nodding a silent thank you as she took her seat. 'I'm very comfortable, thank you,' she said, thinking it was *almost* true now she couldn't feel the warmth of his breath on her cheek, just the tingle it had left behind. There were disadvantages to the sense of intimacy this room gave.

The housekeeper lifted the lids from the dishes on the trolley, inspecting each one before she nodded and turned back to the diners. 'Eloise...just put it down.' The young maid nodded and put a dessert she carried onto the serving table.

'Right, I'll leave you to open the wine, shall I?' She looked at Zach and at the champagne cooling in a cut-glass bucket.

'So does he...my grandfather eat here when he's alone?'

Selene gave a choke that might have been laughter before she whisked from the room.

'Did I say something wrong?'

His sensual lips quirked into a half-smile 'Actually, Alekis eats in the main dining room, which is the size of a football pitch, and he would find it strange if he had to pour his own wine...or, for that matter, water.'

'So this is?'

'This is a private dining room used exclusively when your grandfather is entertaining one of his...*friends*.'

For a moment she looked blank, then comprehension dawned. 'He has...' Her eyes widened some more. 'But he's *old*!'

Zach's lips twitched. 'Not *too* old, apparently.' He

leaned back in his seat and looked at her. 'So is any of this what you were expecting?'

'I'm not sure what I was expecting. Mum used to tell me that one day I'd have beautiful dresses, and I have.' She had found a wardrobe the size of her flat in London crammed with designer labels. A small smile played across her soft lips as her wistful gaze drifted to the fluttering candles on the table. 'A birthday cake with lots of candles. Apart from the birthday bit, it's all here.'

'Do you like seafood?'

She jumped a little, jolting away the memories that curved her lips into a soft smile. 'I like everything,' she said honestly. 'But I'm allergic to nuts.'

Zach could tell by her expression that another memory had been triggered—he didn't want to ask, didn't want to find himself rediscovering how uncomfortable empathy was. It was masochistic, but somehow, he couldn't stop himself.

'What are you thinking about?'

Her eyes fell from his as he walked with his own plate back to his seat. 'This looks delicious.' She looked up from her plate and their glances connected. 'When Mum... When the police went to the flat.'

Kat could remember but hadn't understood at the time the glances the policewomen had exchanged when she'd given her name and address. Though pretty gentrified now, at that time it was not a *nice* area.

'She had left a note. I have it. I had access to my files after I decided to look for her,' she explained. The decision had not been made lightly. She'd known there were risks, most importantly the risk of being rejected all over again. 'I thought she might have another family and I might be a reminder of a past she wanted to forget.'

'You went ahead anyway.' They had both retraced their pasts, but with very different aims. He had wanted closure and, if he was honest, to rub his success in their faces, show them what he had achieved despite them. And she, as far as he could tell, had simply wanted to reconnect, to satisfy her craving for family.

She had forgiven, he never would. This would always set them apart.

She gave a little shrug. 'It took longer than I thought. She seemed to have dropped off the grid after she… left. It never even occurred to me that she might be… not alive.'

He watched as she lowered her eyes so he couldn't see the tears and waited as she speared a prawn onto her fork and slowly chewed it, cursing himself for asking for an answer that he knew was going to make him feel emotions that had no purpose, and yet he was being controlled by something stronger than logic—a primal need to protect.

He might have been able to fight his reaction to her beauty, but when that beauty came attached to a vulnerability not masked by her air of independent fighting spirit, it awoke something in him that he had never felt before. He didn't want to feel it.

'The note she left said…' Kat stared at her plate as she began to recite, '"He made me choose, and Katina is a good girl, and I'm no good for her anyway. PS: She's allergic to nuts."' Her flat delivery did not disguise the fact that reciting the words hurt her.

The fingers around his heart tightened as she lifted her head and said defiantly, 'She wanted me to be safe.'

If she ever had a child, Kat thought, he or she would *know* they were safe. She would never leave them, not for a man, not for *anything*.

Zach bit back the retort on his tongue. Maybe she *needed* to think that her mother had cared about her. What did he know? Maybe the woman had. Why was he worrying one way or the other? he asked himself, resenting how she had intruded into the emotional isolation. Yet when he looked at her, he couldn't be angry. He felt empathy; like a limb deprived of blood flow, the reawakening of this dormant emotion was painful.

'And were you?'

Deliberately misunderstanding him, she grinned and patted a pocket. 'I always carry my EpiPen just in case.' She speared another prawn. 'This is delicious.'

'I'll let the kitchens know about the nut allergy.'

'Don't worry, if in doubt I don't eat it. The allergy is not as serious as some. I know someone who went into anaphylactic shock because she kissed her boyfriend and he'd just eaten a curry with nuts in.'

'So your boyfriends have to swear off nuts?'

The way he was looking at her mouth made the heat climb into her cheeks, and other places. She shifted uneasily in her seat. 'I'm not that bad.' She pushed aside her plate and took a sip of the champagne. It seemed a good time to change the subject. 'So it sounds like Selene has known you for a long time.'

He arched a satiric brow. 'You mean she doesn't treat me with sufficient deference.'

The fact that he could mock himself was a pleasant surprise.

'I was quite young when I first visited the island.'

It frequently seemed to him that Selene still saw him as the young truculent teen with a massive chip on his shoulder and on more than one occasion the family silver in his pockets. His convalescence had been eventful for the new housekeeper, as Selene had been back then.

Kat, trying to imagine what young Zach had looked like, wondered if Selene had some photos of him too. She laid her napkin down on her side plate and decided against another sip of the fizz. The first had gone to her head after the long day. Her appetite after the first few bites had vanished too. She lifted a hand to hide a yawn.

'You're tired.' Of course she was—how could she not be after the day she'd had? He felt the painful twisting sensation in his chest as he watched her stifle another yawn, realising she'd been running on adrenaline all evening.

She shook her head. 'No, not really.'

'You are,' he said, laying down his napkin. 'You need your rest. Tomorrow is another long day. We'll go over the guest list in the morning.' The morning made him think of the night that preceded it. Waking up together, her head on his chest, their limbs tangled. *Tangled*—the word jolted him free of the images flickering through his head.

He did not do *tangled*—emotionally or in any other way. He liked clean-cut defined lines, minus entanglements, which were far more likely to occur if a man spent the entire night in a woman's bed. *Any* woman, let alone the granddaughter of his mentor!

Her brows twitched. 'Guest list?'

'I've compiled a who's who list of the guests for tomorrow along with a bio.'

Her eyes widened. 'Is there an exam…?'

Her comment wrenched a bark of deep laughter from his throat. Then, as their eyes connected, dark on amber, the amusement faded first from his, and then hers.

The air suddenly crackled with a sensually charged tension that seemed to suck the oxygen from the atmosphere, drawing them deeper into a sensual vortex that swirled around them.

Light-headed, Kat didn't connect the sound she could hear with her own laboured breathing, her heart thudding like a dull metronome in her chest as she experienced a surge of deep, strength-sapping longing.

Zach watched the pupils in her eyes expand until only a rim of gold remained. He could hear the roar of hunger in his blood and wanted… *Theos*, how *badly* he wanted to give himself up to it, sink into her softness and… The muscles in his brown throat rippled as he swallowed and dug deep into the reserves of his frayed self-control.

Kat blinked, confused as Zach suddenly surged to his feet, not quite meeting her eyes as he bent forward, the flickering candlelight throwing the planes and angles of his face into stark relief as he blew out the candles.

The gesture seemed weirdly symbolic to Kat because, along with the candlelight, the intimacy had vanished. Been snuffed out, to be replaced by a cool, businesslike atmosphere as he walked towards the door, having donned the persona of the ruthless tycoon with computer chips, not emotions, in his eyes.

'I'll get someone to walk you back to your room.'

She blinked, getting to her feet in confusion as his mercurial mood change made her head spin. 'Aren't you—?'

His quick smile was impersonal and distant. It seemed to her he couldn't get out of the door fast enough. 'I have some work to get through.'

In the corridor, Zach propped his broad shoulders against the wall and released a long, slow, sibilant sigh. It was not pride enhancing to realise that the only effective way he had been able to see to remove himself from temptation was to remove himself physically.

He levered himself off the wall, aware that if he had escorted her back to her room he might have ended up saying good morning and not goodnight. Even the thought of it now heated his blood in a way that drew a low snarling sound from his throat as he strode off, putting as much distance as possible between himself and the witch who had put a spell on him.

CHAPTER EIGHT

THE PLACE BOASTED a state-of-the-art gym that Zach
doubted Alekis even knew existed, but he chose the
beach ahead of the treadmill. Two hours of flat-out
pushing-himself-to-the-limit running later, he felt
he had regained a sense of proportion, enabling him
to think past crippling lust and recognise that being
thrown into the company of someone whose early life
mirrored his own to some minor degree had dredged
up some deeply buried memories, and added an intensity to his feelings when she was around.

A logical explanation, without falling back on the
tired old clichés of soul mates, made him feel more
comfortable and confident he was able to deal with the
next few days without betraying Alekis's trust.

He just needed to keep her at an emotional arm's
length and fulfil his commitment to Alekis.

Having breakfasted alone, Kat asked directions to the
study, where apparently Zach was waiting for her.

The question in her mind was, *which* Zach?

It seemed to Kat that there were more than one.
There was the Zach who seemed warm and interested,

even sympathetic, when she told him about her past, or the one who was the distant and cool executive hiding behind defensive walls to keep emotions out.

She understood the decision to protect her heart in an emotional armour, but her heart had always ached for people who didn't realise they had imprisoned themselves at the same time. *Not your business, Kat,* she told herself firmly.

The thought had been a recurring theme through the long night that had been punctuated by fitful dreams, a session of trying on shoes from the cavernous wardrobe and minutes spent on the balcony, listening to the soothing sound of the waves.

Thank God for caffeine!

'Good morning, did you sleep well? Excellent.'

She blinked. So this was how it was going to be?

'Coffee?' He stood there with pot in hand, more good-looking than any man had a right to be in a black T-shirt and jeans. If his manner had been as informal as his clothes, she'd have been toast. It wasn't, so she wasn't. All positive— this was not the right time to develop a crush and this was not the Zach whose opinion she would ask about the outfit she had chosen for this evening.

'Yes, please, black.' Matching his manner, she took a sip of the scalding strong brew, though the effort was wasted on him as he'd already turned to the desk. 'Right, there will be thirty-five guests tonight. I have subdivided them—society, business and social.' He stabbed a long finger towards the screen of the tablet that was on the desk and tagged on casually, 'Only one royal.'

'Only one?'

He flashed her a look. 'He won't be a problem,' he

promised, dismissing blue blood with a snap of his long fingers. 'However, these might. You can see...'

She couldn't. She was still standing on the other side of the room. Seeing his look of impatience, she overcame her reluctance to move closer, and after a moment's hesitation she reacted to his gesture to step in and look, planting her hands palms flat on the surface as she leaned in.

'As you can see, I have red-flagged those who might be a problem,' he explained. 'Number one is probably Spiro Alekides.' He leaned across her, causing her breath to hitch as he scrolled down the screen before moving back to a distance she found comfortable once more as he explained, 'He can be slippery and has an unsavoury reputation when it comes to women.'

Kat turned her head. He had said that with no discernible trace of irony in his voice, and, yes, there was none at all on his face that she could see—staggering!

'Unfortunately, Alekis has a joint venture with him,' he tagged on, explaining the man's presence.

'You don't sound as though you approve?'

'Alekis does not need my approval.'

'Who is she?' Kat asked, looking curiously at the glamorous blonde woman whose photo was next to the red-flagged man.

'That's Ariana.'

Something in his voice made her turn again in response to a little spurt of something alarmingly close to jealousy tightening in her chest. 'You know her?'

'That sort of intuition will do you no harm,' he complimented her smoothly. 'We have both dated Ariana, as it happens at the same time. Spiro sent her to do a little industrial espionage and I used the situation to my advantage to plant a little false information. He has never actually forgiven me, so keep clear,' he warned.

Kat caught her breath. This was not *close* to jealousy, and more a flood than a spurt. This was the real thing with bells on! The shaft that pierced her was so intense that she would not have been surprised to see a knife hilt protruding from her chest.

Kat was as deeply shocked by her visceral reaction as she was scared by it. Lowering her gaze to hide the emotions she felt were written across her face in neon letters, she amazed herself by responding in a relatively calm voice.

'So she used you, and you used her. Does that cancel out all the using?' she wondered in a voice that sounded too bright. 'I'll look at this myself later. Don't worry, I always did my homework.'

Aware that Zach was watching her with a puzzled frown, she struggled to control her expression and presumably failed; she could hear the suspicion in his voice as he asked, 'What's wrong?'

'Not a thing.' She tucked the tablet under her arm. 'I promised myself I'd explore this morning.'

'Want a guide?'

'I think I'll be fine on my own.' She had to get out of the room before he guessed, which would be the ultimate humiliation!

He stared at the door, fighting the impulse that gripped him to follow her before he slumped down into one of the chairs. It was time to stop pretending and face facts. When it came to this woman his normal iron control did not apply.

* * *

More by luck than good judgement, she found her way back to her suite. Nobody had cleared the shoes that had littered the bedroom floor since she had pulled them out of the cavernous closet in the early hours of the morning. She kicked one of the soft-as-butter lemon-coloured pumps that were lovely, almost tripped over the striking red loafers, and picked up one of the cute kitten heels in one hand, and one of the spiky, far too high ankle boots, sexy as hell—even with pyjamas—in the other.

With a low moan, she threw them both across the room, then, feeling guilty that she was leaving someone else to pick them up, gathered up the shoes and, pairing them all up, stacked them neatly in their boxes, telling herself that she needed to get a grip. She needed to focus and *not* think about Zach Garros.

She spent the next hour lying, head propped in her hands, on the bed, poring over the guest list and the cream of Athens society. But for some reason it wasn't sinking in, so she welcomed the interruption when a maid tapped on the door.

'Mrs Carras asks me to tell you that there is morning tea in the small salon if you wish it, miss?'

Why not? thought Kat, closing the tablet.

'Lead the way,' she said to the girl, who looked startled by the informality.

An hour later, as she sipped her second cup of tea, Kat walked to the high, deep windows. The sea shone in the near distance like silvered turquoise in the morning sun. As the place was built on a peninsula projecting into the water, she assumed that most rooms would have similarly breathtaking marine vistas.

Selene bustled in. Kat found herself envying the woman's vaguely harassed air and realised she was bored. She was used to being busy. She would make a very poor lady of leisure.

'Good morning. Did you sleep well?'

'Perfectly,' Kat lied. 'I thought I might explore a little this morning, if there's nothing you want me—?' she began hopefully.

'Gracious, no. I'll send Della. She can be your guide and she's too teary this morning to be any help—she's in love,' Selene added with an eye-roll.

'No, don't worry. I'd prefer to wander alone, if that's okay?'

'Of course. Enjoy yourself.'

A little exploration had proved her assumption was right: the scale of the building was daunting and then some. She hesitated to call it a home. It seemed more to her like a massive status symbol. *Surely* no one needed this much space?

She got turned around several times during her exploration until she realised that the place was built on a grid system. After that her attempts to get her bearings got a little easier. Everything fanned out from one central living area. She supposed that you got your head around massive in time—less so the presence of staff, discreet but liable to pop up and take you by surprise. She hoped some of them were temporary additions for the evening event.

It was her first test and one she hadn't decided if she actually wanted to pass. Who was she trying to please and impress? The grandfather she didn't know, or the man who didn't care one way or the other?

Maybe, Kat, you should try pleasing yourself?

It was a plan.

The first of the two wings she explored seemed to be dedicated to private suites, like her own, and some slightly smaller guest suites. After half an hour of opening doors and admiring views she wandered back out to the terrace that ran the full length of this side of the building. Beautifully manicured lawns ran down to the sea. She took off her cardigan. It felt like spring as she took a seat on one of the long stone benches surrounded by tubs of flowers. Selene appeared, along with a young girl in a maid's uniform who she introduced as Della.

The appearance was so perfectly timed that Kat imagined her every move being picked up by CCTV cameras. She smiled at the girl, recognising the name, but didn't get a smile back, just a quick curtsey and a look that mingled tragic with sulky. She was not a recommendation for love with the black mascara rings around her eyes.

Selene noticed this, too. 'Go on, run along and wash your face,' she said, and the girl rushed off.

'It's such beautiful weather here, I can't get over it.' She had as little control over that as she did her visceral response to Zach, but the weather was much easier to live with.

'Yes, and such a relief after the heat. The summer was hot even for here. You are finding your way around?'

Kat's smile was a poor disguise for the fact she was overwhelmed by everything. She fought her way through a wave of longing for the comfortable predictability of her old life and nodded. 'There is a lot to explore.'

'Are you sure you don't want someone to show you around? Not Della,' she added hastily. 'That girl is just… She is really trying my patience today.'

'Actually, it's quite nice discovering things on my own, and if I have a guide to rely on it will take me for ever to find my way around.'

The older woman nodded and smiled. 'Oh, I should mention that the room is being prepared for this evening, so there might be a little disruption. Can I get you anything—tea, coffee, cakes?'

'Tea would be nice,' she lied, thinking, *This is how bored people put on weight*. 'So, I'm assuming the guests will be staying overnight?' It wasn't as if there weren't room.

'Normally they would, but, no, Mr Zach has arranged transport. They will be leaving by eight-thirty sharp.' Kat picked up on the 'whether they like it or not' silent addition. 'Hence the early start this evening. If you'll excuse me, the musicians have arrived and they are being a little…artistic.' She rolled her eyes and whisked away.

When the tea arrived it came with some delicious little honey pastries embedded with nuts and jewelled candy fruit, which Kat, who told herself she was still making up for her half-eaten dinner, demolished.

Exploring the second wing didn't really work off many calories, Kat discovered. It was dedicated to the domestic area. Her appearance in a food-preparation room created a bit of a shock panic moment for the staff working there.

She apologised and backed out, then promptly lost her orientation once more and ended up outside again where she discovered that there was more than one swimming pool, and this one was in an enclosed courtyard. A shaded area lay to one side of the marble-floored space complete with what appeared to be an outdoor kitchen; on a raised plinth on the opposite side, a massive spa pool bubbled away happily.

She lay down on one of the loungers with a bump, marvelling at how different this world was compared to the one she was used to.

Not my world, but I'm still me.

The recognition eased the tightness in her chest. Her chin lifted. If she was going to do this, she'd do it her way. For starters, she'd do what she always did. Focus not on the negative but the positive. Yes, heiress was a bad fit for her, but she'd worn ill-fitting shoes before now and survived, she reminded herself, and they'd always looked good.

She'd already saved the refuge... If she was going to inherit money and power, there were a lot of worthy causes out there who just needed someone to notice them.

When a menu appeared for her lunch, Kat requested a sandwich. She intended to explore the gardens and beach.

'Just a sandwich?' Della looked confused. 'What will I tell Mrs Carras?'

'That I want a sandwich.'

Her irritation fell away as, without warning, the young girl's face suddenly crumpled and she burst into loud sobs.

'Fine, I'll have lunch,' Kat said, alarmed. The girl continued to sob.

'*He's* sending him away and I'll never see him again, and I love him!'

'Take a seat.' She got up and the girl took her own, scrubbing her face with her apron. 'Della, is it...? Who is *he*? The first *he*.'

'Mr Gavros. Alexi thinks he's marvellous, but he's not—he's cruel and heartless and he's sending Alexi away because he thinks I'm too young! And he doesn't want anyone to be happy!'

Kat had never been so glad to see anyone as she was to see Selene. The older woman took one look at the scene and bustled the weeping girl out. A few moments later she returned.

'I am so sorry about that.'

'It's fine. She says that Zach is sending her boyfriend away.'

'Oh, I know. She's telling anyone who will listen the same thing.'

While Kat was the first to believe that Zach was no saint, that he was cynical and manipulative, the girl's story just didn't have a ring of truth to it. Why on earth would Zach go out of his way to blight young love? Mock it, yes, but not... No, she was sure there was another explanation.

'So, is he?'

The other woman gave a chuckle. 'Well, I suppose he is. Alexi is one of the placements, one of the big successes, and, as you might know, Zach has an arrangement with the university: if the youngsters he recommends pass the interview and entrance exam they are admitted without formal exams to do a foundation year. Alexi is starting next semester. The boy, as bright as they come, is over the moon.'

Kat tried to pick her way through the information. 'So, this Alexi was originally—?'

'Much like Zach, living on the streets, though obviously his situation was not as dire as Zach's.' The older woman, unaware she had just dropped a bombshell, shook her head while Kat's imagination went into riot mode. 'Not all the youngsters end up in academia, obviously, but they are all offered a way out, a safe way out.'

Kat shook her head. Zach had lived on the streets? She knew his family situation had been bad...*outsider*, he'd said. Now she fully understood what he had meant.

'So, he escaped his family by living on the streets.' The ache in the little corner of her heart was not just for the boy he had once been, but the lone wolf he had become.

Presumably it had been her grandfather who had taken him out of that old life, which perhaps explained the loyalty he seemed to feel towards the older man.

She gave a sudden laugh as she realised that, ironically, it turned out that Zach was as much of a member of the *do-gooding* fraternity he claimed to despise as she was!

Happily, Selene misinterpreted her amusement.

'I know, young love. The thing is,' she said, lowering her voice to a confidential whisper, 'I think young Alexi is quite relieved. Della is a rather *intense* girl and very young for her age.' She hefted out a sigh. 'Better to give her the day off than risk any more meltdowns, I think. I'll leave you to your exploring.'

Her exploring took Kat to the beach, where she

peeled off the clothes over the black swimsuit she'd put on earlier. She could not swim but she could paddle. She waded out, thigh deep, staring, eyes scrunched against the sun, out to sea. She let her thoughts drift—the tide took them inevitably in the direction of Zach. Would she challenge him with his background, ask him why he was so afraid anyone might suspect he was a good guy?

It was almost as if he had tried to make her think the worst of him earlier. Maybe there was a worse but there was also a *better*. A better he seemed not to want anyone to see...*or is that just me?*

She shook her head as she collapsed onto the warm sand. The man was a confusing mass of contradictions! As she shook back her hair she let the sun dry the moisture from her skin, rubbing the sand away as it dried on her bare arms and legs.

It was only when she removed her watch from the pocket where she had put it for safekeeping that she noticed the time. With a yelp, she jumped to her feet, dragged her clothes on over her now dry swimsuit and began to jog up the deserted beach.

She had reached the green manicured lawns that ran down to the sand when she collided not with one of the palms, but a solidity that had warmth.

If his hands had not remained on her shoulders she would have fallen over. Her hands clutched his hair-roughened, sinewy forearms as she inhaled a deep breath of his warm male scent, causing her stomach to violently clench in hopeless desire.

Slowly, her eyes lifted, over the clinging T-shirt stretched across his broad chest to his face. Like the rest of his skin, it was filmed with salty moisture.

She didn't say a word; she couldn't. She ached for him. Quite literally. She hadn't thought it was possible.

It took every ounce of his willpower to resist the longing in her eyes as she looked up at him. Alekis's granddaughter who needed...*deserved* more than someone like him could give.

'You don't look in the party mood.' Hair wild, skin glazed with a sun-kissed look, her lips lightly crusted with salt that he longed to kiss off, she looked the ultimate in desirability.

Kat swallowed the occlusion in her throat; her chest felt constricted and tight. He was close, *too* close. She couldn't breathe, or think, just feel. Too much feeling.

'I'm in panic mode. I'm cutting it a bit fine, probably.' She lifted a hand to her tangled hair and took a step back. His hands fell away as she looked at him through her lashes.

'I should run,' she said, thinking, *Don't let me.*

'Yes.'

She was still running as she entered her suite, brought to a panting, shocked immobility by what waited for her there.

'Good evening,' she said pleasantly to the small army of assorted people assembled inside her private salon. *What the hell?*

She looked to Selene, brows raised, for explanation, even though the hairdryers, tongs and assorted brushes sticking out of a couple of bags was a clue.

'I thought you might like to start getting ready now?' Selene's anxious glance at the ormolu clock over the fireplace that held a massive flower arrangement suggested that she thought this process should have begun some time earlier, and, considering Kat's salty hair had taken on a life of its own, she couldn't really blame her.

'Oh, have you been waiting?'

'Not at all,' came the polite lie.

'Actually, you can all have the evening off,' she said, addressing the small makeover army. 'I'm more than happy to get myself ready.'

The expression of shock and consternation on the older woman's face almost made Kat smile. Clearly the idea that Kat could dress herself, do her own hair and apply her make-up shocked the present company deeply. They *wanted* to argue, Kat could *feel* it.

'Honestly, I've been dressing myself for years.'

Nobody smiled. Kat felt her impatience edge up; she enjoyed a spa day as much as anyone, but she couldn't see it becoming part of her daily routine, or even *big* day routine.

She'd read about freak shows and she supposed this was the modern version—she being the freak!

Damping down her mounting panic, she tried again. 'Honestly, I'll be fine, but if I have a problem I'll yell.'

She utilised a smile aimed at robbing her refusal of any offence and firmly closed her bedroom door on their collective shocked faces. It took her a moment to find the music selection she was looking for and turn up the volume. It wasn't as if there were any neighbours to worry about.

One of these days she was going to take up yoga, but in the meantime her tried-and-tested relaxation method of choice was what it always had been —a five-minute session of wild, unrestrained, let-your-hair-down dancing to a rock anthem while quite frequently singing along.

When the track came to an end, she switched the music off and fell back headlong onto the canopied bed. Staring at the ceiling, she waited for her heart rate to slow to a gentle trot.

To say she was relaxed would have been an exaggeration, but she was willing to accept exhaustion as a substitute—she was just too tired to run away. The thought brought an image of her running away from Zach on the beach. She had stopped once and he'd still been standing there staring after her. The image in her head made her stomach flip.

'Oh, God, this is crazy!' she groaned as she padded to the bathroom. Sadly, she hadn't left herself enough time for a long and lazy bath. The deep double-ended copper tub that took centre stage in the bathroom... now that was one luxury item she might get used to quite quickly.

Sniffing some of the lovely oils lined up, she stripped and walked into the shower, which was big enough to house a football team, though the image that slid into her head did not involve a team, just one man...who was constantly on her mind!

But not your bed, Kat, mocked the voice in her head.

It was about time she remembered she was not the sort of woman who undressed men, even in her imagination, let alone... She scrunched her face and threw a mental bucket of cold water over the febrile images.

Wrapped in a towel, duly anointed with some delicious moisturising lotion, her hair clear of salt, the last traces of sand washed from the crevices it had crawled

into, she looked at the dress she had finally selected
in the early hours from the racks in the massive walk-
in closet.

It was midnight blue, so dark it looked black in certain lights—basically it was a slim ankle-length slip,
not that there was anything *basic* about the cut of the
heavy silk, high at the neck and low enough at the back
to expose her delicately sculptured shoulder blades.

After blast-drying her long thick hair, she tried a
couple of styles, almost wishing she had not rejected
the services of a hairstylist, and then as she pulled her
thick glossy skeins into a knot on the nape of her neck
things clicked. She smoothed it properly and gathered it
again, winding the sections into a smooth loose knot at
the nape of her neck before sticking in several hairpins
to secure it, then finally pulling out a few face-framing
strands for a softening effect.

Her normal make-up was a smudge of shadow, a
touch of gloss on her lips. So the fifteen minutes she
did spend felt like a long time, but the end result, if not
perfect, satisfied her. The dusting of blush on her cheeks
lifted her pallor and the highlighter along her cheekbones worked. She carefully highlighted the almond
shape of her eyes with liner before adding a sweep of
mascara over her already dark and lustrous eyelashes.

She struggled to adjust the narrow straps of the dress
so that they left the delicate architecture of her collarbones exposed, before slipping into the heels. She was
viewing the overall effect with a critical eye when there
was a knock on the door, a polite reminder from Selene.

She took a deep breath and straightened her shoulders. She couldn't pretend this wasn't really going to

happen any longer, but she could pretend her stomach wasn't churning in apprehension.

Smile in place, projecting a confidence she was far from feeling, she pulled the door open. Her smile wilted and died like a rose exposed to an icy chill. A myriad sensations and emotions that were impossible to detangle hit her simultaneously as she saw the tall figure, no longer in running shorts and vest, but in the dress suit, dark hair still visibly damp as though he had just stepped from a shower. An image that did not help her composure, or her heart, which literally stalled. For several moments she felt as if it would never start again.

'You scared the life out of me!' Breathless, and sounding it, she lifted a hand to her throat, where she could feel a pulse that was trying to fight its way through her skin.

Zach cleared his own throat. It had been less a jolt and more an earth tremor to see her standing there and for several heartbeats he'd stood, literally transfixed.

'I really didn't think you scared that easily.'

She was the most fearless woman he had ever met and—as he looked at her standing there now, there was no use pretending otherwise—the most beautiful.

Against the dark fabric her skin gleamed pale gold. Her body, under the figure-enhancing cut of the midnight fabric, was slender and sensuous. The way she wore her hair displayed the length of her slender neck and her delicate collarbones. She looked exclusive and sexy—a hard look to pull off.

He leaned a hand on the doorjamb above her head. 'If you are dressing to impress you have succeeded. You look very lovely.'

Her breath caught at the compliment.

'I wanted to blend in,' she said in a small husky voice, worrying that he might assume she had made the effort to impress him. Worried even more because she couldn't swear she hadn't!

It was hard to smile with the ache in his groin, but he did anyway. 'Ah, well, you failed.' Straightening up, he gestured to her to walk beside him and after a short pause she did, her perfume making his nostrils flare.

'How was your run?'

He flashed her a frowning look. *'Hot.'*

'When is Alekis's surgery scheduled for?'

'First thing Thursday if the rest of the tests are clear.'

'Should I go there to see him before?'

'If you want to.'

'Is the surgery dangerous?'

'Another bypass and a valve replacement, I believe.'

It was weird but hearing all this life-and-death stuff suddenly made the lies she'd been telling herself all day seem petty and ridiculous.

For someone who had spent her life avoiding excitement and danger, it was not easy to acknowledge the idea that had been growing in her head. Because if danger had a name and a face and a really incredible body, she was thinking of throwing herself at him, *giving* herself to him. The thought was scary and liberating at the same time.

Zach just tapped into a reckless part of her. It had required no effort on his part; just breathing did it. Her response would require more effort. Forget instincts, she needed to use her brain.

It would have been helpful if he had remained the

unacceptable but very handsome face of capitalism; instead, she knew more, knew there was nothing two-dimensional about him. She understood when people did not want to discuss their backgrounds for fear of others assuming they were using it in some way, but why hide the things he was giving back to society?

She took a shallow breath and closed down the conflicting theories whirring around in her head. She had to get through the next couple of hours first.

'Well?'

He arched a brow. 'Well, what?' And carried on walking, requiring her to skip on her heels to catch him up.

'Well, isn't there a list? Don't eat with your mouth full, don't get drunk and dance on the tables, don't talk politics, insult the guests or slag off the powerful and influential even if they are total sleazes?'

'I think you have covered the essentials and the file had everything you need in it.' He paused. 'But actually no one here should give you a hard time. This *will* get easier.'

'Well, at least I won't get drunk so there will be no online pictures of me dancing on the table. I only got drunk once and I didn't like it.' The memory made her wince, but underneath she was feeling moderately pleased she was proving they could have a normal conversation without any sex stuff getting in the way. *It had all been in her head anyway.*

He looked amused. 'It rarely stops anyone repeating the process.'

'I had my drink spiked.'

The amusement slid from his eyes. She had the impression he didn't even know that he put his hands heavily on her shoulders, but she knew they felt very heavy; she couldn't move.

Actually, she wasn't really trying.

'What happened?'

'I was at a nightclub for someone's birthday. It was all right, my friends got me out of there.' She chose not to think what might have happened if they hadn't, if the two men trying to half-carry her out to the waiting car had succeeded. 'For a while I struggled with trust, but then I realised I was letting fear rule my life.' She stepped a little ahead of him, paused and twirled around to face him, hitting him full blast with her golden stare, leaving him no escape route.

'You have to trust someone sometime, don't you think, Zach?'

He could feel the pulse pounding in his temple. 'Is there some sort of message in there for me?'

She shrugged. 'Just throwing it out there. Some people are bad. They hurt you, but there are a lot of people that are good, too. You miss such a lot by pushing them away.'

'And if someone spikes your drink?'

'I refuse to live in fear...' Her beautiful smile flashed out. 'I had friends to look out for me and here... I have you, *I think*?'

He ignored the voice in his head that yelled *coward*, his eyes sliding from hers. 'Tonight you do, but there are a lot of tomorrows. There is such a thing as too trusting, Katina.'

'How so?'

The exhaustion came over him in a tide; fighting

the uncontrollable urge to take her in his arms became in the space of a heartbeat just too much. He stopped fighting and surrendered to the roar and the hunger, the ache of wanting.

Holding her wide eyes with his, he placed one large hand in the small of her back, noting the flare in her golden eyes as he curved his free hand around the back of her head and dragged her into him.

She did register that the combustible, exciting quality that she was always conscious of in him was not in the background but right there, in her face, reminding her he was too male, too *everything*. But nothing running through her head had prepared her for what his intention was. She was in denial right up to the moment that his lips covered hers.

The warm, sensuous movement of his mouth drew a deep, almost feral moan that emanated from deep inside her as her lips parted. Her fingers closed around the fabric of his shirt as she raised herself up on her toes, her body stretching in a slim, urgent arc as she invited the invasion to deepen, expanding the cell-deep hungry ache until she simply hung on for the ride, helpless to resist the tide of attraction, the sparking electricity between them. She felt the deep quiver run through his body.

Then it was over. She wasn't quite sure how, but she was on her feet and not plastered up against him and he was standing there looking down at her as though… Actually, she wasn't sure he was seeing her at all. There was a hot blankness in his eyes that slowly receded.

'So what,' she began in a voice that really sounded nothing like her own, 'was that about?'

'Does the unknown that waits for you in there suddenly look so very scary?'

It didn't, but as explanations went that seemed more
than thin. 'Why did you kiss me?'

Breathing hard, but looking insultingly composed
considering the chaos inside her body and head, he
brushed an invisible speck off his shirt before replying.

'A moment... I... I wanted to know how you tasted.'

The blunt words, drawn from him almost against his
will, sent a slam of hot lust through her body.

CHAPTER NINE

'OH!' HER RESPONSE gave *inadequate* a new meaning, but she didn't know what else to say. What would be an improvement?

Don't do it again wouldn't be appropriate, or, more likely, *don't stop...*

'We'll be late.' Suddenly she was the one that couldn't hold *his* eyes.

'It's allowed—you're the guest of honour.' He dragged a hand over his dark hair, thinking about how warm and perfect she had felt in his arms. The promise of passion he had always sensed in her had burnt up into life the moment he'd touched her.

It was easy to see that Kat could become the drug of choice to any man, so long as he didn't mind sharing her with a multitude of good causes.

Theos, he really didn't envy that man!

Even as he congratulated himself he recognised that, but for the obligation he felt to Alekis, *he* would be that man, at least for a night, which was in itself another problem.

The insight he had gained into Kat's character led him to doubt that she had a casual attitude to sex. He

doubted she would look on it as a healthy physical outlet. For her it would come wrapped up in sentiment. Of
course, there were many men out there willing to accept those terms for the joy of bedding her.

Nothing of his thoughts showed in his face as they
continued to walk side by side the last few yards, not
touching, but he could still sense her leaping pulse.

'You'll be fine, you know.'

She gave an odd little laugh and lifted her head at the
abrupt comment. 'Will I?' At that moment she didn't
feel as if she knew anything. She ran her tongue across
the outline of her lips and gave another laugh. Hell, she
hadn't even known her own name when he'd kissed her.

'Be interested...' he said, the effort of dragging his
eyes off her mouth making him sweat. 'Be yourself.'

Kat swallowed down another bubble of hysterical
laughter. How was she meant to be *herself*, or even sane,
after he had just kissed her like that? Being herself and
kissing him back was part of the problem. *Herself* would
be grabbing him and making him do it again.

'Now that is something I never thought I'd hear you
say!' Wow, not even a quiver. She was extremely proud
of herself.

He arched a sardonic brow. 'Why?'

'Because I get the impression me being me irritates
the hell out of you tonight.' Maybe he had kissed her to
shut her up, she thought, nursing her resentment.

He stopped short of the open door, from which the
sounds of music and the hum of conversation and laughter emanated, and looked down at her.

'It isn't you I find—'

'Irritating?' she supplied, slightly confused and at

the same time excited by the intensity in his manner, though next to the post-kiss confusion that still blocked her normal thought processes it barely even registered.

'Not the right word but it will do. It's the situation, Katina, that I find extremely...*irritating.*' *Theos*, wanting her was killing him.

'I don't know what you mean,' she said, thinking of the warm, clean but musky male smell of his body when he had kissed her. *Would he do it again?*

'Are you sure about that?'

She looked away, suddenly more nervous of the glow in his eyes than what lay in the room. Not nervous, excited. She ran her tongue across the dry outline of her lips. *It was just a kiss...stop trying to read things into it.*

She hefted out a deep sigh. 'Right, let's get this thing over with.'

He nodded.

She was incredibly glad for the light touch of his hand on her elbow as they walked into the room, because walking into a room beside Zach made it a dead certainty most of the room would not be looking at you. When Zach walked into a room, any room, he would always be the focus of attention.

There was a short static pause in the audible social hum as more and more people turned to look at them, from where they were already gathered in small groups, chatting, laughing, drinking the wine being offered by the staff.

The sea of faces was actually more a small pond, she told herself as she willed her feet that felt glued to the floor to move.

'Showtime, Kat.' He heard her whisper before flashing him a look from her topaz eyes and lifting her chin and walking away from him.

Zach watched her, while he wrestled with the flood of unfamiliar emotions surging inside him. He knew how scared she was but no one would ever have known it, despite her pallor, and even if they had it would have been her warmth they remembered, a warmth that could not be feigned.

He surprised himself with that thought.

He watched as she approached a man who stood excluded from a small laughing group nearby. Zach's admiration and pride went through the roof as he watched her smile and move forward, touching the arm of the housekeeper before she lifted her head to the solitary man that Selene was offering the drink to.

Zach stood, his shoulder braced on one wall, his attitude possibly not as nonchalant as he intended because nobody approached him, not even one of the guys with the fizz, which was a pity because he could really have done with a drink.

He finally managed to grab one and downed it while fighting a strong urge to march over there and tell Kat that it didn't matter what anyone thought and this wasn't a test.

What the hell was wrong with Alekis, making her jump through all these hoops? And what was wrong with him for helping? If anyone needed to change it was them, not her.

He was shocked by this thought that came from he knew not where—unlike the urge to kiss her; that source was no mystery.

He willed himself to relax. He knew she could cope

and so could he. He took a swallow and grimaced, finding he was holding an empty glass. If he could relive the moment…but he couldn't so why waste the energy? The kiss, while not being ideal, had at least taken the edge off his rampant hunger.

Yeah, you keep telling yourself that, Zach.

Tuning out the ironic voice of his subconscious, he watched as the austere diplomat melted under Kat's charm offensive and took a drink for himself before handing her the fruit juice option she must have requested. He saw her press a hand to her temple and carry on smiling… It was not the first time he had seen the gesture since she had begun to circulate.

The diplomat leaned in and said something that drew a laugh from Kat, a laugh so warm and spontaneous and *genuine* that it made other people smile, including him.

In the periphery Zach was aware of two people separate off from a nearby group and move to join Kat and the diplomat. One was a journalist that he didn't actively dislike, the other… He frowned as he recognised the other was Spiro Alekides, the business rival who had *not* been gracious in defeat and had made his humiliation worse by giving several unwise interviews that had harmed his reputation more than his financial losses.

Zach began to slowly weave his way through the jostle of bodies, not questioning or analysing the protective instincts that directed his feet.

Even without Zach's warning Kat would have summed up Spiro Alekides, who she had instantly recognised from his photo, in a heartbeat. She had encountered the type before. He smiled a lot, but not with his eyes, and tried very hard to say what he *thought* you wanted to hear.

'Oh, yes, I so agree all that talent out there is going to waste. It's not about charity, it's about investing in our future and the youth are our future.'

The man sounded as though he were reading the label on a packet of cereal, but Kat nodded, repressing a wince as the headache moved behind her eyes. Experience told her if she didn't take measures it would become a full-blown migraine and all that entailed—which was *just* what she didn't need.

'Not everyone understands that,' she said, thinking, *Like you,* before adding, 'Sorry, Mr—'

'Call me Spiro, my dear.'

'Spiro.'

The older man turned quite slowly, arranging his features into a smile. 'Why, Zach, what a nice surprise, meeting you here like this.' He beamed at Kat and the journalist and extended a well-manicured, plump hand to Zach, who raised both of his. One was holding a glass, the other a plate.

Zach smiled, making Kat think of a large sleek predator. She suspected that every woman present would have jumped straight into his mouth if the occasion arose—she had. The thought made her blush.

'So where is your lovely lady tonight?'

The reference to the woman that they had both slept with increased the tempo of the throb behind Kat's eyes. If she was going to get a migraine every time anyone mentioned a woman Zach had bedded she could spend her life with a headache!

'She couldn't make it.'

'Such a shame,' Zach murmured. 'Well, gentlemen, I hope you'll forgive me for stealing away our lovely hostess.' He planted a hand lightly in the small of Kat's back. 'But there is someone who is dying to meet her.'

Not happy that she liked the supportive feel of his hand as much as she did, she frowned and asked, 'Who?' without enthusiasm as they wove their way across the room.

'Do you have a headache?' Zach asked without looking at her.

Kat's jaw dropped and her eyes flew to his face, which sent a fresh spasm of agony along her nerve endings. *'How...?'*

His hand went to her elbow as she caught her heel in the hem of her dress and lurched. 'I thought as much,' he said grimly.

'What are we...?'

She stopped as he paused as they reached Selene and explained in an undertone, 'Kat has a headache. I'm taking her outside for some fresh air.'

'But you can't— This is— I have to stay. Some aspirin, Selene, and I'll be fine.'

'That too, please, Selene. You nearly passed out,' he condemned.

'For heaven's sake, I tripped, is all! It's the damned heels and don't blame me—you bought them for me! Not bought as such,' she tacked on hastily in case anyone had heard and got the wrong impression.

Zach stood over her as she swallowed the painkillers and, ignoring his frowning disapproval, washed them down with a mouthful of wine.

'I thought you didn't drink.'

'A mouthful and, anyway, what did you *think* I was going to do—spit them out?' She took a deep breath and massaged her temples. 'OK, back to it.'

'You need some fresh air.'

She looked up at him, exasperated by his insistence. 'I need to get back in there.'

'They can wait.'

'Make up your mind. I thought this party was ultra-important...first impressions, burying bad news with my stunning personality, and all that stuff?'

'The pain is making you cranky. You need some fresh air to clear your head.'

She sighed. It was easier to give up, and the idea of escaping for a few moments had distinct appeal. The lively music the live band struck up made up her mind.

He didn't say anything until they got outside. 'So, you met Spiro.'

She inhaled as they stepped out into the scented night and she let her head fall back. 'Uh-huh, a real charmer, isn't he? If you go for snakes, that is.'

'Not a man to be underestimated, though.'

She lifted her head and walked alongside him onto the sloping lawns that ran down to the beach. The breeze tugged at her hair, dislodging several strands from her updo. She stuck them back in haphazardly.

'He is a poor loser. He takes pleasure from revenge...'

She flashed a look at his profile in the moonlight. 'What did he do?'

'He tried to sabotage something that is...important to me.'

It had taken a while to work out there was actually a pattern to the seemingly arbitrary flurry of false, damaging stories circulating online. The near career-ending false stories about abuse, about a dedicated and vital staff member at the charity for street kids that few knew had anything to do with Zach, and simultaneously the exposé about bullying in the mentoring scheme set up for teens emerging from care.

A firm specialising in forensic investigation had taken about five minutes to reveal that the older man's grubby hands were all over the mess.

The threat of litigation had made the problem vanish. For good measure Zach had explained that he didn't need to resort to lies to bring Spiro down, and that he had in his possession several verifiable documents that would ensure the older man did jail time. As bluffs went it was a no-brainer. A man like Spiro always had dirty secrets.

'Your mentoring scheme for street kids, you mean.'

He stopped dead and looked at her in astonishment. 'How the hell do you know that?'

'What?' she said, dancing ahead and turning around to face him as she continued to skip backwards on her crazy high heels. 'That you are a bleeding heart do-gooder...?' she taunted, allowing herself a triumphant little laugh, frustrated that the shadows across his face meant she could only see his mouth, not his eyes. 'I talk to people. They open up to me. It's a gift.'

He swore.

'I don't know why you act like it's a dirty secret. I think it's marvellous!'

'You know nothing about me—the things I've—'

Her smile faded. 'I know you lived on the streets, and you survived.' That he'd had to protect himself and he had never learnt how to stop; it wasn't a matter of didn't, he *couldn't* seem to open up to anyone.

'Selene?' he growled as he strode out at a pace that made her skip to keep up with him.

'Don't blame her, she assumed I knew already. You ran away from your uncle, the one who died?'

He nodded.

'And you never went back?'

His face was in shadow and when he finally responded his voice was wiped clean of all emotion as he reacted to the question. 'I went back looking for what… I suppose some sort of closure. He was gone. Dead, I found out later, and my grandmother…dementia, final stages.'

Kat gave a little gasp, feeling his pain as sharply as if it were her own as she fell into step beside him once more. 'What happened?'

'Nothing. I put her in a home and haven't been back since the first time.'

'So, she is having the best care?' It said so much about him that he would do that for someone who had abused him so badly.

'Oh, I can provide her with the best care, but I can't… *feel*…anything.'

She reached out in the dark and curled her small fingers around his. She could feel the raw tension emanating from him in waves. 'Sorry.'

'I suppose you think I should forgive her?' he flung out.

'No, I think that you should celebrate the day you escaped every year. I'll help you if you like?'

He looked down just as the moon came out from behind a cloud. It illuminated her beautiful face with breathtaking clarity, toasting her skin with moon gold.

CHAPTER TEN

HE STARED DOWN at her, drinking in each individual feature before gorging himself on the perfect whole. Then slowly, he lifted a hand and framed her face. Kat shivered at the contact and pushed her cheek against his hand, turning her face so that her lips brushed his palm.

His hand dropped.

'How will you help me?'

Her heart gave a painful jolt; her body was humming, her nerve endings raw as though all the insulation, the protection, had been stripped from them. 'I'd do anything you need,' she whispered.

A sound like a groan was torn from deep inside his chest. 'Don't say that, Katina.'

She lifted her chin. 'Why not?'

'Because I need everything.'

The heat between them scorched the air as he bent his head and kissed her. Kat kissed him back with equal abandon, locking her hands around his neck, arching her back to crush her breast into his chest, the little gasps of shocked pleasure as she felt the hardness of his desire against her belly lost in the warmth of his mouth.

They broke apart as the sound of a helicopter overhead cut through the sigh of the water.

Zach swore and took her hand. He studied it for a moment, an expression almost like pain contorting his features before his fingers tightened and he led her onto the moonlit sand.

Kat tripped.

'You're going to break your neck on those damned things. They are lethal.'

'But sexy.'

His eyes glowed hot and hungry. 'Hell, yes!'

The moonlight lent everything a silvered glow and the night-time silence made the hush of the waves breaking into a white foam hiss seem louder. There was no wind at all, just a warm stillness as, hopping on one foot and then the other, she whipped off the heels to walk beside him, her heart pounding in anticipation as they reached the point where the waves were breaking.

He turned, allowing himself to look at her. The fall had shaken free her hair from its elegant knot and it now spilled down her back and blew across her face in silky tangled strands that she pushed impatiently away with her free hand.

'I want to touch you.' He closed his eyes, trying to get some sort of grip on the raw primal instincts that had him in a stranglehold. The muscles in his brown throat worked as he stared at her, but it was the heat in his passion-glazed eyes that made her insides dissolve and made her feet move of their own accord to close the distance between them.

Kat, her heart thudding, forgot what she was about to say, forgot how to speak, how to think; the raw need

stamped into his strong, beautiful features thrilled
through her and into a secret place nothing had ever
penetrated before.

'This is a bad idea, Kat,' he slurred, struggling to
think past the roar, the tidal wave of emotion rising inside him as he dragged a not quite steady hand through
his hair.

'It's too late to go back,' she said, thinking, *In more
ways than one,* as a surge of sheer hopeless longing
made her tremble. He really was the epitome of male
beauty as he stood there in the moonlight, his shirt
open to the waist, his dark hair standing in sexy tufts,
the shadow on his jaw and chin highlighting the angles
and planes of his face.

'You're perfect,' she whispered, utterly dazzled by
his perfection.

'Agape mou!' Zach looked into her eyes, saw the
heat and hunger and felt his control burn away. It was
impossible to tell who moved first but suddenly they
were colliding, the impetus of the contact driving the
air out of her lungs; not that it mattered—Kat couldn't
breathe anyway.

They sank to the sand together, lay side by side,
thigh to thigh, for a moment breathing hard, staring
into each other's eyes.

Zach moved first, reaching out to lay a big hand
against her cheek, then, holding her gaze, he moved in
with nerve-shreddingly slow deliberation to claim her
trembling lips.

Kat's eyes squeezed closed as she focused on the
taste of him, the feel of him, greedily absorbing the

musky smell of his hard, male body mingled with the salty tang in the air.

The touch of his hand on one breast drew a soft feral whimper from her aching throat. She felt the air cool on her hot skin as he pushed the fabric away, revealing the turgid pink peak. The air around them crackled with the passion that burned away oxygen, leaving them in a bubble when, as if responding to some silent signal, they both began frantically tearing at each other's clothing, their mouths connected as they kissed with a wild lack of restraint, a desperate drowning feeling that Kat had never dreamt existed, let alone would ever feel.

Her entire body felt sensitised. She was aware of every touch, every abrasive point of friction between them and most of all the hot ache of arousal between her thighs.

Zach raised himself onto his knees, pulling Kat with him, his lips not releasing hers for a second as his hands moved to the zip at the back of her dress. The need to see her was part of the madness consuming them both.

The dress slithered down to waist level.

Kat squeezed her eyes closed and felt, rather than heard, the vibration of his deep gasp, a gasp that was drowned out by her louder groan as she felt the touch of his mouth against the tip of one quivering soft breast and then the other. Her fingers speared into his dark hair, holding his head there against her to prolong this nerve-wrenching erotic sensation, giving herself over to the bliss.

By the time his head lifted, she was shaking every-where and burning up. They faced one another, still kneeling as behind them the waves continued their relentless advance, retreat, hiss.

The pounding in Kat's blood did not retreat. It kept pushing forward, harder and harder, driving her deeper into the sensual maelstrom.

Zach leaned in to trail kisses down her neck, one hand cupping her breast, before pressing a fierce kiss to her parted lips.

'You feel like silk—so very soft,' he husked against her mouth.

'I want to feel...touch you...'

Their breath mingled, their tongues tangled as they continued to kiss with hungry, bruising intensity. Kat felt him quiver as she pushed aside the fabric of his shirt that hung open to allow her palms to slide down the smooth, slightly hair-roughened skin of his chest. She loved the feel of him, the hardness, the amazing definition of every individual ridge of muscle, every perfect contour. His skin felt fever hot under her exploring hands as he started to kiss down her body.

His tongue had found her nipple again when he felt the moment she encountered the scar, not from the knife but the surgical scar where they had opened his ribcage to save his life and massage his heart.

He lifted his head, the hot colour edging his cheekbones lending them a hard definition in the moonlight. Holding her eyes, he fought his way out of his shirt, allowing her to see the white line that ran midline along his breastbone and the more raised scar just under his ribs.

'What hap—?'

Her words were lost inside the possessive heat of his

mouth as he pressed her back down onto the sand, the weight of his body pressing her deeper. The first skin-to-skin contact sent all questions, all thoughts from her head. She moved her hands over his broad shoulders, excited by his strength. The heat flaring between them as they continued to kiss and touch.

'Have you any idea how much I want you? Have wanted you from the first…the very first moment I saw you?' The expression of fierce concentration on his face, the molten hunger in his eyes as he stroked a finger down her cheek as much as his erotic admission drew a throaty whimper from Kat's throat.

'I wanted you, too. Inside me. So much.'

The admission burned the remnants of his shredded control away; he gave a grin and levered himself off her.

He watched the protest die on her lips as she realised what he was doing; he was aware of her eyes following him as he unfastened his trousers and slid them down his thighs, kicking them away.

His boxers followed.

'Oh…!' She swallowed and felt the blood pool in the juncture between her legs. He really was magnificent, the level of his arousal was shocking, yet she wasn't embarrassed; his primitive male beauty fed the urgency in her blood.

She lay there, aching for his touch, and perhaps her desperation communicated itself because his hands moved down over the feminine curve of her hips as he freed her from the folds of dress fabric that had bunched across her. Her panties—scraps of lace—followed suit and he knelt back down beside her.

Kat reached out and touched him. He gasped and she

felt him quiver as she stroked down the hot, hard length of him, then, emboldened, curved her fingers around him, touching the velvet tip with the pad of her thumb.

Nostrils flared, teeth clenched, he watched her, unable to tear his eyes from the expression of carnal concentration on her beautiful face. He bore it as long as he could before he grabbed her hand and, ignoring her protest, pushed her back, lowering his body onto her.

Hands held at the wrists above her head, all she could do at that first nerve-searingly perfect moment of skin-to-skin was moan. Then moan a lot more and squirm against him as she felt his hand slide between their bodies and in between her legs, exposing the heat in her sensitised core to his clever touch.

She tried to breathe, moving against the heel of his hand at the intimate exploration until it got so intense that she couldn't bear it. The pleasure moving close to the pleasure-pain line.

'Please,' she whispered, her teeth closing around the lobe of his ear. 'I can't...' she begged. 'It's too... You're too...'

'Relax, it's all right,' he slurred against her neck as he gave into the primal roar in his blood and parted her legs. 'Wrap your legs around me, hold me.'

She did, happy to take instruction. She was in uncharted territory, and he really seemed to know what he was doing. Zach was an intuitive, passionate and generous lover. She knew from conversations she had frequently felt excluded from that this was a rather rare combination.

She stopped thinking anything when he slid into her, his powerful thrust slowed by the tightness of her warm female body as it adjusted to him, relaxing and contracting as he began to touch deeper inside her, waking nerve endings that sent rush after rush of mindless bliss through her body.

'You feel...oh, Zach...you feel—' Her words were lost in the warm moisture of his mouth.

She felt as if she were on fire as she pushed towards an unseen goal and when she reached it the shock of release jerked her entire body as the pleasure spread from her scalp to her curling toes.

Her muscles had started to relax when she felt the hot rush of his climax; a moment later he rolled off her and they lay side by side, panting.

It felt like coming back to earth after floating far above it; it wasn't a thing that happened in a moment.

When she did Kat was smiling.

He watched as with fluid grace she rolled on her side, then he took her hand to kiss her open palm before he drew her warm, pliant body to him.

Relaxed... As it seeped through his body it took him a while to recognise the feeling. He did not associate sexual release with being relaxed; lowering your guard to that degree, opening yourself that much, required trust.

Then it hit him like a wall, the knowledge that scared him more than anything else could—in the few days he had known her she had burrowed her way through all the barriers he'd thrown up into his soul, his heart. If he loved her this much now, how much deeper, stronger would it grow if he let it?

How much harder it would be when it ended, when

he let her down; there was a terrible inevitability to it.
No one had ever been there for him and he had never
been there for anyone else; a genetic flaw or something
he'd never learnt, it remained a fact.

It was in his genes. Who would pass on a heritage
like that? It would stop with him.

He closed his eyes and lay there, feeling her hands
on his body, exploring. She was a giver and he was a
taker, but he didn't have the will or the strength to stop
her. He wanted the moment to last.

She watched Zach. He appeared to be sleeping, his
breath even and steady, his chest rising and falling. The
rest of him . . Her glance slid lower and she blushed,
remembering the pleasure his body had given her. The
rest of him was perfect. The only flaw, if it could be
counted as such, was the long surgical scar she had
seen.

Zach tensed and kept his eyes closed as he felt her
fingers move down the scar on his chest; he'd known
it was coming. In a moment she'd find the more messy,
less surgically precise scars on his ribs, which the knife,
luckily for him, had just glanced off, not penetrated. It
was the one underneath that had thrust upwards, sever-
ing some major vessels, that had caused all the damage.

The only people who knew the truth of the scars
were Alekis and Selene, plus the surgical team who
had saved his life, the *real* heroes. He was indulgent
of a little morbid curiosity from his bed partners. He
even had a few ridiculous lies he wheeled out on occasion to amuse himself, safe in the knowledge they really didn't care about his pain or his trauma or the fact

his uncle had knocked seven bells out of him—these were all pluses.

This was different. Kat's curiosity would not be morbid. Her empathy had quite a different quality and would include sympathy and pity, two things he had a strong allergic reaction to.

He opened his eyes and turned his head and, despite everything, experienced a shock-level surge of possessiveness as his eyes slid over her lovely face and beautiful body.

She smiled.

You made a mistake that was human and, if not, forgivable as such, but at least you could have a free pass; you repeated it and there were no free passes because you were a fool.

He was not a fool.

He'd made a mistake and he was not about to repeat it. This was going nowhere, because he didn't do tomorrow and she very definitely did. The kindest thing in the long run—and she might appreciate it one day, when she had her family and her brood of children— was a clean cut. Not that there would be anything clean about it if Alekis found out.

She had edged a little closer, planning to put her head on his chest, pushing her long leg against his hair-roughened thigh, enjoying the contrast in their bodies. They were two very different halves that had made a total perfect whole. At the last moment something in his face, or rather the *lack* of it, made her pause.

'Is something wrong?' Fear of losing this happiness made her tense.

'I didn't protect you.' The only time in his life.

It took a moment for his words and the self-contempt in his voice to make sense.

'I'm sorry.'

'I was there, too,' she reminded him quietly. 'It was my responsibility, too.'

He closed his eyes and shook his head. 'You would say that.' Because she was good...too good for him, but the truth was she had given and he had taken.

She reached out again and touched the scar, pale against the deep gold of his skin. 'What happened?' she asked, her tender heart aching as she thought of the pain those marks represented.

He took her hand off his chest, dropped it as if it were something contagious and sat up. 'One of those "wrong place wrong time" things.'

She blinked and felt the trace of unease already stirring in her belly take serious hold. 'Is that all I get...?' She smiled to lighten her words and added half jokingly, 'You really could do with some lessons in sharing.'

He looked at her again; the coldness in his eyes made her stomach quiver in apprehension. She reached for her dress as the self-consciousness she had shrugged off returned. Pulling herself onto her knees, she slipped it over her head but didn't attempt the zip.

He didn't offer so she knelt back down again.

'We are not sharing, Katina. Yes, we had sex, but it was not the beginning of some special sharing, caring relationship. But if you want to know, the scars are why I am who I am. I was in the wrong place but so was Alekis.'

'You saved him.'

'I am not a hero, Kat. Do not look at me that way.

I hate bullies and I didn't think before I acted…much like tonight.'

It wasn't just what he said, it was the fact he seemed to *want* to hurt her.

'You sound as though you regret it.'

She left him the space to say no, that it had been one of the best things that had ever happened to him, but the space stayed empty and instead his eyes drifted away from hers as if the contact was something that made him uncomfortable. 'It was a mistake—you must see that.'

Kat said nothing. She was actually afraid if she tried to speak she'd start crying.

'For starters, Alekis trusted me. I have betrayed that trust and betrayed someone I respect.' *But, man, is he good to hide behind.* Ignoring the sly insert of his subconscious, he appealed for her understanding. 'You must see that.'

'Why should I care about what Alekis thinks?' she flared back. 'Anyway, what about me? Don't I deserve a little bit of respect?' she choked out.

'Please do not become emotional…'

'*Seriously!* We just made love.'

'Had sex.'

The rebuttal made her pale.

'And do not imagine this is the start of some sort of love affair.'

She sat there shivering while he got to his feet and dragged his clothes on. There was a pause before he extended his hand to her; she ignored it and got to her feet.

'I know you want a happy-ever-after thing, a husband and children, which is fine, but I'm not the man for that and if I'd known you were so inexperienced I would have—' Innate honesty made him pause. If he'd known he would not have stopped—nothing would have stopped him.

'Don't put me in one of your little boxes, and don't presume to know what I want from life! You know something, Zach, I really don't think *I'm* the one with the problem. I didn't expect you to declare undying love. I just wanted a little bit of…well, respect would have been nice. But no, you had to spoil what happened by turning it into something nasty and sordid, because you're too scared to risk feeling anything that you can't control. You know what I think?'

His jaw clenched as he struggled to control his anger. 'Is there any way I can stop you telling me?'

'You won't have any sort of a future until you come to terms with your past and stop letting it rule you.'

'Who's presuming now?' he growled out.

She picked up her skirts in one hand, decided not to look for her shoes—they had killed anyway—and started back across the sand toward the lights of the house.

Zach, who experienced a stab of visceral longing as he watched her progress, dignified despite the fact her entire back, including the upper slopes of her pert bottom, was exposed, managed to wipe his face of expression as she suddenly swung back, her anger cancelling out mental censorship as she had the last word.

'You're not the only one with trust issues, Zach. Why the hell do you think I was inexperienced? Though, for the record, I was a virgin! And as it turns out a stupid one because I thought I had found someone I could let my guard down with. You know what, though, I'd prefer to be me and make a mistake than you, who spends his life pretending you don't feel anything...' Her eyes searched his face. 'But I don't believe that—you did and for me!'

The level of his self-loathing went up several notches as he watched her flounce away.

CHAPTER ELEVEN

'How did it go?'

Selene saw Kat's face and her own melted into one of concern. 'Oh, dear, is it bad news?'

Kat shook her head as she laid her handbag down on the table and turned back to the housekeeper. 'No, no, nothing like that really.' She was not ready to share just yet what the *something* was that had put the worried look on her face. 'The doctors are really pleased with his progress. If all goes well with his next round of tests, they are willing to discharge him next week.'

Kat was visiting the clinic in Athens once a week, but talking to her grandfather during the week online. This time she had taken herself off to see another specialist after seeing her grandfather.

'Things are definitely getting more relaxed.'

'He must be pleased he's coming home.'

'No, he's mad as hell that he can't escort me to this charity auction.'

'Never mind, there's next year.'

'That's what I said only he…yes, thanks, tea would be lovely,' she said with gratitude to a maid who brought in a tea tray.

'Only?'

'He has roped in a stand-in. He says as he has donated a sports car, an Azaria should be there. I said I'm not an Azaria but, well…' She shrugged. She had discovered her grandfather was a hard man to argue with and when faced with a defeat he fell back on chest pain, and who was going to risk disbelieving him?

Not Kat.

'Join me,' Kat begged when the woman poured her tea.

Smiling, Selene poured another and took a seat. 'So who is the stand-in? Anyone we know?'

Selene had already guessed, the way she had figured out at least some of what had gone on between Zach and Kat.

'Zach,' Kat said quietly. Unlike for Selene, the news had come as a massive shock when Alekis had announced his stand-in for the charity auction.

Kat had excused herself and gone to the ladies' room to cry her eyes out, but then she had an excuse for being over-emotional. Her hormones were all over the place—she was pregnant.

She'd had her suspicions for a few days and the consultant had officially confirmed it today.

To keep things private—the island was a very small place—she'd asked Sue to post her the test kit. Her friend had been sympathetic but she had promised her that *nobody* knew that early, but Kat had, and she'd been right.

Two weeks to the day since Zach had left, never, it seemed, to return, she knew she was carrying his child. The shock was still there, even the occasional moment of blind panic, but a level of acceptance had started to kick in and, to her surprise, *excitement*.

While her emotions were all over the place, she was totally sure of one thing. This baby would have a mother who loved her or him. Her baby would never feel alone and be scared. She was absolutely determined to give this child the childhood she had not had.

Sadly, she could not guarantee the baby a father. And the great-grandfather? Well, the jury was still out, but she suspected, hoped, that Alekis would be over the moon about having a great-grandchild.

And if he wasn't, well, she would deal with it. The baby came first as far as she was concerned and if other people had a problem with that—tough!

It was the father's identity her grandfather might have a problem with. It was a problem the father himself might have, too. She had lain awake half of last night trying to decide when and how to tell Zach and had come to the conclusion that she needed to get used to the idea herself before she shared.

It made sense.

Or she might just be a big coward!

'It's a really stunning event with the cream of society and—'

'But Zach...,' Kat wailed, still blaming her hormones.

Kat had taken to her room and cried for a day when Zach had left, claiming a migraine, and when she had emerged she had known that Zach wasn't the only person in denial.

Hard enough to accept she had wanted him physically, but accepting that she had fallen in love with Zach had been one of the hardest things in her life. She prided herself on being truthful but this was one truth she had been avoiding because she had known it would hurt—she just hadn't known how much!

'You could make an excuse...'

Kat's chin went up. 'Why should I?' She wasn't the one who had done anything wrong.

Zach, drawing eyes and more than a few camera clicks in his dress suit, stepped back into the shadows, and the limo that drew up disgorged the members of a new girl-band group.

The paparazzi went crazy and Zach's patience grew thin. His offer to travel over to Tackyntha to escort Kat had been politely refused by someone who was not Kat or even Selene.

He was being given the runaround. The only surprise was that nothing of what had happened between he and Kat seemed to have filtered through to Alekis as yet.

The past two weeks had been a sort of hell Zach had never experienced before. Normally in times of stress he was able to bury himself in work until it passed, but not on this occasion. He couldn't concentrate, a unique experience for him, so work was impossible.

His volatile mood had swung from anger and frustration—he hadn't asked for any of this—and then on to black despair. It was crazy but he was missing her, not just the physical stuff, although that had been incredible, but stupid things like the sound of her voice...her laugh, the way she wrinkled up her nose.

The woman was haunting him.

Logic told him that a man couldn't fall in love so

quickly, but the same logic told him that love, the romantic variety, didn't exist outside romance novels.

He'd believed that before Katina had walked into his life.

And now? Now he didn't know what the hell he felt, and her words kept coming back to him. *'You won't have any sort of a future until you come to terms with your past.'*

He was the one with the problem.

It still made him angry, but Zach had started to wonder if she could be right.

He had rejected the idea that he was a coward hiding behind his past and unable to face the future, but the more he thought about it... Tonight would give him a chance to connect again. Maybe there was some sort of middle ground?

He dashed a hand across his head. *Middle ground? What the hell was he thinking?*

He was thinking of kissing her—just sinking into her warmth—as he had been from the second she had walked away from him. He had struggled not to run after her. He had begun to wonder what would have happened if he had—maybe their passionate affair would already have burnt itself out?

Or she might have killed him.

A half-smile on his lips, he stepped forward again. This time the limos had arrived in a block of three.

The door to the first opened and a platinum blonde got out, wearing a glittery silver dress that was so figure-hugging it appeared painted on. She rocked a little on her heels as she paused to pose for cameras even though no one seemed that excited about her and her escort's arrival.

'Well, I hear that Alekis's little heiress will be here tonight. I wonder if she's as much of a slut as the mother was.'

'Was she?' the man asked.

'God, yes, and a druggie… I hear that the girl is just like her. Alekis found her in some sort of refuge and I hear that before that she was actually living on the streets.'

The woman with the uniquely unattractive voice had begun talking as she emerged from the car. Standing at the top of a long flight of stone steps, Zach nonetheless heard every word of this conversation.

He stepped in front of the doormen.

The woman looked him up and down, her painted lips widening into a smile. 'Oh, hello, how nice to see you again, Zach. Darling, it's Zach.'

Zach, who had not to his knowledge ever seen either of them before, waited until she had finished listing to her long-suffering partner all the times they had met him previously.

'I heard you speaking—actually I think several people heard you speaking—about Miss Katina Parvati,' Zach observed, pitching his own voice to carry. It was a message he did not mind sharing. 'I did not like what I heard. Obviously anyone with an ounce of sense will recognise spiteful lies and malice when they hear it. But I feel it only fair to warn you that should I hear those lies repeated anywhere online or in person I will have no compunction but to put the case in the hands of my *very* litigious legal team. And after they have finished with

you I am sure that Alekis Azaria might enjoy watching
his own team picking at your bones. His granddaughter
is a person so superior to the likes of you that I find it
offensive that you breathe the same air!'

'Zach!'

At the sound of the voice he turned. Kat was standing
at the bottom of the steps, wearing a dress a shade paler
than the one he remembered stripping off her body. This
one was much more formal: a strapless bodice that revealed the upper slopes of her breasts and the dazzle of
a diamond necklace.

He rushed down to her, taking the steps two at a
time, shedding his doubts with each step he took. What
he felt for her was not going to burn itself out. She was
part of him and if he ever won her back he would never
let her go!

'Do you make a habit of making public scenes?' Oh,
God, he looked so gorgeous she could not take her eyes
off him. The ache of longing she had struggled to deny
was a physical ache that went soul deep.

He looked blank for a moment, a little dazed, and
then glanced up the stairs. The couple had vanished.

'Not usually.' His shoulders lifted in a shrug.

There was so much he needed to say but now she was
here and he was acting like some tongue-tied kid, or
maybe just the Neanderthal who had taken her virginity on a beach she probably thought he was.

Kat lowered her eyes and struggled to collect her
fractured composure. Seeing him standing there had
shaken loose a million conflicting emotions. The idea
that she could distance herself from him emotionally
or any other way had vanished.

He was the father of her child and she loved him.

'I heard what you said,' she said, not even bothering to try and project the illusion of calm control—who was going to believe it? 'I think maybe a lot of people did.'

That was the problem: there were way too many people and he wanted her all alone. 'Let's get this over with,' he said, taking her elbow and mentally figuring out just how soon they could reasonably leave without causing massive offence. While he had zero problem with offence, he suspected that Kat might not be on the same page as him with this.

'You've not lost any of your charm,' she said, hating the fact he had the ability to hurt her.

He looked down at her, frowning. 'No, I didn't mean... I need to talk to you alone and I avoid these things like the plague normally.'

Warning herself not to read anything into his words or the possessive blaze in his eyes when he looked at her, she allowed herself to be escorted into the room.

Selene had warned her that everyone crowded into the small space for drinks and finger food before the auction, which was to be held in the marquee outside. And it was crowded, very! The jewels she had been so reluctant to wear were not the most extravagant baubles on display. Kat had never seen so much bling in such a small space in her life, though maybe the impression was exaggerated because the walls felt as if they were closing in on her.

'Fruit juice, please,' she said as she was offered champagne. 'I feel like everyone is staring at me.'

'They are. You're the most beautiful woman in the room.'

It might have given her more pleasure to hear him say this had her head not started to spin in a really sickening fashion. She lifted her head as the lights above began to blur.

'Zach?'

He caught her before she hit the floor and when she opened her eyes, he was kneeling beside her looking pale while he emptied the contents of her small bag onto the floor.

'Where's the EpiPen...? Does anyone have an EpiPen? This is anaphylactic shock. Will someone call an ambulance?'

'No, Zach, it isn't.'

A look of intense relief washed over his face. '*Agape mou*...no, don't move, you fainted. I think you might have eaten something with peanuts in.'

'No, I haven't.' She hadn't eaten a thing; she'd been too nervous about tonight. 'You remembered!'

'I remember every word you have ever said to me.'

She ran her tongue over her dry lips and tried to lift her head. 'No, stay there, wait for the ambulance.' A large hand on her chest made it impossible for her to defy this edict.

'Will you stop it?' she said, batting his hand with both hers. 'I'm not ill, you idiot, I'm pregnant!'

Her exported admission coincided with a lull in the conversation that had started up when people had guessed she wasn't dead. The room had excellent acoustics so at least eighty per cent of the people present heard the happy news.

Beside her, Zack had frozen. The blood had quite

literally drained from his face; he looked much more in need of an ambulance than she did.

'*Pregnant.*'

She nodded.

A long sibilant hiss left his lips as he leaned back onto his heels.

'Only just…obviously.'

His hand lifted from her chest, but her relief was short-lived. He needed both hands to scoop her up and carry her out of the place, magnificently oblivious to the hundred pairs of eyes watching them.

Outside, a car appeared as if by magic. Zach slid her into the back seat as if she were a piece of porcelain before joining her.

'I don't know… I don't know what to say.' His dark eyes slid to her belly. 'You're sure?'

She nodded. 'Sorry.'

His dark brows lifted. 'Do not say sorry. A child is, is…' A child was scary. 'A blessing. At least that was what one of the nuns who taught me in kindergarten said. I think she decided I was an exception when I asked her how many she had.'

'You don't have to pretend, Zach,' she said, sounding understanding but feeling miserable as hell. If he could allow himself to love her even half as much as she loved him, they could have a wonderful life. A family, because, even if he did not know it, she knew he was a marvellous man who had overcome more than most people could imagine. 'I know that this is the very last thing you would have wanted and I'm not going to ask you for anything.'

'You shouldn't have to ask.' He stared at her for a

moment before giving a cracked laugh. 'And you don't have to. Obviously, we're getting married.'

It was Kat's turn to laugh. 'Is that meant to be funny?'

'You tried telling Alekis that yet?'

'This is nothing to do with Alekis.'

Rather to her surprise, Zach nodded. 'No, it isn't.' He leaned forward and lifted a hank of hair from her face, tucking it behind her ear with such tenderness that it brought tears to her eyes. 'I came here tonight wanting to talk to you, to say some things. How about I do that first and then we talk about…?' His eyes dropped, a smile curving his lips, as her hand lifted to cover the flatness of her belly protectively.

'So you don't want to discuss the elephant in the room.'

'I want very much to discuss it, but there are things I need to say first to put what has happened into perspective. Would that be okay with you?'

She nodded warily and glanced at the partition between them and the driver.

'He can't hear us.'

'All right.'

'Firstly, you were right. I do have a problem. The past is…has been stopping me moving on. I've been alone for a long time and I decided that was a strength, but I realise now that it is in fact a weakness.'

'It's lonely,' she said quietly, her heart aching for the lonely boy he'd been. 'I know. It's not weak, Zach, it's just…sometimes you need to give a bit of yourself to get something back.' Kat knew she'd been lucky she'd had foster parents who had taught her that. Zach had had no one; he'd been alone.

'It's *easier* to be alone,' he said with a self-recrimina-tory grimace. 'I was willing to walk away from the best thing that ever happened to me because I was scared. A coward. I've been wrong about a lot of things in my life but this here with you… I was insane to let you walk away.'

'You didn't let me walk, Zach, you threw me away.'

A look of shame crossed his face as he heard the bit-terness in her voice. 'You're right. I'm an idiot. I think that part of me cannot believe that I am allowed to be happy in that way—to have something so precious and lose it… I think that was my fear. I was afraid that I couldn't look after you like I couldn't look after my mother.'

Heart aching for the pain drawn on his face, she caught his hand and pressed it between both of her own. 'You were a child, Zach. It wasn't your job to do the looking after.'

'Being alone was my way of feeling in charge…but I'm not going to think of being alone now, and I'm going to think of that time when I was as the time I was wait-ing for you, until that moment I saw you, in that grave-yard, looking like a sexy angel.'

'There was someone there!' she breathed, recalling the day when she had sensed a presence as she'd laid flowers at her mother's grave.

He gave a half-smile. 'I couldn't get your face out of my head.' He took his phone from his pocket and showed her the snapshot. 'Have you any idea how many times a day I have looked at that?'

The tears that had filled Kat's eyes as he spoke

spilled out, sparkling on her lashes. 'You're not saying this just because of the baby? I really couldn't bear that.'

'The baby… Now that is something I never thought I would have, but now I am claiming it.' He pressed a possessive hand to her stomach and his mouth to her lips.

The kiss was deep and tender and life-affirming.

'I love you, Kat!' Just saying it felt liberating, so he said it again, aching sincerity throbbing in his voice. 'I love you and I hope you will one day learn to love me. Marry me, Kat. Let us be a family.'

'That's not possible, Zach, because I'm already totally insanely in love with you!' she cried, throwing her arms around his neck.

EPILOGUE

'I WANT TO see the person in charge!'

Kat's eyes lifted from the baby in her arms to see her handsome husband standing at the side of the bed.

'He is just so perfect…yes, I think Alek suits him?' Her husband looked as exhausted as she had felt, but it was a good tired that came with a deep feeling of contentment.

'I think so. You should really get some sleep, you know.'

She nodded. 'We have a family, Zach.' There was wonder in her face as she looked down at the baby who had arrived at six that morning.

Zach covered her hand with his own. 'We are a family,' he corrected, looking deep into her eyes.

The bellowing voice interrupted the tender moment, making itself heard once more. This time the baby's eyes opened; they were dark, flecked with amber.

'Hush, Alek, we will not let Great-Grandpa wake you up. You'll get used to him.'

'If he's anything like his mother he'll have the old man wrapped around his little finger in no time at all.'

'What can I say?' Kat said with a smile. 'I'm irresistible. You know, you really *should* go and tell him to come in. You know he's creating havoc out there.'

Zach gave a resigned sigh and levered himself off the bed, pausing to touch the dark head of his son and press a warm kiss to his wife's lips. 'You did good, kid.'

'A joint effort,' she protested.

'Hardly. My contribution required much less effort,' he said with the wicked grin she loved so much.

'Oh, I helped a little bit with that too, as I recall.'

His grin deepened. 'Well, I have to say I'm really relieved he doesn't look like Alekis. That was my secret fear all along.'

'Oh, was that what your secret fear was?' she teased lovingly. 'I thought it was I might slip, I might get too hot, I might get too cold, I might—'

'All right, all right, a man is allowed to be protective, isn't he? And now we have this... He is very beautiful, isn't he?'

'Of course he is, he looks just like his papa.'

'Doctor!' the voice outside thundered scornfully. 'I wish to speak to the person in charge, not a child.'

'Oh, really, Zach, go and give him the news before he starts telling everyone how there would be no baby if he hadn't thrown us together, and that it was all part of his grand plan...' She broke off and gave a laugh of delight as the baby's tiny perfect fingers curled around one of her own. 'He is so strong, aren't you, my precious?' She looked up. 'You don't think there was a grand plan, do you?'

'You know something, *agape mou*? I really don't care. I am here with you and our baby. I don't care if the devil himself arranged it. I am just happy.'

Kat nodded. 'Me too.' She lifted a hand to stifle a yawn. 'Tired and happy.'

The addition made him smile. 'Right, I will go and tell your grandfather that you are not allowed visitors until tomorrow.'

'But the midwife said—'

Zach kissed her to silence. 'Tomorrow.'

'You are a very good husband.'

'I am a work in progress, but my heart,' he promised, pressing his hand first to his own chest and then against Kat's beating heart, 'is definitely in it.'

'Seen the name outside the surgical wing, young man? That is *my* name. I think you'll find I have some influence in this place!' Alekis shouted from the hall-way.

'But he doesn't in this room,' Kat promised the sleeping baby in her arms.

Zach nodded his agreement. 'Oh, everyone at the refuge sent their love when I texted the news. Sue made a flying visit to the new refuge and she said to tell you there were no problems.'

'Oh, that is good news!' In the months after they had joined forces there had been five more refuges opened and Zach's mentoring scheme had started up in two UK cities.

'She also says everything is under control, so relax and enjoy the baby.'

'I—' Kat broke off as a loud bellow outside made the
sleeping baby stir. 'Go and save the poor staff, Zach.'

Laughing, he obeyed, because after all Kat had saved
him from a lonely life. She had given him the greatest
gift there was—unconditional love.

* * * * *

COMING SOON!

We really hope you enjoyed reading this book. If you're looking for more romance, be sure to head to the shops when new books are available on

Thursday 8th August

To see which titles are coming soon, please visit
millsandboon.co.uk/nextmonth

MILLS & BOON

Coming next month

HIS CINDERELLA'S ONE-NIGHT HEIR
Lynne Graham

'So…er…the job?' Belle prompted tautly.

'The job would be a little unusual but completely above board,' he assured her and then, as though suddenly recollecting his manners, he moved closer to extend a lean hand. 'My name is Dante Lucarelli.'

'Yes.' Belle barely touched the tips of his fingers. 'The bartender identified you before you'd been seated for five minutes. He's a business student.'

'Tell me about yourself,' he urged.

'There's not a lot relevant to tell,' Belle retorted uncomfortably, wishing he would just get to the point instead of keeping her in ignorance. 'I'm twenty-two. I left school at sixteen with a bundle of GCSEs and I haven't had any educational input since then. I'd like to change that when I get back to London. These days you need training and qualifications to make a decent life.'

'If you know that why did you skip that opportunity until now?'

'I never *had* the opportunity,' Belle countered wryly, settling down on the concrete bench beneath the trees. 'My grandmother died and then my grandfather fell ill and needed looking after. After they were both gone, I took a job here, which was basically housekeeping but which turned into full-time caring as well.'

Dante lounged back against a tree trunk, all lithe, lean power and thrumming masculinity. He was as relaxed as she was tense. 'Is caring for older people what you want to do going forward?'

Belle stiffened. 'No, definitely not. I think professional caring's a job you need a vocation for and I don't have that.'

'Fair enough,' Dante murmured, increasingly surprised by her cool, unapologetic self-containment because at the very least he had expected bubbly encouragement and flirtation from her. In his experience women came onto him whether they thought they had a chance with him or not, but Belle wasn't making the smallest effort in that direction. 'You may not have a vocation for the job I'm about to offer you either, but it *would* eventually get you back to the UK and I would *pay* you handsomely to do it.'

Belle twisted round to get a better view of him, wishing he would step out of the shadows so that she could see him better. 'Tell me about it…'

'I need a woman prepared to pretend that she's my live-in girlfriend. Faking the part would be *all* that was required from you,' Dante assured her with calm emphasis. 'The job would only last for a couple of weeks and then you would be free to pursue your own plans with the cash I give you. It would be a win-win proposition for both of us.'

Belle was rarely deprived of speech, but the shock of the nature of his job offer was sufficient to glue her tongue to the roof of her mouth because such an exotic possibility wouldn't have crossed her mind in her wildest dreams. 'But…er…you don't even know me,' she protested weakly when she could find her voice again.

'Why would I need to know you? Steve vouches for your trustworthiness. It's a job, a role if you want to call it that. It's casual and temporary but also financially rewarding,' he completed smoothly.

'But pretending to be someone's girlfriend would mean knowing stuff about each other, that sort of thing,' Belle protested in a rush. 'And we're complete strangers.'

Continue reading
HIS CINDERELLA'S ONE-NIGHT HEIR
Lynne Graham

Available next month
www.millsandboon.co.uk